The Crystal of Light

"I know who you are," Bailiwick whispered.

Bronwen started--he was not so innocent after all. She took a moment to poke at the fire and collect her thoughts "Of course you know--I am the prophetess."

"No. No. No." He flipped in the air and came to rest on the floor again. "You became the prophetess after you left here. After you left your infant son behind."

Bronwen's heart stopped beating and she felt her face drain of all color.

"How do you know this?"

"I'm sorry. I didn't mean to upset you." Bailiwick looked contrite and somewhat worried.

"You have upset me. Who else knows this?"

"No one, I swear. I've told no one. It's not my place. I know that. I swear I'll never tell anyone, cross my eyes and spit at the moon."

Bronwen sighed. "Fine, I'll have to take your word that you'll keep the secret. But tell me how you know of such things."

"Well, to tell you the truth," Bailiwick's voice lowered to the merest whisper. "I am magic."

Wings

The Crystal of Light

by

Catherine Anne Collins

A Wings ePress, Inc.

Fantasy Romance Novel

Wings ePress, Inc.

Edited by: Patricia Evans
Copy Edited by: Elizabeth Struble
Senior Editor: Elizabeth Struble
Managing Editor: Leslie Hodges
Executive Editor: Lorraine Stephens
Cover Artist: Richard Stroud

Wings ePress Books
http://www.wings-press.com

Copyright © 2009 by Cathy Walker
ISBN 978-1-59705-652-6

Published In the United States Of America

February 2009

Wings ePress Inc.
403 Wallace Court
Richmond, KY 40475

One

Swirling mists muted the sounds of nature, wrapped around the nearby hills and settled into the valleys of the faerie realm. A mournful howl mingled with the mist, echoed into the distance, and wended its way to every creature within hearing.

Adoneesis, king of all the faerie races, shivered at the loneliness ringing within that howl, but continued on the familiar path that wove around the outskirts of his home, Dunraven. The scars on his back burned with the memory of a long ago beating resulting from doing exactly what he was now doing. Except his father, Raegar, was no longer alive to beat him.

He felt grim satisfaction in knowing that no matter how hard he'd tried, Raegar hadn't learned the existence of the tree from Adoneesis. And Raegar had tried his best. First with a fierce beating and then days locked in the newly dug dungeons of Dunraven with no food or water.

That was when Adoneesis had learned to hate his father.

But he'd never told the secret of the tree.

He couldn't, or Raegar would have destroyed it as he had every other magic tree in Dunraven. Faerie lore was rampant with stories of trees of magic, but before Adoneesis was born, Raegar had razed many of them to the ground in an ill-tempered rant that Adoneesis dared not ask about for fear of a beating.

In spite of the constant yearning that had led Adoneesis to the tree in the first place, he'd never again returned to the secret clearing until Raegar's death these ten years past. Then he'd followed the tree's song each year since with the advent of the blue moon. He knew the tree held answers. He just had to understand what the questions were.

Stepping over a jutting root and weaving past a muddy patch, he followed the timeworn path that led to the tree. A tug of power boiled Adoneesis' faerie blood as he approached the familiar clearing. Silken strands of moonbeams bathed the clearing in a luminous glow, while shadows wavered like dancing ghouls among the surrounding trees and created a more surreal effect than usual. His heart thumped with expectation as he stepped off the almost overgrown path and into the shadow of the ancient tree. He breathed in deeply, relishing the crisp air and the musty scent of damp leaves.

As tall as four trees with a trunk that spanned the outstretched arms of ten human-sized faeries, the tree's graceful arch of limbs curved out from the trunk, reached to the heavens and swept down to touch upon the earth. The willow had probably sat upon the land as long as Duir, the ancient tree of life, and she had assuredly seen many rituals performed under her sweeping limbs and delicate leaves. Branches quivered on an unseen breeze and the majesty of the tree's presence prompted Adoneesis to thank the fates that this tree had been spared Raegar's insane fit of destruction.

He knelt. Cool, damp earth soaked his pants, but he ignored the discomfort as he fixed his eyes on the tree and could have sworn that a branch lifted and reached out for him. A distant hum distracted him. Strange, this was the first time he'd heard the humming since his first visit here as a youth. He relaxed into a warm state of meditation and felt the pulsing energy of the tree, much like tendrils of prickling energy, wind about him.

Mingling with the rising wind, the cadence of the hum changed, as if trying to form words. Strands of Adoneesis' hair lifted and danced with the breeze. One flick of his wrist swept the dark hair back over his shoulder as he struggled to understand the language of the tree. He gave himself up to the sensations washing over him, knowing that he should be able to understand the swelling power that rose within, and frustrated that he couldn't.

His head ached as words thrust into his mind in an attempt to force him to understand. Frustration at his own lack of ability angered Adoneesis, but somehow he knew that emotion wouldn't lend itself to enlightenment. With maturity that he'd lacked his first time here, he breathed deeply, trying to rein in his emotion and concentrate on the words in his mind.

A dark cloud passed over the moon and cast the clearing into shadow. Adoneesis' mind clutched at the swirling words, which, indistinguishable at first, slowly formed a melody so sweet that Adoneesis could have drowned in it.

Adoneesis, young you may be
Come closer here, closer to me
Years have melded in a haze
I've waited, waited out the days
Now that you hear me, I can rest easy
I am named Wyllow Wood
You'd do well to remember my name
Now we are one, one and the same

3

A blast of heat shot through him with such force that Adoneesis feared he'd ignite into flames. Instead, his knees melted beneath him and he sank to the ground with one triumphant thought in his mind. He finally understood the language of the tree.

~ * ~

Returning to consciousness was a slow process. Adoneesis was barely aware as someone lifted him, placed him over their shoulder and carried him through the night to an unknown location. He sensed no danger, so he didn't struggle. In fact, whoever was jouncing him around exuded a sense of familiarity and comfort.

Wavering on the hazy edge of awareness, Adoneesis remembered the words that had emanated from the tree-- Wyllow Wood. After all this time, he finally understood what she'd been trying to say to him. He grunted with satisfaction.

"Well, it's about time you came about. I was beginning to think we'd have to find a new king."

The gruff voice jolted Adoneesis to complete consciousness. No longer slung over someone's shoulder, he was now lying on a hard surface in a large room. The smell of broth, warm bread and ale tickled his nostrils and set his stomach to growling. He clutched his head, fully expecting to reawaken the pain, but it felt fine. Carefully, he sat up and looked around, not expecting to recognize anything. But he did. He was in the eating room, a huge space carved out of dirt and rock below the main dwelling tree of Dunraven. Such a location had been necessary, since the tree trunk itself had not been large enough to provide the room needed for all of Dunraven's faeries to gather. With solid bedrock and dirt for a floor, the room weaved itself around the base of the giant tree and used the tangled roots to provide support for the tables wherever space allowed.

"Here, drink this." A beak nosed, red-haired giant of a faerie who moved like a seasoned warrior, all stealth and strength, thrust a battered copper mug into his hands. Adoneesis accepted the mug and drank the ale in one gulp. He grinned at the faerie who stood with arms crossed and a scowl on his face. "Krickall. You carried me here?"

"Of course. See anyone else around?" Krickall turned and threw some cheese and bread onto a plate, which he then slapped onto the wooden table where Adoneesis had lain unconscious. "Eat."

Adoneesis greedily bit into the warm, crusty bread and followed it with a mouthful of tangy cheese. He watched Krickall ladle some broth into a bowl and place it on the table beside the bread and cheese, more carefully this time so as not to spill the liquid. Thirst and hunger sated somewhat, Adoneesis wondered about his friend's unwarranted, albeit welcome, presence at the sacred moon tree. But knowing Krickall and his gruff manner, Adoneesis worried that the wrong words could set the faerie into an unwanted barrage of castigation, so he spoke carefully.

"Ahem... Krickall..."

In a whirl of anger, Krickall turned and jammed his finger at Adoneesis' face. "What were you thinking? Do you realize the danger you placed yourself in? The goblins have been raiding too close to Dunraven for you to be sneaking around after dark. Have you learned no sense of responsibility after ten years as king?"

Taken aback by all the barrage of questions, Adoneesis opened his mouth to speak, but Krickall slammed his hands to his hips and began to rant again. "How can I be expected to fulfill my duty if you slink about at all hours? What were you doing in that clearing anyway?"

His gaze drilled into Adoneesis with the fierceness of a warrior stalking his adversary. Adoneesis stared back, but couldn't hold Krickall's gaze, so he looked away.

"Well?" Krickall demanded.

Steeling himself, Adoneesis drew his gaze back to Krickall and straightened his shoulders in an attempt to appear in control. After years of friendship, they were almost equal measure of height and weight and, even given the fact that Adoneesis was king, Krickall still managed to intimidate him. He cleared his throat.

"I think I'd like an answer or two as well." He locked his gaze with Krickall and noted eyes of darkest blue. "How did you know where to find me? And what duty are you talking about fulfilling?"

Without breaking for a breath, Krickall replied, "I followed you, of course, which is my duty." He folded his arms across his massive chest and waited.

"You followed me. By what rights do you do such a thing?" Adoneesis' face flushed with anger as he regarded Krickall. Imbued with the blood of giants inherited from some distant ancestor, Krickall's size made him perfect for the responsibility of protector and he'd done the job well for Raegar. Adoneesis had often wandered how anyone could shift allegiance so easily, but he had eventually come to trust the faerie. Now he wondered if his trust had been given in haste.

"I do so by the rights of protection I swore upon attaining my knighthood to give any faerie who sat on the throne of the realm. First, your father, and now, you. If, fates forbid, I should outlive you, it is a protection I'll give the next king. It's what I do."

Adoneesis shook his head. "It's what you do. Does that mean that you've been following me everywhere for ten years?"

Krickall shifted his feet, glanced at the ground, and mumbled.

"Speak up, I can't hear you."

"I said yes." Krickall thrust his chin out belligerently.

Adoneesis didn't know how to react. Anger at the intrusion was his first thought, but that anger melted away with one glance at the stubborn look on Krickall's features and the realization that the faerie would die in Adoneesis' place if need be. He pondered the situation and finally understood that Krickall's loyalty hadn't been to Raegar any more than it was to Adoneesis. Rather, Krickall's loyalty was to the land of faerie and an oath given to protect whoever ruled the realm. Therefore, Adoneesis had no need to doubt Krickall or worry about any misplaced devotion to a dead king.

"I suppose I should be grateful you happened to be so close tonight."

One corner of Krickall's mouth lifted in a half-smile. "Sure, you can be grateful, but I was only fulfilling my duty." His narrowed gaze ran across Adoneesis' face, as if checking for injury. "What happened in that clearing?"

Adoneesis shoved the last piece of bread into his mouth and chewed thoughtfully before answering. "I'm not sure, but the tree communicated with me on some level. Said that we were now one, or something like that." He shrugged, moved by the occurrence, yet afraid of setting Krickall off on another tirade by talking about something that seemed so rooted in magic.

Krickall shifted uncomfortably. "You know that Raegar didn't approve of such talk..."

Anger, as well as the lingering effects of the tree, prompted him to say what he'd wanted to for so long. "But he was wrong. Magic is an inherent ability in all faeries, from pixies to brownies. Even the goblin faeries have their share of magic, as little as they might deserve such a thing. It is the part of us that helped shape the realm of faerie. Raegar was wrong to say that magic corrupted."

A grin split across Krickall's rough face. "About time."

"What?"

Krickall threw a leg over the wooden bench and sat down facing Adoneesis. "Raegar didn't approve of such talk, but his motives were selfish. Your father outlawed magic to keep us under his own power. What you don't know is that he used magic himself to control those around him, but disallowed others to develop their abilities." He grunted. "If the trees are talking to you, you should listen."

Adoneesis considered his friend and realized that nothing was ever what it seemed. "Do others feel the same?"

"Of a certainty. We are, above all, faeries. Raegar suppressed our heritage, but couldn't stamp it out."

"So why have I not seen anyone practicing the old ways and rituals?"

"They are afraid."

"Of me?"

"You're Raegar's son. As far as they know, you follow his cruel ways. Many a faerie was beaten for lighting a fire at Beltaine, or leaving an offering to the ancient ones. Raegar's ego and need for control lent way to bondfaeries, beatings, the construction of Dunraven's first dungeons, and this unknown hatred that Gar as the goblin leader holds for you. Your father's cruelty has cast a pall on the faerie realm."

"Ten years is not enough for them to judge my actions? Have I once issued orders for a beating? Did I not close the dungeons? What do I need to do to prove I am not my father's son?"

Krickall stood and placed a hand on Adoneesis' shoulder. "My suggestion. Stop being embarrassed about the power that springs from you. As long as you deny it, they will wonder why and be nervous about showing their own. Other than that, keep doing what you do. You'll earn their trust."

While Krickall grabbed the jug of ale and refilled both their mugs, Adoneesis considered Krickall's words and understood the wisdom of his advice. Fear's memories cast long shadows and if he denied his own magical abilities, how could the faeries not worry that he did it out of distaste for magic and not fear of his own unpredictable abilities?

"So what do we do about Gar?" Krickall plunked a mug of ale on the table in front of Adoneesis and sat.

Adoneesis gulped a mouthful of spicy sweet mead and asked, "Are our scout teams out every night?"

"No. Gar and his goblins strike sporadically and we don't have the faeries to cover all of Dunraven every night, so the scouts go out two or three times a week. We don't use any set pattern and hope to keep the goblins off guard since they'll never know when to expect us."

Adoneesis watched a pink ray of dawn's light wend its way through a knothole and across the dirt floor. A new day was beginning. He considered the feeling of unease unfurling in his stomach and wondered what the day held. More appropriately, what did the night hold?

"Make sure they patrol tonight. Gar will strike."

Krickall frowned. "How do you know?"

"I've heard rumblings." Years of pretense and hiding of his abilities brought a lie easily to his lips and he didn't mention that the rumblings originated with a tree and an inner sense of unease. He hoped he was wrong, but day would pass to night and Gar would strike. Adoneesis was as sure of that as he was the fact that his experience with the tree, Wyllow Wood, had changed him on some elemental level. Only time would tell.

Two

He'd been right. Fates be damned. Sighing, Adoneesis cursed and paced the hard-packed earth of the dungeon he'd suddenly found a reason to use. Roused from his slumber by an insistent pounding on his door and confronted with the news that brought him here, he was in a sour mood. The stench of stale urine and rancid vomit assaulted him, while the gnarled roots of the dungeon tree taunted him with bitter memories of his youth. Overwhelmed, he snapped at the one responsible for bringing him here. "Fangs, Krickall, I cannot stand the smell. Bring him to me outside."

Without waiting for a reply, he took the stairs two at a time, threw open the heavy oak door and gulped a lungful of the fresh, pungent night air. Summer scents of hay, lavender, and sweet moss melded on the gentle night breeze and helped to relax Adoneesis, if only for a moment.

He loved his home, and since inheriting the throne from his father, he'd come to accept the responsibility of ruling the faerie realm. He took the responsibility seriously. Now, the realm was in danger and decisions must be made.

Sounds of a scuffle carried from within the darkness of the open doorway. A growl mixed with a cursed proclamation. Krickall's deep voice escaped into the night, followed by a thud. Seconds later the peace of the night was shattered as Krickall ousted an unconscious goblin on to the dew-covered grass by his feet.

"Krickall, how can I question him if he is unconscious?"

"Won't be but a moment and he'll come round. I didn't hit him hard." Krickall nudged the figure with his cloth bound foot and managed to elicit a moan from the scraggly looking creature. "See." Krickall smiled. But it wasn't the kind of smile that boded well for the goblin.

"Tell me again, but don't leave out any detail," Adoneesis demanded.

Krickall shook his massive head and ran his fingers through his red hair. "Last night, a band of goblins attacked one of the outer trees. They trampled the garden, killed livestock, and torched the tree." A quiver of disgust threaded his voice. "They raped and killed Rina, the female tree dweller, forced her family to watch, and were about to slaughter her mate and their two young ones, when they were set upon by neighboring faeries who heard the screams. This one was captured, but the others escaped."

Anger rose within Adoneesis, darkened his emotions, and set his pulse to beating fiercely. It didn't make sense. The goblins pestered the faeries with an occasional raid, but they'd never resorted to such violence. Slowly, deliberately, he reached down and grabbed the shackled goblin by his throat. Feigning unconsciousness, the goblin had no choice but to open his eyes and gasp for breath as Adoneesis squeezed hard. "Tell me, is this violent act of your own accord, or that of your leader, Gar?"

Slobbering and choking, the goblin shook his head. Whether that meant he didn't know or wouldn't tell, Adoneesis wasn't sure. He released his stranglehold. "Tell me."

The goblin choked, hunched over, and spat blood onto the grass. The shadow hours of night reflected the blood as a black stain on the earth.

Krickall kicked the goblin's leg. "Your king asked you a question. Answer him."

"It was Gar. He sent us."

"Why has he started raping and killing, and how does he expect to get away with such vile actions?"

Fresh fear lit the goblin's dull gray eyes as they flicked from Krickall to Adoneesis. "I... He..."

A low growl sounded in Krickall's throat as he raised his fist. The goblin cowered and words rushed from his mouth. "Gar hates Night Gloom. Says the trees haunt him. He wants to rule all faeries and goblins and live at Dunraven. He hates you too, Adoneesis. He plans to anger you by attacking the borders of Dunraven, and then use the duergarrs to guard the pathways to the world of man." The goblin raised a hand to cover his head as if expecting to be beaten, but Adoneesis and Krickall stood silent.

"The duergarrs." Krickall's whispered words fell into the silence.

"Yes," Adoneesis replied. "They hate humans enough to mislead or torture any who enter the faerie realm--usually killing them in the process."

Adoneesis' mind raced with the implications. Generations of inbreeding had taken a toll, as was apparent in the deformities of newborns and the weakening of powers that once rang strong and true. Now, the faerie bred responsibly, with only a few babes born each year. Some years, the change of seasons passed with no mewling cry of a newborn to light the day. With no hope of a new generation to replace them, faeries would soon cease to exist. Now that the duergarrs guarded the

13

pathways, there was no hope of breeding with humans to strengthen the faeries.

And Gar had turned to murder.

Adoneesis jaw twitched. Lifetimes ago the faeries had been a peaceful race, only rarely resorting to battle, and even then it was usually just a skirmish. How had they fallen to dealing with the foul tactics of last night's raid? Goblins creeping about in night shadows and killing the innocent? Some would say that the faerie bloodlines had become too tainted with human blood and the frailties that came with human characteristics. Others swore that as the power of the faeries weakened, so did the veil separating the two worlds, and the increased exposure to the primal world triggered the violence. Now it was necessary to patrol borders and train peace-loving faeries in battle strategy.

Adoneesis considered his options and tried to ignore a lifetime of his father's taunts declaring that he'd amount to nothing. A brief snicker shattered his thoughts and he glared at the goblin who wasn't fast enough to hide the gleam of triumph that lit his eyes.

The tide of anger that swirled inside Adoneesis lent itself easily to his latent powers. Not comfortable with his powers, Adoneesis fought a constant battle to suppress what he couldn't understand. But that night, beneath the shimmering silver rays of the moon, he lost control. Swirling anger gave way to pulsing power and Adoneesis was consumed until he could no longer breathe without choking. Lusty vengeance wound from deep within and in one shaft of focused power, he unleashed his fury upon the goblin.

A chilling scream of pain arced from the goblin's mouth and his face twisted into a mask of intense agony. With his feet jerking uncontrollably, the goblin's heels dug divots in the grass, while his fingers clenched clods of dirt from the earth in a death grasp. Then he lay still.

A startled look of fear crossed Krickall's features and Adoneesis' heart raced at the implications of what he'd just done. To kill with mere thought and emotion. How? What other abilities did he possess that would show themselves unbidden?

Krickall's deep blue eyes clashed with Adoneesis' gaze and Adoneesis cursed the fates that had caused him to explode into a red haze of emotion and kill the goblin. Krickall recovered quickly and lowered his gaze to the now dead goblin.

"I'll bury him where he won't be found."

Adoneesis laid his hand on Krickall's arm. "Thank you."

Krickall shrugged. "I can't leave his body here, can I?"

"That's not what I mean. Thank you for your loyalty and belief in me."

"I've known you my entire life. Of course I trust you, Adoneesis." His gaze flickered to the goblin and he grinned. "Even if you can decimate a goblin with nothing more than a glance.

Adoneesis smiled, but it was a hollow gesture. Krickall joked, but the truth was that Adoneesis had lost control and someone was dead. If his hold over his own emotions was so tenuous, how could he be trusted to control an entire realm with each faerie dependent on his decisions and actions? He fisted one hand and jammed it into the other hand.

"I don't know what to do. Gar has always posed a minor irritation, never a threat to life. What's happened that he's escalated his attacks?"

"I'd guess that he's been planning this for years, but only now feels confident enough to strike in such a manner." Krickall shook his head--the mass of red hair making a shuffling noise as it brushed across his neck. "Not a good sign. We can't waste time. Whatever we do, it must be quick and decisive or we'll find ourselves cut off and slaughtered. Last night was Gar taunting you, much like what a hunter does before pouncing on the prey that has no way of escaping."

Cold fear gripped Adoneesis in a frozen moment. Raegar's face loomed in his mind's eye, with familiar, hateful features twisted into a mocking grin. *Failure. You'll never be anything but a failure.*

Responsibility and doubt slammed into Adoneesis, but lessened with the dawning understanding that the future of the realm didn't depend solely on him. The fate of the faerie realm rested with the faeries of the realm. That knowledge gave him the freedom to act.

"There is but one thing to do. I'll have the banshee send out a Sound of Gathering. We'll meet at the clearing to the north of the main tree."

"Sound of Gathering. But that's not been done in... hmmm, I can't say as I remember it ever being done. Such an act will be perceived as one of desperation. It is so... final." Krickall grabbed the goblin's body and hoisted it over his shoulder. "Are you sure there's no other way?"

"Gar is at our throats and the duergarrs have cut us off from the world of man. It is necessary."

Krickall bowed his head and melted quietly into the nearby forest. Adoneesis shook his head that one of such size could move like a wraith. He sighed and sent out a brief mind feeler to locate one of the banshees. Another ability he possessed, but one he did not fear. It was harmless, not like the power that had lashed out and killed the goblin.

He easily located the presence of a banshee not far away and set off at a lope to set into motion an act that he knew would instill fear in every goblin within hearing distance. Such a Gathering of all races of faerie would prove an intimidating adversary. Even for the goblins.

~ * ~

16

Those faeries in close proximity to Dunraven arrived quickly in spite of the late hour. Banshee broke into the clearing first, as they were the ones who had sent out the call. This was the one time they used their keening wail for something other than the announcement of death. Their white silk gowns shone bright in the dim evening light and highlighted their stringy hair and sharp features. Adoneesis bowed his head in a gesture of acknowledgment. Corrigans followed closely, presenting a contrast of beauty to the harshness of the banshee. Of course, the morning light would show the corrigans differently when daylight turned them to ugly hags.

The first to arrive were set to the task of feeding and arranging places to rest for the influx of faeries, as it would take at least half a day for most of them to arrive at their fastest pace. The area hummed with frantic whispers and speculation while Adoneesis set about fortifying Dunraven. He'd chosen a meeting place that offered the best defense against attack. Surrounded by dwelling trees and lying on the highest spot of land, the clearing offered a view of the only road that led to Dunraven as well as the encompassing hills and valleys. He sent faeries to collect firewood and pile it at strategic points so fires would light the night sky and he posted a lookout on the top branches of the main dwelling tree to raise the alarm at the approach of any goblin.

The day passed in a flurry of activity as faeries flew, flitted, or fell into the clearing. Flickering spots of light, golden globes of energy, large and small, young and old, all faeries within distance of hearing arrived. Finally, they waited for only one-- the Lady of the Lake. But rather than come herself and tax her aged self, she'd send her emissaries, the ellyllons. These guardians of the Lady would speak for her in all matters.

Dusk descended on the unsettled group and brought with it a cloying mist. A raspy voice broke the muttered whispers of speculation and cut through the mist. "I hate waiting so long. Why are we here? Tell us now."

Adoneesis looked at the speaker and sighed. Eora. A phooka. A temperamental breed at best that could take on the body of horse, dog, or bull, while retaining the head of a faerie. Currently, Eora had shape-shifted into a stamping, snorting bull whose eyes blazed with impatience and dull-wittedness. Scattered around him were about a dozen phookas, the only ones left in existence. As with many faeries, their numbers had decreased over the decades.

"Eora, I will speak when all the faeries are here."

The phookas pranced about in a temper. Eora narrowed his gaze and pinned it upon Adoneesis. "Tell us why we are here, or we will leave." His snarling tone was challenging and disrespectful.

Adoneesis hesitated at further confrontation because tendrils of anger he'd raised with the goblin still fought to gain hold over him, but decided he couldn't leave the phooka's attitude unaddressed. Being overly soft would do nothing to gain the respect of those he was responsible for. "No one leaves. This concerns the welfare of all faeries." Bending down, he pulled at some leaves until he found what he was looking for. Armed with a simple rowan branch from a nearby tree, he raised his arm and waved. In reply, the trees swayed, as if in a gentle breeze, and the leaves danced, not haphazardly, but rather a purposeful crackling of leaves piling together to form a circle about the clearing.

A simple manipulation of energy.

Adoneesis had sealed the clearing so that no one could leave. The phookas screeched, while shocked dismay crossed the faces of others gathered and whispers spread like wildfire.

Adoneesis knew he'd shocked those assembled. Their king had resorted to magic and since most faeries were not even aware of his powers, the fact that he chose to display his abilities only enforced the penetrating urgency.

Impeded now by the circle cast about the clearing, the surrounding forest mist was unable to cast its pall in the gathering of faeries. Wings ceased to flutter, grunting stopped, and all movement stilled. Silence descended.

It was a gentle buzzing at first, circling around the outer shield of the clearing. Slowly, the buzz increased to an insistent whisper that formed a request to open the circle and allow entrance. Adoneesis raised the rowan wand. The motion cleared a path through the swirling leaves and pervasive mist.

The ellyllons had arrived.

Small and winged, they flew into the gathering and found their way to the front, close to Adoneesis. They were the emissaries of the Lady; it was where they belonged.

With a nod, Adoneesis gave them fair greeting and cleared his throat. He gazed out over the assembled faeries and wished for an easy answer, but knew that times ahead would separate the weak from the strong, while circumstances would shape characters and meld relationships. Krickall's words that they must act quickly and decisively gave him strength to share the knowledge gained from the goblin. He left out some of the more graphic details as well as the freshly dug grave on the edge of Dunraven's forest that was a testament to his own inner demon. At least he'd managed to gain information from the terrified goblin before sending him to the Netherland of Tarnished Souls.

Fidgeting turned to statue stillness. Eyes at first filled with anger and indignation turned to fear as Adoneesis completed his tale with the final statement of fact. "Not only has Gar declared war on us, but he's enlisted the aid of the duergarrs to prevent us from calling humans to us for breeding or for help."

A voice drifted from the middle of the shifting crowd. "Why can't we travel to the world of man and mate with them there?"

"Travel to the human world means assuming a denser form to adjust to their slower moving energies. Since we must be in our true form to mate, it means the humans must find their way here."

Despair and pain crept into Adoneesis' words and lent truth to the severity of the situation. Sounds of shuffling feet and tearful whispers reached Adoneesis, and he felt each tear as if a knife in his heart. The faeries were his responsibility, and he had failed them. He did not know what to do and he searched the pleading gazes looking to him for answers. Ugly and beautiful, they were all the same to him and they were his responsibility.

A strange sensation slowly pulsed in his mind, and Adoneesis pulled himself from the mire of emotions to send out sensing feelers. Undetected by anyone, his mind ran over the faeries one at a time. Nothing. Suddenly, he felt the twinge again, but not enough to find the source. Rather than rely on his overloaded senses, Adoneesis used his vision.

His eyes came to rest on Toran, leader of the dryads. Toran was ancient and the only male dryad left among a race of females--another effect of too much inbreeding. Wisps of colored light, all dryads held within them the wisdom of the ancient trees. They were the guardians of the trees, and over the ages, they had learned the secrets of nature, in some cases even passing their information to humans--such as the human druid, Merlin.

The dryad's aura shimmered in a state of flux, and a flicker of hope flared. Did this age-old dryad know of a way to save the faeries?

"Toran, what do you know?"

The wisp of light that was Toran stilled and a dense shape--not unlike a human--formed. When Toran spoke, he sounded like the wind in the trees and the storm in the sky. Powerful, yet subdued, his voice echoed around the clearing and garnered silence from the faeries.

"I have no knowledge."

The faeries grumbled in dismay. Snuffling, flitting, chattering, and flustering, they darted about the clearing and drowned out any further conversation. They grew restless, and their king was doing nothing to give them hope.

"Quiet." Adoneesis' command brought silence to the clearing and all eyes turned to Toran, and then back to Adoneesis. Two great souls, young and old, they stared into each other's eyes and each took a reading of truth, lies, and honor.

~ * ~

Toran tore his gaze from Adoneesis and looked to the expectant faeries. He smiled ironically. For years, younger faeries had taunted or ignored him and held little respect for wisdom and age. They knew nothing of the battles he had waged, the lives he'd changed, and the part he'd played in the history of man and faerie. Now they looked to him for salvation and the thought crossed his mind to leave them on their own. Bah! They were foolish and the situation was of their own making.

A glimmer of movement from the edge of his sight drew his attention and he looked down to see a small pixie sitting cross-legged on the ground by his feet. It was Bailiwick, a pixie with the purest of hearts and sweetest of souls. Bailiwick smiled, his pointed nose crinkled and his blue eyes shone bright. His six-fingered hand reached up to tug at his green tunic that always seemed too big for him, and then he folded both hands into fists, settled them under his chin, and sat in rapt attention. The young whip was like a sponge waiting to soak up any words or knowledge that came from Toran's mouth.

A smile tugged Toran's lips, but he hardened his mind against the innocent. What would it say of his character if he did not speak what he knew? He would probably be banished to the Netherland of Tarnished Souls, and he would deserve it if he condemned these souls to their certain death. A nervous murmur grew among the faeries and in a moment of panic Toran raised his pulsing hands of light.

"I have been too long gone from my tree, I must return."

With the power of one older than most, he shimmered himself through the barrier raised by Adoneesis and came to land by his tree, Duir. Gnarled and old, the huge tree had withstood centuries of life and nature's elements, a testament to Toran's protection. With a gentle rub upon the rough trunk, Toran melded with the oak he had long ago claimed as his own.

Worn out from the meeting, he needed to rest. Like his tree, he was old--too old to be caught up in the current problems of the faerie folk. He'd lived his life, fulfilled responsibilities, and dealt with death and despair. He sighed deeply and listened to the soothing of the wind whispering in the branches of his beloved tree. It seemed as if nature was speaking to him and softly whispered of the past and his duties of the present.

No. He bolted up and refused to listen. With a shake of his fist, he yelled at the circling wind he suspected had been sent by the Lady. "The time is past. Let them take care of themselves. They have shown no care for me over the years with their taunts and disrespect."

It did no good. The wind whispered like a subdued hive of bees. The brush of a warm sliding breeze touched upon his cheek and whispered seductively in his ear. *You cannot ignore their need.*

"Bah!" Toran snorted, though his resolve weakened. He had never been able to withstand the Lady's sultry powers of persuasion.

"Toran." Intruding on his solitude, an all too real voice demanded his presence.

"There is no one here."

"Toran, come out from your tree. We need to speak."

"King Adoneesis, I have nothing to say."

"Yes. You do."

Increasing from a whisper to a gust, the wind blew about Toran's tree--the very motion letting Toran know the Lady of the Lake would brook no argument to her wishes.

"Toran, don't make me hurt your tree." An empty threat thrown out by Adoneesis, but it was enough to pull Toran from his tree instantly. One of the most sacred dryad rules was that they must show themselves if there is threat of danger to the tree they protect.

"Fangs on you, Adoneesis." Toran flickered light and bright, reflecting his anger.

Adoneesis was not alone. Bailiwick and the leader of the ellyllons were with him. Toran narrowed his gaze and snorted.

"It is only because of my respect for you that I did not call you to task in front of the other faeries, Toran. What I don't understand is your hesitation in sharing knowledge that would help us."

"Your respect--maybe, but others of the faerie race show me no respect. They laugh at me and bombard Duir with stones. We are old." Toran reached out to stroke his beloved tree. With his fingers he caressed the deeply etched furrows that had formed over many centuries. His voice tugged with tears and emotion. "We deserve respect."

"Please, Toran, this is not the time for grudges. I will decree a law that all must show you respect. Just help us," Adoneesis pleaded.

Toran settled his flickering light and sank to the ground. "All right, all right." Weariness crusted his ancient voice. "This is not the first time such troubles have been faced by elemental beings. Lifetimes ago, there existed an island where everyone respected the forces of nature and the universe that gave them life. They didn't show disregard like the faeries these days."

"Toran..." Adoneesis prompted, warning him to stay on subject.

"Fine." He waved a shimmering hand and continued his story. "Humans, faeries, gods, and animals lived in harmony until greed, lust and corruption took over and destroyed the island. A few survivors managed to find their way to a new land, and over time, they changed the land to create a place that drew all creatures of mystery. Various life forms drew together and altered the very atmosphere, pulsing with the vibrations and enabling this new place to shift away from the world around. They were there, yet not there."

Bailiwick jumped up and down waving his hand.

"Yes, Bailiwick?" Toran questioned.

"I know, I know--it's Avalon, am I right?" His excited voice squeaked out his question in a quick jumble of words.

"Yes, young pixie, I speak of Avalon. The island survivors created Avalon, a place for elemental and primal beings to exist. But when Avalon disappeared into the mists of time, the humans of Avalon had evolved into entities far too light to return to the primal world, so they worked with the faeries to create the realm of faerie from what was left of the land of mist."

Bailiwick jumped about in circles and bounced off Toran's aura. Coming to land on the ground, he straightened his peaked cap and blushed. "This is the time you spoke about. The time when faeries were in danger."

"Yes, yes. The end of Avalon was a hard time for us."

Toran looked to the leader of the ellyllons, emissaries for the Lady of the Lake, and guardians of her domain. "You know of that time, guardian?"

"Yes. I was there."

"Ahh. What is your name?"

"Raven."

Toran bowed low. "I remember your name. You were part of the plan."

Before Raven could answer, Adoneesis spoke. "Toran, please, our need is great. With all respect, what plan do you speak of?"

"Always in a hurry. Fine. The first Lady of Avalon, Niobe, possessed the ability to look into the future and saw this time of trouble for the faeries. She confided in me with instructions not to speak unless the situation could be resolved in no other way." Toran sighed and whispered, "Niobe came from the island I spoke of earlier and she was a lover of one of the original old gods. The Thunder God himself.

"Unknown to any, Niobe placed their child with humans and intended that the power of the god and magic of the Lady would one day save the faeries."

"How was this kept secret? Do we know if the bloodline of this child still exists? Even so, how could a human child possibly save us? It would be far too tainted with human blood, would it not?" Adoneesis paused to take a breath.

"The child's birth was kept secret because the Lady feared for its life. Too many enemies would have used the child to gain power. The child, a male, grew up and produced a child, who in turn produced a child. Each generation there has only been one offspring--whether male or female does not matter, they pass on the full power of the firstborn. The Lady made sure of this when she cast her spell." Toran passed a wavering hand over his brow. He was not young anymore, and grew weary.

Raven spoke up. "Let me continue, Toran."

"*You* know the story?" Adoneesis questioned sharply.

"Yes, but I had forgotten the tale until now." He sighed and turned his gaze to the distant mountains, as he spoke, his voice revealed untold depths of anguish. "So much has happened, so many lives gone. The Lady was wise enough to make certain that the powers of the child would remain hidden and stagnant unless they were ignited by a faerie who chanted the words she wrote long ago. That way the child would remain undetected and safe from any dark forces of magic."

"But how was the child placed with humans? If the Lady had ventured among them, it would have been known far and wide."

"She had help. A spunkie."

"Of course, spunkies were notorious for switching faerie babies with human ones; that was one way our ancestors introduced fresh bloodlines into the race."

"Yes, until the spunkies slowly died out themselves."

"How is this child supposed to be our savior? Even if he, or she, possesses the power, how can that benefit us?"

The question Toran dreaded. His answer was quiet-- apologetic. "I have no answer to that."

Like a fire raging out of control, panic flamed in the king's eyes, and he whispered, "To be so close to a solution, only to find that it is no solution at all. What are we to do?"

Raven raised his hands and appealed to Adoneesis. "The answer lies in the mind of the child. We must find him, or her, and open the lock that was placed there many years ago by the Lady."

"Wait. Why not ask the Lady? She placed the spell, so surely she can tell us how to use the power of the child. Right?"

"The Lady's recollection of past events has faded with age, so I'm afraid she'll be no help to us. If she even still lives."

"She still lives. Her essence was here but a moment before you arrived."

Raven smiled. "That is heartening to know, but I'm sure she drained herself with such an act."

Adoneesis cleared his throat. "I'm sorry for the Lady. She is a living legend whose death will be our loss. So it is up to us to find this child ourselves, make sure it is safe, and bring it here. Then we must find a way to unlock the secret of its mind. There must be someone who knows how to do that."

"There was someone, but he disappeared many years ago. Kypher, one of my fellow ellyllons."

"Then we will use combined magic and find a way. We have to."

Bailiwick settled on Adoneesis' shoulder and whispered in his ear. "How do we find the child?"

"I..." Adoneesis looked from dryad to ellyllon. "Do either of you know?"

Both shrugged.

"How can you not know?"

"So many battles have been fought, so many souls born and withered. We did not feel the need to keep track of a human child--even if it had the blood of the Lady in its veins," Raven answered for both Toran and himself.

"We are lost." Adoneesis brushed a weary hand over his brow.

"No. There may be a chance," Toran remarked. With a flicker, he turned and connected to Duir with a sliver of light. The sliver grew and pulsed with luminescence. Light around Toran paled and then grew bright--bright enough to make the others cover their eyes. With a final blast of light Toran and Duir disconnected, becoming two entities, and the light dimmed to normal.

"The prophetess. She can help us find the child."

"The prophetess?" Raven, Bailiwick, and Adoneesis looked to each other questioningly.

"I thought she died. Is she not dead? Yes, I'm sure I heard she died." Bailiwick jumped from Raven's shoulder to Adoneesis' shoulder.

"Hmmm, if Duir says she lives, then she lives," Raven remarked with only a hint of uncertainty. "Although none have heard of her in such a long time."

"Where can we find her?" Seeking an answer, Adoneesis looked from Toran to Raven.

"You will find her eight days ride to the west. At the base of Blackthorn Mountain." Toran stretched a shimmering finger and pointed westward. "Could be done in five days if you push your horse to the limit. I have done my duty, so leave me to rest. I am tired." Toran's formless shape melded with his beloved tree, and he was gone.

~ * ~

The moon rose like polished marble through the branches of the ancient tree Duir, where the fate of the faeries had been discussed. As if sensing the gravity of the situation, even the animals remained silent. The result was a place of emptiness-- except for one thing. The muffled sound of cursing and stumbling broke hard through the silence. Leaves crackled and branches swayed as a figure clumsily emerged from the denseness of the woodland thicket.

"Jeez and jeepers, bugs and creepers, why is it *always* up to me--why is it *always* on my shoulders--why do I *always* have to do the dirty work?"

Picking leaves, dirt, and grass from his ragged clothing, the goblin stumbled his way from the clearing and down the path he knew would lead him back to his leader.

"Carts and farts, bats and cats, do I have a tale to tell. Hee, hee!" Gwepper chuckled and snorted through his nose and ignored the spit and slobber running down his chin. He came to a fork in the path and had to stop to consider his options. "Oh, yes, Gar will give me a reward. I have no doubt." He rubbed his hands together in anticipation of lustful fulfillment.

Deciding upon his direction, he ran up the pathway muttering, "The child. The child. We must find the child. They will search for the prophetess, who I am sure is dead, while we find the child." Gwepper bounded across the lands of Dunraven and made his way towards the realm of Night Gloom, the goblin's stronghold to the north.

Three

Everyone feared the prophetess. Tales of dark magic and curses emitted mumbles of protest when Adoneesis asked for a volunteer to ride out and find the mythic faerie. He considered commanding someone to go, but the importance of finding her dictated he trust whomever he sent do their best to find her. It was a task better set upon him anyway, mainly because he was curious--having heard tales of her as far back as memory served--but also because his horse, Brachus, could outrun any faerie steed and would allow no one on his back but Adoneesis. Time was too valuable to waste. Issuing strict orders to Krickall to stay at Dunraven and protect the faeries and armed with Toran's directions King Adoneesis set out to find the prophetess.

He pushed Brachus to his limit, and sensing the urgency, Brachus gave with all his heart. The duo galloped through forest, marsh, desolate wasteland, and only the occasional pocket of rich crop-filled field. Gar's goblins had obviously raided the land, leveled small forests to gain wood for building, and picked over vegetation without planting anything in its place.

Upon seeing the damaged land, Adoneesis wondered how he had been so blind to what was happening beyond the borders of Dunraven. The faerie races, once devout in natural ways and beliefs, now abused the very land that gave them life. Raegar's influence, Adoneesis was sure, as well as Gar's.

After five days of travel over winding trails amidst low-limbed trees that brushed against him with grasping branches, Adoneesis was relieved to come within sight of a widening of the trail. His relief was short-lived as the sound of a falling tree ripped through the forest.

"That is not possible," he muttered. "The ancient trees have withstood centuries of weather and natural upheaval. Why would they give up their roots now?"

But his heart knew the answer. They would not--unless taken down deliberately.

He urged Brachus into a gallop and it soon became clear that the widening of the trail was in fact the unnatural clearing of the ancient trees. He felt a ripple of disturbance in the way of nature, a thickening of the air and pressure in his chest. As he broke into the carnage of the clearing, even Brachus snorted and pranced in uneasy fashion. Before him lay the wasteland of a once great forest. Newly gashed scars marked the earth. Trunks of trees long-lived, now dead, exposed their roots of life to the onlookers. Small animals, birds, and even some tree faeries flitted and scampered about in search of a home that no longer existed. Confusion, death, and greed tainted the afternoon breezes that blew across the land.

In the midst of destruction stood the faerie troll, Rufus, cocky and abrupt, squat and ugly, dark and hairy. His harsh voice harangued the workers. Bondfaeries, much to Adoneesis' dismay. An ancient practice revived by his father and one that Adoneesis thought he'd managed to stamp out over the last few years. Timeless ages ago, when the land of faerie had come into being, the various races had been given a portion of the land as a kind of stewardship. No one could own the land, just care for it with the respect intended for all living things. As time passed and the exposure to the human world had crossed over the barrier between worlds and tainted good intent with greed, a certain hierarchy had developed among the faeries. The races had divided their loyalties, each race claiming their portion of land in ownership. Unfortunately, the stronger took advantage of the weaker and bondfaeries had come into being. Faeries bound to the overlord by fear and forced to work as slaves.

Since becoming king, Adoneesis had managed to wrest control away from many of the overlords who made claims of ownership and he managed to restore many of the older customs of respect and sharing of the land. Obviously, Rufus had managed to avoid him.

"Leave no trees in this entire area." Rufus waved his hand to emcompass the entire valley. "Let me know when the job is done, and don't slack or I'll flay the skin off your backs myself." With a snap of his cloak, Rufus turned for his horse only to face an enraged Adoneesis.

"Damn!" he whispered. His eyes lit with fear that turned to conniving consideration.

Confrontation was delayed by pounding hoof beats. Three riders, all trolls like Rufus, approached with two packhorses in gallop behind them. Ignoring anyone but Rufus they slid to a halt and displayed the packhorses. The horses pawed the ground and snorted in obvious distaste of their load. Each horse carried a couple of bloody deer carcasses. Once alive with grace and regal beauty, the deer's lifeless black eyes now stared at nothing.

Covered with mud and blood splatters, one of the riders cleared his throat and bragged. "We followed them for a bit, then lost them up around the outer border of Dunraven, but Eckherd here circled around and flushed them out. Right over the old canyon cliffs, we were able to run them to their deaths."

He chuckled and puffed his chest. "They'll make fine food for the feast."

Livid with seething anger, Adoneesis spoke in a harsh whisper. "Fangs, Rufus, you have gone too far this time. You have broken the laws by which we live and I will not let this go unpunished."

His hands clenched the reins and he forced himself to remain calm or he would kill the arrogant fool before him. Maybe he should. But he battled the urge that rose so insistently, that part of him that could kill without a thought. Such an action would lower him to the level where Rufus now wallowed, and he did not want another grave to add to the one already dug for the marauding goblin. Fierce pounding in his head made it hard for him to concentrate as his hand moved towards his sword. He touched the smooth leather handle and imagined drawing the steely length of the long sword and thrusting it into the disgusting creature before him.

Rufus saw the action and lowered a hand to his own sword. Thoughts of his journey's purpose calmed Adoneesis enough to withdraw his hand. He was not sure enough of his untrained powers to engage Rufus and his followers single-handed and the worker faeries did not look strong enough, or bold enough, to back him up.

"Not now. There is a time and place for everything." Adoneesis pinned Rufus with a gaze steeped with barely controlled rage. "You disgust me by eating the meat of living creatures and destroying the ancient trees of life. Your actions clearly align you with Gar and I will deal with you after I deal with him."

Rufus puffed his chest and lay his hand upon his sword. "This is *my* forest and the animals that live in it belonged to *me*. It is my right to kill the animals and serve them on a platter. It is my right to take the trees down and use them for whatever purpose I want." With a flick of his wrist, he withdrew his sword and waved it at the nearby workers. "Why are you just standing there? Work," he snarled. Terrified, the faeries hastened to their work with renewed purpose. They may not agree with what Rufus was doing, but subservience had been beaten into them and they could no more break free than could a sprite trapped in a mud hole.

Rufus smirked in satisfaction. "They will do as I say. Now, get off my land."

Adoneesis looked at the laboring faeries and despair seeped into his bones. They did not deserve Rufus for a lord. No one deserved the treatment Rufus forced on those below him. Adoneesis locked his gaze on Rufus and the troll faerie matched his stare, unblinking. Adoneesis wondered at such lack of deference to him as king but realized that now was not the time to exert his authority and challenge Rufus. He couldn't risk injury or death. Not now. Tapping down his anger, he snapped, "I will leave, but hear this--I will see you destroyed, your lands restored to someone who will treat them with respect, and your bondfaeries set free to live their own lives."

Without waiting for a reply, Adoneesis spurred his restless mount. Brachus, in a deliberate maneuver, dug his hooves deeply into the ground and rained divots of dirt into Rufus' face. Seething anger followed Adoneesis through the rest of his journey and increased with each stride Brachus took toward the base of the mountain that supposedly lent a home to the legendary prophetess.

~ * ~

Bronwen rubbed her aching back and silently cursed the aged body that gave her such grief every time she gardened. But in spite of the pain and awkwardness of using her gnarled hands, she loved working the rich soil. The garden faced the full light of the sun, gave life to vegetables, herbs, and fruits, and provided a connection to the earth's energy that sustained her powers as nothing else could.

She wiped the back of her hand across her forehead, sighed, and inhaled deeply of the perfumed wildflowers dancing in the noon breeze. Their gentle perfumes drifted on the far reaches of the wind. Their vivid colors bathed in the golden rays of sun.

Her valley. Her home. Her prison. Wrapped in rolling hills and age-old trees, rooted deep into the soil of time, the valley provided a haven for fox, deer, rabbits, birds, and other animals. Untouched by time and untainted by dark forces, the valley almost glowed with succulent abundance.

In the midst of the splendor, Bronwen had built a small hut of clay, fallen limbs, and underbrush. It was crude, yet had withstood the tests of nature. It was where she'd lived for decades and where she would likely die.

Her reverie was interrupted by the jolt of awareness that a stranger had entered her valley. "Someone approaches." She shaded her eyes with one hand and patted the head of a nearby goat with the other, while tendrils of anxiety wound a path to her stomach. Visitors had been rare in the decades since she'd been banished to this outlying land of solitude.

Just then, a stunning silver flash of fur burst from the shadows of the forest walls--Gray Wolf responding to her mood. Protector of the prophetess, Gray Wolf had wandered into her life one day and planted himself firmly. Bronwen enjoyed his company, not that she needed his protection, but it pleased her to please him, so she let him stay.

Within no more than a moment, Gray Wolf sat on his haunches by her side. Resting her hand lightly on the wolf's broad head, Bronwen felt a warm surge of familiar energy followed by a spike of fear. "I sense the king himself. I suppose that means we must act with a semblance of diplomacy."

A rumble of a growl that had been building in the throat of the silvery wolf faded into a whimper of disappointment. Bronwen chuckled and waved her hand in a gesture of dismissal that sent the wolf loping back to the shimmering shadows of the forest where he would stay until their visitor was gone.

"Farewell, my friend," she whispered, her mind reeling with uncertainty and possibilities. She turned to face Adoneesis. The king's approach would explain her restless night. With her sleep wrought with nightmares and memories too hurtful to relive, she'd tossed and turned until dawn rose across the distant horizon. What did his presence mean? He couldn't know the truth--could he?

Folding her arms across her chest, she waited anxiously. The first thing she noticed was the steed that he rode. Dark brown, like the rich soil of the earth, the creature obviously held ancient blood within. He tossed his massive head in greeting. Bronwen understood the gesture of salutation, though Adoneesis merely gave a tug on the reins to settle his beast.

"Greetings of the day to you, prophetess."

His confused thoughts lay open to her probe and she forced herself not to flinch at one thought in particular. *This cannot be the prophetess. Where is the beauty she is renowned for?* Tears of hurt gathered in her eyes, but she blinked them back. "You are mistaken, I am not the prophetess. I heard she passed on to the next world many years ago."

He studied her face, his eyes boring into her in a manner that suggested keenly developed senses. The sensation of a mind probe surprised Bronwen and she was barely able to set up a block in time. Was the king aware of his mind probe? The ability for such things had been forgotten by many, but would occasionally show up in a faerie of exceptional ability. She was not surprised that Adoneesis had inherited such things.

Adoneesis frowned, making Bronwen think he was aware of his intended probe and her deliberate block. "You have to be the prophetess."

"Why?"

Adoneesis hesitated. "My father told me about you, and I have no reason to doubt his word."

Bronwen's blood ran cold. With a shaking hand, she reached up to brush a stray hair from her cheek. "Your father told you," she whispered. "What exactly did he tell you?"

Adoneesis waved his hand dismissively. "It's not important."

"Tell me or the conversation ends now." Her voice was harsh, commanding the elements and rippling the currents of air surrounding them. Gray Wolf growled from the shadows of the woods but Bronwen knew he wouldn't attack without reason.

Wrinkling his brow into a frown, Adoneesis answered. "When I was young, many faeries told whispered tales of a beautiful faerie of immense power who lived across the mountains to the west. When I questioned my father about her, he slapped me. He said that the witch had been condemned to a life of seclusion by her own hand, and there she would stay until she died. A few times, when I had done something very wrong, he threatened to send me to the witch and let her deal with my disobedience. I never asked of you again, but I remembered the stories of your power. The dryad, Toran, directed me to you. He said you could help."

Bronwen heard only the first part of Adoneesis plea. Sorrow took her breath from her and left a pulsing hole deep within where she'd locked away her emotions. Her throat clutched open and shut and she was barely able to whisper. "He threatened you--with me."

"What?"

"Your father. He used me to threaten you."

"Yes." Adoneesis had the grace to look sheepish, as if realizing the insult.

Sorrow turned to hot anger. "You are brave to come to the home of a witch so evil that she is used to threaten young ones."

Adoneesis said naught, just sat upon his steed and waited.

She narrowed her gaze and considered the young king before her. "You may call me Bronwen."

Adoneesis breathed in relief and Bronwen sensed the seething of strong powers dormant just below the surface and probably beaten out of him when he was younger. Raegar's ego would have demanded such an act.

"Since you have come such a distance to speak with me, I assume your needs are great. Maybe a vanishing spell, or better yet, a love potion?"

Adoneesis waved his hand in dismissal. "No. None of those things. What I need is much more important."

A chill crossed the sunlight valley. Gray Wolf's mournful howl rode the rising wind and set the trees to shivering in its wake. Adoneesis pulled his wrap tighter as if he were cold, but Bronwen recognized the whisper of death and nothing could protect against its call.

She sighed. Even though death called, life was not finished with her yet. Adoneesis was here for a reason--a reason she was not ready to hear. She looked intently at the king. He was handsome enough with his dark-toned skin, determined jaw, and moderately slanted eyes. His dark walnut colored hair was long, but no longer than the collar of his leather vest, and his eyes were the dark brown of molasses. By the looks of his beard, he hadn't shaven in days. Rugged. Rugged and handsome even by human standards. What set him apart from others of good looks was the flashing intensity in his eyes that bespoke depths of intelligence and understanding. Bronwen opened her senses further--what she felt made her proud. Here was one who cared about those around him. Not only did he care, but he would go out of his way to help those he felt responsible for. His sense of duty was strong, as was his compassion.

"Lady Bronwen, are you all right?"

"I am fine. Tell me King Adoneesis..."

"I have not told you who I am."

"It's not necessary. Your circle of life radiates around your body and tells me all I need to know."

"I see. Does this circle of life also tell you that the faeries are in desperate times and need the benefit of your powers?"

"I have only the humble powers of a backwoods witch."

"Bah! Do not fool with me. I am your king and as such demand your co-operation." Even as the words left his mouth, his eyes filled with repentance for the arrogant words.

"Ahhh. The young pup has sharp teeth." She was amused rather than insulted.

Adoneesis flushed with embarrassment. "Lady, you may have been alive as long as the ancient trees growing in the forest of Night Gloom, but that does not mean you could shed your allegiance to the people of the faerie world."

Bronwen bowed her head. "I am sorry. I suppose I have lived with only my own company for too long."

Adoneesis inclined his head. "No, I apologize. I was raised to respect my elders, and given your great powers, you deserve my respect."

"Your parents raised you well." Bronwen stated and watched his face drain of color.

Coldness and tension crept into Adoneesis voice. "I never knew my mother, but my father raised me as befitted a future king." He snorted. "Sometimes, it seems I knew him naught, either."

Bronwen clenched her fists to restrict the tears from falling. "I'm sorry."

"No need for you to be sorry, but I thank you for your concern." He pulled on the reins to quiet his horse that shifted impatiently. "I fear that Brachus has run out of patience. I ask you--no, I plead with you to come with me to Dunraven where others await us. I will explain then." He paused. "I do not know why you have become a recluse, but I do know that you are needed. Please."

Silence fell heavy. Not a bird sang and there was not a breath of whispering wind as the world waited in breathless anticipation, or maybe fear.

"I will come."

Adoneesis breathed deeply with relief. "How much time do you need to prepare? I can send a cart back to help collect your things."

Bronwen smiled. "No, that would take too long. The trip around the mountains is not an easy one. I'm surprised you made the trip at all. You should have sent someone else."

"I ride faster."

"I see. I would also wager that everyone is afraid of me. Still, the faeries should do your bidding no matter what, and since you are king, you should have commanded. By placing yourself in danger, you place all faeries in danger."

"We are already in danger. That is why I am here."

"Fine, I will gather a few belongings and come with you now."

Adoneesis dismounted. "Let me help you."

"No!" Heart pounding, Bronwen took a deep breath and softened her tone. "Why not water your steed. He must be thirsty." Without waiting for a reply, she disappeared into her hut. She hoped she had not raised suspicion with her sharp retort, but she hadn't been expecting him, so she hadn't had time to hide certain items he shouldn't see--mementos of her past and paltry possessions of a heart broken and torn asunder. No, Adoneesis was not ready to know the truth.

~ * ~

Adoneesis watched Bronwen retreat into the dark hut and wondered what she was hiding, not that it was any of his business. But he felt the urge to confront her and demand... demand what? Why did he feel such a need to help the faerie who denied her powers and place in the world? Who was she really? Her looks were of a dried prune, yet her laughter whispered like the softest chime in a summer breeze and her words fell from cracked lips like warm maple syrup. He was drawn to her elusive qualities in a way he couldn't understand.

Adoneesis drew water from the well and laughed as Brachus slurped from the old wooden bucket. Scratching the muscled neck of his faithful steed, Adoneesis remarked, "Tell me friend, when did life get so complicated? And why do I find myself with all these conflicting emotions?"

As if to attest to his words, the back of his neck tingled strangely just a moment before a crashing sound echoed from the forest. Instinct bade him to reach for his sword as he turned to face a slobbering beast that broke from the forest. The beast--a rare muckraker--cast a huge shadow on the ground with his misshapen body. His single-horned, bullet-shaped head moved from side to side, while his nostrils flared in an attempt to find prey. They were not known for having great eyesight. What they were well-know for was eating the flesh of any living creature, usually after burying their prey alive and then digging it up once the flesh had a chance to season with the earth.

A snarling screech reverberated as the muckraker scented his prey and his loping gait covered the distance from the forest to Adoneesis. Brachus reared. The unexpected jolt of horseflesh against his shoulder knocked Adoneesis off balance before he could draw his sword, but he righted himself quickly enough to confront the frenzied beast. The stench of rotten breath, his sharp teeth, and wicked claws garnered untold fear in Adoneesis, who narrowly missed death by diving to the other side of the nearby well to avoid deadly claws. Brachus screamed a ferocious, belly-deep battle cry, while flames flashed from his nostrils and singed the attacking beast.

Adoneesis stumbled to his feet just in time to watch Brachus charge the muckraker, teeth bared, mane flying, and flames flashing. Fates, Adoneesis had never seen Brachus breathe flames. What kind of a beast was his steed? What else did he not know about the animal who had been his constant companion since youth?

The battle between beasts raged and it soon became evident that Brachus needed help. The muckraker's massive weight gave him an advantage and he was overpowering Brachus. Adoneesis drew his sword--the sound of metal sliding against wood igniting his own battle juices--and as he stepped from behind the well, he screamed his own war cry. The hills came alive with rage, fear, anger, and blood thirst. In a flurry of flying hooves and slashing claws, Brachus and the beast collided again.

Sword pointing at the muckraker and without thought to himself, Adoneesis jumped straight into the flurry of battle. Before he was able to break into the battle, a strange thing happened. The sky suddenly darkened to winter blue and thunder rumbled its way across the valley. In a blinding display, a snap of lightning streaked the darkness and struck right into the heart of the marauding muckraker. Pain-filled screeches ripped the air, as did the stench of burning flesh. Smoke rose from the twitching creature while Brachus stood, quivering, over the body of his opponent.

Adoneesis was stunned. What had happened? The clear blue of the sky hid well the secrets of the sudden storm that killed the muckraker. His question was answered when he saw Bronwen outlined in the doorway of her hut. Hands lifted in supplication, she glowed with a luminescence that connected her to the bright sky. *She* was responsible for the lightning that killed the muckraker? How was that possible? The sound of Brachus stamping the body of the beast invaded the surreal sense that had pervaded the once peaceful valley.

Bronwen approached the confused Adoneesis. "Are you all right?"

"I am fine, thanks to you. But how..."

"I did what needed doing."

"I have heard legends of such power, but never imagined that anyone could command the forces of nature."

"I did not command nature. I merely asked for her help. Now, I believe we have an emergency awaiting us in Dunraven?"

"Yes, and suddenly I feel that maybe we stand a chance of surviving."

"Do not make the mistake of resting all your hopes on my powers. Other factors will be involved in the future of the faeries. Now, gather your steed." She waved to the waiting animal. "And let us leave for Dunraven."

Caught up in the surprise of lightning cracking from the sky, Adoneesis had forgotten about Brachus. A hand run gently over his body assured Adoneesis that Brachus had suffered no lasting damage, just a couple of scratches. He gathered the reins of his lathered steed and held him steady as Bronwen stepped into the stirrups and onto the saddle with a spryness that surprised Adoneesis. Just as he was about mount, the memory of flashing fire crossed his mind and he hesitated.

"You've never seen him throw fire before, have you?" Bronwen asked.

"No, and I wonder what else I do not know about him."

"He will protect you with his life, as he has just demonstrated. What else do you need to know?"

Feeling shame for his moment of doubt, Adoneesis stroked Brachus' neck in apology for his sudden unfounded fear. Brachus merely snorted and tossed his head impatiently. With a laugh, Adoneesis threw his leg forward over Brachus' neck and settled into the saddle in front of Bronwen. Turning for home, the trio set a steady pace to the top of the valley.

"Hold for a moment," Bronwen requested. "I need one last look. This valley has been my home for many years and it pains me to leave."

Adoneesis detected a flash of silver approaching from the shadows of the forest and his hand flew to his sword. Bronwen stayed his hand and smiled.

"Some beasts of the forest offer friendship not death." She smiled. "Come, let us ride for Dunraven."

~ * ~

Gwepper the goblin came to awareness and wondered if maybe he had died and gone to the Netherland of Tarnished Souls. He felt as if a muckraker had chewed him up, and not finding him to his liking, spit him out to lie there suffering. He couldn't decide what was worse, his splitting head or his throbbing ribs.

"Oh shits and tits, I feel awful." He groaned and attempted to sit up.

A voice broke through his fog of pain and Gwepper was sure he must have gone to the Netherland, because the voice was wondrous to his ears. Soft, melodious... "Jeez and sneeze, get a hold of yourself, you rat-face goblin." Gwepper reprimanded himself for getting soft in the head.

"I ask you again not to use such language in my home." That same feminine voice interrupted Gwepper's personal tirade.

With an effort and an imaginary axe pounding his head, Gwepper looked towards the voice. Yep, he had definitely died, but he hadn't gone to the Netherland of Tarnished Souls, because there stood one of the celestial faerie nymphs. Hair of spun gold, eyes of heavenly blue, lips meant to kiss away your troubles and a nose... of a pig? Gwepper's heart leapt in his chest--she was a goblin.

"I'm not dead?"

The feminine apparition smiled. "No, of course not. Why ever would you think you were?"

Gwepper couldn't find his voice. This was ridiculous; he was a goblin for mercy sakes. Not just any goblin, but the favorite of the Lord Gar, king of the goblins. This female creature should be on her knees begging for his favors. Instead, she hovered over him as he lay in bed, a soft bed, but a bed nonetheless. In an attempt to restore some semblance of dignity, Gwepper forced himself to rise. Placing his four-toed feet upon the dirt floor, he stood--and promptly fell back on the bed.

"Relax. You are in no condition to be standing. You cracked your noggin hard when you fell down the hill, you know."

"When I *what*?" Gwepper had no memory of how he came to be in this small hovel.

"It is not a hovel, and I would thank you to show respect since I saved your life." The words were spoken softly, with no hint of anger.

"How did you know... dung heaps and tongue seeps, you can read minds. You must be one of those witch goblins." Gwepper wiped his runny nose on his arm and prompted his savior to pass him a cloth of linen to blow his nose with.

"I don't need that, my sleeve works fine."

"Use the cloth. That is what it is for." Blue eyes pleaded with Gwepper to show some manners.

Gwepper's emotions spun out of control, but he attributed it to his head wound, not the blue eyes of the female goblin. "I can force myself, but only if you tell me your name."

"I am Ghilphar."

"Hmmm. I'm Gwepper." Gwepper thought her name was pretty, but would never say that aloud. Instead, he blew his nose and changed the subject. "I didn't fall down any stupid hill. You must be wrong. Maybe a muckraker attacked me and I hurt myself fighting him off?"

"No."

"Well, maybe a band of roving humans threatened you and I fought *them* off?"

"No. Sorry. You simply fell down a hill."

Frustrated at looking clumsy to this female goblin, Gwepper tried to find a way to retain his dignity. "Well, I *am* on an important mission for King Gar, so it makes sense that I fall down the hill if my mind was on such important matters."

Ghilphar frowned. "Gar is not king. Adoneesis is king."

Dung it all. When would he learn to keep his big mouth shut? "Farts and carts, of course Gar is not king. It is just a private joke. After all, he is Raegar's son as well, you know."

"I don't think so. I should check your wound. Maybe you banged yourself harder than I thought."

Dung it again. It was as if this female somehow loosened his tongue. "It is your fault. You practice dark magic to make me speak. Your ways have been outlawed. I should leave before trouble befalls me. Bloody death and fetid breath, let me pass."

"Pshaw." Ghilphar's previously serene attitude showed a crack. Frustration and anger singed her words as she jabbed her finger into Gwepper's chest and didn't allow him to go anywhere. "My ways are the ways of ones such as the old gods, the great Merlin, the Lady of the Lake, the Earth Mother herself. It is the narrow mindedness of ones such as you who condemn faeries of all kinds to trouble."

"Baw, I argue with no measly female." Gwepper deliberately snorted into his sleeve and then proceeded to fall to the floor in a state of supreme dizziness.

"Hmmm, would you like this measly female to help you back to the bed?" Ghilphar teased.

"Drats alive. Why is the world out to get me today?" Gwepper moaned. "There's not time to lie about. I must get back."

"At least let me make you a snack. You need to keep up your strength." Gracefully, she sidestepped around Gwepper, who still lay on the floor, and opened the door of a small wooden cupboard that sat in the corner of the one room dwelling.

Gwepper took a deep breath to focus his mind on ignoring his throbbing head. With a mighty effort, and support of a rickety wooden chair, he hauled himself to his feet and gave his head a gentle shake. All seemed to be in working order. His gaze fell to the goblin witch as she wrapped a slab of bread into a cloth and added a chunk of white cheese to the package. Gwepper's traitorous stomach rumbled and he didn't miss the smile that curved the side of Ghilphar's full mouth. Humph! Females, they always thought they were right.

His thoughts were cut short by Ghilphar's warm breath on his neck. "Here, take this on your journey, and go with my best wishes."

Gwepper looked to the lips hovering, oh, so close to his. His mud-gray eyes met her dulcet blue ones and he felt the effects of another spell the witch must be casting. His limbs were melting, and his heart pounded as if to come forth from his chest.

Just then, the sound of hooves pounded just outside the small wooden hut. Ghilphar frowned. "Strange, I rarely get visitors. I'm kind of far away from things, you know."

"I'd never have guessed," Gwepper mumbled sarcastically as he followed Ghilphar from the small hut into the brightness of the afternoon sun. Cresting the hill that Gwepper assumed was the one he had taken a tumble down appeared a familiar figure. The mahogany majesty of the horseflesh alone would attest to the fact that royalty approached.

"Rats and cats, rats and bats. The king can't see me." Gwepper dove for cover behind a large woodpile beside the door.

Ghilphar didn't know what to make of such strange behavior, but any questioning she wanted to do would have to wait.

"Good day to you," the king greeted her. "We hurry to Dunraven and would like permission to cross your property."

Ghilphar knelt and bowed her head. "Goodness, you do not need my permission. I am honored by your presence." She raised her head and found herself confronted by the black eyes of the old hag who sat behind the king. A jolt of awareness ran through her veins and she felt a kinship. Though the power that came from this one was such that she herself would never attain in ten lifetimes.

Bronwen smiled and set Ghilphar at ease. "I feel your thoughts." Her eyes looked to the well-tended garden, and offerings to the goddess. "I also see your work. You have created a beautiful home. Tell me, why have you chosen such a solitary life?"

Ghilphar pursed her lips and tried to think of the reason for leaving her own kind and seeking out a lonely place in nature.

"I used to live in Night Gloom, until Gar banned customs that had been passed through generations. With thoughtless greed, he desecrated the land and destroyed the trees. An act that left all tree faeries homeless. Will-o-the-wisps lost their bright glow and the forest faeries mysteriously disappeared." Ghilphar gave a smile of pained remembrance. "When the ones who gave me life died, I had no reason to stay."

Memories of the short period after her mother and father's death flashed in her mind and she shivered. Gar had cleared a room at the main tree for her to live and stated that goblins always took care of their own. Unfortunately, his generous concern for her welfare soon turned to stifling obsession and his warped motivation obvious when he moved her things to his bedchamber and locked her there until he could return later that night when he'd, *Give her a lesson or two in pleasing her master.*

Even now, memories of his grasping hands and bestial treatment of her sent her into panic and it was only with great effort she was able to take a deep breath and face the prophetess and speak. "I ran away, found this place, and have been here ever since."

The prophetess fixed her black eyes on Ghilphar, who stood tall and proud against the scrutiny. Gar was the one who should be ashamed, not her.

"As I thought, you and I share a similar history. I have a feeling that you will accomplish more in this lifetime than you may think."

Ghilphar gasped. Such a decree by the prophetess was like words carved in stone. "I thank you."

"It's encouraging to see that you honor nature and have not followed others of your kind," Adoneesis remarked.

"I was taught these ways by my mother, and she by hers; so it goes as far back as any written word or shadowy memory. I will not give that all up, because we are told it is wrong." Ghilphar's voice held bitterness and her words ached with memories and pain not shared with anyone.

"We must go." Adoneesis' prompting broke the emotional tension. Inclining his head, he turned the stallion who gave a mighty leap--his pounding hooves digging into earth and sending divots of dirt showering in all directions. The threesome disappeared in the haze of the hot sun that lingered in the afternoon.

Gwepper poked his head above the woodpile. "Are they gone?"

"Yes, you mighty oaf. And why are you hiding from the king?"

"Things that do not concern a mere female such as yourself." Gwepper preened at his own importance.

"Ah, well, now that this mere female has saved your life, tended your wounds and provided food, I guess you'll be on your way," Ghilphar spouted indignantly. It bothered her that this goblin could upset her usually calm manner. And she wondered what he was up to that he did not want King Adoneesis knowing about. It probably had something to do with the fact that he referred to his lord as King Gar. A joke indeed. Her brains were not that addled.

"Gwepper, a word of advice. Give carefully of your loyalties. Greed is not a worthy motivator."

"Words of wisdom from a witch," Gwepper taunted. "Who was the old hag who traveled with the King?"

"Who... you are not serious?" She noted his wide-eyed look of emptiness. "Yes, I see you are. I'm not sure I should tell you. I mean, being a male and all, you may not understand."

Gwepper shuffled his feet and dug his toes into the soil and grass.

"Gwepper, I'm only teasing. The female was one I thought all would recognize, but I was wrong." She placed her finger under Gwepper's chin and raised his gaze to meet hers. Tingling warmth fluttered in her stomach. "She was the prophetess." Reverently whispered words wound their way into the sunlit meadow and danced among the tree limbs of the nearby forest.

"No! I say no! She has died. I know it." Gwepper wrung his hands. "Farts and darts, I need to get back. I have been too long gone. Gar will kill me. Oh, woe is me--the prophetess. This does not bode well. Dung it all!"

"Gwepper! You are driving yourself into a fervor. Settle down." She laid her hands on his shoulder in an attempt to settle him, but he shrugged her off.

"No, you have no idea. I must get back." With a jump, he took off in a full, albeit jerky, lope across the meadow. Watching him leave, a numbing pain wound its way into Ghilphar's stomach. Tears fell from her face as she realized the stupid goblin had ignited an emotion she thought she'd conquered--loneliness. Without consideration, whispered words fell from her lips.

> "*This moment that we part,*
> *Blessings on you I shower,*
> *Find somewhere your hidden heart,*
> *And you'll find somehow your power.*"

With a heavy heart, Ghilphar found solace working in her garden. Sinking her hands into the soil of Mother Earth always gave her the comfort of a connection with a power far greater than any. Her mind raced over the events of the day. Why the ugly goblin affected her so, she knew not. Why the prophetess had said those words, she knew not. The cycles of nature had taught her many things--one of these things was patience. All would happen in its time--when it was time.

~ * ~

The flapping of the food-filled cloth banging against his leg brought Gwepper back to awareness. The proximity of the hated half-brother of Gar, and the presence of the prophetess, had spurred him into fleeing from the cottage like firedrakes snapped at his heels. Shaking his head, he stopped and turned his gaze to the place he had just left. An involuntary sigh left his lips. How beautiful Ghilphar looked next to her cozy cottage and garden. Life here would be peaceful. Gwepper smacked himself across the face. "Eeeeks! You stupid goblin. It is not the life for you. Your loyalty is with Gar. You swore to him."

Snarling at his moment of weakness, Gwepper raised his hand in a brief farewell and turned the direction of Night Gloom forest, the home of Gar, and the rebellious goblins.

Four

The sound of Brachus' hooves pounding the ground and the air rushing past them negated any attempt at conversation, which was fine with Bronwen who needed to put up a mental barrier against the turbulent emotions rolling off Adoneesis. With awkwardness the mood for the first couple of days, it wasn't until the third night that Bronwen came to understand at least part of the reason for his discomfort.

After reining Brachus to a halt Adoneesis helped Bronwen off the tired steed and followed easily with a light thud. The spot was strategic with its outcrop of rock on three sides and small pebbles on the trail leading up to the flattened area where they set camp. After a meal of nuts, cheese, and sweetened fruit, they settled down and stared into the fire as they had the previous two nights. Bronwen knew why she'd been sought out, but she wouldn't ask any questions until Adoneesis felt comfortable enough to explain. Until now, he'd been respectful, if somewhat distant, but Bronwen was patient.

The distinct crack of a branch interrupted the silence and Adoneesis had sword in hand before Bronwen could even blink. In a battle ready stance, he stalked to the trail's edge and peered into the forest. Another crack was followed by an uneven step of hoof upon stone and Adoneesis clenched his sword and raised it to strike if need be. A deer, as majestic and stunning as any Bronwen had ever seen, stepped from the darkening shadows of the woods and into the firelight. His head hung low as if his antlers were too heavy to hold high, and the poor creature limped forward while a trail of blood marked his advance.

Cursing, Adoneesis sheathed his sword and reached out a welcoming hand to the injured deer. Seeing that he was not alone, the deer tensed and pranced back a step where he stood quivering, whether in fear, pain, or both was not clear.

Bronwen moved with a speed that belied her aged appearance. No hesitation did either she or the deer show as she made her way to the injured animal and laid her hands on him. A shivering shudder wrenched through his body as his knees folded and he slid to the ground where he lay and gratefully accepted the healing offered.

"He must have escaped Rufus' minions," Adoneesis offered when he noticed the mark of an arrow creasing the deer's side.

"Who is Rufus and why would he do such a thing?" Bronwen kept her voice deliberately soothing, although she throbbed with the pain transferred by her healing of the deer, as well as her own anger at such an unjust act.

"Rufus is the culmination of what the faerie realm has become." He clenched his fists and squatted on the ground beside her. "I came across him on my way to find you and was horrified to see him ripping down the trees and killing animals such as this one for food."

Bronwen moved her hands deftly over the deer, searched for the places that needed her energy, mended the wound and opened channels for the energy to flow at an optimum rate for healing purposes. Warmth flooded her hands and transferred to the deer that moaned and lifted his head to gaze at her in adoration--his liquid brown eyes filled with gratitude. She smiled and gave him a gentle pat of acknowledgment before continuing her ministrations.

"How could you let this happen? After all, the realm is your responsibility." Her voice cracked more harshly than she'd intended and had an effect she hadn't expected.

Adoneesis swore and slammed a fist into the nearby rock wall. He stood and paced the clearing, unmindful of the blood that welled on his fist. Patting the deer and sending a mental caution to lie still and rest, Bronwen straightened and considered the pacing king. Her throbbing bones protested the move from her enforced crouch and she absentmindedly rubbed her aching back. Sighing, she reached out and grabbed his arm.

"Give me your hand before you bleed all over our campsite." She spent a few minutes stemming the flow of blood and closing the ragged skin. "I'm sorry, I might have spoken out of anger and blamed you for something not entirely your fault."

"It is my fault. Everything that happens in the realm is my responsibility."

Bronwen smiled. "You feel your responsibility too much. That the goblins had turned from their beliefs and planned revolt is not a fault to be laid at your feet. It's not due to anything you've done that a sense of lust and greed pervades the land and chokes the life from the once fertile fields. You certainly did not inherit Raegar's sense of justice and responsibility--or lack thereof." She let go of his now healed hand.

"You knew my father?"

His searching gaze pierced into her uncomfortably. How she longed to tell him the truth, but feared his rejection, so she merely turned to the fire with a shrug of her shoulders. "As much as anyone. Come, I am tired. Let's sleep."

As if sensing that questioning would get him no answers, Adoneesis stretched out on his blanket and locked arms behind his head. "What about the deer?"

"He'll sleep for awhile and then be on his way. Hopefully, he'll avoid Rufus until we can do something about him and others like him."

"So, you'll help."

Damn. She hadn't decided anything yet, so why had she spoken? "We'll see. Goodnight."

~*~

The deer was gone when Adoneesis and Bronwen awoke and neither of them spoke as they ate porridge and continued on their way. As they traveled further from Bronwen's home, she became increasingly aware of the seeping of life from her limbs. She felt weakened and considered deeply what the faeries wanted from her. She also couldn't discount the peril-beyond-return that she moved closer to each day. Was it a chance she was willing to take? Especially since her sacrifice would be for those who had forgotten her and had ceased to pay their respects to the ways of Mother Earth.

She would make her judgment--in time.

Brachus snorted and kicked up his heels. The landscape changed, and Bronwen felt strength return to her limbs. The land they approached was verdant and powerful with the natural energy of the woodlands, grasslands, streams, and wildlife. Bronwen breathed in fresh air that tingled and sparked with life. All the elements were strong--earth, water, air, fire and spirit. Mostly spirit, because it was the spirit that kept the rest alive. Someone cared for the life around them and gave respect where respect was due. Bronwen wanted to meet the person who still practiced the old ways.

"We are now on Dunraven land--my home," Adoneesis announced proudly.

Dunraven. The words sang to Bronwen's sense of belonging and nostalgia. The land flourished under Adoneesis in a way it never had while Raegar ruled. Trees that held the wisdom of life thrived in the rich soil--their limbs blowing in the breeze, extending to the mysterious portals of the sky above. Untouched and free, wildlife bounded about the forests and fields.

The narrow dirt road they traveled meandered across the land of Dunraven and led them toward the main section. It followed the fresh sparkling stream of crystal water that supplied the people of Dunraven. Within Bronwen's breast grew a sense of admiration, respect, and pride. It seemed the old ways had not disappeared into the past. Maybe there was hope for the future.

"It is beautiful."

"Yes. It is." Adoneesis kicked Brachus into his last gallop towards home.

In a smite of energy that streaked in time with the stallion's pace, a pixie made his presence known. Flitting from Adoneesis to Bronwen, between Brachus' ears, up to the sky and back down again, the tiny pixie flew.

"You are home. Oh, glory, the king is home. Is this the prophetess? Will she help us? I still think you should have let me go with you. No one would care for you better."

"Cease your chatter Bailiwick, I am weary," Adoneesis requested as he reined Brachus to a prancing walk. "Do Toran and Raven wait?"

"Yes, yes. Anxious as two black cats at full moon--if you know what I mean?" He slapped his hand over his mouth. "Prophetess, I didn't mean to offend. Such a dunce I am."

"It is all right, young one. I gave up blood sacrifices centuries ago." She said with a hitch of laughter in her voice. "You gave no insult, and please, call me Bronwen."

"Oh, no, that I could not do." Bailiwick's pixie face took on a reddish hue.

Just then, a shout went up from the walls of the main residence. "The king returns, the king returns." The call announcing their return was punctuated by the clank of swords clashing.

"Why do I hear swords?" Adoneesis frowned.

"It is Krickall and Mayard again. They have been at odds since you left."

"The usual reason, Bailiwick?"

"Yes."

Anxious now for his oats, Brachus planted himself by the stable tree and would not move, even at the urging of Adoneesis.

"Fangs on you, Brachus, why must you be so stubborn?"

His curse was rewarded with a backward look from Brachus who had the light of determination shining from his bright eyes. A shake of his head set his mane to flying about and tickling Adoneesis nose.

"Fine. Damn stubborn beast, I see you need a firm hand and some training, but for now, you can find your way to your stall." Adoneesis swung Bronwen from the steed's back and Brachus smugly trotted into the stable where oats and water waited.

Bronwen frowned. "Have you no stable attendants to do this for you?"

"Yes, but they're probably watching the sword fight."

"Nevertheless, they would have heard the call that you have returned. Their place is here." Bronwen remembered a day long ago when Adoneesis father whipped a stable attendant for not being on hand immediately upon his arrival home. The young faerie's excuse was that he'd been attending to his sick mother, but Raegar hadn't cared. He wielded the whip himself on the youngster--and found pleasure in the act. Bronwen shivered at what had been the first of many insights into Raegar's true character.

"It is done now. Let us hurry." Adoneesis motioned toward the main dwelling tree. "I have heard the trees of Dunraven rival the ancient trees of Night Gloom." His voice hinted at the pride he felt for his home. "Although, I've never been anywhere near Night Gloom, so I cannot be sure of the validity of such a tale."

The main dwelling of Dunraven was as large as Toran's tree, Duir, but it did not radiate the knowledge of life, as did Duir. Bronwen remembered well the fact that the tree could house up to twenty-five faeries, not pixie-size either, but full-size.

Adoneesis ran his hands lovingly over the gnarled bark that wound its way around the trunk of the tree, while Bailiwick flitted about. The young pixie took it upon himself to fill in the silence and answer Bronwen's earlier musing of the stable attendant's duty. "King Adoneesis is too kind. Others take advantage of his manner. I tell him all the time. I say, 'King, you let others...'"

"Enough!" Adoneesis growled at the well-intended pixie. "There are more important matters to attend."

"Of course, I was only..." One look from Adoneesis quelled any further comment from Bailiwick, who rolled his eyes skyward.

Bronwen smiled at the banter between the two. Adoneesis was obviously very fond of the fluttering faerie. Just then, a couple of young faerie drakes ran by, pushing past as if Bronwen and Adoneesis were invisible. Bronwen noticed the slight deformities in the small drakes caused from inbreeding. Unless something could be done, there would be no more faeries. Which also meant no more realm. Part of, yet not part of, the world of humans, the world of faerie would simply cease to be. If the faeries disappeared or became creatures intent on greed, lust, and power, the magic and beauty of the land Bronwen loved would be gone forever. A legacy passed through the ages of time would be lost in the echoes of time.

Introspective, Bronwen thought it strange how well she remembered her way through the tree; she hadn't tripped over the crooked root haphazardly growing up in the center of the common room and without thought she had turned towards the stairway that led to the upper chamber. She skipped altogether the step that sometimes creaked as if in protest of weight. Noting the puzzled look on Adoneesis face, Bronwen cautioned herself to be careful lest he start asking questions she was not ready to answer.

"We are here. We are here," Bailiwick announced in bright anticipation.

Being the only one strong enough, Adoneesis pushed open the heavy wooden door that guarded his room. The door had been imported from the western shores of faerie. There, the trees grew tall and strong, and legend told that they were touched with a hint of magic--the magic of Avalon. The chamber itself was small and gently curved to follow the natural lines of the tree trunk. A small window graced the room where a large knothole had been punched out to provide natural circulation and light.

In the room waited a flickering aura of light and a fluttering faerie. Toran and Raven.

Toran spoke first. "I was not sure if you could be enticed back here, even with the threat of destruction to the faeries." His incandescent light form bowed respectfully.

Bronwen's heart warmed at the sight of familiar faces--so long she'd been without any companionship. "Toran, it is wonderful to see you again."

"You know each other?" Adoneesis frowned. "Maybe I should have sent you to ask for her help."

Toran shrugged. "I wouldn't have gone. I know her history and wouldn't have had the heart to insist she return. No, it was better you go and demand she come with you."

Adoneesis frowned. "She came of her own free will."

"I doubt it was a journey made willingly, but I am glad to see her nonetheless."

"I don't like being an outsider in my own home. What secrets do you hint at?" Without waiting for an answer, he questioned Raven who stood on the tabletop and still only managed to reach shoulder level. "Are you acquainted with the prophetess?"

"Yes, our paths have crossed once or twice." Raven took two of Bronwen's fingers in his hand and bowed low. "Greetings, how fare you?"

Polite words spoken aloud, threaded with implications of an unspoken conversation. Bronwen sensed a bright flash of fire that gave birth to a dark image of evil and then reassurance from Raven and Toran. A brief flickering image of Adoneesis and his attempt to mind probe invaded her senses and Bronwen hastily put up a block.

Obviously frustrated to have his attempts halted, Adoneesis snapped, "Now is not a time for secrets. What history do the three of you share?"

"Nothing that concerns the present," Bronwen soothed. "It is all better left in the past."

"Maybe it would be better--" Raven began, only to be abruptly cut short by Bronwen.

"No. Let us get to the matter at hand. Time runs short."

"Yes, it does," Toran whispered lightly. "Shorter for some than others."

Bronwen moved to the window and looked out over the lands of Dunraven. Her stance was stiff as her mind drifted into a soft trance of memories.

Silence reigned. Each lost in thought. Bronwen finally broke the uneasy tension. "I know why you have brought me here. At first I was not sure if I would help." She turned back to the ones waiting in the room and whispered, "But, it is my destiny to help, no matter the cost."

"I knew you'd help. I think--"

The rapid flutter of Raven's wings silenced Adoneesis. "What you think does not matter. Acknowledge the wisdom before you and let the prophetess plot her own course. That is what you brought her here for, is it not?"

Flushing, Adoneesis inclined his head. "Forgive me; I know my life span equals a trivial amount compared to the age and experience of the three of you."

Bronwen smiled and brushed her fingers across his arm. "Do not bother with recriminations. You are the king and are acting as such. Toran and Raven must also allow for the respect of your title, and I am sure you will learn to open your mind to the wisdom of others who have lived many lives before you."

"Of course," Adoneesis, Toran, and Raven agreed in a single voice.

"Now, I have said I will help, but there will be certain stipulations that must be followed no matter what." Bronwen looked to Adoneesis who waited for further words. "Firstly, I'd like the chamber at the end of the upper hall facing north for my own."

Adoneesis nodded his head in agreement. "That is my chamber, but I will gladly move to another room."

"Secondly. Some of my ways and rituals may seem strange to you, but they are what they are and must not be questioned."

"I will not question you."

"I mean it, Adoneesis, there must be no obstacles put in my way."

"Fine."

"Thirdly, and most important, there will come a day when you and I will disagree on a course of action. On that day, you must do as I say without question. Is that understood?"

"I suppose, but how will I know when the time is here?"

"You do not have to know. I will."

Adoneesis inclined his head. "I agree."

"Without question, Adoneesis," Bronwen reiterated.

"I have given you my word. My word is my honor. My honor is what makes me who I am. That is all I can say to assure you."

Bronwen sighed. "That will do. Now, I need to rest and then I will prepare a list of what I need."

"But I have not yet explained why you are here."

Raven and Toran chuckled, while Bronwen gave Adoneesis an amused look of indulgence. "Ah, you are so young," Bronwen's voice of dark honey teased gently. "I need no explanation. I know you seek the child. The legends have been alive longer than you or I."

Adoneesis frowned. "Of course, it is that age and wisdom thing again, is it not?"

"See, you do learn quickly," Bronwen teased.

"Visit for a few minutes and I will have your chamber prepared." Adoneesis bowed himself from the room.

The three of age and wisdom looked to each other and sighed. "I hope the legends are true and the child truly exists," Toran commented.

"The child exists. Remember, when Niobe and the Thunder God produced a child, I was the one who enlisted the help of a spunkie to switch the child with a human one. I have seen the evidence for myself," Raven reassured.

Bronwen affirmed the fact. "Yes, the offspring of that first child exists in the human world somewhere. I have felt her many a time over the last while."

"Her?" Toran and Raven questioned at once.

"Her. I know the child is female."

Toran hesitated but asked the question that had hovered in the background since her arrival. "Prophetess, does Raegar's curse haunt your steps?"

"I fear so. As soon as I left my home, I felt the presence of death encroaching on my mind. There are spells I can use to put off the inevitable, but although he denied it, Raegar's power was strong and his hate for me increased his curse tenfold."

"Does King Adoneesis know of his heritage?"

"No. And he must not know he is my son."

Raven pleaded, "But, lady, if his bringing you here is to be the cause of your death, do you not think he should know of the bond?"

Bronwen spoke softly. "No, he cares too deeply sometimes. I am afraid if he were aware of our connection, he would be presented with an untenable decision. The fate of the faerie people is more important than my life. This I say, and this I do."

Her voice brooked no argument, and all had been said that would be.

Five

A raging fire crackled in the huge fireplace and licks of flames danced to the ceiling of the newly hewn wooden keep. Canine beasts snarled and fought for food scraps thrown to the dirt floor by feasting goblins who sat on chairs long past better times.

A large wooden table, scarred and stained from abuse, held center spot in the room and provided somewhat of a barrier between slobbering goblins and more sedate duergarrs. The two faerie breeds usually did not co-exist well, but these had a common purpose. Even so, they faced each other at opposite ends of the table. The distance served only to highlight their differences.

The duergarr's standard of dress included a lambskin jacket and a green hat. They were short, usually about two feet tall, and mean looking, much like a troll. The goblins themselves had no particular look about them--tall, short, one-eyed, two-eyed, skinny, fat, it didn't matter. The one common feature the goblins shared was the fact that they did not bathe--ever. This made for a rather rancid atmosphere when they assembled in one place.

On a raised platform at the head of the table sat the leader of the goblins, Gar. His dull gray hair stood in haphazard spikes from the top of his head, and his eyes were of a darker mud gray and crossed, so that when he looked at you it was always in question whether he was *really* looking at you. His teeth were rotten from years of abuse, and his breath was rancid from the dead meat that stuck between his few existing teeth. His clothes had once fit well and been clean, but now, on a steady diet of meat, gravy, and rich foods, Gar's gut had overgrown his clothes and dark food stains attested to many meals eaten.

The growing din of confusion wore Gar's temper. One smack of his hoary fist upon the table brought silence to the room. "Take those blasted creatures from my sight." He waved to the marauding canines. "And bring more mutton."

Servants stumbled to fulfill his commands--afraid that if they didn't obey instantly, they would be beaten--or worse. Scurrying about, the goblins attempted to separate the scraps of food from the snapping, snarling dog-like animals. Gar watched the procedure with a satisfied sneer. Power was a heady emotion. Too bad for everyone else he was the only one who wielded such a thing with a mere snap of his fingers and direction of will.

He took a slurping sip of mead and grumbled as angry voices carried from the front hallway and over the growing din of drunken goblins. A flurry of tangled arms and flying fists fell through the door and tumbled to the worn carpet. Gar frowned. It was a tough life being the one in charge and responsible for bringing order to chaos. He thumped the table again. "Who dares interrupt my dinner?"

His bellowing voice instilled fear. The struggling trio of goblins froze. Just as suddenly, not wanting to be outspoken by another, the three of them started to speak at the same time. Onlookers snorted and anticipatory whispers flamed through the masses--each one thankful not to be on the receiving end of Gar's anger.

"Shut up," Gar snarled and peered at the trio. He recognized two of his guards, but the third goblin was unfamiliar... or was he? Squinting, he leaned forward in his chair in an attempt to see more clearly in the dim room.

"It is I, your lordship--Gwepper." The goblin spoke hopefully with only a twinge of fear.

Gar hesitated. He knew the name, but couldn't remember this goblin's place in the scheme of it all. Wait--yes, that was it. "Well, Gwepper it is about time you returned. Have you brought me the skin of a unicorn?"

Gwepper swallowed. "Yikes and spikes, the unicorn. I forgot to find a unicorn hide for your new bed chamber." Obviously terrified by the thundering look on Gar's face, Gwepper slobbered. "Please listen before you beat me. I have news. Yes, news." Arms open and palms forward, he advanced and knelt on the floor at Gar's feet. "In my travels I saw rats and bats, bears and hares, gnats and cats, but nowhere did I see a unicorn."

Anger distorted Gar's features and he raised a fist. Gwepper covered his head with his arm and quickly continued his story. "My news is important news from Dunraven."

It was forbidden to speak the name Dunraven anywhere within Night Gloom. That Gwepper had the nerve, or the stupidity, drew gasps from the other goblins. Eager goblins waited in suspense for the terrible punishment that would surely be bestowed upon Gwepper.

Gwepper stumbled over his words as he imparted his news to the leader of the goblins. Gar sneered at the measly goblin who cringed as if struck. Gar found great satisfaction in Gwepper's reaction.

"King... I mean, Adoneesis requested a Sound of Gathering." Peering from beneath his bushy eyebrows, he continued. "Jeepers, creepers, it was such a sight as you never seen before. Faeries from all over gathered to the clearing at Dunraven."

Again, the word elicited gasps from the onlookers--such was the influence of habit. Gar grew restless. The Sound of Gathering had never been called for in his lifetime. His latest raid must have rattled that bastard, Adoneesis. What euphoric power that thought elicited in Gar's warped mind. Anxious now, he leaned forward, prompting Gwepper to speed up his tale.

"The faeries are dying out and they are feared of us goblins." Gwepper snickered in stupid arrogance. "Adoneesis runs scared with his tail tucked."

Gar considered Gwepper's words. True, they had been hounding the faeries for years, but more so lately. Gar grew impatient with his self-appointed role of king of the goblins. He wanted what Adoneesis had--everything.

"There is more," Gwepper imparted, puffing up his chest importantly.

Gar hated arrogance. It was fine for him, but it was not acceptable in those below him. How dare this filthy creature think himself equal? Gar's snarl made Gwepper fall to one knee and beg. "Sorry, sorry, but the news is very important."

"Then tell me, you blithering dufus," Gar bellowed.

"Farts and carts, there is a child."

"So. The faeries still breed rarely, but a child here and there will make no difference, especially since we have cut them off from the world of man."

"No, no. The child was born to Niobe and some ancient Thunder God and lives in the man world. Adoneesis knows this."

Gar frowned. How this mattered to him, he didn't know. "Gwepper, I care not for child born to the bastard line of these two."

"Farts and darts, you should." Gwepper overstepped his bounds again, and he slapped his grimy hand over his mouth. His eyes widened in terror.

Gar narrowed his eyes and, without taking his gaze from Gwepper, summoned his guards. Gwepper cowered to the ground and groveled.

"Please, let me finish." The guards grabbed him and dragged him screaming to the doorway. "A legend says this child can save the faeries. Adoneesis found the prophetess. I saw them together. Toran and Raven waited at Dunraven for them."

"Wait." Gar gestured for the guards to back off. "Toran, Raven, and the prophetess you say?"

"Yes," Gwepper gasped, relieved to be released.

"The oldest and wisest are those three."

"Yes, lord."

"What is the legend?"

"Cripes and yipes. Don't know. Niobe saw the future and made the child for the man world. Only one child is born each generation, but all the power of Niobe and the Thunder God gets passed to each child."

"So, do they know where to find the child?"

"No." Gwepper smiled slyly.

"How do they plan to find the child?"

"The prophetess knows how."

"You're sure it was the prophetess you saw?"

"Dirty men and flirty hens, I saw her myself riding on the back of the beast owned by Adoneesis."

"Oh." Gar raised his eyebrows. And where did you see this pray tell?

Gwepper gulped. "Ahh, I saw them at the home of a goblin named Ghilphar."

Gar shot upright in shock. That name sent rivulets of emotion through him. "You *know* where this Ghilphar lives?"

"Yes, I saw her," Gwepper whispered.

"How did she look?"

"Nice." A gleam lit Gwepper's dull eyes.

Jealousy flared in Gar's breast. "You did not dirty her with your touch, did you?"

Gwepper sensed that his life rested on the line. "No. No. She helped me after... after I saved her life. Yes, that's it, she was being attacked by a wild beast and I saved her life."

"Hmmm. Your news of the child and of Ghilphar pleases me. Grud will take you to my chambers where you will show him Ghilphar's home on my map. Then you can rest."

Gwepper looked as if he could have wept at his reprieve. "Many thanks. Thanks, ranks, and stanks."

Just as Gwepper was about to leave the room, Gar bellowed, "First thing tomorrow, you will set out to find me my unicorn. This time you will not fail--understand?"

Gwepper deflated like a fried mushroom ball. "Yes, lord," he whispered and obediently followed Grud out of the room.

The hide of a unicorn was the last thing Gar cared about in light of the latest news, but the fact that Gwepper defied him by returning without one was not to be tolerated. The stupid goblin could die trying and Gar wouldn't bat an eyelid. Infused with power and purpose, Gar hollered, "Assemble a trio of goblins. I want Ghilphar brought here. I also want to visit the mage rotting in the bowels of my dungeon. I think he may finally earn his way back into my graces. Yes, there is much work and little time."

~ * ~

Gar's malevolent laughter echoed deep within Gwepper and touched a place he had no idea existed. He remembered the feeling of peace when he looked into Ghilphar's face, how the butterflies and birds flitted about her home, how his heart tugged when he had to leave. He feared, not for himself, but for the lone female goblin about to be brought forcefully to the arrogant and cruel Gar.

Upon reaching Gar's chamber, a voice whispered to Gar to give the wrong directions. In his mind flashed a brief image of himself as a savior and the female goblin throwing herself to his feet in gratitude. But the fear of Gar, and a lifetime of servitude, was strong.

With a weary sigh, and knowing the fate he set upon Ghilphar, he directed Grud to her home. Somehow feeling less heroic than he had earlier, Gwepper slunk away, glad to be done, but sick with himself for being a coward, and angry with himself for caring.

~ * ~

Gar wrinkled his nose in distaste at the stench that assaulted him upon entering Night Gloom's dungeons. Darkness hid the source of the smell, as well as the hapless souls condemned to live their lives deep in the womb of the earth. Once Gar passed judgment on someone, he rebelled at any reminder of his or her existence. But the mage might be useful and, under other circumstances, Gar would have had the prisoner brought to him, but the mage was special. In order to secure his powerful magic, the mage was imprisoned in an unusual manner--a manner that forced Gar to drudge through the depressing pathways of the condemned. Extreme circumstances called for extreme sacrifices.

"Here." Grud pointed to last door looming out of the murky dimness of the hole of perdition.

Just then, a pain-filled howl screeched through one of the many doors that harbored forgotten souls. Blasting through the shadowy corridor, the howl echoed, not only with pain, but with a hint of derision and triumph as well. Despite his resolve to not show fear, Gar shivered.

"Who screeches such vocal insults?"

"I think it comes from the cell of Kypher, one of the ellyllons," Grud replied in a shaky voice.

Gar frowned. "He's still alive? I thought he'd be fodder for a muckraker by now."

"He is weak, but we seem unable to kill him, even with starvation. It is almost as if..."

"As if what?"

"As if he receives energy from some source. Some say the energy of the Lady lives in all her emissaries."

A shiver crept up Gar's spine. "Foolish, stupid talk. More likely, we have a traitor sneaking food to the prisoner. Find out who and kill him."

"Yes, Gar."

Satisfied, Gar motioned Grud to open the mage's cell door. In his wildest dreams, he couldn't have prepared himself for what he saw. Untold years had taken a toll on the former mage of King Raegar. Once admired for his good looks, the mage, Lapis, now resembled a living corpse. Suspended horizontally just above the ground by the use of leather straps and ropes, Lapis had been denied any connection to the earth from which he drew his power. Given only the bare minimum of food and water to keep him alive, his body had shriveled, lank, gray hair hung about his gaunt face, and haunted blue eyes stared into a nothingness that spoke only to him. Nary a word had passed his cracked lips in all his years of imprisonment.

Gar prodded the mages body with sword, which he had drawn in readiness before entering the cell. Nothing happened. Short on patience at the best of times, he needed the attention of the mage for his immediate plans and wouldn't tolerate insolence.

"Speak, mage."

No response.

Gar snarled. "I have no patience for your obstinacy. Talk now."

Still no response.

"Clod's feet, speak or I will have that bitch, the prophetess, killed before the week is out."

A glimmer of interest sparked in dull blue eyes.

"Ahh, that catches your attention." Gar gloated. He was not prepared for the sound of a word spoken. "What did you say?"

With a voice unused to speaking, Lapis repeated himself. One word, raspy and barely audible. "Coward."

Gar snarled. He drew his sword and thrust the tip into Lapis' thigh. Droplets of blood fell from withered body to mingle with the dirt floor.

"By what right do you call me names? You, who were a traitor to your king," Gar gloated.

With an effort, Lapis mumbled, "He betrayed first."

"You speak treasonous arrogance. No wonder he gave you to me," Gar snorted.

~ * ~

Lapis ignored his enemies taunting words, as matters of more importance needed his attention at that moment. Drops of his blood from Gar's sword ran deep into the ground, made a connection with the untainted soil of Mother Earth and sent tendrils of energy back to its source. The tingle of power seeped into his veins and Lapis almost smiled at the irony of his enemy unknowingly returning to him his power.

"What do you want of me, goblin?"

"I need you to find a child for me."

Lapis coughed up phlegm and spat it at the feet of Gar who immediately backhanded him across the face. Swinging wildly in his imprisonment of ropes, Lapis reveled in the goblin's anger. Another blood droplet fell to the ground and the tendril of power that connected Lapis to his long forgotten earth, strengthened. Lapis was not yet sure what child Gar spoke of, but a suspicion formed in his mind. There were not many things that would draw the goblin to this cell, and not many faeries that had the power to scare Gar into this visit.

Unbeknownst to Gar, the ability to send out mind feelers had remained with Lapis through the years of his imprisonment. Thusly, he had been able to keep himself in touch, to a degree, to the outside world. He had hidden a lot from the self-proclaimed King of the Goblins, including the fact that he could have broken his chains of imprisonment at any time. His powers were of the ancient gods, and it was stupid of Gar to think that he could ever have imprisoned the powerful mage. Granted, the long imprisonment had worn Lapis' powers down, and eventually he may have died. But he had his own reason for wasting away in this bowel of hell, and it had nothing to do with Gar's imposed imprisonment. Guilt could be a powerful motivator.

"I have no time for games. Time runs short." Arms crossed, Gar slowly paced around the hanging mage. "Tell me, mage, does your heart still burn with love for the witch?" Gar's question was no doubt meant to rattle the senses of the prisoner.

With no answer forthcoming, Gar lowered his face and snarled in Lapis'ear. "I think you ache for her forbidden love and I think you would do anything to ensure her safety."

"Do you tell me she is in danger?"

Gar sneered. He leaned close to Lapis and whispered, "Yes."

Not trusting Gar, Lapis' heart still jumped in fear that the one he loved may be in danger. Would he not sense the danger? Maybe not--his powers had weakened over the last years. He needed to stall Gar to allow himself time to gain strength from his renewed connection to the earth.

"I will listen, but first you must release me."

Triumph and power coursed through Gar's veins and glowed in his goblin eyes of mud gray.

Seeing the hesitation and lack of trust, Lapis said, "I can do you no good from here. My powers are not available to me, especially if you need me to find someone. A child, you said?"

"Hmm, you are correct." Gar paced and mumbled to himself, "But how can I trust you?"

After moments of silent consideration, each opponent weighed options. Gar pinned Lapis with his gaze and then a sudden dawning awareness of power tinted Gar's mud-like eyes.

"I will release you, but first I will tell you something I have learned while you have been rotting in my dungeon."

"Come, Gar," Lapis prompted. "You are the one in such a hurry."

"Yes, well, your animal rutting with the witch was fruitful and it is your blood spawn who sits on the throne--my throne--not Raegar's. The bitch you feel so much love for lied to you both."

Sweet dismay rose in Lapis' chest only to be felled with the thought of the power Gar held over him--if his words were true. "How do I know you speak the truth?"

"I speak truly. Think back," Gar prodded.

Lapis was afraid to remember, yet remember he did.

~ * ~

A soft, summer solstice breeze wafted over the mountains to the west and brought with it the taste and smell of new life to the land of Dunraven. With that year's cold, bitter winter, the weather was a much-needed change. Lapis had taken the day for himself and left the main trees of Dunraven--and Raegar--

behind. On foot, he had only a sack of food wrapped and slung over his shoulder, and his wolf for company.

Gray Wolf. His companion since childhood so very long ago. No one knew of his canine protector, since he only came to Lapis' side when the mage left his duties behind. Like today. Lately, his duties had worn him out. Actually, Raegar wore him thin. The king was a being of few morals. Strict, disciplined, unforgiving, unrelenting, narrow-minded, and strong-willed were all words to describe him well.

That was why Lapis had such a hard time understanding. No, no sense trying to reason it out. The wrenching truth was that Bronwen, the one he loved, belonged to King Raegar. Maybe she saw something in Raegar that others could not. Maybe when they were alone, he complimented her, held her close, and caressed her slender body.

"Fangs, you dunce. Stop thinking of her in that way, or you *will* find yourself in heaps of trouble." His words earned a nuzzling inquiry from Gray Wolf who loped easily at his side. "I am fine, friend. Just an old man's meanderings of life and love. Come; let us settle ourselves by the river. My hunger grows."

The river flowed from the mountains. Wild and untamed, the crystal blue water rushed in undulating froth and foam over craggy rocks and down the primeval icons of nature that reached to the heavens. Into the valley of Dunraven came the water, where the land became smoother and gently rolling hills silhouetted the horizon. Lapis found the place where the wild land tamed into graceful gliding water and provided a haven for all creatures.

After finishing his meal of cheese, bread, and fruit--all of which he shared with Gray Wolf--Lapis' eyelids slowly drooped and his breathing slowed. He had not felt so relaxed in a long time. Since before coming to Dunraven.

One might ask if he were so unhappy, why did he stay?

Two reasons. One of them being the Lady Bronwen.

Her eyes were black, yet when she looked at him, they radiated warmth, not cold. Her hair fell freely in silken strands of honeyed gold down her back to touch upon her rounded buttocks. The attraction was not one-sided; the ache of longing ran through both their veins and bound them together in an unbreakable bond. Yes, she was one reason he stayed. One day, Raegar would tire of her. One day a sweet, young virgin would take her place in Raegar's bed and shatter Bronwen's naive belief in Raegar's love for her. On that day, Lapis would take the Lady Bronwen and they would leave the land of Dunraven and the reaches of Raegar. She would have been replaced long ago if not for her powers of prophecy that Raegar used to his own advantage.

Lapis lay his head upon the soft grass and gave a contented sigh; it was nice to dream. Unfortunately, as Lapis had learned over the years, the Fates sometimes had their own plans. His body relaxed and his vivid imagination found an open mind in which to weave dreams.

His arms wrapped around the softness of a willing female body; lush lips brushed across his brow and found his parted lips. Tongues--hot and wet--danced together and raised the aching senses to a fever pitch. Lapis' limbs became limp, unlike his manhood, which rose into a turgid probe. Fates above, could the sweetness get any better?

In a dark recess of his mind, he knew it had to be a dream, but his heart's fulfillment was at hand, even if in phantom form. He let his hands wander in delightful abandon and found all the secret womanly places. Moans of pleasure filled his mind as his physical needs overwhelmed him. Unable to hold himself any longer, he plunged deep into the sweetest place he had ever dreamed of being. Eeyiah! He screamed his release and swore that the earth shook beneath him.

Then she was gone.

His dream was over.

Slowly waking, he was embarrassed that he had spilled his seed like an untrained youth, and over a dream no less. At least that is what he thought until he found the footprint by the water. The small print had not been there before his nap, he would swear to that. His heart pounded. Gathering his belongings he did something he had not done in many years--he used his powers to time shift from one place to another.

His breath short with anticipation of seeing Bronwen, he did not have long to wait as she dashed across the open field of clover toward her rooms in the main dwelling tree. Ready to confront her with his knowledge of their joining, a glimpse of blue beyond the forest trees held him in place. Damn! It was one of Raegar's attendants, and he followed Bronwen. He must have seen them at the river.

Maybe he could stop the spy before he reached the king. He raised his hands to render a spell of silence but was stopped by a familiar raspy voice that whispered in his ear.

"Let us hear what he has to say--else I will send the Lady Bronwen to her death with a mere flick of my wrist," Raegar threatened and gestured to the surrounding warriors in full gear.

Lapis would have laughed at such a threat, waved a spell in Raegar's direction, and absconded with Bronwen, except for the fact that Raegar held the crystal somewhere in his possession.

The second reason for Lapis staying at Dunraven.

The crystal had been stolen from the Tuatha de Danann and lost somewhere in the realm. Rumor bespoke of a confrontation between Raegar's father and a rebel with Tuatha bloodlines who'd had the gall to steal the Book of Time and the Crystal of

Light. Word also spread quickly--for the sprites of the woodland loved to gossip--that Raegar's father had overcome the rebel and hidden the legendary stone somewhere at Dunraven.

Lapis meant to retrieve the crystal and return it to the Tuatha de Danann. It was his destiny as surely as his love for Bronwen warmed his heart. So far, he had spent years searching all of Dunraven and the surrounding country, to no avail. Raegar's father had hidden the legendary crystal well. Each morning that the sun rose, Lapis was certain Raegar would decide he did not need the powers of the mage. Each day he breathed a sigh of relief that he was able to continue his search another day. Sometime over the last years, he had decided that Raegar did not realize the existence of the crystal. Now, his senses tingled in full battle cry that his time here was over and he feared the crystal's hiding place would be lost in the vortex of time.

That afternoon of pleasure was such that the gates of hell blew open and changed the lives of all for years to come. Struck from behind by a heavy battle club, Lapis lost consciousness. Sight and sound receded as his body hit the dirt and the blackness took over. His last sight was Bronwen's face and her black eyes shimmering with pools of unshed tears-- these same eyes silently begging forgiveness for her solitary act of weakness. He barely managed to twist his mouth into a smile of reassurance before he fell into oblivion.

~*~

Remembering it all brought his senses back into overload and it was a shock to have Gar's voice bring him back to his present state of imprisonment. Lapis never knew what became of Bronwen, but the stark fear in her eyes had been etched into his mind for the last thirty years. Once in awhile he had been able to sense a flickering of a mind probe. He had not responded at first, wanting the isolation, and later he had become too weak to send his thoughts over such a distance. The years had passed, and being locked in a living hell had worn him into a shell of his former being.

"A male was born exactly twelve cycles of the moon to the day you and the bitch mated at the river like the wild animals you are."

The crude words sent Lapis' already reeling emotions into a spiral of dizzying anger. With a mighty roar, he collected the earth energy, and using his droplets of blood as a connection, he sent all his thoughts into striking out at Gar. It worked. Heat filled the dungeon and Gar screamed in pain.

Lapis felt infinitely better until Gar recovered from the blast of heat and viciously beat Lapis with the hilt of his sword. The pain invaded his ancient soul and filtered into the depths of the darkness he had been living for so long. He would have howled but had not the strength and did not want to give Gar the satisfaction--he still had that much pride.

The beating stopped and Gar stepped back to wipe sweat from his brow. He whispered to the hovering Grud, who smiled and scampered from the dark room. As Lapis refocused his strength Gar lovingly caressed his sword before he placed it back in its scabbard.

Breathless anticipation grew in the dimness and quickened the beating heart of both goblin and mage. Footsteps echoed through the hallway, advanced and increased in din until they came to a grinding halt in the doorway. Lapis came to full awareness when he heard the chirping of a firedrake. Weary eyes turned to focus on the latest of Gar's manipulations. Two firedrakes rested in a carved wooden crate that Grud wheeled into the room.

Small creatures that resembled their larger forebears, the iridescent blue firedrakes had sharp teeth, nostrils larger than normal--for the fire breathing--claws like needles and wings that spread out in a fine array of primal wonder. Bred for domestication, at least to the degree such a thing were possible, the firedrakes were the size of a large hawk.

Gar put his finger into the crate and began to coo to the creatures. They preened for him and presented their necks for a scratch. "You see," Gar bragged. "I've trained them to be my pets. They do what I want."

"Birds of a feather," Lapis mumbled.

"Yes, well, these birds will make sure that you do what I want." A sneer etched itself into Gar's already wrinkled face.

Lapis was tired, weak, and having a hard time understanding the direction of Gar's comments, but Gar seemed to expect some kind of response, so Lapis grunted.

Gar snorted. "Stupid mage. Am I the only one here with a brain?"

Gar's outburst startled the firedrakes who retaliated by nipping at his finger they had been cuddling a moment ago. Lapis smiled, adding anger to the pain of the bite. Gar slapped the side of the crate and sent the firedrakes beating about the enclosed area. Turning to Lapis, he stuck his finger in his mouth and sucked until the bleeding stopped.

"Laugh, but I have a used quiver given to me by Raegar on one of his infrequent visits. A gift that I thought he gave me because he cared, but then I found out it belonged to Adoneesis. One whiff of that quiver will lead these firedrakes straight to him. Within seconds, their sharp teeth and claws will rip him to shreds. You see, mage, the life of the whelp you bred depends on you. I will release you, but if you raise one finger against me in magic..."

Lapis fumed. Gar's plan was a solid one. Once freed, the firedrakes would seek Adoneesis and Lapis knew he wasn't strong enough to deter them from killing the son he'd only now found out he'd sired.

"I see you understand," Gar gloated. "Grud, clean him up and take him to the human's sleeping chamber. I have an idea." With a flick of his wrist, Gar turned on his heel and made his hasty exit. His mumbling words followed him from the dark place that had been Lapis' home for so long. "What a depressing place, how can anyone stay sane here after all this time."

Lapis knew Gar hated him and would try to break his spirit before all this was done. He just had to hope that he was able to find a way to freedom before the goblin was able to use Lapis' powers to hurt Bronwen and Adoneesis.

Six

Hypnotized, or maybe just bone-deep tired, Bronwen stared into the dancing flames of the fire blazing in the stone hearth. She huddled deeper into the soft chair--afraid to look too closely around the chamber she used to share with Raegar. Memories of the past hung in the room like a shroud. Somewhere in the passages of time, she could almost hear Raegar's raspy whisper condemning her to spend the rest of her life alone. With a dull throb, her arms recalled the biting pressure of his thick fingers digging in as he dragged her from the courtyard into this chamber.

Why had she requested *this* room? She had no idea the overwhelming fear would engulf her so. She could not change her mind now though, because Adoneesis would wonder, and she was not ready to tell him anything of the past. He did not know so much. So much he would need to know before all was done.

She took a deep, calming breath and tried to push Raegar's memory from her. She would not let that hog's breath get to her, not now, not when she was finally in a position to help her first and only born. Granted, her time was short. Already, darkness came for her. The curse--Raegar's curse.

She shivered upon recalling how he had beaten her that day when anger claimed his mind and overshadowed anything he may have felt for her. Certainty that she had conceived upon that day ached within her, and she held her arms closely around her abdomen to protect against the hardest blows. When the beating stopped, she lay on the floor, bloodied, beaten, and thankful to be alive. Her mind raced with thoughts of escape. She and Lapis would find a place where they could be together and raise their child.

Unfortunately, Raegar had other plans. "Bitch," he spat. "I should kill you here and now for taking another into your arms. But I need an heir, and your bloodlines are strong." Raegar turned his back to her and stared into the fireplace. When he spoke, his voice was filled with cold calculation. "I will keep you in this room and breed upon you until you conceive. Yes." An evil smile of satisfaction shadowed his harsh features. "Then, once you have birthed my heir, I will have my guards take you to the coldest mountain peak and leave you to die."

His eyes lit with insane rage and an unearthly glow lit the darkening room as he contemplated her. "But even that is not enough for the ill you have done me on this day. If you should survive the bitter cold of the mountains, I curse you to shrivel into a hag that no one can lay their gaze on without recoiling. You will be an outcast from Dunraven, never to return. If you dare set foot here again, you will wither and die from the inside out. Pain will rack your body as organs and bones turn to dust, and your skin shrivels yet more."

"You cannot do this to me," Bronwen had pleaded. "You cannot separate me from my child." Her voice was weak, for she felt the responsibility of guilt--her guilt.

"Yes, I can," Raegar roared. "My word is law, and I will make all faeries swear to do naught to help you. You will be on your own. But I am not completely without heart, after all, we will share a child. The curse will be lifted if you can find someone to love you regardless of your appearance. Similar to the curse of the corrigans, except they show their beauty at night, whereas you will be ugly all the time."

Rage burned deep in Bronwen's heart. 'Twas no wonder she found herself tempted by the love of another. It was hard to believe she ever could have loved Raegar. But still, to be used as a breeding animal and then thrown away with no thought-- torn from the child she was to bear, and cursed to such ill fate.

Raegar had taken her then, by the same fireplace that now burned brightly. Savagely and with hate, he had thrust into her for that night and many others. Bronwen dared not tell him that she had already conceived with Lapis. Raegar would have torn the child from her womb. As it was, she needed to make him believe that the child to be born was his offspring. That at least she had done for her son.

Comforted by the crackling warmth of the fire, Bronwen shook off the heavy memories and made a mental list of all that she would need for the task that lay before her. Tomorrow she would have faeries search for the herbs she needed. She would choose the crystals needed and search for the right spot for the ceremony. She knew the energy lines of this land well and she had a mental sense of three places she would test tomorrow and decide which she would use for her seering ceremony.

A barely there scratch at the door interrupted her. "Enter." The door remained firmly shut and the gentle scratching repeated. "Blither it," Bronwen sighed as she rose from her chair. "I said enter." She opened the door and was almost knocked over by the haphazard skittering of a small pixie flying into the room.

Words like waterfalls careened from Bailiwick's mouth. "Sorry, but the door is too heavy for me to open. How is your room? Is the fire warm enough? If you need anything, just ask me. The king sent me to tend to your needs." He hovered midair and the rhythmic flutter of his tiny wings made a soft hum in the chamber. His face puckered into an expression of wondering. "Lady, I know I am bold, but..." He hesitated as if not sure how to put his thoughts into words.

"Speak, young pixie." Bronwen returned to the chair she had vacated to answer the door. "You have disturbed me now, so you may as well say what you came for."

Bailiwick blushed. "Oh, but, I came only to make sure you were settled."

"Do not lie to the prophetess. I see the truth."

"Oh. Of course." Bailiwick let himself sink, cross-legged, onto the floor at Bronwen's feet.

Chin resting in hand, mouth twisted into a tone of careful consideration, he was the perfect picture of innocence. Bronwen was entranced and refreshed by his directness.

"I know who you are," Bailiwick whispered.

Bronwen started--he was not so innocent after all. She took a moment to poke at the fire and collect her thoughts "Of course you know--I am the prophetess."

"No. No. No." He flipped in the air and came to rest on the floor again. "You became the prophetess after you left here. After you left your infant son behind."

Bronwen's heart stopped beating and she felt her face drain of all color.

"How do you know this?"

"I'm sorry. I didn't mean to upset you." Bailiwick looked contrite and somewhat worried.

"You have upset me. Who else knows this?"

"No one, I swear. I've told no one. It's not my place. I know that. I swear I'll never tell anyone, cross my eyes and spit at the moon."

Bronwen sighed. "Fine, I'll have to take your word that you'll keep the secret. But tell me how you know of such things."

"Well, to tell you the truth," Bailiwick's voice lowered to the merest whisper. "I am magic." His gaze darted about the room and needlessly checked that they were indeed alone. "How do you think a pixie became personal attendant to the king? I do things others cannot. I see things others can not." He preened, his wings spreading to full span. "I made myself indispensable to the king by always being there for him and knowing what was best for him. That is how I earned my name. Everything is my bailiwick."

"Well that is most interesting, little pixie. But most faeries have some magic left in them that has filtered down from before."

"Yes, yes, I know that. But my magic is strong." Bailiwick fluttered his wings incessantly and leaned closer as if to share a secret. "For example, when King Adoneesis cast a circle about the clearing to prevent the phookas from leaving--they really are obnoxious--anyway, afterward the king had so drained his energy, he had to lie down to recuperate. Such is the price of using magic for most faeries these days." Bailiwick sat up straight and pointed his finger to his puffed out chest. "I could do that blindfolded and still be raring to go for more. I can snap my fingers and make anything happen."

With these words, he snapped his fingers and a spark of flame burst from the fireplace to land on the bed. "Oh, no." Bailiwick panicked. "I did not mean for that to happen." He snapped his fingers again in an attempt to stop the flame. "Oh, Lady, I can not put it out. Use your magic, douse the flames."

In a flash so fast, the movement barely registered, Bronwen leapt toward the bed and threw a pitcher of drinking water on the small flame.

"That was hardly spectacular," A not so contrite Bailiwick complained. "Why did you not use your magic? It would have been so much more fun."

Bronwen sighed and turned to the overeager pixie. "One should never abuse the power of magic. For every action, there is a reaction and you cannot always prepare yourself for the consequences. Trust me, I know of what I speak."

"Oh." Bailiwick's face took on a thoughtful glow. "Can you maybe teach me in the ways of magic?"

"I thought your magic was already strong."

"It is. It just does not always follow my wishes."

"I understand. Tell me, how did you come by your knowledge of magic?"

"I... well... I do not know if I should..." He lowered his voice to a whisper, "I found something one day."

Before he could confide any further, a faerie of slight stature and fine features entered the room--her arms laden with fruit and refreshment. "The king requested that I make sure you are comfortable, Lady."

Bronwen raised her brows and arched a questioning look to a sheepish Bailiwick. "The king you say?"

"Yes, Lady. Can I get you anything?"

"No thank you. This will be fine for now."

"Good, I'll see you on the morrow then." The faerie bowed and took her leave.

Bailiwick was quick to follow. In a wisp of fluttering wings and a goodnight, he quickly flew out the door before it had a chance to fully close and successfully avoided having to reveal his secret.

"I will deal with you later, little one."

With a sigh and a stretch, she stood and with deft fingers unclothed herself. She avoided looking in the small oval mirror resting in the shadowed corner of the room. Many years ago,

her body had been taut and smooth, her flesh ripe like a summer peach. Now, withered and pasty, her skin hung from a hunched frame and recessed wrinkles littered her once beautiful face.

Raegar's curse.

As she climbed up into the wood-framed, feather bed, Bronwen prayed she lived long enough to help Adoneesis save the faeries. She closed her eyes and drifted into a troubled sleep.

She'd been asleep for some time when a sudden jabbing in her chest woke her. Darkness cloaked the room and Bronwen panicked as she realized she couldn't move.

Someone was choking her.

Her breathing was labored, and her eyes watered as pain jabbed her chest again. A voice drifted on the cool night breeze. *You betrayed me. You will suffer greatly before you die.* The disembodied voice drifted away to a mere hum. *You should have stayed away.*

With a jolt of adrenaline, Bronwen jerked up to a sitting position--her hands clutching her chest. The curse. The curse that would rage a war from the inside. Ravaging her, destroying her, aging her into a painful death.

~ * ~

Adoneesis sipped his nectar and tried to ignore Bailiwick who had returned from somewhere in an agitated state. Not succeeding, he raised his hand. "Bailiwick, settle down. I have much to think about and you're distracting me."

"I am sorry, so sorry. I'll sit right down here in the corner until you need me." Bailiwick darted to the furthest corner and sat, cross-legged.

Adoneesis regretted his harsh words, but was glad for the peace and quiet. He surveyed the small room and, as always, felt Raegar's presence strongly. Equipped with a table, chair, bed, and desk, the room was one known only to Adoneesis--and now Bailiwick.

Raegar's words from years ago still rang in his mind, *Trust no one! As long as no outsiders know of this place, you will have a place of safety. This will be your sanctuary in times of stress, as well as a place to hide if your enemy overruns you.*

Adoneesis remembered how Raegar had taken him by the shoulders and stared into his eyes. *You are soft and pliable, and think to bind the people to you by showing caring and understanding. Ha! You must overcome this weakness because you will earn enemies, regardless of your governing skills. Someone will always feel left out, unappreciated, or taken advantage of, no matter what you do. Heed my words and keep this place to yourself.*

Adoneesis thought how typical it was of Raegar to temper advice with insults. No matter how hard he had tried, Adoneesis had never been able to satisfy Raegar's desire for a son worthy of the family name. He had never been fleet enough, strong enough in contests of hand to hand, able to sit a horse properly, or witty enough in conversation. Worse, at least in Raegar's mind, magic had coursed strongly through Adoneesis from the day he was born.

After a few successful attempts at levitation and making his favorite sweet treat appear out of nowhere, Adoneesis had been beaten until he swore never to use magic again. But that was the past. The present needed to be dealt with and it seemed magic would be the order of the day, yet it felt strange for Adoneesis to access that part of himself that had been denied for so long.

He sighed and brought his mind back to Gar's pillaging and killing of innocent faeries because of some unfounded hatred he held for their king. Adoneesis rested much hope on the prophetess, more than he liked to admit, because lying just below the surface of his understanding he felt a sense of shadows and darkness. That is what troubled him. He had no doubt the prophetess could find the child, but at what cost? And would the child be able to save the faerie realm? Did they even deserve to be saved? That small question rolled about in Adoneesis' mind and caused him no end of guilt. Of course, the faeries deserved to be saved. Why wouldn't they?

With these questions in mind, his thoughts wandered to the desecration of nature he had seen more of lately. The old ways of harmony and respect had gradually melted into a way of life more resembling the confusing world of man where greed, lust, and a self-centered attitude ruled. None of the old gods and goddesses existed, except in legends and the minds of some of the older faeries. Yes, there was the original Lady of the Lake, but he doubted that she would live much longer. With her would go a way of life Adoneesis found his blood singing for, a knowledge that existed only in his mind, yet he found himself aching for daily.

With a sharp pound of his fist on the table, Adoneesis released some frustration and startled Bailiwick into a state of confusion.

"What's wrong? What happened? What did I miss?" Bailiwick rubbed sleep from his wakening eyes.

"Nothing. Settle back. It is just that I am king, yet can do nothing. I must rely on the questionable power of a hag from the middle of nowhere."

"Adoneesis!" Bailiwick raised his voice and admonished the king in a way he had never dared before. "Don't talk like that. The faeries look to you for strength. Your words keep them strong and rally them together. Your courage leads us all. As for the prophetess, trust me, her powers are as strong as legends recount. Our entire world was created from legends, the legends of our forebearers. If the prophetess has a smidgen of their powers, she will help in our salvation. I know that the two of you will each fill your destiny and save our world."

"My, my Bailiwick. You are quite the storyteller."

"It is not a story--it is destiny."

Adoneesis smiled a crooked smile of indulgence. "Well, I guess the wheels are in motion and we must deal with whatever fate sends our way."

Bailiwick spun high into the air, flipped a double somersault midair, and dived straight at Adoneesis who, not fast enough, found himself with an armful of excited pixie. Trying to keep his kingly composure, Adoneesis held him at arm's length and snorted, "Yes, well, enough of that. To bed, pixie. I am tired."

~ * ~

While Adoneesis drifted into a restless slumber, Bailiwick used all the persuasion he could to keep his eyes open. When soft, gentle snoring reached his ears, he shook himself awake. Creeping across the wooden floor of the tree, he sent a prayer to the heavens that nothing would creak and wake the king. Bending down in the corner, he reached under and around a twist of gnarled wood. For a minute, he thought it was gone. His heart gave a leap in his chest and then settled as he felt the familiar smoothness of the crystal he sought. Reverently, he pulled the crystal from its hiding place. Large enough that he needed both hands to hold it, the crystal was of a rough rounded shape. The ragged edges may have fooled the casual observer into believing it was of little or no consequence, but if one looked closely, they'd become aware of a warm light that bathed the crystal in a luminescent glow.

Ahhh, an instant stab of pulsing energy surged up his arm as he held the crystal close. Glowing like a luminescent moonbeam, the crystal connected to Bailiwick and gave its gift of vitality. On some remote archaic level, Bailiwick sensed greatness. Visions raced by at an intolerable speed--screaming people, rushing water, falling buildings, and then darkness. From the darkness came light and a place of peace. Bailiwick's tension eased and then the disruption began again. This time it was more intense. Bailiwick felt closer to the destruction and ached with the loss of the faeries. He held on as long as he could but when it became too intense for his small mind to handle, he let go of the crystal.

Brimming once again, he placed the crystal back where he had found it so long ago and tapped down the feeling of disappointment that always accompanied one of his sessions. The crystal's power overwhelmed him, yet he comprehended only a small part of what the crystal tried to pass on to him.

He understood the destruction of the land surrounded by water, as well as what he assumed was the creation and eventual disappearance of Avalon. But underneath those visions had been a subtle knowledge--a thread he needed to unravel as if woven through his mind.

Pursing his lips, he forced his eyes shut and concentrated on the thread. Suddenly, as if there all along, his mind was cognizant of a fact. A single fact that made so much clear. The birth of a child--unwanted and unacknowledged. King Raegar had another son. Gar.

Hog's breath. That explained so much. But how to let King Adoneesis know the source of Gar's anger without exposing his possession of the crystal? Maybe he didn't have to. If Bailiwick could figure out the crystal's latent abilities, he could save the faeries. They wouldn't need to find the human child, the goblins could be put in their place, and King Adoneesis could loose the tight mask that had recently become his face.

All he needed to do was learn how to work the crystal. Maybe he should have told the prophetess of his found treasure? No, that didn't feel right. Another path would be presented to him when the time was right. He was sure of that.

With a shrug of his tiny shoulders and a final look at Adoneesis, who snored the song of sleep, Bailiwick tiptoed from the secret chamber and made his way to the root of the tree where his chamber lay. With a satisfied sigh, he closed his eyes to dream of becoming the hero who saved the faeries.

Seven

Despite her bitter memories, Bronwen fell quickly into a state of slumber. Steadily she fell, aware on some subconscious level that she had gone beyond the realm of peaceful dreams. Swirling in a mist of lost souls and unfulfilled dreams, she was drawn into her past. Deep into a void of suppressed emotions, she relived her first years of isolation.

She had given birth to a male child--Lapis' child. Of course, Raegar, in all his masculine ego, claimed the child as his own. That was fine. That meant the child would be safe. As Raegar had proclaimed, Bronwen had been torn from her newly born child, taken to the farthest mountain, and discarded. The faces of the faeries transporting her held pity, but their fear of Raegar was stronger. The one favor they did was to leave her at the base of the mountains, just below the line of snow that capped the peaks.

That act saved her life.

That, along with the strange appearance of a wolf.

Stumbling toward the warmth of the lower lands, Bronwen knew she needed to find some food or perish from hunger. Raegar's orders had been to leave her with no food, tools, or water. He had consigned her to death--a slow horrible death of starvation or mauling by one of the many creatures that roamed the land. That is how she would die. She already heard the howling from a distance coming closer as she stumbled over the wild terrain.

At least it was getting warmer. She left the shadow of the mountain and made her way to a valley that sparked with life. Maybe there was a chance she would live. But she needed food, oh, how she needed food.

At that moment, a figure broke through the line of dense forest and Bronwen's heart danced in fear. It was the embodiment of Raegar's curse. It had to be. Large, muscular, and furry, the creature loped towards her and Bronwen sighed in acceptance of her death. There was no way to outrun or outfight the creature. She closed her eyes and waited for the blessed release of death. She said a silent farewell to the child she never knew. She waited--nothing happened. Slowly, she'd opened one eye. Expecting to see the open jowls of death's creature, she was astounded to see the body of a rabbit on the ground in front of her.

Her eyes rose to lock with shimmering silver eyes of a gray wolf. Tentatively, she reached out to touch the rabbit. The body was still warm. She would never have killed an animal to eat of its flesh, but when offered by the bounty of nature, it was a gift received.

Satisfied that his gift was accepted, the wolf formed an unspoken bond with the faerie, and from that day on the two became inseparable. She became used to his presence and one day he told her his name. Gray Wolf. Her savior. He'd helped her survive Raegar's edict and if ever Bronwen needed help, the wolf was there. The bond between them was that strong.

Years passed quickly and Bronwen etched a place for herself in the small meadow surrounded by forest. As her connection to the earth grew, so did her powers. She remembered the exact day she realized her powers went beyond those of a normal faerie. Some number of years after her exile, she was practicing one of her usual moon rituals when something unusual happened.

The rituals were to enhance her connection to the earth, harmonize with nature, and relate to the moon goddess. That time there was a different snap in the air as she prepared her altar for ritual. The candles burned brightly, the herbs decorated the altar, and the moon shone in luminescent beams upon her secluded valley. But the air was charged with a restless wind that swept across the grasses and disturbed the branches of the trees.

A tingle shivered across her arms as she disrobed to present her natural presence to the heavens. Chanting her dedication to the Goddess and nature, she knelt on the softly grown grass of her valley. Her body vibrated with the force of the power that came to her that night. She ached with longing, and thrummed with an understanding that she would never be the same again. Racing ever more forceful down the mountains and into the valley, the winds brought with them a vision.

Girlish voices intruded on her vision--or maybe they were part of the vision. A flicker of unfamiliar, foreign surroundings and a whisper of an ancient voice stroked itself across her hearing. Her vision focused on the face of a young human girl.

~ * ~

The young girl, Bryanna, snuggled deeper behind the bank of built up snow. Beside her, her friend giggled in breathless anticipation. At the sound of an approaching car, the two cohorts looked at each other in mute agreement, quickly gathered snow, and packed it tight between damp mittens.

Silence, except for the sound of snow dripping from the limbs of gnarled apple trees. Wisps of misty breath blew from mouths curled in anticipation. As the car came closer, bouncing down the country lane, the two girls raised their arms for the attack. Waiting, waiting--launch. The snowballs flew through the air and landed right in the middle of the windshield. Snow splattered all over the window and blinded the driver for a split second. The car swerved to the right, then the left and then came to a full stop on the side of the road.

"Oh, oh. Let's get outta here," Bryanna yelped and made a mad dash for the crumbling split rail fence at the far side of the orchard. Her friend, Trudy, followed closely behind. They were spurred by the sound of a man yelling for them to stop. Was he crazy? Like they'd really stop and go back so he could yell at them some more.

Legs pumping, heart pounding, blood rushing, Bryanna let her coltish legs fly over the freshly fallen snow. Exhilaration colored her face, and the glory of running free made her feel as if she could conquer the world. In a split second, the fence rose before her. It looked too high to jump, but Bryanna felt strong. With one single bound of energy, she cleared the fence and landed on the other side in a steady stance of readiness.

"Bryanna, I can't make it over the fence. Help me." Trudy's voice quivered with fear.

Jeez, sometimes Trudy was such a pain. What was so difficult about getting over the fence? She'd cleared it in a single bound--kinda like Superman. Bryanna giggled at the picture of herself leaping over buildings in a single bound. "I'm coming," she reassured.

They both heard the man coming closer, stumbling through the snow. They only had a minute or two and he'd be upon them. Bryanna grasped Trudy's hands and tugged with all her might. Trudy's feet kept slipping on the fence rails and she was beginning to whimper.

"Why did I let you talk me into this?" Trudy cried.

"Stop whimpering and keep climbing." Now Bryanna was getting scared. She couldn't leave Trudy behind. That wouldn't be right. But she sure as heck didn't want the man to catch them. He was close enough that she could see his face turning red with exertion--or was it anger. Either way, they had to get Trudy over the fence before he reached them. Why couldn't he fall down or something? Trudy was almost over.

"Come on Trudy," Bryanna demanded. "You've got to try harder."

Everything happened at once. A humming heat filled Bryanna's body and then released in a whoosh. Suddenly, the pulling pressure on Bryanna's hands eased as Trudy practically flew over the fence, and the man let out a yell as he tripped over a log and fell flat on his face. In a split instance, Trudy was standing on the ground beside Bryanna and the man was lifting a snow filled face from the snow bank.

Bryanna was stunned. She wasn't sure what happened, but it felt as if she'd literally lifted Trudy up and over the fence with nothing more than a thought.

"Wow, that was cool." Trudy tugged at her arm and with a laugh of relief; they raced up the trodden pathway, through the field, and into the back yard of Bryanna's home.

"Shhh, Aunt Shirley will hear us," Bryanna cautioned.

"She'll probably know we've been up to something. I don't know if you've noticed," Trudy lowered her voice, "but your aunt's kinda weird."

Bryanna snorted. "Duh. Of course, I noticed. Why do you think I stay away from the house so much?" She spoke with all the wisdom of her eleven years.

"Oh. I guess. Hey, let's go inside and check out some of her stuff," Trudy prompted.

"I thought you said she was weird."

"Yeah, but in a cool way." With the comfort of a long-time friend, Trudy opened the door and entered the small house. Sigh resignedly, Bryanna followed.

Adjusting her eyes to the dimness of light after the bright sun, Bryanna was aware of the rumble of voices from one of the rooms down the hallway. "Aunt Shirley has a customer. That means we're free to look to our heart's content. Just don't move anything," Bryanna whispered.

"Okay. But won't all the good stuff be in the room where she is?"

"No, that's just her work room. It's her personal meditation room that has all the good stuff."

On tiptoe, the two girls crept through the overstuffed living room--their feet sinking into the luxury of the outdated green shag carpet. They dodged under the hanging baskets of plants and flowers, passed through the hallway papered in swimming dolphins, and climbed up the stairs to the upper rooms of the house.

The meditation room occupied the southside of the building. That way the room was exposed to sun as it rose in the west and made its way across the sky to the east. It also let in the rays of the full moon, which according to Aunt Shirley was a good thing. Bryanna didn't really care about that kind of stuff; it was just too weird. Although, for a second, she remembered the feel of pulsing heat that had raced through her body and released itself as Trudy flew over the fence.

"Come on, Bryanna, we don't have much time," Trudy prompted her into the small turret room with smooth walls that circled in a never-ending path. Windows were everywhere, displaying a panorama of snow covered rolling hills, old growth forest, and the shimmering ice on a pond dug long ago.

Wherever there was no window, shelves had been built into the wall. The shelves sagged under the weight of books, mysterious bottles, candles of every size and shape, decks of cards, crystals, rocks, and more that was hidden amidst the clutter.

"Wow," Trudy stated. "Every time I come in here, there's more stuff."

"Yeah. Aunt Shirley sure likes to collect. Look, here's her newest deck of tarot cards."

The next few minutes were spent ogling the cards, which just happened to be a deck that had a few more bare butts and breasts than normal.

"Can someone really tell a person's future with a deck of cards?" Trudy wondered.

"Of course not." Bryanna threw the cards down because the warmth radiating from them made her uncomfortable. "Come on let's get out of here. I think I hear my Aunt moving around."

It had only been a ruse to get out of the uncomfortable room, but when Bryanna and Trudy descended the stairs, Aunt Shirley was waving good-bye to a matronly woman making her way through the snow to her car.

Bryanna had mixed feelings about her aunt. She loved her, but was quite uncomfortable around her at times. Since Bryanna's parents had died in a car crash when she was younger, her aunt was the only parent she had ever known. Living in an isolated area in the country didn't give her much to compare family life to. Bryanna knew her aunt was unusual. That was enough to make her feel uncomfortable. On the other hand, her aunt loved her, was tolerant of her occasional bouts of troublemaking, and asked her opinion about things instead of treating her like a child.

Bryanna supposed her biggest complaint would be that they lived so far away from anything that resembled a city. Her aunt explained that it was necessary, but she wouldn't say why, which only made Bryanna wonder even more about what her aunt was trying to hide.

"Earth to Bryanna," Trudy's voice interrupted.

"Sorry, I was just thinking," Bryanna mumbled.

"I just asked, dear, if Trudy was staying for dinner," Aunt Shirley asked.

"Sure, if she wants to." Bryanna's mind wandered, and for some reason she was having a hard time focusing on the present. She felt dizzy and warm. A strange voice whispered in her ear--beckoning her to the fringe of a place she'd rather stay away from. Like maple syrup, the voice warmed her, hypnotized her and asked her questions she had no answers for. Though distant in her vision, she was aware enough of her surroundings to realize that she was falling. The colorful braided rug in the front hallway rose to greet her in its welcoming softness.

She had fainted, but not before she heard her aunt's fearful resigned whisper. "It's begun."

~ * ~

Pale and fearful, the innocent eyes of youth had connected with Bronwen's eyes of age. Shivers arced across Bronwen's spine and she struggled to understand what was expected of her. In an attempt to reach out to the human child, she spoke a greeting, but the young girl only shivered in fear. Bronwen asked a couple of questions in an attempt to find out who the girl was, but her questions resulted in the girl falling in a dead faint to a floor covered with a strange looking mat.

~ * ~

Bronwen woke from her dream to face the darkness of the night and the harsh familiarity of the bedchamber she'd shared with Raegar. She shivered and poured a cup of cool water to soothe her parched throat. That had been her first contact with the girl. That one brief moment when past, present, and future weaved themselves into a single thread and Bronwen had known that she had a purpose. A purpose that involved a young girl and forces from the past. She had used her time wisely to enhance her newly gifted skills in preparation.

Then Adoneesis had shown up with his request for help.

Bronwen only hoped she could help before Raegar's curse destroyed her. With a sigh, she settled back on the firm straw mattress and sent a prayer to the Lady that all would be well.

Eight

Morning dawned with a glorious display of nature's beauty. Rich colors painted their palette across the horizon and bathed the realm of faerie in surreal shades of life. Beauty and perfection--unless one looked closely. From the north, a dark aura smudged the land. Creeping like mist, it tainted the land and heightened the unrest that was already prevalent among the faeries.

From the window of his secret room, Adoneesis looked over his land and his throat tightened. His senses were attuned to the atmosphere change and he knew something was wrong. Something more than the threat from the goblins. He hated being so useless. All his hopes were pinned on a child that he wasn't even sure existed. He sighed.

"King Adoneesis." Bailiwick fluttered to the window's edge. "I am sure that everything will work out. Besides, everything looks fine to me."

"No." Adoneesis shivered. "I sense evil approaching--darkness creeps from the north."

Bailiwick frowned. "Yes, Gar is quite a nasty goblin."

"It is not Gar that I sense. There is something else. I know not what, but I fear this new presence because I do not understand it." His voice lowered to a quiet whisper. "How can one battle what one does not know?"

"Don't worry so. You will know what to do when the time is right. All the faeries have confidence in you."

"That is the problem. The responsibility lies with me and I am helpless." His voice hardened in irony. "King Raegar would know what to do."

With a mighty burst of unusual disrespect and anger, Bailiwick snapped, "No, he would not. It is his fault that the faeries are in this crisis. His curse..."

"I will hear no more, Bailiwick. No fault lies with Raegar." Adoneesis smiled at the young pixie. "I appreciate your loyalty but it is not necessary to make things up to soothe me."

"But..." Bailiwick tried to speak.

"But nothing. Enough self-pity, there is much to do." Adoneesis strode to the inner trunk wall, twisted a knot of wood that protruded and stepped through the opening that swung open into a small room. "Come, we should find Bronwen and discuss her plans."

They found her in the eating room. As if holding court, Bronwen sat at the largest table. Enraptured fairies surrounded her and soaked up her every word. Her soft, flowing voice held power sheathed in a blanket of velvet and drifted like gentle mist through the room. The king was hypnotized. At that moment, the creature before him was someone who truly lived up to the title of prophetess, not merely Bronwen. He wondered again how a wrinkled hag could produce such a melodious voice.

As if his thoughts had reached her, Bronwen turned the full power of her black eyes on him and Adoneesis felt as if he were drowning in a weight of emotions. She could not have known his thoughts--could she? Although her gaze stayed on him, her voice continued its mission of storytelling to the enraptured audience of faeries.

"And once the lord of hawks realized he had been hoodwinked by his love, he cast her from the nest and condemned her to a life of lonely existence. Occasionally, I see her circling above the valley where I live. She cries out, her lonely screech echoing like a beacon, warning others of the desolate price of deception."

Her story ended, yet her gaze remained locked on Adoneesis. His heart ached with emotions he could not understand and wistful memories of something unexplained teased the edges of his mind. Hypnotized, he moved toward the prophetess only to be knocked against by faeries with legs long ago numb, standing up to stretch. Chattering and movement broke the spell woven a moment ago. The prophetess was Bronwen, laughing and joking with the faeries.

"Lady, we must speak. Have you finished your morning meal?"

"I have eaten. I have also sent some faeries out on tasks of gathering and preparation for my ritual. There is naught else to do for the moment."

Adoneesis looked at the etched features of the face before him and the black eyes seeming to beg for his trust. But the kingdom and everyone in it were his responsibility. He had the right to know what was going on.

As if sensing the emotions within Adoneesis, Bronwen spoke gently. "Trust me. I will find the child. You must prepare for possible war with the goblins. I will leave you to your duty, if you leave me to mine."

Before Adoneesis was able to answer, loud voices echoed from the stairway. Two arguing faeries descended into the eating room. Krickall and a shorter faerie, Mayard, who--some would say--was more pleasing to behold, with his smooth face, pouting lips, and lithe, wiry stance.

Between them, and being bandied about by both, was a faerie as fair any. She was delicate, blond, and visibly harried. Over the curses and arguing of the two males, her voice stood not a chance of being heard, yet she tried. Her lips moved, but any sound that she made was lost in the exuberant voices of the two males who held her between them.

"She will eat with me this morn, I tell ye." Krickall stated as he tugged on a delicate arm.

"No Krickall, she ate with you last eve. This morn she eats with me." Mayard tugged on her opposite arm.

Bronwen frowned. "She is the reason the two of them drew their swords yesterday?"

"Yes, her name is Analiese. They both desire her and neither will give up their claim."

"Their *claim*. Pray tell, what kind of *claim* does either hold upon her?"

"Well, her sire died many years past and since Krickall was his closest comrade, he feels a responsibility."

"Humph! You mean he feels heat between his legs," Bronwen snapped.

Swallowing in embarrassment, Adoneesis ignored her words and continued, "Mayard grew up with her and was the first to kiss her. He feels that gives him prior claim."

"There is that word again. Why should either one of them claim her? She is not a prize or an object. Do not tell me you have let this go unaddressed in your kingdom. You are a king. Act like one."

The harsh words hit Adoneesis like a stone upon still water. What had he been thinking? By showing disrespect to one of his people, Krickall and Mayard showed disrespect to him. Blast it that Krickall had earned his place as a warrior, and forget that Mayard was a smooth talking scholar--he was the king. If he had not the guts to stand up to these two, how could he ever hope to stand up to one like Gar? Hog's breath, what had he been thinking?

"Cease! Krickall and Mayard, unhand her." Bellowing with previously untapped depths, Adoneesis voice fell like a hammer upon everyone in the room. Shock showed on the faces of the faeries and breathless silence descended in anticipation of the growing entertainment. Krickall and Mayard let go of Analiese, who sagged in relief.

"But, King Adoneesis," both scorned suitors protested.

"Silence." Adoneesis voice held determination. "Lady Analiese, do you desire the attention of either one, more than the other?" He waved his hand to the offending faeries.

Swallowing deeply, shy at the sudden attention focused upon her, Analiese answered quietly. "King, I have not had the chance to decide. They hound me constantly until my head spins." Analiese stepped away from Krickall and Mayard, smoothed her skirt, and pushed her hair back from her face. The fact that she was free, even if for a moment, seemed to give her renewed strength.

"Would you say that you might possibly have a lasting interest in one or the other?"

Analiese snorted in a quite unladylike manner. "If either buffoon would give me a chance to gather myself, I may find an attraction for one--or the other."

Adoneesis considered the situation a moment. Turning to Bailiwick hovering close by as usual, he requested, "Give me a coin."

With the flick of a hand and wave of his wing, Bailiwick produced a coin. "Oh, what a morning of entertainment. First, a story from a witch, now you're putting those two mush heads in their places for running roughshod over the fair Analiese and spreading their argument through all of Dunraven. Oh, what fun. What fun."

Adoneesis smiled. "Top or bottom, Krickall?"

"Lord?"

"Speak now," he commanded as he tossed the wooden coin to the air.

"Top," Krickall proclaimed.

"I do not think that surrendering her on the toss of a coin is a fair end to the situation." Bronwen's voice quivered with suppressed anger. Adoneesis silenced her with a wave of his hand.

Twitters of interest and speculation punctuated Adoneesis next words. "The coin shows top. That means Krickall wins."

Cheers greeted his words and Krickall slapped his hands on the table in delight. "Come to me, Analiese. It seems you are mine."

"That is not what you win, Krickall."

"What... but, you said..."

"I said you win. *What* you win is the first month to woo Analiese, with no interference from Mayard. That leaves the second month for Mayard, with no interference from you. At that time, the fair lady will make a decision as to whom *she* wants to spend her life with--if in fact she decides on either one of you creatures. If it were up to me, I'd toss you both over and find another who has shown me more respect."

Bronwen was the first to laugh. It started as a delicate chuckle and then grew into a robust release of tension. Others followed her example. Even Krickall and Mayard looked relieved at having the situation taken into hand and settled.

Understanding dawned in the soft blue eyes of Analiese who gave no hesitation in taking advantage of the situation. "Krickall, I do believe I am hungry and desire some fruit. Maybe a bowl of oatmeal as well to start the day." With a sly smile of feigned innocence, Analiese sat down, crossed her ankles, folded her hands on the table, and waited.

Stunned into a state of disbelief at the sudden turn of events, Krickall sputtered, mumbled a few curses at the unfairness of life, and then did exactly what Analiese had requested. With all eyes upon him, he ladled steaming oatmeal into a bowl, poured rich cream over it, and spooned a heap of brown sugar on top. Then he took some fruit from the serving table--selecting the plumpest, juiciest fruit--and placed his offering in front of Analiese.

Adoneesis almost laughed aloud at the absurdity of his friend, who knew little of proper manners and played the chivalrous one to a female. Then, there was Mayard who watched carefully as Analiese carried on a lively conversation with Krickall. Of course, Analiese was doing all the talking while Krickall mumbled his replies. Mayard smiled, and Adoneesis could imagine that the scholar was quite likely thinking that Analiese would grow quickly tired of the big oaf and when it came turn for his month of wooing, Mayard would dazzle her with his intelligence and wit.

Adoneesis breathed deep and relaxed in the knowledge that he had averted a growing problem. Yesterday's swordplay could have turned into something much more serious--it would have, eventually. It had been so easy to fix, why had he not done something sooner?

"It feels good to flex the kingly muscles of power, does it not?" Bronwen whispered to him.

"I never wanted to be king." The whispered confession seemed to be a form of excuse for his actions, or lack thereof.

"Yes, well, in spite of that, you settled the dispute with authority and fairness. You performed well."

Bailiwick, pumped from the excitement, turned flips in the air and tittered a small poem.

"The mighty King has spoken
The restless trio is broken
Breathless, we shall wait to see
Who wins the hand of the fair faerie"

With a laugh and a final flip, Bailiwick landed on the table beside the King and Bronwen. "Oh that was so much fun."

Bronwen laughed. "You find amusement in almost anything, do you not, little one?"

"I try. Oh, how I try."

"You are quite the little poet as well."

"Of course, it is just one more of my many talents. I can do so many things. Why do you think the king has me serve him? I am indispensable."

"Do not let your head swell, or I may replace you, pixie," Adoneesis teased. "Truth is, Bailiwick earned his name because it seems that almost anything is in his ability. Life is his bailiwick. He is useful."

"Yes, I suppose he is."

Adoneesis watched Bronwen fix a narrowed gaze on Bailiwick which caused the little pixie to jump to his feet and declare, "I have many chores. I must be on my way." With a flicker of wings, he disappeared up the stairway.

"He is quite energetic," Bronwen said. "Now, I must prepare. I trust you will be readying for further invasion from Gar." Her voice was steel covered in the softness of a summer breeze. It brooked no argument.

"Yes, Lady Bronwen, I will leave you to your duties and I will tend to mine." He rose from his seat and raised his hand for silence. All eyes turned his way, some with the dawning of a new respect for their king.

"As you know, events have been set into motion and it is time for us to defend our lands, nay, our very existence. Gar moves in from the north and we must put an end to his constant aggressions against us. The time to bear arms and defend our borders is at hand. It has been awhile since we have gone to battle and our forces are weak, so we must train hard over the next while. Krickall." The warrior reluctantly turned his attention from Analiese, whose hand he had just taken into his. "You are the most experienced among us, so you will lead the forces in training exercises. I will be leading the defensive battalion; therefore I will take my knocks in training along with the rest of you."

Murmurs of approval whispered about the room. Some of the older faeries remembered King Raegar had always left the battle up to his forces and stayed behind the safety of the walls of Dunraven.

"There are faeries to the north, east, and west who are vulnerable to attack, we must send out the strong to defend the weak. The fastest riders will take word to the outlying areas and bring the faeries there back to Dunraven. They cannot be protected properly at such a distance. Those who go to the borders will need to be outfitted with weapons, battle gear, and food. You will be responsible for your own weapons, whether those be bow and arrow, spear, or sword. Those who do not leave for the borders will be responsible for sewing cloth for tunics and extra clothes, and preparing foods that will withstand the rigors of travel and time. Planting extra crops and harvesting can be tended to as well. Though it is late for planting, at least some of what you plant will grow to see the light of day. We will need the extra. Now, there is much to do, let us get started. If there are any questions, talk to Bailiwick, he will know where I am at all times."

Adoneesis paused for breath and looked over the expectant faces of those who sat before him. How he prayed he was saying the right things, making the right decisions.

Sensing his hesitation and uncertainty, Bronwen touched his arm and whispered low, so only he could hear. "You do fine, continue."

"Mayard, you are well studied, so you will remain here to tend to correspondence which will be carried back and forth."

Krickall gave a grunt of dissatisfaction. "That means he will be close to Analiese."

"Then it's good that the first month is yours. It will take us that long to prepare. When we leave, Mayard will have his month. If the Lady Analiese chooses you, then you will not have to worry about Mayard being here because she will be waiting for your return."

Since there was no response to such logic, Krickall just shrugged his shoulder in acceptance.

Heavy consideration of impending hardships replaced the previously spirited atmosphere and whispered speculation was the order of the day as the sun passed across the sky and each went about their required tasks.

Nine

In the end, there was no choice. Bronwen choose the clearing to

the far west of Dunraven--the clearing where grew the Sacred Moon Tree. One of the trees of the gods, it was purported to hold the secret of immortality and Bronwen would need the tree's connection to the full moon above to complete her ritual. She would also need the lustrous glow of the Thunder Moon to create magic for astral travel, telepathy, and a connection to the ethereal world.

Bronwen prepared her surroundings to bend the powers of the moon and bounty of the Moon Goddess to her will. Candles of silver, pearl, and white perched in circular array about the outskirts of the clearing while a mixture of cinnamon, dragon's blood, and fern burned warmly in the censor. Cinnamon, to enhance clairvoyance and spiritual vibration, the fern and dragon's blood were for protection.

Never in all her years of craft and ritual had she intentionally undertaken this quest, so protection must be maintained, as Bronwen had no idea where she would be taken, or what forces she might encounter on the way. The few times over the years that she'd seen the young girl had been by accident and she'd never tried to repeat the process--not wanting to expose herself to the plunge through swirling mists of darkness.

Bronwen had pondered over her experiences for a long time but understanding never came--until Adoneesis had approached her. In a split second of total understanding, she knew the visions had been given to her as a way to guide her now. The trip upon which rested the fate of the faerie realm and all the faeries who lived there.

All her studying had been for this one moment in time. All her life had been focused toward this one duty that she would fulfill for her kind. It was time to call the elements to her.

Crumbling salt between her fingers, she lifted her face to the moon and chanted an ancient rhyme of forgotten powers.

> *Earth, fire, wind, and water,*
> *Four elements from four corners*
> *Sun, moon, dark, and light*
> *Guide me by your hand this night*
> *Past, present, future, and beyond*
> *Touch briefly in this common bond.*

At first, nothing happened. Then, in a slow quivering orchestra of nature, the branches on the Sacred Moon Tree trembled and the roving wind circled its way around the clearing. Flickering candle flames burst into shooting torches of light that illuminated the forest and dispelled the pervasive shadows. Though no clouds adorned the sky, a gentle mist sat lightly in the air.

Bronwen was aware of her surroundings as if in a wavering dream of surreal visions. She felt light-headed and her ears hummed monotonously. Droning in the background of her awareness, the sound gradually became decipherable as words of song--the song of the Sacred Moon Tree. Bronwen knew that as certainly as she knew her senses had deserted her. On the wings of belief and fate, she gave herself up to the words and let herself be led through the doorway of light and down the pathway of travel from one world to another.

Her journey was so different this time. More real, more certain, more controlled. Light as the breeze, yet as strong as the ancient trees, her heart sang with wonder and release-- release from the physical form that so constricted one's abilities. Threading her essence through dimensions of past, present, and future, love and hate overwhelmed her. She experienced firsthand the pain of loss, battle torn countries, violent uprisings, and religious fanaticism. Through it all shone the Sacred Moon Tree, a beacon to guide her on her journey.

Finally, gliding to a hovering stillness, she saw what she had been sent to discover; the young girl from Bronwen's earlier journey, now a beautiful woman--a sad woman. Kneeling on the ground by a gravestone, the woman wept such that Bronwen ached with her loss. Intruding on such a moment of sorrow was the last thing Bronwen wanted to do, but she would not get another chance.

In a flash of focused intent, she placed her essence within the woman's mind and probed for information. She grew weaker, it seemed her connection to the moon tree lessened as she mixed with the soul of another, and so she had best hurry or be caught in the mind of another for eternity.

Calling upon nature's force, she opened the woman's mind to her and in that moment re-lived an entire lifetime of loneliness and loss. Hers and the woman's. They had both lost loved ones; they had both lived in exile. Oh, how Bronwen wanted to comfort this being who so touched her own heart.

In the recesses of her languid mind, Bronwen became aware of a distant, haunting murmur. "Nooo, you must make haste or lose yourself forever. Remember your reason for being here." Like a hundred voices of reason, the murmur pulled her into awareness.

Sorting through child-like memories and bittersweet adult emotions, Bronwen took the information she needed and discarded that which was useless. Like one of the ancient keepers of knowledge, she assimilated the knowledge within herself.

When she had all that was needed, Bronwen withdrew from the soul she had invaded, although she could not resist one last melding--one last comforting touch of her mind to the mind of the woman, and then she was gone.

In a lightning flash of cracking energy, Bronwen found herself catapulted back to the clearing. No visions of other worlds and lives, no singing of the Sirens, no pulling of her emotions. Weak and disoriented, she returned instantly to the Sacred Moon Tree and became aware of the touch of the moon upon her face. Without conscious thought, she drew on the potent lunar energy to help feed her physical body. It took a couple of moments before she returned to full awareness of what she had done, and all she had experienced.

Her journey had been successful. It would not be an easy journey but she knew where to find the descendant of the Lady and the Thunder God.

~ * ~

Bryanna knelt by the freshly turned grave and felt empty. The funeral was over and everyone had left her alone. Granted, Trudy had offered to stay with her, but truth be told, Bryanna wanted time to herself to say good-bye.

How did one say good-bye to a loved one? Bryanna shivered in her silken black dress--not because she was cold, but because she was alone. Her aunt had been such a force in her life, the only person Bryanna had ever loved. Sure, Trudy had been a friend for years, but her friend had a family of her own and Bryanna sometimes felt as if she intruded on their life more than she should. Trudy assured her she would always be welcome, but Bryanna made sure not to overburden their friendship by hanging around too much.

What was she to do now, though? Her aunt had left her the house in Vermont, but Bryanna didn't think she'd be comfortable living there without her aunt. The house would be too full of memories. God, thirty-two years old and she was alone in a world she had never felt comfortable in, and she only now realized that her aunt had been the one thing that kept her sane.

Fear rose in her chest, constricted her breathing and made her dizzy with a plethora of emotions. Aunt Shirley always insisted on living far from any kind of large town or semblance of civilization. Bryanna thought it was because of her aunt's strange ways, but as time passed, Bryanna began to suspect it was because of her.

There had been strange occurrences during her childhood-- until she learned to control whatever it was that was inside her. Plates falling from shelves, candles flickering wildly when she entered a room, predictions of upcoming events that turned to truth. Most vivid of all had been the time when she was young, the time she had seen the hazy face and heard the distant voice calling her. That voice haunted her for all the years after, mainly because Bryanna had felt a connection, an urge to answer back.

A gentle fall of light mist brought Bryanna back to awareness of her surroundings. Strange, there were no clouds in the sunlit sky, so where was the mist coming from? She shivered, and wondered how the afternoon sun had faded into a dim shadow of its earlier glory so quickly.

When she shifted her position, a crinkling from her pocket reminded her of an envelope that her aunt's solicitor handed her only that morning. *Your aunt wrote this, years ago, with instructions to give it to you immediately if anything should ever happen to her.* Bryanna had forgotten all about it until now and her curiosity surged to the surface. What could be so important to be held in the hands of a lawyer all this time? It had nothing to do with the will, because that had been settled easily enough. She'd inherited everything.

Reluctant to leave the graveside, Bryanna fingered the envelope and considered reading the letter there. After all, Mr. Drake had said it was important. Just then, the rustling of leaves in tree branches captured her attention. The wind picked up. Her short jacket flapped about her hips and her dress hem lifted in the rising breeze.

Something wasn't right; this was no ordinary breeze. With it came the whisper of a dimly familiar presence. She stood and brushed grass and dirt from her dress as the wind blew about her. Was that someone singing softly? But it seemed to be coming from all around her. How was that possible?

Scared, she hastened to leave the cemetery, but before she could move, she was struck with a blinding headache. Bryanna clenched her head and knelt to the ground she had just risen from. The singing increased, but not as softly. The words assaulted her brain in ferocious abandon. She screamed, at least she thought she screamed. Why did no one come to help her? The pain melted into her brain, as if searching.

Just when she could no longer stand the pain, it was gone. As the final fingers of pain left her almost numb brain, Bryanna felt a touch of warmth in her head. Soothing and comforting, the heat traveled throughout her entire body to heal and strengthen. Strangely enough, feeling no worse for her ordeal, Bryanna was aware of a lingering familiar impression, an old memory that niggled on the edge of her consciousness.

Before she was able to grasp the fleeting sensation, the mist disappeared and left her standing in the last heat of the sun's afternoon rays. That was when the fear set in. Was she going crazy? No, she was just stressed.

From her pocket, the envelope prodded again. Deep inside, without understanding the why or how, Bryanna felt absolute certainty that her life had taken a sudden and drastic turn into the unknown.

~ * ~

Adoneesis tripped over a tree root but recovered quickly. Hopefully, his presence remained unknown. Low in a stance of expectation, he listened for a shout of discovery, but breathed a sigh of relief when Bronwen's advance through the forest continued unchecked. Cursed be the thickness of the forests growth that prevented the brightness of the moon from shining his path. Stepping as lightly as possible, he picked his way carefully with his softly clad feet. Adoneesis followed the prophetess to her eventual destination. The clearing of the Sacred Moon Tree.

Of course, that was just a guess on his part, but Adoneesis could think of no other place situated on this area of Dunraven that would serve her purpose so perfectly. Yes, the only place for the prophetess to perform her ritual would be in the clearing of Wyllow Wood. He wasn't sure why he'd followed her except that he had a connection to the tree and felt himself drawn.

As he approached the familiar place, Adoneesis was ever aware of the prodding song in his mind, although his adult mind was better able to handle the intrusion. Wyllow Wood recognized his presence and greeted him with a warm taste of welcome. Afraid the prophetess may be made aware of his presence, he tried to back off his mind connection to the tree, but she was having none of that. Insistently, the sacred moon tree sang to him and drew him closer to the clearing.

He was barely aware of the prophetess, except as a distant distraction. His mind grasped the image of her as she lit candles, spread her ritual tools, and began her chant. Wyllow Wood's song became the song of the prophetess. Together their voices rose to the heavens and raced across time, taking Adoneesis with them. Out of control, his physical body became a vaporous substance and his surroundings nothing but mists of color and emotion.

On the heels of the prophetess, he experienced what she experienced. His senses were aware of battles of glory, feats of honor, desecration of loyalties--and his soul cried as he realized how insignificant his entire life was. Crying, he was enabled by the sacred tree to see through the eyes of the prophetess.

Beauty incarnate. Glorious radiance of fire and ice struck him breathless. Had the world ever seen such perfection? Luxuriant flaming hair beamed in late day sun, eyes of ice blue melted his heart as Adoneesis watched the mist that was the prophetess reach out to engulf the crying woman of the strange place.

Maybe not so strange, it looked to be a place of funeral pyres. Yet the ground was flat, not raised, and there were no piles of hay and wood to begin a ritual fire. And the crying woman's clothes, never had he seen such. Aching to touch the porcelain face of beauty, he tried to get closer, but found himself stuck in place. Then, suddenly, quicker than the river's running from the mountains in spring, he felt himself shot into the clearing in Dunraven.

"No," he protested. How had his return journey been accomplished in the blink of an eye? He felt cheated and empty. Scrambling unsteadily to his feet, he peered into the clearing just as the prophetess came into awareness. Satisfied she was safe, he plopped back onto the now cool ground. He was stunned at the power and mystery of his journey.

What now? Had that beautiful creature been the one of ancient bloodlines? What strange world had he found himself entering?

Before he could figure out the answer to any of his own questions, a voice beckoned to him. "King Adoneesis, you may as well come out from hiding. I know you are there."

Trying to embody an aura of contriteness, Adoneesis stepped into the moonlit clearing to stand among the wavering flames of countless candles. Thrown far and misshapen, his shadow danced upon the tree he knew as Wyllow Wood. "I beg your forgiveness."

"Do not mock my intelligence with your apology, because there is not a single iota of your soul that is sorry for your actions." Though her words were stern, her eyes teased. "I felt you from the start, you know." She peered into his face. "You must have a strong tie to the sacred tree for her to allow you to journey with me."

"Truly, I did not intend anything like that to happen. I merely wished to watch your ritual."

Bronwen frowned. "You mean your journey through space and time was not deliberate on your part?"

"No. I would have no notion of how such things are done."

"Stranger still. It seems the sacred moon tree plays with fate."

"Wyllow Wood," Adoneesis spoke before he realized.

"Pardon me."

"The tree, her name is Wyllow Wood." With these words spoken, the wind lifted the languid limbs of the tree and sent them rustling about in the air to softly touch upon the face of Adoneesis--a lover's touch.

"Ahh," Bronwen whispered. "I see she is drawn to you. I think perhaps the tree dabbles in your destiny. Let us hope her meddling is without repercussion--the hand of fate should not be forced."

"How do you know that her meddling, as you say, is not fate itself at work?"

"Hmm, intriguing possibility. I suppose we shall see as time progresses." Beginning to pack up her tools of ritual, Bronwen casually remarked, "I had no idea the powers of the ancient ones ran so strong in your blood."

Adoneesis hastened to deny the fact.

"Do not insult me more by denying your powers; they are as clear as a fresh mountain stream. You radiate mage's magic."

"That is impossible." He snorted. "Granted, I have practiced some minor spells of magic, but to have mage's blood and abilities, I would need a relation to such a creature, and I do not."

"Are you so sure of that?" Bronwen turned to Adoneesis and her steady gaze pierced him in a questioning manner.

"Stop. You will not gain answers to my soul with your powers." He gestured impatiently and asked the question that burned his mind. "Tell me of the woman. Is she the one we seek?"

"Yes. She is the one." Bronwen lifted the flap of her saddlebag and set her tools gently inside.

"And you know where to find her?" His voice shook slightly and he cleared his throat. Blast the human for affecting him so easily in the confines of a mere vision.

"Yes." Bronwen closed the flap of the saddlebag and turned to Adoneesis, her eyes wide with enlightenment. "You found her attractive."

"No."

Bronwen chuckled. "Lie to me, but don't lie to yourself. Fates, I hope this does not cause trouble."

Before Adoneesis could make another denial, an impatient snort sounded from the forest, and Adoneesis silently thanked the creature for the distraction. "I think Brachus grows restless, so if you have everything, we can make our way back together."

"Humph. Your beast needs to learn manners. You are king, not he. His ego inflates muchly with his illustrious roots."

"You hinted before about his bloodlines. Tell me more."

"Yes, the tale may make for a pleasant journey back to Dunraven."

Bronwen mounted easily, but Brachus was not about to allow Adoneesis the same benefit. Snorting and stamping, the great beast snapped at Adoneesis and sidestepped in agitation.

"Fangs, I agree with you. This animal needs to be taken to task."

"No, not this time." Bronwen dismounted and raised her hand for silence. "He reacts to the approach of someone... or something." Her black eyes searched the dim shadows of the surrounding forest.

Breathless, they waited. Bathed in lustrous beams from the moon, Wyllow Wood's shadows danced like phantoms on the encompassing forest. Nary a sound touched the ears of those who listened--just a sense of expectation that drifted upon the night air.

"Are you sure?" Adoneesis tightened grip upon his sword hilt.

"Yes. Brachus and I are sure. Listen."

Adoneesis was aware of a swiftness of movement, but still no sound. Then, as if the earth itself opened up to reveal a secret, there began a song of nature as trees shook their branches, flowers bloomed in a midnight display of color, and even the lowliest weed in the fields flaunted their truest beauty. The sense of expectation increased.

"What godly presence approaches?" Bronwen whispered. "I feel an echo of the ages such as I have never felt before."

Adoneesis loosed his grip upon sword as he felt no evil approaching--quite the opposite. His heart sang in harmony with all of nature. He straightened his shoulders and stood true to his height in an attempt to inspire, while Brachus stamped his mighty hooves, cleaving the soil--his welcoming whinny reaching into the heavens.

Then it happened. In a blinding flash of iridescent shimmering light, a creature stood before them. As pristine and perfect as either of them had ever feasted vision upon and glowing like the finest of pearls, the one-horned steed pranced about in a manner as befits royalty. Nostrils flaring, she stepped forth to greet Brachus who pranced his way toward the unicorn. Between them was spoken a secret language of past races and forgotten times.

Adoneesis knelt to the ground in reverence and astonishment. "Fates that be, I have heard tales but never believed with any truth in the words."

Bronwen had knelt beside him. "Oh, yes, a legendary creature. The pure innocence and benevolence of the unicorn has been their downfall, and now only a few remain, but they stay hidden for self-preservation. The cruelty of the world cuts them too deeply."

Adoneesis was unable to do naught but whisper as he rose to his feet. "Why has this one appeared to us?"

"I do not know." Bronwen rose to stand beside him.

"Brachus seems well acquainted," Adoneesis remarked as he watched Brachus and the unicorn touch noses in greeting.

"Yes, well, his bloodlines can be traced back to the unicorn."

Adoneesis was stunned. "I had no idea. I thought him a horse like any other."

"Then you were looking with your eyes and not your heart. How did he come to be your companion?"

"As a child, I wandered the lands of Dunraven--somewhat more than Raegar permitted. One day I fell asleep at water's edge--you know the stream that stretches west to east--and I awoke to the velvety touch of something upon my cheek. I opened my eyes to find the muzzle of a horse stuck in my face. Quite insistent he was that I rise, he nudged me firmly until I stood. Just then, the piercing cry of a muckraker bellowed from the other side of the stream. My heart fell to my feet, as I was unarmed and unescorted. The muckraker leapt into the water and I froze. Brachus saved me. Kneeling on one knee, he allowed me to jump to his back, and then he carried me so far away that the muckraker's horrid cry could no longer be heard."

"He has been with you ever since?"

"Yes. Even Raegar could not claim Brachus for his own, although he tried." Adoneesis voice fell to a soft cadence. "He tried to beat Brachus into submission. When that did not work, he then turned his whip on me. Nothing worked; Brachus would not let Raegar near him. Look, the unicorn comes this way," Adoneesis whispered. "And she is not alone."

A figure cloaked in a dark robe and hood accompanied the unicorn. Neither Bronwen nor Adoneesis could have stated from whence the specter came. They only knew that the robed silhouette approached on silent feet. In awe they waited, neither sure of what greeting to give the strange apparition. It felt only natural to kneel to a single knee and offer respect.

The airy wave of a robe covered arm bid them to rise, which they did. A raised hand pushed silken robe aside to reveal a face hidden partially in shadow and partially lit by a moonbeam. Bronwen seemed to know immediately who stood before them, but Adoneesis was only aware of a niggling of familiarity.

Wisdom and an endless aura of life's experiences etched themselves into the man's leathered face. Luxuriant hair with streaks of gray and white hung long past his shoulders and mingled with his beard. Eyes of amber looked into the very souls of Bronwen and Adoneesis; perhaps searching for the answer to an unasked question. Fingers, long and adorned with various gem rings, scratched the beard in quiet contemplation.

Slow, hypnotizing, and deep as the ocean's mysterious bottom was his voice when he spoke. "I was expecting only one. How have the powers of the moon and tree worked to fool me tonight?"

Bronwen replied, "Great Merlin, I as well found myself surprised by events this evening. It seems that fate has a mind as to what transpires and we are mere pawns."

"Ahh. Well, if the prophetess can be fooled then who am I to feel slighted by the mysterious turn of an errand. Tell me, who is the young buck who stands tall before such powers as have been instigated on this eve?"

"King Adoneesis himself, Merlin," replied Bronwen.

Sharp eyes became sharper, while amber flamed to a hot orange-gold as Merlin turned to Adoneesis. "I see. That explains much." The white-haired wizard stroked his beard and hummed a gentle tune of contemplation.

Adoneesis stood in awe, unsure whether he was awake or in a dream state of awareness. Before him stood a legend who had only crossed his mind in songs and tales of faerie magic. He remembered the tale of the evil manipulations of Morganna, how the witch had led Merlin and Nimue into believing each had betrayed the other. When Nimue assumed the title of Lady of the Lake from the original Lady, Niobe, she had also taken on the responsibility of the Sword Excalibur and discretion of its use. Morganna had stolen the sword in the dark of night and given it to Merlin, with staunch assurances that Nimue had given her blessing.

Adoneesis remembered not much more except for a curse that had carried down through each of their bloodlines and culminated on a fiery battle in the human world where the sword had been recovered and used to destroy Morganna. Realizing that lies had kept them from each other for many lifetimes, Merlin and Nimue disappeared together, never to be heard from again. Their bonds of responsibility had been cast off once Avalon became lost in the passages of time and most assumed they had disappeared to live their lives in peace and discretion.

The title of Lady of the Lake had not been passed on to anyone, and faeries had, out of respect for a long ago tradition, used the title once again in reference to Niobe.

Merlin spoke. "I hear echoes of the past singing their haunting tune; what has gone full circle now comes to rest itself upon this land, and in the heart of this king."

"What does that mean?" Adoneesis questioned, only to be hushed by Bronwen.

"Listen carefully, as he will not repeat his words."

Threaded with the power radiating from Wyllow Wood, Merlin's voice permeated into the very essence of time. His lips moved, but somewhere along the way, the words melded into thought and became reality. Adoneesis and Bronwen found themselves enthralled within the premonition.

"A once great land disappeared into the ocean only to reshape into the wonder of Avalon. Destroyed by greed, and dishonor, Avalon also became lost. In the ever-changing dance with time, the magic that has lived for centuries rests within the land of faerie. No place, no time, no world is left that can be home to this age-old magic. The faerie realm *must* survive. That is why I have been summoned from my rest."

Soft and gentle as a summer mist, the unicorn approached. As if understanding the gravity of the conversation, the unicorn sought out the hand of Merlin for comfort--whether to offer or ask, was uncertain. Merlin smiled and scratched the offered muzzle. Both man and unicorn glowed in an unearthly manner of love and peace. Comfort was given and accepted.

Merlin's voice wavered as he continued his story. "A gift. She is a gift from the Lady to the human child. Only one of magical blood can ride upon the back of such a creature." Merlin gave a loving last rub upon the unicorn muzzle. "Treat her well and she will never steer you wrong. Listen to her with your heart and you stand a chance of surviving these dark times."

"Do you speak of the unicorn or the human woman?" Adoneesis lost the thread of Merlin's meaning.

"You decide," was the cryptic reply.

Brachus took that moment to bellow out an ear-wrenching cry and stamp his mighty hooves upon the earth as he pranced about in royal splendor.

"Ahh, I see your steed shows off for the unicorn. I think the mixing of their blood would prove to be interesting in their offspring," Merlin mused.

"I thought no normal creature could mix with the blood of a unicorn; that they must mate with their own."

"It is true." Merlin frowned. "Do you not know the noble heritage of the steed upon whose back you are allowed to ride?"

Adoneesis flushed and looked to Bronwen for support. "I have heard mutterings of such a secret."

"Fates preserve us," Merlin muttered. "Brachus is as pure of blood as the unicorn, except that his talents lie in, shall we say, another direction." Merlin chuckled. "Your creature is blood of the dragon steeds of Atlantis, where they were bred for passion, loyalty, and protection against enemies. He is the last of a line of royal steeds that pledges their loyalty to one master for life. If anyone dares to attempt harm to their master, the animals will fight to the death, otherwise they usually outlive their master, as their lifespan is thrice that of a faerie. Unfortunately, Brachus is the last of his kind. Oh, yes, and he breaths fire from his nostrils as well."

Stunned into silence, Adoneesis stared at the burnished dark copper of the steed he had ridden since boyhood. Odd, it hadn't occurred to him to wonder why Brachus never aged. As muscled and vigorous as ever, his horse stood tall and proud. "Yes, I had a brief display of his abilities with fire, but I never imagined... Fangs, I have been blind. Look at him; he is a wonder to behold." Adoneesis voice lowered in awe, "And he is mine."

Merlin chuckled. "Do not fool yourself. Brachus belongs to himself. It is he who has chosen you as his."

"Oh." Adoneesis mulled on those words. Somehow, they seemed quite true.

Merlin sighed. One last pat upon the head of the unicorn and he moved to raise his hood to cover his head.

"Wait," Bronwen spoke. "You said Brachus is the last of his kind. Does this stand for the unicorn also?"

"No. But, sadly, there are few left. I could not even hazard a guess as to the remaining number. "Guard her well--guard them both well." His gesturing hand encompassed both the unicorn and Brachus. "I desire your word, as the King of Faerie, that you will protect them with your life."

Not even pausing to consider the ramifications, Adoneesis bowed his head to the great magician and vowed. "Of course, my word is given."

Merlin smiled. "I will trust you to your word. I know your heart races with true magic blood. Now..." He adjusted his hood and robe. "My time here is over. I return to whence I came." A gentle smile touched upon his lips. "I have a loved one who waits."

"Nimue," Bronwen whispered. "So the legends are true. Your love has been fulfilled." Her tone ached wistfully with her own past.

"Do not worry, prophetess. There is hope for you as well," Merlin suggested gently.

"I fear you may be wrong this one time, magician. But thank you for your words of encouragement."

Merlin shrugged. "Only time will tell, my lady." His arms rose to summon the force that had carried him there.

"Wait," Bronwen cried. "What is the unicorn's name?"

"She will let you know when the time is right. In the meantime, you both have a long and dangerous journey, so the sooner you set off the better. I bid you safety and success."

His words created an onslaught of gusting wind to whip up the leaves and send the limbs of Wyllow Wood dancing about in wild array. A bright flash of light snapped from the sky--then Merlin was gone. Adoneesis gasped in amazement, while Bronwen merely smiled as if unimpressed by such a display. The great magician had appeared in silence, as if not to scare. He left in a storm, as if to punctuate the importance of his words.

Adoneesis frowned. His mind had picked out only what was of interest to him and he had questions. "Prophetess, Merlin is a wizard of legendary knowledge and abilities, is he not?"

"Yes, so it is said. Why do you ask?"

"He said that only one with magic in their blood can ride the dragon steed, and that my heart was true because I had magician's blood in my veins? I know this to be untrue."

Gusts of wind had died and an eerie calm fell over the clearing that had held such magic. Bronwen's hand went to her throat and she looked away from Adoneesis. Before she could answer the precarious question, Adoneesis answered himself.

"I suppose I will have to look to Raegar's ancestors. There must be some magician's blood somewhere I know nothing of. Perhaps that is why he was so against forms of magic."

"Perhaps." Bronwen was relieved the truth had been delayed yet again. "Now, we have a journey to prepare for. We need to ride."

"You have a journey to prepare for, and I have a battalion of faeries to prepare for battle."

Bronwen froze in her task of packing her many herbs and ritual tools. Slowly, she rose to meet Adoneesis full face to face. "You will travel with me and the unicorn. You gave your word to Merlin. How can you protect the unicorn with your life if you are not with her?"

"I..." Adoneesis stammered as the full realization of his promise finally dawned upon him. "But, I told the faeries I would lead them into battle."

"Yes, you did. But to Merlin you gave your promise. Krickall and the others can strengthen your borders and prepare for war without you, and they will understand your journey to the Westland Gateway is as important as their battle against the goblins. I think the way is clear, besides..."

"What? What do you know?"

Bronwen shivered. "Your way is with me. That is all I know. Now that you have given your word, you have no choice. You and I will travel beyond the faerie realm to the world of humans. That is our destiny."

Once spoken, energy becomes something real, something that can be heard--or not--depending on who is there to listen. Unfortunately, Bronwen's words carried upon the mists, swirling and dancing the words found their way north across the land to be plucked from their erratic ride by one who was looking for just such a thing.

Ten

Gar paced the antechamber and stumbled more than once over clothing strewn in masses and furniture arranged crookedly. Filled with impatience and anger, his thin, puckered mouth foamed in anticipation of hearing news from beyond the closed door. With a snort of disgust at being made to wait like some lackey, he kicked the post and screamed when a shaft of pain shot up his hairy leg.

Scampering footsteps approached and a fawning goblin servant bowed to his knees. "Master, what ails ye? What can I do?"

Gar's frustration boiled to the surface and he struck out at the closest target--the servant goblin. With a mighty flash of hairy fist, he sent the goblin flying across the cold stone floor and slamming into a grimy wall. Backlit by the single sunray that beamed in the small window, dust, and cobwebs erupted in a hazy display. Floating from ceiling to floor, dust settled upon Gar's rather large bulbous nose and caused a fit of sneezing, which further frustrated the goblin. With a strangled roar of anger, he flung open the door to the room where the secret ritual was being held.

His eyes took a moment to adjust to the darkness, which was punctuated only by candlelight, but ·his nostrils instantly detected the burning stench of bitter herbs and charred flesh. A shadow crossed his vision before he was able to see much of anything.

"You have no business here."

Gar faced the human man who had the audacity to reprimand the king of the goblins. A weasel shaped, pockmarked face was his most outstanding feature, and Gar liked the fact that someone existed uglier than he. From the first day the human, Navarre, had entered Gar's world, things changed dramatically. Armed with powerful magic, Navarre had enticed Gar with a plan for domination, wealth, and immortality in a world that offered delights beyond the faeries realm.

Gar snapped at his cohort, "All that goes on here is my business." Deliberately he stepped around the human to face an unwilling participant in the ritual--Lapis. "What has he found out?"

"Nothing is what I have found," Lapis answered the question himself. "This cretin of a human insists on his rituals of dark magic; it weakens my abilities."

"Bah! Stupid old fool. Your power will never come close to my capabilities."

"Enough!" Gar screamed. "Now is not time for egos. *Find the child*. I wait your news in the dining area." Gar stomped from the room, slammed the door behind him, and muttered all the way down the newly hewn log stairway. "Bloody incompetence, why am I so plagued with idiots?"

His entry into the dining area created havoc, as he hadn't been expected and food was not prepared. "More incompetence," he muttered and banged his fist on the table. "Bring me food and do it quickly or I'll have your heads ripped from your shoulders." There, that should ensure a hasty meal.

With a pitcher of honeyed brew in his hand, he settled into a mood of cunning planning. Would the mage find the child? Was the human, Navarre, trustworthy? Would he ever sit on the throne that belonged to him? Then realization hit him and he sat up straight. Ha! Sitting on the throne mattered little because soon there would be no land of faeries to rule, and being the king of a barren wasteland did not appeal overly much. What did appeal was the thought of conquering a world beyond the faerie realm--the world of humans.

Yes, when Navarre had been found wandering the land of Night Gloom, Gar had almost had him killed on the spot. Now he was glad his urge to torture the interloper had prevailed over his urge to kill him. Of course, the torture had never occurred because by the time they had arrived to the dungeons, the human had convinced Gar the value of an alliance. Gar remembered the manipulations of the human as clearly as if it had happened yesterday.

~ * ~

Gar sniffed the air and his face twisted into a display of grim satisfaction. He and his cohorts had just finished raiding the northwestern border of Dunraven for supplies. Packing the horses with food and precious woven wool for clothing, they were returning to Night Gloom when a shadow ran at them from the woods.

Shouting a warning, one of the goblins tackled the intruder to the ground. Amidst horses rearing and goblins shouting, it had been determined that the prisoner was a human from beyond the gates of Westland. Determined to find out how an inferior human creature human had bypassed all faerie and goblin patrols, Gar ordered him bound and tied to his horse. He would interrogate him when they stopped for the night.

Night fell quickly and Gar demanded fire for warmth and food for his rumbling belly. Never daring to deny Gar's desires, the goblins jumped to obey, quickly gathered twigs and branches to start a fire, found leaves for a soft bed and made food appear from worn leather saddlebags.

Covered in dirt and leaves from Gar's horse dragging him, the human creature still managed to look arrogant. This angered Gar who kicked out and sent the human sprawling to the edge of the newly built fire.

"Tie this cur up. I don't want to look at him while I eat."

Grumbling, Gar dismounted and took no time in stuffing his mouth with food--all the while pondering the human captive. How had he made it to the faerie realm undetected? How had such a stupid creature survived in a land that could be harsh if you did not know the customs? Why was he sitting here wondering when all he had to do was ask?

"Bring me the human."

Three goblins scrambled to do his bidding. They untied the human from the tree where he'd been bound. Unceremoniously, they dumped him at Gar's feet. After landing face first in the dirt and gravel, the prisoner sat up, brushed leaves from his silken clothes and straightened to face Gar--eye to eye.

Gar's fingers itched to slap the smugness from the prisoner's face. Instead, he growled and clenched his fists. "Does your stomach grumble?"

A glimmer of a smile touched upon parched lips. "Actually, I am more thirsty than hungry if you don't mind."

Gar snapped his fingers at whoever hovered closest to him. Within no time, a flask of water appeared before the prisoner who, losing his composure briefly, snatched the flask and drank heartily of the crystal cool water.

Yes, Gar thought, *the stranger can show weakness.* "Tell me your name."

"I am Navarre."

"By what right have you crossed from the world of man to the realm of faerie?"

A piercing silver gaze burned into Gar and the effect staggered the goblin. Visions of splendid feasts, silken clothes, piles of jewels, and sexual exploitations danced across his mind. Full in his chest rose a feeling of utter and complete superiority. Fangs, he felt drunk with power.

Navarre's soft, hypnotizing voice interrupted his euphoria. "I can give you all that--and more."

Gar shook his head to recover his senses. What magic haunted the night? His gaze fell to the stranger and he snorted. "Your wily magician tricks do not fool me." Lowering his voice, he leaned into Navarre's pasty face. "Tell me, ugly one, why I should not end your measly life here in this clearing?"

"I have already shown you what I can give you, now I will show you how." Navarre withdrew from beneath his cloak a book--a book of worn black leather adorned with faded etchings and gold embossing. Reverently, Navarre thumbed the etchings and opened the book to reveal parchment pages covered with indecipherable writings.

At least it was indecipherable to Gar whose eyes strained to see in the flickering shadows of the nearby fire. He wasn't sure, but it looked as if the pages of the book sparked, and the fire's flames reached out in an attempt to touch the ancient pages.

"What have you there?" Gar's voice was abrupt but curiosity crept into its timbre.

"Ahh," Navarre proclaimed. "This book is my father's. He came from the land where we now sit."

"Explain," Gar growled, growing impatient with the game.

"My father was of the land of faerie. How do you think I came to be able to travel here undetected? It is all written in this journal--the passing over into the faerie realm through the gates of Westland, avoiding the call of the banshee, slipping unknown through the land of the phookas and the Lady of the Lake, but mainly how to come into the land of Night Gloom."

Gar's narrowed gaze into thoughtful consideration of the stranger's words. Cruelty and self-serving were only his minor characteristics. Gar was ever known for his thirst for domination and power. The words of the captive, Navarre, interested him.

"Fine, I will let you live for now. Convince me of your usefulness." Gar squinted as a flash of light assaulted his eyes and he wondered how a leather bound book could reflect in such a way. And why did he suddenly feel the urge to retch? With an effort, he fought off the feeling and closed his mind to the low hum of words that subtly invaded his mind. A show of weakness in front of his troops would not bode well for his continued hold on the reins of domination. His vision swam for a moment, and then all became as it was.

Goblins were credited with a low reserve of intelligence, and though they were elemental creatures, their primal instincts ran strong. His senses warned him that Navarre used magic on him, but he knew to keep the knowledge to himself.

Narrowing his gaze, Gar confronted Navarre. "The book you carry bespeaks the language of magicians. How is this so?"

~ * ~

Yes, Gar remembered that time very well. The human had convinced Gar to spare his life, on the understanding that he would deliver the throne of faerie to Gar. Somewhere along the way, the human tried to convince Gar that they could rule the world of man through the world of faerie. Everything that happened in the faerie world reflected ten-fold in the land of man and the prospect of riches and power beyond imagination caused Gar to slobber. Yet, he did not fully trust the human.

The sound of footfalls on the creaky wooden stairs interrupted his meandering into the past. Navarre and Lapis approached. One face twisted into a mask of self-satisfied success, the other looked haunted with uncertainty and fear.

"Ahh, I would say you've been successful." Gar motioned Navarre to sit beside him at the dining table and bid him indulge in the hearty repast the serving goblins had hastily prepared.

Since he had not been bid to sit, Lapis stood by the wall and awaited Gar's wishes. The goblin ignored the mage's presence. Lapis had performed his duty so Gar couldn't care less what he did. Heavily guarded, Night Gloom offered no escape, and Lapis would dare not attempt to harm anyone or Adoneesis would be killed. As far as Gar was concerned, the mage could eat with the curs snarling and fighting for food scraps.

Navarre was quick to stuff his mouth with charred meat, dry potatoes, and stale baked bread. Absentmindedly, he wiped his face and glanced around as if considering the best way to tell his tale.

"Come, give me the news," Gar barked.

Lapis stiffened and directed his gaze to Navarre as if bidding him to be silent. The action pleased Gar, because it meant that Navarre and Lapis had been successful in their magical probing.

Navarre directed a sneer to Lapis and taunted, "The mage is weak. I could have done better without his presence to impede my rituals."

Gar doubted that. He knew Lapis to be one of the most powerful forces he had ever dealt with. More likely, Lapis had been stubborn in his dealings with Navarre in an attempt to stall, which worried him. Did the mage hold some powers in reserve? What did he hope to accomplish by stalling? Yes, Lapis, would bear watching closely.

Aggravated by the blustering attitude of the human and the uncertainty of Lapis actions, Gar snapped, "Don't let your arrogance rule your mind; the mage could smolder you into flames with a single thought. Speak."

Navarre paled at the inference of being turned to flame by one he had belittled. But, he hastened to relate what had been gleaned in the darkness of the tower room. "The child has been found. She is full grown to womanhood now."

Gar salivated at the thought of power that lay within his grasp. If the child truly was the savior of the realm and he destroyed her before she fulfilled her destiny, there would be no one to stand in his way. Not even the stupid human who thought he was so smart with his smelly old book and words of magic. Hah! A swift swipe of a sword would take care of him.

Most assuredly he was unaware of Gar's train of thought, because Navarre continued his tale but arrogance filled his every word. "Adoneesis and the prophetess leave on the morrow for Westland--the gateway to the world of humans."

Words like snow pellets hit Gar and comprehension slowly dawned. Adoneesis was leaving Dunraven, which meant that Gar no longer held power over Lapis. His firedrakes could not travel the length of the realm to the gateway. Acting with an ingrained instinct for survival, Gar leapt from the dining table. Knife drawn and muscles straining he lunged, but Lapis met him with a force of power beyond reasoning.

~ * ~

Lapis felt those beady eyes fall on him and his heart wrenched in fear. He'd had a taste of freedom and wasn't ready to find himself imprisoned by the goblin lord for even a moment longer, but years of imprisonment had worn away his powers. Spells and incantations once remembered without thought had become lost in the memories of past deeds. His movement was slow, his magic even slower, yet as Gar flew at him with knife flashing, Lapis was able to re-direct the attack with a deflection spell. Gar fell to the ground but recovered quickly enough to grab a branch of burning fire from the fireplace. Lapis knew his deflection spell would not hold against fire, but he didn't know if Gar knew. Gathering his muscles to leap at the last minute, Lapis let Gar charge him. With teeth bared, spittle flying and a snarl on his lips, Gar attacked. The smell of burning cloth and seared flesh choked the onlookers, but none of them left. Enthralled with the battle raging they stood their ground and began placing bets on the outcome.

"Two rivlets of silver that Gar wins."

"My sharpest sword I bet on the prisoner."

Shoving, shouting, and secondary fistfights broke out amidst the goblins and created an atmosphere of confusion. Lapis couldn't focus his mind and his arm throbbed with the pain of a deep burn. He needed a spell, but words became suddenly foreign to him. Thoughts of Bronwen and Adoneesis kept intruding and he tried to push them aside so he could take care of the writhing mass of goblin that tore at him.

In the end, Gar came out the victor. It was a lucky shot with a sturdy club that one of the goblins threw to him in the midst of the melee. Lapis saw the club coming and braced for the impending smash to the back of his skull. Mercifully, he felt nothing, though the sound left his world and all became silent as his vision showed him a world of slow motion. His knees turned to water, he slid to the dirt floor and his eyes closed on the confusion that danced about him. Just the split second before he fell face first to the ground, sound returned. In a roaring mass of shouts and whistles, Lapis was able to hear one single sentence that set his heart to beating.

"We leave immediately for Dunraven. When Adoneesis and the prophet bitch return with the woman, we will be there to greet them."

Total darkness and blessed oblivion accompanied Lapis into silence.

Eleven

Controlled confusion was the order of the day and Bronwen used that to her advantage. Waking early after last night's ritual, she tried to go back to sleep, but her mind was haunted with memories. Driven, she pulled on her clothes while shivers of anticipation crept up her spine and pulled her to prowl familiar places she thought she had forgotten.

Busy with chores and hushed anticipation, none of the faeries noticed the old lady who moved like a shadow through their very midst. Of course, Bronwen's seldom-used veiling spell helped her remain as unobtrusive as possible; she needed no prying questions.

Over the years, she thought she'd come to terms with her banishment and the loss of her son, but coming back here opened the floodgates of emotion that had lain dormant for so long. Her feet touched upon the same courtyard grass whence she had met Raegar and her fingers touched upon the bark where barely legible initials of R and B were and intertwined to signify lasting love. Her senses soared with a remembered embrace and kiss that had sent her spiraling down a path of betrayal and treachery.

If only... oh, but there was no sense in sending her thoughts that direction. Raegar had not been the shining star of her young dreams, but she had not been as soon in betraying him as he had her. Bronwen's only excuse was that her betrayal had been motivated by love, while Raegar's many betrayals had been motivated by an innate need to exert control over all around him.

Past emotions threatened to overwhelm her, and Bronwen's veiling spell weakened. Before finding herself exposed to prying eyes, she made haste to the nearby stable. The horses would offer her comfort without expectations. Scents of hay, manure, and horse assailed her nostrils. All smells that she loved and had missed. Raegar had not given orders to leave her with any kind of mount when he'd had her exiled into the nether regions, and there had been no time over the years when she'd found herself in possession of a horse.

A familiar nickering floated from the end of the large stable tree and Bronwen felt a gentle leap of heart in chest at the sound. Anxiously, she made her way to the last stall, and peered hopefully over the carved wooden half door. Eyes of richest chocolate stared into hers and with the quickest of speed; a slobbery tongue ran from chin to forehead. Delighted, Bronwen laughed aloud and threw her arms around the proffered stubbly gray muzzle.

"Oh, Briar, I cannot believe you are still here. How fare you after all these years?"

Most would think the question only spoken in the emotional moment of a reunion, so they would have been surprised to see the horse respond with a flickering of her upper lip and an almost decipherable whinny.

"I see. I have missed you dearly as well." Her voice broke. "I would have given some years of my life to have had you by my side these last years."

Eyes connected and unspoken communication created a pleasing hum in the stable tree. Understanding the energy flow, the other horses hung their heads over stall doors in an attempt to become part of the reunion. Whinnying, whickering, and snorting rose from a quiet murmur to a shrill vying for attention. Bronwen's uncertainty how to end the raucous confusion was ended with one commanding whinny and a stamping of hooves upon earth. Brachus had spoken--and Brachus ruled the stable. Instantly, harmony was restored within the horse dwelling; gentle chortles and quiet snuffling were the only sounds heard.

Bronwen smiled. "Brachus, you are a many talented creature. Tell me, where rests the unicorn?"

The dragon steed directed his gaze and Bronwen was able to make out the luminescent figure of the unicorn grazing in the outer fields. Unicorns were not comfortable within the confines of any structure; nature's bounty was home to the legendary one-horned creatures.

"She is beautiful, is she not?" Bronwen mused.

Brachus' responding whicker was soft, but his eyes blazing the direction of the unicorn left no doubt as to his meaning. With a final stamp of his mighty hoof upon the ground, he arched his neck, tossed his head, and trotted out to the meadow alongside the unicorn.

"Even the valiant dragon steed preens in the face of love." Bronwen chuckled. An insistent nicker from a nearby stall interrupted her thoughts. Curiosity took her to the back corner of the stable--the stall beside Briar. Within the stall stood a delicate creature of golden honey who tossed her creamy mane to gain attention.

Bronwen almost wept at the perfection of the creature. Intelligence shone from golden eyes as the horse stretched out her muzzle in invitation. Bronwen felt strangely drawn as she reached out a shaking hand to place it upon the horse's silken neck. Briar gave a long-winded whinny from the neighboring stall and Bronwen understood. The golden horse was Briar's offspring and the filly had been born and bred with Bronwen in mind. What forces at work could prepare for such eventuality? No force could have guessed her arrival that far in the past, yet there stood a horse--a gift upon her return.

The pervasive weight of approaching darkness cast a pall over the joy of the unexpected gift and Bronwen shivered. She felt its quickened approach. It knew she was here and strived to fulfill its long ago given task. She must prod Adoneesis; there could be no delay in leaving on their journey. If they were fortunate, they could stay one step ahead of the evil released with Raegar's curse. If she were fortunate, she would stay alive long enough to bring the woman back to Dunraven.

Adoneesis chose that moment to enter the stable tree. His body blocked the rising sun which cast his shadow long enough to come to rest on the dirt floor by Bronwen's feet. Their gazes met and a spark jumped. Bronwen understood the familial connection, but Adoneesis only frowned in confusion at the unfamiliar connection.

"I am glad to find you here. I realized that if we are to travel swiftly you'll need a reliable steed." He watched Bronwen stroke the muzzle of the golden horse. "I see you have chosen already." He stepped closer and reached out to the horse, who responded by withdrawing. "That is her usual greeting. Truth is that when I entered and saw you so close, I was surprised. Briar's daughter has ever been fickle. In fact, she has let no one get close enough to her to even indulge in the urge to name her--until now. The honor is yours."

The Crystal Of Light

Bronwen considered. "She shines as brightly as the morning sun rising atop the hills. She is golden like the colors of the earth in fall. I'll call her Aurora." The words evoked a hearty response from the newly named horse.

Adoneesis laughed. "You seem to have a special way with animals. Is it a learned or natural talent?"

"It is an ability that all faeries possess."

"I assure you, I have no ability to converse with animals."

Bronwen smiled. "Yes, you do. It is inherent in all living creatures--this ability to communicate with each other. First, you must believe, and then you must open your senses to the feelings and thoughts that float about freely in the air all around us. With practice you will be able to take the emotions and convert them into a language understandable to yourself."

"I do not think..."

Krickall strode into the stable and filled it with his very presence. "I've assembled everyone in the courtyard as you directed."

Awaiting direction, the loyal veteran stood--strong, tall, and weathered like the mightiest of ancient trees.

Aware of the emotions warring within her son, Bronwen was quick to assert authority and dismiss Krickall. "King Adoneesis shall be but a moment."

Bronwen watched Krickall's retreat and then turned to Adoneesis. "Your emotions write themselves upon your face like a tale."

"I worry about the reaction I'll receive when I make clear my plans to leave after I already declared that I'd stay. Krickall is more than capable, but he is not their king."

"Yes, you are the king, so your responsibilities cannot be compared to others. Your path leads a direction that cannot be measured against the ordinary. Hold your head high, explain your mission--not your reasons. It is not the way of a king to explain his actions."

"Your words sound harsh, yet I'm sure they bear a certain truth." He sighed. "Once I give voice to my change in plans, I will delegate all duties so we should be able to leave in a couple of days."

"No! We must leave sooner--today."

"Today? That's not possible. There are arrangements to make, and I cannot leave until I am sure they are done properly."

"Unless we begin our journey there will be no lands to return to, and I... there are other reasons as well. Adoneesis, you have many loyal and capable faeries; trust them and they will respect you the more for that act of faith."

"Words of wisdom gratefully accepted. But, I wish you would tell me everything. I don't like making decisions based on half-truths."

"The time will come for you to know all, but we need to focus on the task at hand. Go. Speak. But remember, show no sign of doubt--you are the king."

"I will stand strong and true." Adoneesis strode to the arched entrance to the stable tree and turned back to the shadowed interior. His voice rang forceful amid the stalls. "We leave at the break of the midday meal."

"Yes, my son," Bronwen whispered to his retreating back. "You learn quickly. You shall do fine." With a final pat upon her newly acquired steed, Bronwen hastened to do her packing for her fateful journey to the world of man.

~ * ~

Adoneesis stood upon a large stone and looked out over the many familiar faces. The crowd numbered fewer than he'd hoped and he worried that many would not heed his warning and come to Dunraven for protection. It was possible they did not trust him enough. After all, his rule only encompassed ten years, a mere drop in the measure of time. He had yet to prove himself to some of the older, wiser faeries. Always, he felt their eyes on him--judging, weighing, sometimes even condemning his actions. The thought of more faeries being hurt or killed while under his protection tore at his conscience while Bronwen's words edged into his mind and reminded him of his responsibilities. Forcing his voice into a timbre of surety and strength, Adoneesis addressed the assembly.

"Many faces I see here that have lived a life long before I ever drew my first breath. I thank you for your trust in me and I will do all in my power to keep that trust." A light smattering of applause gave him a moment to plan his next words. "I also have trust in those who believe in the realm that is our home. I trust that you will work together, fight together, and yes, even die together if need be. Thus is the spirit of the faeries, thus is the responsibility passed to us from those who ruled the ancient water realm and our sisterland of Avalon. We must endure, or all that has been will perish into a nothingness of existence never to be heard of again. That, we cannot let happen--that we *will not* let happen. I stand before you as the King of Faeries, yet without you, there would be nothing to protect. Together we rule. Together we survive."

His words evoked a reaction amongst the faeries that, quite literally, shook the lands of Dunraven and beyond. Any who may have doubted Adoneesis ability to fulfill the glory of his role as king were put to shame. Each word evoked a palette of emotion, pulled all the faeries into his spell and encouraged them to believe in their king.

Adoneesis filled with pride and wonder. Pride in his people, wonder at his responsibility of preserving an ancient race and the mythical place they lived, but his next words may not find his followers quite as supportive. He raised his hands, palms forward, for silence.

Subconsciously, he noticed Bronwen slip unobtrusively into the crowd, a difficult thing to do at best. As soon as the faeries realized her presence, they parted way and allowed her a clear path to the dais, whether she wanted it or not.

"Please, there is more." Adoneesis paused to take a breath. "The prophetess has located the descendant of the Lady of the Lake in the human world; she leaves today to bring the woman here."

Relief spread through the assembled faeries. With the faeries standing strong against Gar and the magical child on her way, the faerie realm stood a chance of survival.

"I must travel with her to Westland."

"But..." Krickall frowned and uncertainly shifted his feet. "What if Gar attacks? You said you'd be here."

Adoneesis looked to Bronwen, and her words prickled his mind--*it is not the way of a king to explain his actions*. Something did not ring true within those words and Adoneesis struggled with the concept. Trusting eyes looked to him for reasons and hope. What had he done to earn the trust of these faeries? But trust they did or they would not be here awaiting his words. Words he would give them. It would have been the way of his father to leave them wondering as to his actions, even if it had meant their lives. His arrogance was not that which Adoneesis wanted to emulate.

So he spoke.

"Fates have decided my path lies toward Westland, and I gave my word to the great Merlin who appeared last night during a ritual by the sacred moon tree. The prophetess will confirm my words."

Gasps of wonder and disbelief flamed through the crowd. That their king had been in contact with a legend such as Merlin astounded them. What powers were in play here? Obviously more than they understood.

"My journey to bring the woman here is as important as holding off Gar's advances. Wise words recently spoken warned that if we did not return with this woman, there would be no faerie realm to return to."

Krickall asked, "I am awed that you have had spoken with the Great Magician. If Merlin has decreed your destiny, who are we to gainsay his word?"

Krickall knelt to one knee and, like an undulating sea, everyone followed. "As at your crowning, we offer our complete loyalty and trust that you will see us through this time of unrest and uncertainty. So it is said. So it is done."

Following Krickall's example, the crowd murmured the words in unison. "So it is said. So it is done."

With an effort to steady his voice, Adoneesis bid them rise. "Krickall, I trust you to lead the foray to the outer regions. You have the most experience in case you come across any of Gar's men and need to fight. Analiese, you will be in charge of the kitchens and keeping the household running smoothly. Mayard, as I said earlier, you will be in charge of correspondence, now I also want you to keep an eye on organizing the outlying faeries who will eventually find their way here for sanctuary. I also want you to train some volunteers to take care of any wounded who may return here. We must be prepared for anything." Solemn words gently spoken sent a shaft of cold reality into the hearts of the faeries.

Adoneesis looked with fondness over the upturned faces. "I take my leave with wishes that I will see all of your faces upon my return. Do not disappoint me." Adoneesis stepped from the dais and strode to the main tree as he threw a final statement over his shoulder. "Bailiwick, to my chamber."

~ * ~

Bronwen's chest about burst as Adoneesis spoke. He had ignored her admonishment not to explain himself, yet the faeries drew closer to him for placing his trust in their ability to understand. His action was not one of rebellion against being told what to do. Rather, he had weighed his options and judged his people accordingly. Wisdom grew in the character of King Adoneesis and Bronwen thanked the powers that be for allowing her the chance to see her son, even if for a short time.

Her gaze roamed over the face of the faeries left in Adoneesis wake and they looked encouraged. A new feeling of vigor tingled in the air. A hope for the future of the faerie realm.

"Yes," Bronwen whispered to herself. "King of the Faeries."

~ * ~

Darkness fell on the land of Night Gloom and Gwepper was relieved to finally have a chance to rest. "Creepy, sleepy idiots," he mumbled and grabbed another piece of wood off the ground for kindling. "About time they settled down for the night. Stupid to think they can travel so far without food and sleep."

Begrudgingly, he threw the firewood down and stretched his lithe, hairless body. It took only a minute to start the fire, but his grumbling stomach protested even that wait. Dinner. A juicy rabbit or maybe a squirrel. Yes, gray squirrel tasted the best. Pulling a slingshot from his worn sack, Gwepper figured he'd be lucky to find any signs of life with darkness here. "Drats and bats, the stupid idiots," he mumbled.

He directed his curses at Gar's group of goblins who, at that moment, were camped not too far from Gwepper. Of course, they didn't know Gwepper was close by. Not that Gwepper was following them. He was just headed the same direction.

Gwepper set up camp to the side of a rocky hill, where his fire would drift away from the camp of the other goblins. As long as he was quiet, they'd have no reason to know he was close. "Brainless bean heads. I should be leading them on their mission, and not chasing some stupid unicorn."

Preening in the reflected moonlight of a nearby stream, Gwepper decided he was as fierce looking as any goblin. Probably better looking than most. His bony hand with its four fingers brushed across his pointed nose and ran down his cheek to his cracked lips. In his mind, he pictured the lips of another-- full, inviting, colored with purple berry juice. His hand wandered down his chest and he imagined they ran across the bosom of the golden-haired goblin named Ghilphar. Snapped to awareness by the cracking of a twig in the forest, Gwepper smacked himself on the forehead.

"Dung it all, you miserable goblin. You have a duty; leave the female out of your mind."

His eyes pierced into the shadows of the forest trying to pinpoint the origin of the cracking sound. A newly fallen tree limb was the culprit--nothing to get excited about. "Looks like grubs and grass for me," Gwepper bemoaned his meatless fate.

Just as he was about to make his way back to camp, voices drifted from across the stream. Gar's band of goblins. Until now Gwepper had not wondered what they were up to, he had only followed them because they headed the same direction. What was their mission? Why had Gar sent them out when war against Adoneesis loomed? Hmm, might be worth a sneaky visit.

Carefully, Gwepper crept to their camp. Skulking around in silence was something he had learned when he was younger.

Beaten by his father and teased by other goblins, he had found that staying unobtrusive had become a necessity for him. So he was able to come within a breath of the goblins and remain undetected.

His found a place to squat beneath a fallen tree. Animals had dug a hole under the trunk that allowed Gwepper a perfect hiding spot. Burrowing himself under the trunk, he poked his finger through moss and dirt until he'd created a peephole into the camp of the goblins. Yes, he could see the three of them. His nose tickled with the smell of roasting meat--almost to the point where he made his presence known just so he could share in the bounty.

Snapping and snarling, the three goblins grabbed for the now cooked meat and, unknowingly, teased Gwepper with their slurping and dripping of slippery grease down their chins. Gwepper's stomach grumbled in protest. Why did he lay there while they ate hearty? They were fellow goblins after all. What harm could be in letting them know he was there?

Deciding his hunger was more important than continuing to hide, he made a move to stand. He promptly found himself frozen in place and a voice whispered in his ear bidding him stay.

Dungus and fungus, he was hearing things. Just hunger making him slightly woozy is all. He made another effort to stand only to feel a gentle pressure push him into place and the same voice whispering to stay. Rats and bats, he covered his ears with his hands. Was he going crazy? Yes, he could see it now. He'd wander the forest of Night Gloom, and stories would be told about the crazy goblin of the woods. Parents would warn their faerie children to avoid the crazy goblin.

Calming and quiet, the voice whispered and Gwepper knew it came from his mind, as his hands covered his ears. *Stay. Your fate does not rest with them.*

Words spoken in his mind became more solid until they melded with the voices of the hobgoblins in the clearing. Relieved that the voice had stopped badgering him, Gwepper leaned closer to hear the goblins.

"What good is this goblin bitch to Gar anyway?" questioned the skinny goblin with bug eyes.

"Don't know, don't care," the big ugly one with broken teeth mumbled.

"I think if we hurry to get there, maybe we can have a wee bit of a rest before we come back." The skinny goblin giggled

"You mean with goblin bitch resting with us, right?" Broken teeth sneered back at his cohort.

"Of course, what fun would there be otherwise?"

Broken teeth pondered a moment. "Gar says leave wench alone. We hurt her, she tell Gar. Gar hurt us. Painful hurt."

Eyes glazed in contemplation of sinful delights so close, yet denied them. Leaning forward, pointed features highlighted by firelight, the third goblin spoke for the first time. Words softly spoken can sometimes elicit fear more than those shouted can.

"There are ways to make sure she can't speak." His smile painted a grotesque line across his ugly features. Satisfied with his settling of the situation, he sat back, arms folded and waited for the accolades to follow.

Broken teeth and skinny did not disappoint. Drool dripped from their mouths to mingle with congealed animal grease as they laughed at the prospect of immoral gratification.

Gwepper was stunned. Could they mean...? Were they talking about... no, no, no... he had a mission. Fangs on them all. His mind worked into a fervor. Broken teeth and slimy breath tortured his conscience. Golden hair and cerulean blue eyes tweaked at his emotions. His mind recalled the mysterious whispered words--*your fate does not rest with them.*

Sweat rolled down his face to blur his vision until the three goblins became mere specters of evil. For the first time in his life, Gwepper decided to do something that he wanted to do, not what someone told him to do. With glee dancing at his intestines, he slowly crept from his hiding spot. Once well enough away from the goblins campsite, he exploded to a run. Yes, this felt right, he didn't question why. Leaping to his small camp, he grabbed his few possessions and thrust them into his sack, which he flung over his shoulder. He must make haste, the deep forest of Night Gloom and a mountain pass stood between him and his fate--him and his golden goblin.

Twelve

Adoneesis and Bronwen left the lands of Dunraven far behind on their first day of travel. It was a pace they meant to keep up for the entire trip. Beneath them were steeds whose veins ran strong with the blood of early breeds and beside them ran the unicorn. She was grace, beauty, and strength, a contrast to Brachus with his virile, muscular power.

Supplies were only what they could carry, so they would rely on nature for as much as possible. Adoneesis had no doubt they would find what they needed, as they needed.

Hooves pounded over virgin turf. Adoneesis had rarely traveled far from Dunraven and the journey was exhilarating. He noticed the untouched lushness of the land, and was pleased that most of the faeries in the outlying regions had maintained the beauty and peace of their inheritance. Even the energy sparking in the air took on a new feel for Adoneesis; he felt more alive and invigorated. He noticed that Brachus and Aurora as well gained a renewed strength and their pace quickened with natural playfulness and delight.

Within a few days their intense pace had taken them far enough from Dunraven as to leave any signs of faerie civilization far behind. Conversation was sparse, stops for food even more so, and time ran together in a blur. It was the sameness of each day, as well as the distance from their enemy that lulled Adoneesis into a false sense of security. It was at that time that Brachus snorted and almost unseated Adoneesis as his great hooves rose from the ground and pawed the air in warning. Heart pounding, Adoneesis calmed Brachus and looked to see Bronwen's position. She and Aurora where at his side and both were intent on the trail ahead as if sensing danger. The unicorn kept to herself and appeared only sporadically as if to reassure them that she was still around. Presently, she was nowhere to be seen.

Silence prevailed while Adoneesis decided a course of action. He saw nothing on the trail ahead, no sound came from the forest, and the countryside offered him a view of distant mountains, rolling hills and green grass, but no threat. He pressed his knees gently to Brachus' side and advanced. Nothing at first, then his ears prickled with sounds of revelry drifting down the trail. Without thought, he settled his hand on his sword handle. Smooth, worn leather warmed easily with his touch and he was comforted by the protection offered by sharpened steel.

"I thought that no faerie existed this far west," Adoneesis remarked as he glanced at Bronwen. The look of confusion on her face gave him no reassurance.

"There should be none, yet..."

"Bronwen, if you know something, tell me."

"I know nothing except that a lifetime ago a race of faerie inhabited the lands between Dunraven and Westland. The common tale is that they appeared through the final swirl of mist that once covered Avalon and laid claim to the lower hills of the mountains. Supposedly, they appeared just as mysteriously in Avalon." She shrugged. "But no one knows for sure. Skilled, with great knowledge in the arts of magic, music, poetry, and weaponry, they lived apart from other faeries until one day something happened and they disappear as mysteriously as they appeared. Like wraiths."

Adoneesis considered her words. "We have no choice. Westland is ahead and we have to get to the gateway. Steel whispered against leather as Adoneesis drew his sword from its scabbard. "Let's proceed."

No more than two minutes later, they stepped into a sunlit clearing to the sight of an assembly of faeries in the middle of preparations for some ceremony. Probably a summer solstice celebration. Adoneesis counted thirteen faeries, each face shining with particular beauty and intelligence. Trying to pinpoint the exact characteristics and breed of faerie was difficult, as he had not seen any like them before. Like the clearing surrounding them, the faeries chimed with a sense of peace and strength. Their features were splendid, strong, and regal. Their stature was tall, straight, and proud.

The clearing itself looked much as others they had come across the last couple of days. Abundant with rich green grasses mingling with wildflowers, the clearing was a meadowland of vivid color. Mountain heather, lavender, and forget-me-nots provided shades of purple from pale to bright. Pansies, basket-of-gold, welsh poppies, and marigolds gave a spectacular contrast of yellow to the purple. Wafting on a gentle breeze, the flowers' fragrances bore tale to the care the faeries gave to nature's gift. But the color did not stop there; Adoneesis eyes took in the grandeur of the surrounding trees and he was awed. All around the clearing and rooted into the forest itself grew such trees as he had never seen before. Resembling trees of such distinction as magnolias and flowering dogwoods, they held a strangeness in their appearance that took Adoneesis a moment to determine. All the trees had a double trunk.

Shock must have shown on his face but before he could question the phenomenon, one of the elderly faeries spoke.

"Hail and good day to you." The faeries eyes touched briefly on Adoneesis' sword. "You are in no danger here. Your weapon is not necessary."

Strangely prompted by the words, and not of his own volition, Adoneesis sheathed his sword.

"Much better." The faerie spoke and waved a hand that encompassed the surrounding land. "Welcome to our home. Here you can relax and rest after your long journey."

"You are right. We have traveled far." Adoneesis frowned. "But how do you know that?"

"Anywhere from here is a long way. It was not a difficult guess."

Adoneesis flushed. "Of course. You are also right about us being weary. If you can indulge us for the night, we would be on our way as the sun tops the horizon."

His words elicited a chuckle from someone in the back of the gathering. "It seems we are to host our king for an evening." An elderly faerie with hair of gray that touched his shoulders stepped forward.

"How do you know I am the king? We have traveled many days and the farther we go from Dunraven, the less I am known."

"My soul may be old but my mind still remembers faces from the past with ease." The faerie swept his gaze over the two of them and Bronwen pulled Aurora back a step so she was angled away from the faerie. "Are there just the two of you?"

"Yes, we are two in number." Adoneesis reined Brachus over a step to enable Bronwen to share in the conversation, but she shifted her position to be hidden from view. Adoneesis couldn't understand Bronwen's obvious need to hide herself. He let his gaze wander over the faeries to see if any looked hostile, but all seemed normal except for the surreal beauty of the place and trees that grew into double trunks. It took him a moment to realize something other than the ordinary.

"I see no dwelling trees. Do you live around here?"

A hissing sound from Bronwen's lips was the first sound she had made since entering the clearing. Urging Aurora a step closer, Bronwen leaned forward and whispered, "Are you so blind that you cannot see. These faeries are of the Tuatha de Danann; their homes will be in yonder hillock."

Adoneesis was stunned. The Tuatha de Danann. His eyes grew wide with wonder as he took a closer look at the faeries before him and the truth came clear to him. Royal faerie lineage, the Tuatha de Danann had supposedly been obliterated centuries ago, and he had heard nothing over the years of their continued existence.

"All will be explained. But first, let me show you our dwellings while one of the others tends to your mounts." He motioned to a younger faerie to bestow food and water upon the hard working Brachus and Aurora. In the distance, another faerie tended to the cautious unicorn. The magical creature seemed ever needful of keeping her distance, which was no wonder as most of her kind had been brutally slaughtered.

"I am Lir." The faerie broke Adoneesis from his reverie. "I bid you follow me, King Adoneesis and Lady Bronwen."

Adoneesis was aware of a thread of tension and hesitation between Bronwen and Lir, but he had no time to question as Lir led them to the entrance of the Tuatha de Danann's home under the hillock. Upon entering the ivy covered wooden door, a resplendent sight greeted their gazes. Being underground should have made the living quarters dull and stifling, yet the opposite was true. The room was lit with sunlight streaming in from above by way of circular holes to the sky and enhanced by crystals reflecting the light into itself. This effect created an atmosphere of intense glowing splendor.

Adoneesis lifted his hands to shield his eyes as they adjusted to the uncommon brilliance. Bronwen gasped but remained uncommonly quiet as if not wanting to draw undue attention to herself.

"I apologize for the light. We are accustomed to the luminescence, but your eyes will take a moment."

"It's amazing. I've never seen such a way to cast light." Adoneesis eyes had adjusted and he began his perusal of the underground living quarters. As if expecting the arrival of guests, the hosts laid a bountiful feast of fruits, vegetables and sweets upon a table of gold in the middle of the large room. Adoneesis reached out to touch one of the walls and found it smooth and cool.

"We are in a system of underground caves," Lir replied to Adoneesis questioning gaze. "We are in the common area, but you see all around the doorways to other areas such as sleeping quarters, the kitchen, and the place of meditation."

"It's beautiful," Bronwen whispered and then quickly covered her mouth as if she had not meant to speak.

Lir looked at her and his gaze probed as if delving deeply into her mind. A silence ensued in which Adoneesis felt quite ill at ease. But he said naught as he sensed something at work here in which he had no part.

Breaking the silence, Lir remarked, "We celebrate summer solstice tonight. We would be pleased if you would join us."

Bronwen answered in haste, "I celebrate in my own manner. Thank you for asking, but I would rather be alone."

"That is fine. We have sleeping chambers arranged for you both where you can have some privacy."

Adoneesis frowned. "How is that? You could not have known we would pass by here."

Lir and Bronwen laughed, which made Adoneesis feel quite foolish. What magic wound its way through these hills and in the blood of these ancient faeries? Did destiny dictate that they play a part in events unfolding? Why was Bronwen acting so strangely?

Too many questions. Too few answers.

"You have been expected since before you left Dunraven. Your journey has led you here, as Merlin foretold."

"Merlin. You know Merlin? How could he have told you? He could not have reached here before us."

"No, we have not seen Merlin in many ages of the earth cycle, yet his information manages to reach us." Lir smiled at Adoneesis obviously seeing his confused look. "Many of the old ways and abilities have drifted from this place of faerie, yet still there remains magic, enchantment, and sorcery within many of us--you included."

Words much the same as Merlin had spoken, words that confused Adoneesis and made him question his upbringing. He had no memory of the faerie female who bore him, as Raegar had always avoided any conversation that required answering questions about her. The most Adoneesis had ever been able to glean was that she had been blond and of reputed beauty and intelligence.

One day when Raegar was in a drunken state and feeling quite put upon by the entire world, he had kept mumbling a name over and over until such anger had built up within him that he had beaten to death the steed that had thrown him into the mud earlier that day.

Adoneesis had been huddled in a corner of the stable tree and witnessed the entire event, and although he couldn't quite hear the name Raegar mumbled, Adoneesis somehow knew Raegar's fierce anger was directed at the faerie who'd given birth to Adoneesis. He never had the nerve to confront Raegar and find out more because the sheer hatred that burned hotly within Raegar was such that Adoneesis never wanted it directed at him.

"Adoneesis?" Bronwen's voice ruffled his bitter remembrances. "Are you all right?"

Brushing a hand over his flushed face, Adoneesis cleared his throat and reassured. "I am fine. I just wandered into memories for a moment. Lir, I would be honored to take part in your festivities this eve, although I am sorry you feel the need for solitude, Bronwen."

Lir and Bronwen exchanged another hesitant glance, with the latter keeping her face in shadows. A difficult feat considering the crystals cast such a radiant light. Feeling awkward and on the outside of a situation of which he had no understanding, Adoneesis took a step towards the food laden tables in an attempt to refocus the mood.

"Forgive me. I am sure you would like to wash up before eating. Let me show you to your room and I'll have someone bring your things from your steeds."

"I've grown quite used to sleeping under the stars, so don't put yourself out on my account, although the Lady Bronwen may desire the comforts you offer."

"I am sure you both would benefit from the comfort of a soft, warm bed. Besides, I insist. A room has already been prepared for each of you." With a swish of his silken cloak, Lir turned on heel and made his way to one of the far doorways. He hesitated not, nor glanced back to make sure they followed.

Adoneesis envied such certainty and ability to command. Taking Bronwen's arm he remarked, "It seems we have no choice, though I for one admit to looking forward to a night of sleep without the hard, uneven ground poking into my back." His banter was light, yet he felt Bronwen's fear, and it worried him. So far, he had seen nothing that would lend itself to such an emotion, quite the opposite. How he wished for the presence of Bailiwick at that moment; the little pixie had a knack for deciphering emotions and situations.

They came to Bronwen's chamber first and left her with directions to meet for food in the main chamber.

"After food, you may then take your ritual tools to an area that suits your needs and celebrate the solstice there--alone," Lir instructed.

"Thank you." Bronwen closed the door and left Lir and Adoneesis standing in the passageway.

"I apologize for her. She's not usually so quiet."

"I am sure she is merely weary from traveling. She will find her strength tonight as she connects to Mother Earth in her summer solstice ritual."

"You're probably right."

A few paces down the passage and they came to another door, which Lir indicated for Adoneesis to enter. Adoneesis made a move to enter but instead looked to Lir. "I will see you in a couple of hours in the main room, and I thank you so much for your hospitality, even if I don't exactly understand how you came to know of our approach."

"Until repast time then, have a pleasant nap, as the night will be a long one." Lir disappeared soundlessly into the shadows of the passageway, which was not lit with crystals, and left Adoneesis in awe of such graceful elegance. No doubt, this was a strange place with strange inhabitants. Sighing wearily, he closed the oaken door, and without even looking to his surroundings, collapsed onto a feather soft bed and attained a dream state within seconds.

~ * ~

A lunar glow mingled with firelight and cast shadows upon the ancient tree limbs. Scents of lavender and wisteria drifted on the soft midnight breeze and carried their scents lazily to the starry skies above. Bronwen had set up her altar for the occasion. She needed the help of sprites and spirits--now more than ever. To journey to the world of man on an astral plane was difficult enough, but this physical journey through realms of magic, ancient powers and uncertain obstacles, gave Bronwen pause for doubt. So certain within the safety of Dunraven, she now experienced the pangs of fear of failure. All the realm of faerie rested on her being able to direct Adoneesis to the woman and bringing her safely to Dunraven. It would be up to the Fates what events transpired then, but without the woman, there would be no next step.

The appearance of the Tuatha de Danann also bore some consideration. What role had they to play? Their bloodlines ran as far back as any could remember and they retained the forgotten powers of those times, so why did they not bear some responsibility for the future of the faerie realm? They would cease to exist as much as the rest of the faeries when there was no place left on Mother Earth to seek sanctuary.

Bronwen knelt to the lush grass to light her ceremonial candles; silver for the Moon Goddess, gold for the Sun God. She cushioned her wand of rose quartz between both palms and raised her arms above her head so the wand was above her crown energy center. Focusing her mind, she concentrated on pulling energy from the surrounding area into her wand and her own aura. As the vital hum of power rose within her, Bronwen extended her wand outwards and turned a circle clockwise encompassing her and her makeshift altar in a circle of protection and power.

> *I cast this circle once around*
> *All within by magic bound*
> *A healing place, a sacred place*
> *Safe from harm by love's embrace.*

Bronwen traced a circle and imagined a bright white shaft of light beaming from her wand, tracing a pattern upon the ground and creating a protective circle where only the well-intended spirit was welcome.

Focusing her mind was difficult. Questions still nudged at her mind and prodded at her senses, but years of circle casting and ritual had been ingrained within, so she was able to cast the circle with no area of weakness. Once satisfied, she knelt down to her altar and cleared her mind so she could communicate with the powers that would be attracted to her call for magic. Summer solstice was a time for healing and love magic, and Bronwen intended to call upon the spirits she needed to grant her the benefit of vision and guidance.

Goddess above who shines so bright
I ask of you your help this night
Guide me to the place I seek
Beyond the hills and through the veil
To a place of vision for those not frail
Guide me to the place I seek

Lightheadedness fogged her mind, while ringing battered her eardrums. She sensed a foreign, yet familiar, presence hovering on the outskirts of her perception. The presence wanted something from her and Bronwen had to concentrate hard and reach deeply into otherwise untapped powers to understand the ethereal request. On some level, an understanding grew and Bronwen gave permission for a melding of her soul. Gradually, a sense of sureness bubbled inside and a completeness of self and power. Strange, she had never felt such sensations in her rituals before. A connection--a powerful connection had wound its way within and made itself a part of her. Bronwen was uneasy. She felt invaded, but not necessarily in a bad way, just an unusual way.

She shivered.

What ancient powers took a part in her ritual? She had no doubt that the essence was one of times long ago; such life force was unknown of these days. How and why had her ritual drawn such power? By taking the life force within her, however unwittingly, what was she to become? Naught could be done now, the evening passed and her ritual must come to an end. Whatever had transpired had become reality--her reality. The days to come would unfold the reasons.

With a sigh, Bronwen took her wand and performed the closing of circle ritual. This time she turned counterclockwise and spoke different words.

I close this circle, all is done
Magic forged by moon and sun
All who came here, thanks to thee
Go in peace, and blessed be.

Enjoying the song of the crickets and calmness of the moonlit night, Bronwen disassembled her altar and packed her ritual tools carefully within the softest silk. She was not aware of any presence until a hand upon her shoulder startled her from her task. In a move swift as the most graceful deer, she jumped to her feet and turned to face the intruder.

Standing on the edge between shadows and shimmering moonlight, Lir smiled at her.

"I am sorry to startle you. Sometimes I forget that we are undetectable to the ears of others."

Bronwen's pounding heart slowed to a more peaceful pace, yet her mind sped into a state of fever. The link that had been established during her ritual--it had been with Lir. The Tuatha de Danann leader had been inside her mind, prodding, exploring, searching into the recesses of what she wanted to keep hidden.

"Please," Lir pleaded. "Do not fear me; it is unnecessary. It is not my place to tell your secrets, only to guide you."

This is what she'd feared from the very moment she realized they had entered the land of the Tuatha. Her secrets revealed. "My secrets." Bronwen took a couple of steps towards Aurora and placed her tools into the saddlebags. It was a gesture meant to stall. "I knew you would see into my very soul, just as I knew your bloodlines were of the Tuatha de Danann as soon as I lay eyes upon you." Patting Aurora upon her golden muzzle, Bronwen received a sloppy tongue in return. "It is thought that your kind died out long ago."

"Yes. It was necessary. 'Twas a time when many evil ones wanted to destroy us. Much like Gar and the faeries now. In order to preserve ourselves, we needed to disappear."

"Is that what the faeries will need to do in order to survive?"

"No, other pathways are in the process of being presented to all involved. The choosing of the ways will be up to the individuals, and those decisions will determine the outcome of the realm of faeries."

"But this also affects the Tuatha de Danann. Without the realm of faerie you will disappear, just as the rest of us."

"That is why your knowledge and abilities have been heightened. Your journey is a rough one--one that must not fail."

Bronwen felt dizzy. The connection had been so much more than she understood. It still was. "What have you done?" Her whispered words of fear fell into a sudden silence of nature as the breeze stilled, the trees froze, and all sounds of animals ceased. Breathlessly, the world waited for an answer.

"Prophetess, you are now one of us. It was a necessary feat in order for you to accomplish your goals. Otherwise the darkness invoked by Raegar would have destroyed you before you reached Westland."

Chills crept down Bronwen's spine, and she clasped her fists to her side. "The darkness approaches. I can feel its relentless pursuit of me." Her black gaze locked with the surreal beauty of Lir's azure eyes. "Tell me, is there naught that you do not know of me and my past?"

A flash of pity blazed in blue and disappeared as if it had never been. "No, I know all. But as I spoke earlier, your secrets are yours to reveal."

Bronwen paced across the grass and barely noticed the pink of a sky as the sun peaked above far off mountains. "Some secrets are better veiled."

"Some, but not the one you keep."

The thought of telling Adoneesis the truth scared Bronwen more than the approaching darkness. How does one tell such a story of deceit and betrayal? As circumstances allowed now, she had his friendship and respect. If she told him the truth-- chances are she would only earn his contempt. That was something she was not sure she could handle. Better to ride through a herd of muckrakers, or battle an army of vengeful goblins than tell Adoneesis the truth.

"You will do as you will." Lir obviously was aware of the direction of thought.

Bronwen stopped her pacing and ran her hand lovingly over Aurora's silky mane; the motion calmed her. Aurora responded by shaking her head and nickering her delight at her owner's attention.

"Lir, if you know all and have the abilities and knowledge of the ancient ones, why do you not go to the world of man and bring the woman here?"

"Ahh, that would be the ideal solution." Lir paused and looked to the sun rising in the distance. "We come from that direction you know; it has been said that the sun rises in the land of the Tuatha de Danann."

His voice grew wistful as if repeating an oft-told tale of sadness to himself. "Our home was linked to another place of similar properties. I think your Lady of the Lake refers to the people of that place as the Ones Who Came Before."

"I have heard mention of them. They came from a land in the middle of the ocean and settled in Avalon, or at least it came to be known as Avalon."

"Yes, Avalon. *An inland haven that rose from the destruction of an island paradise.* What we did not realize is how strong our bond was with those people, that somewhere in our history we are linked. As long as they remained strong, so did we. As soon as they were in peril, we grew weak. Once Avalon disappeared into the mists, we became merely wraiths in this world. As potent and invincible as we thought ourselves, we quickly became mere shadows of ourselves. Now, we are no longer able to function much more than the barest of magic-- soon we will be gone forever."

"But the Lady of the Lake is one of the Ones Who Came Before; as long as she lives do you not stand a chance of recovering your former strength?"

It took a moment for Bronwen to see the slight shaking of Lir's broad shoulders. Though he'd turned his back to her, she was aware that tears flowed down Lir's cheeks. The meaning of those tears was as clear to Bronwen as the moon that shone in full glory. The Lady was dead.

"I am sorry." Words could never be adequate for the loss of such a treasure of the realm of faerie.

"No, do not be sorry. Niobe gave her essence so that the realm of faerie may survive, thus allowing all faeries a chance to live. She dreamed that one day faeries would return to ways of old and regain so much that had been lost."

"She gave her essence?" Bronwen was puzzled. She should understand something, but couldn't quite grasp what that was.

When the realization hit her, nausea did as well and she immediately knelt to the ground and spewed her last meal.

Lir's gentle hands rubbed her shoulders and his soothing words whispered their comfort to her soul. "It was her time. She merely decided where to place her essence for the best of all involved. The gesture is one of beauty and valor, not something to make yourself sick over."

As the heaving of her insides slowed down, Bronwen gave heed to Lir's words. She had been scared of failing before, but now--the survival of the legendary Tuatha de Danann was upon her conscience, and the essence of Niobe within her body.

She could not fail.

"There is more."

Words spoken so softly Bronwen thought she might have imagined them.

"We all have secrets and it is time I told you one of mine. A piece of knowledge I have had for a long time."

"I do not think I can take more on this day." Bronwen tried to discourage Lir from speaking the words. Her connection to Lir enabled her insight to the words, but if she could prevent them from being spoken, they would not be true. Years would not have been wasted.

But the fickle will of fate must be adhered to and so Lir spoke. "Lapis still lives."

If one's heart could be crushed from inside one's body, that is what happened to Bronwen on that night. Memories both wonderful and terrifying rushed through her mind and tortured her as if it all happened at that moment. Pain-filled years of guilt, longing, and banishment haunted her as years of waste. She tried to speak, but only silence crossed her quivering lips. There then rose within her anger so intense she feared her actions. Blinding red flushed her vision and her hands clawed at the air in front of her--to find only emptiness. Gentle hands of persuasion massaged her mind and a soft voice calmed her senses until a normal state of being returned to her.

Niobe's voice.

Suddenly strong in the light of all that had happened, Bronwen demanded of Lir. "Why not tell me sooner? Why tell me at all?" Conflicting sentences that mirrored Bronwen's unsettled emotions.

"If I had told you sooner, you would not have become who you need to be to help the realm of faerie. I tell you now because Lapis has a part to play as well."

To see her one true love after all this time, Bronwen did not know how to feel about the possibility. Where had he been? Why had he not come to her? Clod's breath, why now when she had so many other things on which to concentrate?

In his inscrutable way of reading her mind, Lir said, "I cannot tell you anymore, but trust that all will become clear. Now, time runs short. You must return to Adoneesis who waits impatiently. You are almost at your destination. That is when the difficult part of the journey begins."

"The difficult part?"

"Yes, you will have trouble convincing the woman to come with you. Then your return to Dunraven will herald a dark time."

"But we will succeed in saving the faeries, right?"

"I cannot say."

"Cannot, or will not."

Lir smiled. "You are guided by powerful forces, but the decisions you and others make, will determine the outcome. There is one more thing you need to know, another important piece that will effect the outcome."

Bronwen rolled her eyes. "Is it not complicated enough? Must the Fates insist on a rockier road?"

Lir smiled. "One of our own stole some important items many years ago and managed to cross over to the world of man. There he married a human and produced a son. The items he stole were a book and a crystal. Combined with the power of the child, these items are more powerful than you or I could ever imagine."

"Yes..." Bronwen waited for further explanation.

"Just be aware of this fact."

The azure blue of Lir's eyes looked slightly more faded than they had earlier. Bronwen felt a tug of pity and did not push, although she was frustrated with the lack of explanation.

"I am honored by what you have given to me and I promise to do all in my power to make things right. To lose such as the Tuatha de Danann would be a great loss indeed."

Lir's essence glowed, and then gradually disappeared into a mere morning mist. Alone in the clearing, Bronwen shivered. Too much rested on her shoulders, but as Lir had said, the decisions that *all* made would determine the outcome.

Thirteen

Out of breath and sweating, Gwepper plopped onto a log to rest. "Won't do no good to run yerself into the ground, stupid goblin." He spoke the words aloud and could have kicked himself in case the other goblins were within hearing distance.

Upon hearing last night's conversation, he'd set off running. Though traveling by foot, while they traveled on horseback, Gwepper had the advantage of a night's travel as well as fear to spur him. He consoled himself that the goblins, glad to be away from Gar's oppressive presence and constant threat of beatings, would take time to enjoy their freedom.

Warmth from the rising sun touched his face and he looked to the horizon to enjoy the pink and peaches of the sky. Trees as tall as the distant mountains basked in the morning sun and reached out dancing branches as if in greeting.

"Bah! Creepy, sleepy goblin. You're going soft in the head." Even though no one had seen him enjoy the sunrise, Gwepper felt embarrassed by his moment of weakness. This whole, stupid mission of saving some female goblin was a weakness, Gwepper thought. Why was he even pushing himself so hard to save her? But visions of golden hair, cute pig-nose and a rear end that swayed allayed his doubts.

"Gotta get there first. Gotta go faster." The litany repeated in his mind and gave strength to his skinny legs to pump faster and harder.

Ghilphar. A name to inspire kings.

Ghilphar. Gwepper leapt over a moss-covered log, feeling as if his feet had wings.

Ghilphar. He imagined that she loved him and awaited his return.

Ghilphar. Even the dense forest and rushing streams at the base of the mountain range south of Night Gloom did not impede his progress.

For the first time in his life, he had a mission that meant something to him. Not cleaning up after others, not mucking out the stables, not even spying for Gar. This was for him!

He climbed to the top of an ancient oak and wailed a cry of freedom from deep inside his chest--from within his very soul. "Yaaaaa!" The sound carried across the land in all directions to cast a pall upon some and give hope to others. When he realized what he had done in the moment of emotion, he hunched his shoulders and peered through the tree branches to see if anyone had heard him. Of course no one was around, he assured himself. He was in the middle of nowhere.

"Gotta go, goats and ghosts. Have no time to waste." He scrambled down the tree and wondered how in the fates he had ever climbed such a monstrosity in the first place. The trunk was as wide as three trees and as high as most trees in Night Gloom--yet somehow different. He'd never been one to climb trees. Every time he'd tried, he'd ended up thrown to the ground as if by some unseen force. Sometimes he thought the trees themselves had dispelled him from their branches. But this tree... he paused to rub the trunk in wonder. This tree felt right. It felt strong and caring. If he listened carefully, he could almost hear a song of peace wafting among the forest trees.

"Yikes! Stupid goblin, there you go again. Gotta go." He jumped the last few feet to the ground but couldn't resist one last pat to the tree trunk. One of the branches, most assuredly directed by the wind, swung over to touch upon his head and ruffle his hair. Eyes rounded in shock Gwepper bound off into the distance muttering, "Gotta go."

~ * ~

Ghilphar knew trouble approached. She'd known from the day she fled Night Gloom and Gar's unwanted advances, That was why she had developed her mind, senses, and natural abilities. All would be necessary to protect her against the self-proclaimed king of the goblins whose mind probes had searched her out over the years. Though practices in the dark ways of old magic were frowned upon, Gar still practiced blood sacrifice, subjugation, and lust for total power that had leant a dark pall upon all practices of magic.

Ghilphar was scared, but consoled herself with the thought that light always overcame dark. Good was stronger than evil. Right transcended physical powers of might.

Ghilphar believed this, yet she felt the stink of Gar's evil coming her way. How had he found her? How could she stand up against him? She couldn't. She needed to run.

Scrambling to stuff essentials into a sack, Ghilphar allowed herself only a second of regret. She loved the place that had been her home for so long. Granted, the hut was not of any luxury, but it withstood the weather and suited her purposes. She'd blessed the fallen trees as she had stripped them of their bountiful limbs and strapped them together with sturdy vines. She inhaled the aroma of pine as she laid the branches upon the frame layer upon layer. The stone fire pit in the center of her abode cooked her meals and kept her warm in winter. Over time she had furnished her home with hand-twined twig furniture and always made sure to take only what had been discarded by the trees.

With a sniffle, she packed her herbs so lovingly planted and grown in her garden and stuffed enough food into her pack to last for a few days. Anymore her mule would not be able to carry, not with everything else she had packed. With a silent blessing and promise to return if possible, Ghilphar closed the pine-decorated door and stood in the warm sun of the afternoon.

It was at that moment that she knew she would not be alone in her ordeal. Echoing from a distance, yet sounding as if it were in her very mind, a howling screech of freedom and self-awareness echoed across the land. She shivered, but not in fear. Her heart beat fiercely as if in sympathy with the creature that howled and her limbs filled with anticipation for what was to come. Such strength tempered the yell that was reminiscent of an ancient warrior battle cry. Joy surged in her chest--the Goddess sent her a defender, a champion, one who would travel with her through these uncertain times. A smile tugged her lips and she imagined him to be tall with shoulders the width of the tree trunks of the ancient forests to the west. Handsome, at least handsome in a goblin sort of way, and strong enough to sweep her into his arms and carry her from the approaching danger.

"Thank you, Goddess." Her whisper had barely left her lips when a crashing sound came from the northern forest line. Her protector had arrived and he was being very clumsy.

"Oh, my." Ghilphar could think of nothing else to say as she became aware of the familiar form loping down the hill. Gangly, not especially handsome, with a rather large nose and spindly legs was the form of her imagined hero. Something must have gone wrong, how could this goblin protect her against the danger she knew approached?

She didn't have time to wonder as Gwepper slid to her side and pulled at her arm. "Come, there is no time, no time. Three come from Night Gloom. Ikes and spikes, hurry!"

Ghilphar's mind refused to send signals to her body. She stood and sputtered like an idiot. "What... but..."

Clearly agitated at Ghilphar's lack of response, Gwepper slapped his hand to his forehead and moaned, "Females, why must they be so slow?"

That did it. Ghilphar regained her composure and immediately snapped back at Gwepper. "*Females*. What about you, you silly goblin? You're brain must have gotten lost somewhere between here and Night Gloom if you think you're going to save me from Gar." She threw her pack over the back of her mule, Glory, and laced the bands tightly about the belly. Glory hee-hawed her protest at such rough treatment and turned her mournful brown eyes to Ghilphar in admonishment.

"Sorry, sweetie." Ghilphar patted the mule gently in apology.

Gwepper looked to the already packed items and the hut, which was obviously closed and deserted. "Hmmm, maybe you're not so slow after all."

Ghilphar snorted her reply and lugged a cask of water from beside the hut to Glory. Before she could even attempt to lift the cask, Gwepper grabbed it and grunted his way to placing it on the back of the mule. With a humph of satisfaction, he looked to Ghilphar with his head a smidgen higher and his shoulders pulled back a little further than before.

It wasn't until their eyes met that Ghilphar fully appreciated the champion that had been sent to her rescue and she felt shame for the disappointment she had felt at his looks. His eyes radiated goodness, love, respect, and the humble emotion of shyness. Gwepper's shyness slammed into Ghilphar's heart and she was lost. The world suddenly took on a rosy hue that had nothing to do with the sun and everything to do with the goblin standing in front of her. The goblin, who had risked his life to come to her rescue, didn't even know if she would accept him.

Voice trembling and emotions reeling, Ghilphar reached out her hand to touch Gwepper's cheek.

"Powers above, powers that be
My faith and life I bind with thee
Through the dark times that come
I trust in you as the one
No other's words shall I heed
No other path shall I lead"

Completing the verse, Ghilphar knelt down in front of Gwepper and placed her fingers to her forehead to complete the uttered vow of allegiance.

Gwepper stood with a frozen look of amazement on his face that such beauty could place her in his trust. "Rats and bats, stupid female goblin. Get from your knees. This is insanity. Plain, insane insanity," he sputtered and took the reins of the mule. "Let's go, the three goblins come fast. Their thoughts are of bad things. I must save you."

Ghilphar stood and smiled. He had come to save her with no thought to himself. She had felt the deep sense of honor and rightness in this funny looking goblin from the start. It was right that he was the one to come to her rescue.

With one last sad look to the clearing that had been her home, Ghilphar fled with Gwepper and Glory. They had danger fast on their heels and no destination. Although Gwepper said they would head for Dunraven and safety, Ghilphar knew they wouldn't reach Dunraven quite as easily as Gwepper hoped--if at all.

~*~

Ghilphar and Gwepper hurried through the paths and trails that Ghilphar knew so well. Gwepper's relentless pace tired them quickly as they passed through marshes, mountain foothills, and streams of cool mountain water. The only thing that kept Ghilphar from complaining about the pace was the prickling awareness of danger. In her mind's eye, she saw the arrival of the three goblins shortly after the hasty departure that had set them on the road to Dunraven.

As clearly as if they stood in front of her, Ghilphar saw an ugly goblin with broken teeth, a skinny one with a whiny voice, and the scariest of all--the large, silent one who rode the lead. She heard their shrieks of anger when they found the hut empty and she smelt their rancid fear that Gar would flay them alive if they returned without her. Ghilphar felt a wrench as the goblins, angered at having their quarry escape, lit a torch to the hut and burned it to the ground. With slobberings of destructive glee, they ripped up any remaining herbs and knelt in the hand-sown garden to defecate.

Ghilphar felt weak as the devastation wrought by the fearsome goblins played itself out in her mind. Gwepper must have seen her stumble for he placed his hand on her shoulder.

"No time for rest. We must hurry... I'm sorry." Though he couldn't be aware of what was occurring at Ghilphar's home, he must have sensed something. His eyes softened from mud gray to soft brown and he touched his finger to Ghilphar's cheek in a gesture of comfort. "We must hurry."

They left the well-traveled trail and headed deep into the forest and headed south to Dunraven. They planned to stay off the well-traveled trails, but terrain grew rough and they had too hard a time navigating in the forest. In a hurried conference, they decided to travel the trail at night when they wouldn't be so easily seen. Ghilphar swore that the moon above and trees of the forest would lead them. Gwepper wasn't so sure, but he agreed, grumbling that being given orders by a female was bad enough, but to rely on being guided by the *trees*--well, that was a tale he would rather not tell anywhere.

Ghilphar just smiled, knowing his bellyaching was a cover for a soft heart. In a spur of the moment action, she reached out and took Gwepper's hand in hers. Surprise lit Gwepper's eyes and they sparkled a startling silver sheen of delight. Glory gave her approval by nudging Gwepper so he stumbled closer to Ghilphar. This is how they made their way through the forest toward the trail that would lead them to Dunraven.

Ghilphar would have reason to berate herself for getting distracted from danger. Maybe then, she would have been aware of the fact that the danger now lay before them, not behind. Maybe then, she would have been able to avoid seeing the glint of evil delight rise in Gar's eyes as she, Gwepper, and Glory broke through the thickness of the forest directly into the center of Gar and his battalion of goblins.

Fourteen

"We stop here for the night." Bronwen declared.

"But daylight still marks the sky, and we are so close."

"Yes, we are." Bronwen dismounted from Aurora and stretched her weary limbs. "I need to perform some rituals before we cross over to the world of man. The Westland gateway lies upon that rocky peak."

Adoneesis' heart pounded as his gaze rose to the peak of the winding hill where a stone monument of simple design stood. They were so close to the world of the woman who would save the faerie realm.

As if reading his thoughts, Bronwen warned him. "Do not stay all your hopes on the woman. Other factors will play a role."

"I do not understand. If the woman is not the savior, why are we spending our time searching her out?"

"She is necessary to the survival; she just isn't the only factor involved."

Adoneesis shook his head and dismounted from Brachus who shifted his hooves restlessly. With a pat on Brachus' chocolate rump, Adoneesis set him free to forage and rest for the night. Kicking his hooves up in a masculine display, the steed galloped across the grass to the tree line where the unicorn waited. Prancing and snorting, the ethereal creature presented a sight of luminescent beauty as her pearl hide reflected the golden sun. Brachus and she touched noses then disappeared into the forest.

Bronwen chuckled. "I foresee a young foal in the future. A foal that will be the beginning of a new breed of animal."

She relieved Aurora of the load of saddle and bags and took time to sort her ritual tools for the night's work while Adoneesis gathered wood to light a cook fire for dinner. It was a mindless task and Adoneesis took the time to consider what lay ahead tomorrow. He was used to relying on himself and always made sure to know all aspects of a situation before involving himself or making a decision. Now, he found himself in an unusual situation traveling across the land of faerie solely at the behest of this woman and her visions.

Slowly Adoneesis chewed on an oatcake and pondered Bronwen. Her facial features danced in the firelight creating an image that was her--yet someone else. Memories and familiarities flitted the outskirts of Adoneesis mind rendering him frozen in a moment of confusion. How could he have memories of someone he had never known before? Yet, he was certain that the female who sat across from him possessed a part of his past that he wanted. Bursting with the certain knowledge, he was still reluctant to question Bronwen. His senses told him that all would be revealed in time, so he continued to chew his food and left things well enough alone.

Lately, awareness had become more a part of him. Traveling through the land of Dunraven, coming upon places where ancient powers still trickled in the land and most especially finding the Tuatha de Danann alive, had opened gates to places within. Now, more than ever, he questioned his own ancestry and Raegar's anger whenever he'd tried to explore his burgeoning abilities. Harsh words and even harsher beatings.

You will not sully my throne with such teachings of magic. It is evil and stupid to attempt such things. Do you not wonder why none of the ancient ones still live? They destroyed themselves in their arrogant attempts to place themselves at one with nature. Power and total subjugation of those below you is the only way to stay strong and rule a kingdom.

Yet, Adoneesis became more certain with each passing day that the blood of magicians ran through his veins, so why would Raegar be so against any use of magic? As far as Adoneesis was concerned, magic was merely a way of making use of natural abilities. The drifting away from such practices is what endangered the realm of faerie, and the arrogance was in not respecting the trees, animals, and living being that was Mother Earth. Sureness of this grew in Adoneesis as swiftly and strongly as Brachus' ability to fly across the land with his power of the fiery dragon steeds of Atlantis.

"Yes, I believe you are now ready," Bronwen whispered into the growing darkness of the night.

"Pardon." Adoneesis state of mind remained hazy from his self-analysis.

"It is time. You will be part of the ceremony tonight. The sacred moon tree accepted your ability, and now you have accepted your ability. Therefore, you come with me to the world of man."

Adoneesis was stunned. Traveling to the world of man was a journey of danger, yet the thought appealed to his sense of adventure. Crossing from one realm to another was seldom attempted, although it used to be a common practice. "But how can this happen? You are the prophetess. You have the powers of the ancient ones strong in your blood, but I... I am merely a faerie of common abilities."

"Do not spout such foolishness. I have seen awareness of your strength shine on your face this eve." Bronwen paused as if contemplating her chosen words. "Adoneesis, there are things you do not know, things that will become clear to you eventually. Trust in what you feel and trust in what you know. Tonight, you come with me."

Bronwen stood--tall and strong, looking remarkably like one of the Tuatha de Danann. Adoneesis drew in his breath at the transformation from hag to beauty and expelled it as the figure before him shrank and again became a hunched figure of age. Silently, she reached for her sack of ritual tools and melted into the surrounding forest and never once looked back to see if Adoneesis followed.

He did.

Without thought or doubt, he followed her from the bottom of the hill where they camped, up the winding, rough-hewn path that led to the crest of the hill. It was a challenging climb, with the natural terrain presenting an obstacle course. Adoneesis muscles screamed in protest as his breath caught in his chest and seemed nothing more than a shallow intake of air.

Adoneesis paused but a brief moment, only to see Bronwen disappear around a crooked bend in the path above. How in the Heavens was she able to travel this course sprightly? More physical training was definitely in order if he couldn't even keep up with someone so aged. Sighing, Adoneesis prompted his sore muscles into movement.

Thick, lush foliage hid the destination from Adoneesis, so he was awestruck when he finally broke from the treed pathway into a hilltop clearing. His first impression was one of standing in the heavens and riding on a mist of clouds. Spearing into the sky above was a stone monument of simple splendor that it radiated a luminescent glow onto the swirling mists that surrounded its peak.

"Beautiful, is in not?"

"Yes." Adoneesis stood in wonderment. "It is a beauty that defies the senses. Not only sight, sound, and smell, but I feel the touch of this place on a deeper level--inside." Adoneesis struggled with placing these strange sensations into words, and he looked to Bronwen with a pained look of confusion. "Suddenly, I do not understand myself." His voice fell to a whisper. "I feel as if I am so much more, yet at the same time, so much less."

Bronwen laid her hand upon his arm and gave a smile of consolation. "It is how I felt my first time here. By understanding the powerful energy of this place, you become greater and stronger than you were. Yet, you also feel small and inadequate, somewhere deep inside wondering if you can ever fulfill the greatness such a place expects of you. Yes, it can be a fearsome experience."

"Your words are as if right from my heart. How can you know so well what I feel?"

Stillness filled the hilltop with only a gentle, warming wind to circle the great stone Tor. Black eyes met with brown and a small spark leapt from one to the other.

Adoneesis broke the silence first. "I think there is more to us than I know. One day maybe you will trust enough to confide in me."

Bronwen touched her hand to his cheek. It was a soft touch with a withered hand, and Adoneesis wondered once again at the contrasts within this complex faerie of magic.

"It is not a matter of trust. It is a matter of complication and maybe a touch of fear that truths revealed may forever change the course of what is." With tears upon her cheek, Bronwen took a deep breath and turned to her tools. "Now, we have a tough journey ahead of us, we must begin."

Frustrated, he realized that Bronwen was right, the night ahead would be long. "Just guide me. I will follow your directions."

"You need only relax and clear your mind. I will perform the ceremony, and with the help of the Goddess, we will find our pathway from this world to the human world. The Tor is a place where veils between worlds are at its thinnest. In times gone past, this same place could have easily taken us on a path to Avalon. Unfortunately, that realm no longer exists." Her gaze became thoughtful and she pondered to herself as if forgetting Adoneesis knelt beside her. "I think that somewhere in the mists, Avalon still exists. Occasionally, I feel a tendril of someone--or something, calling to me. Almost as if trying to reach out and assure me. But enough, we have no time for such sentiment. Let us begin."

Adoneesis knelt on the cooling grass, took a relaxing breath, and waited in anticipation. Bronwen prepared the ritual space by casting her circle and lighting an array of colored candles. From her bag, she pulled a branch and laid it on the flat rock she had improvised for her altar. Upon the altar, she also placed her athame, and at either corner of the rock, a single white carnation and white gardenia. The two flowers soaked in the rays of the moon and between them possessed properties of protection, strength, peace, love, and a greater connection to the spiritual. The spicy aroma of cinnamon and sage drifted lazily on the night breeze to mingle with the flowery scent of lavender and frankincense.

"How do we know we'll even be close to the woman when we reach the other side?"

"The gateway takes us to the place we visualize in our mind. I have the essence of the woman from my last visit; therefore, I will direct us close to her. With the Fates on our side, we will hopefully land in the same place together."

Bronwen began to talk quietly, as if to herself, yet the words were spoken for them both. "We must relax our minds, let go of all pre-conceived beliefs. The stone before us looks solid, yet will open a door to lead us where we venture. In order to step through the door, you must believe in can be done."

Panic rose in Adoneesis chest. What if the door opened and he saw nothing? What if his belief was not enough to take him where he needed to go to save the faeries? He suddenly felt unworthy of the belief others had placed on him. As he doubted, his subconscious became aware of a change in the atmosphere. In the background, Bronwen's chanting voice seemed to reach out and create a heavy thickness in the air. Adoneesis watched as she raised the branch she had taken from her bag and held it to the moon.

> *"This branch I have been granted by your Sacred Tree*
> *Its powers I call upon and now bring to me."*

She repeated the verse until the words ran into one. Adoneesis tried to lift his arm but could not move in the thickness surrounding him. Bronwen did not seem to be having any trouble moving. She had replaced the branch with her crystal wand which she now pointed the direction of the stone Tor.

> *"As life passes through the wheel of time*
> *I unlock its door with this rhyme*
> *As we now are*
> *We shall be again*
> *But now we cross the line*
> *And leave our essence behind*
> *Show us the world of man*
> *As only you can."*

Bronwen's words mingled with the air and fast became a wild restless wind. A vortex of dirt and small pebbles circled about the Tor, and in an instant, a flash of light and tremendous sound shook the earth to her very core. The hilltop trembled and the stone spear looked as if it were about to tumble onto the two onlookers. In a breath of fear, Adoneesis leapt to his feet and grabbed for Bronwen only to find his hands clutching nothing. A swirl of mist had reached out from the Tor and engulfed her. Blindly, Adoneesis grasped about the mist in an attempt to feel her. Instead, he found himself surrounded by the mist and lifted from the ground. Spiraling into the unknown, he felt dizzy with the sensation of weightlessness. Visions of nameless faces and sounds of voiceless words whirled all around him until everything stopped and he found himself thrown onto a hard surface.

Sound returned, but they were unfamiliar sounds of noise and confusion. Afraid to open his eyes, yet afraid not to; Adoneesis slowly peered out from beneath one of his eyelids. Before he was even able to comprehend what lay before him, a familiar voice whispered in his ear.

"Get up before you make a spectacle of yourself." Hands pulled at his clothes urging him to rise.

His eyes flew open and relief swept over him as he found himself looking directly into Bronwen's black eyes. "Thank the Fates we didn't get separated."

"Yes, that worry crossed my mind as well. But we are here and people are looking, so please stand up."

Adoneesis hastened to his feet and observed their surroundings. What he saw awed and frightened him. "Where is the earth?" He pointed to the hard, gray surface they stood upon. "And the trees, where have they gone?" Panic rose in his voice as his eyes searched for something familiar and his ears were assaulted with noises of mass confusion. All around them stood strange looking structures. Alike, yet unalike, these structures obviously held the humans inside because he watched them as they came out clear doors onto the gray walkway.

They had their share of monsters here in the man world as well. At first Adoneesis jumped when one of them roared past, until he realized they were not harmful creatures--just noisy and fast.

"Do not let them scare you. It is a mode of transport for the humans."

Adoneesis looked closer and noticed that, yes indeed, each of the noisy conveyances held at least one human. His mind still had a hard time with wondering where the earth had disappeared to though. He voiced his concerns.

"Mother Earth is here." She pointed to the gray walkway. "Beneath this is the earth. Humans build upon the earth to make travel easier. And the trees are stripped away to make room for their buildings."

"But that does not make sense. To cover the earth is to cut yourself off from her energy, and it is a sin to take down trees that still hold life within their limbs."

"In our world yes, but not here in the human world."

"Then I am glad I do not live here. How can they even breathe properly? The air smells stale and dead. The lack of true fresh breathing air makes me feel nauseous."

"Yes, I agree. Let's not tarry here longer than we need. The woman is close by. I feel her."

~ * ~

Bryanna hummed in tune with a Gordon Lightfoot song on the bookstore radio. She had decided long ago, when the store was still a dream, that she would play music that would appeal to the relaxation of book buying. There was nothing she hated more than going into some of the large chain stores and having loud and raunchy music blast you so much that you couldn't even concentrate on reading the back cover blurb.

Her dream had been to open a small store that catered to people wanting to spend the day browsing, reading, and eventually buying something. Shelves overflowed with new and used books, as well as a small selection of artsy ornaments and pixie-like figurines that her friend Trudy designed and crafted. A coffee machine and a cappuccino machine sat in the back corner by a large picture window. Customers were welcome to drink and sit in any of the various cushy armchairs strategically placed about the store. Plants were everywhere; English ivy, fichus, angel wings, grape ivy, philodendron, chrysanthemum, and even orchids. They crept, crawled, ascended, descended, and hung from all parts of the bookstore. A splendid display of color and greenery gave a feeling of privacy to customers who opted to settle in for a coffee and afternoon read.

Since her aunt's death four months ago, Bryanna had thrown herself into expanding and decorating her small bookstore. Her main purpose had been to forget the mysterious death and the following letter that had intruded on her well-ordered life. Her friend Trudy had cautioned her about putting too much thought into the letter.

"*Your aunt was a wonderful woman, but we both know she wasn't always thinking with all cylinders intact.*"

Leave it to Trudy to always get to the heart of the matter, and in this case her friend had been right. Bryanna had loved her aunt dearly but didn't always agree with her rituals or beliefs. Upon reading her aunt's letter, Bryanna had been upset. How dare Aunt Shirley write one last weird letter and leave Bryanna with that final impression? How dare she write a letter that cast doubt on the death of Bryanna's parents?

Trudy talked her into throwing the letter away and pretending it had never been written or read. Bryanna agreed. The problem was that the words had etched themselves into her memory and reasserted themselves in her dreams on a regular basis.

> *Your parents were killed by an evil force that has lived in various forms through many lifetimes. That is the reason we always stayed away from cities and people. I had a responsibility to keep you safe for your destiny. Within you runs blood of the ancient ones, and you hold a power that will shape worlds and change lives. It is not something you should ever have had to become aware of, but forces have searched your parents out and killed them because of the power your father possessed, the same power he passed on to you. I am sorry you have to face your future alone, but I warn you with everything that is within my soul. Beware! Trust what you have been raised with and trust your own heart. If events come to pass, you will need to act fast and trust in the light. I know this doesn't make sense to you now, but it will. I love you dearly and watch over you to the best of my ability from wherever I am bound.*

Bryanna slammed a book she was pricing onto the counter and took a deep breath to settle her senses. It was all so stupid and she felt responsible for not seeing that her aunt had been crazy. Maybe if she'd gotten her the proper help, Aunt Shirley wouldn't be dead now. Maybe she would have spent more time with her while she was alive. Who knows? Now it was too late.

"Jeez, woman, your eyes look like thunderstorms." Trudy's cheery voice interrupted Bryanna's morbid thought process.

"Trudy, what are you doing here?" Bryanna reached out to hug her friend.

"I had a few more trinkets to add to your collection, so I thought I'd drop them off." Trudy placed the wooden box she carried onto the counter and lifted the lid to reveal about a half dozen figurines of various sizes and colors. The one thing they did have in common was their resemblance to a sloppy, cute, pink-cheeked pixie.

"They're adorable. I'm glad you stayed on the pixie theme for a while longer, I've already sold most of the others you left me."

Trudy rubbed her hands together. "Great, that means you owe me some money, woman."

"Oh, well, if you insist." Bryanna withdrew some bills from her register and handed them over. "Can you stay around for dinner? There's a great Italian place just around the corner."

"I suppose..." Trudy never finished her sentence because she was too busy staring at someone who had just entered the store. She whispered, "I've died and gone to heaven. Is that who I think it is?"

Bryanna looked to see who had entered the store, actually, everyone in the store turned to look. It couldn't be... no, it wasn't. "No, it just looks like him," she whispered to Trudy who still stood frozen in place.

"Are you sure? He looks as if he just stepped from the Lord of the Rings with that long, dark hair, smoldering eyes, jaw of granite..."

"Trudy, snap out of it, he is not the actor you're thinking of."

"Viggo."

"What?"

"Viggo. The name of the actor he looks like. Are you absolutely sure, it's not him?"

Bryanna rolled her eyes and laughed. "I should be. I've seen each of the movies four times."

"Yeah. I guess if anyone would know, you would. But he is gorgeous isn't he?"

Bryanna took a closer look. She'd never been attracted to any of the actors in the LOTR movies; it had been the movies themselves that had held her captive. Epic adventures of loyalty, redemption, honor, life and death. She shivered at the concept of such an ultimate battle of good over evil. Faced now with someone who so resembled Aragorn, she found her heart doing an unfamiliar flutter about her chest. He truly was gorgeous, in a masculine way of course. Long walnut colored hair that brushed his collar, dark eyes of passionate depths, and a strong jaw covered in a growth of stubbly beard and body to die for.

His eyes connected with hers.

She blushed. She was sure she blushed. Stupid, there was no way he could know what thoughts raced through her mind. His nostrils flared as if an animal scenting its prey, and Bryanna shivered again. He walked toward her and Bryanna lost awareness of everything except him. Her heart pounded fiercely until she felt it would break loose from her chest, yet still he came.

Graceful, yet predatory. Handsome, yet deadly. Of this world, yet not of this world. All these thoughts came into Bryanna's mind as she waited for him.

When he spoke, his voice was deep and strong, yet hypnotizing in its softness and simplicity. "You are the woman."

Bryanna frowned. Beside her, Trudy laughed. "I'm sorry?" Even to her own ears, her voice sounded weak.

"You are who we have come for."

We? Only then did Bryanna notice there was a woman with the Viggo look-a-like. Unobtrusive and elderly, the older woman stood off to the side and left the conversation up to the man. Bryanna returned her attention to the man--no hard task.

"Has someone recommended my bookstore to you? If there's a certain book you're looking for, I'm sure I can help." Good, she sounded reasonably capable and businesslike.

"No, you don't understand, it is *you* we have come for."

The older woman stepped forward and spoke. "Greetings. My name is Bronwen. We have something very important to discuss. Maybe if we could have a few minutes of your time in private." She was painfully aware of the customers listening so intently to their conversation.

"I close in a couple of hours. Maybe we could talk then?"

"No, it is too important. We must talk now," the intense man insisted. With a sigh of frustration, he turned and started physically pushing confused people out the front door.

"Wait a minute. You can't do that," Bryanna protested as he closed the door behind the last customer. Trudy protested but quickly found herself outside the door where she pulled a cell phone from her purse and frantically pushed buttons.

Bryanna stood in stunned silence at such high-handed handling of her customers. She literally sputtered her words before she was finally able to speak clearly. "Who do you think you are? This is my bookstore and those are my customers you just herded out the door. I can't afford to lose the money they might have spent."

"What is this money of which you speak?"

"It is a human form of barter," Bronwen replied.

The course of the conversation was strange enough to give Bryanna a surreal sense of confusion. These people were crazy. "Look if you don't leave right now, I'm going to call the police." She laid her hand upon the nearby phone ready to dial nine-one-one if necessary.

The clock ticking on the wall was the only sound as the three of them faced each other--considering, weighing, anticipating.

"You will come with us. We have a long journey ahead and no time to explain," The man spoke firmly as he took a step closer to Bryanna.

In one smooth motion, Bronwen stepped forward. Her attempt at convincing was more eloquent and softly spoken. "Child, it is a long story, but trust me when I say many lives depend on what you do right now. We beg that you come with us no questions asked and we will protect you to the best of our abilities."

"Protect me?" Bryanna shook her head as if to clear her hearing. "I'm sorry, I have no idea what you're talking about, but I guarantee I'm not going anywhere with either one of you. Now, I'll not ask again--leave my store!" She lifted the phone to her ear and poised her finger to dial.

She didn't get the chance because Bronwen waved her hand and the phone disappeared, an action that shocked Bryanna into a muted scream. The Viggo look-a-like moved like lightning. Pulling rope from his waistband, he grabbed Bryanna and tied her hands behind her back before she had a chance to even react to his actions.

"We have no time to argue. You are coming with us one way or another."

Bronwen shook her head. "Adoneesis, you may well regret your hasty act."

"I will deal with that when the matter arises. For now, we must get away from this strange world that saps my strength. My mind and body ache for the familiarity and freshness of the faerie realm."

Bryanna's mind raced. They were kidnapping her. Trudy was outside talking into her phone. Bryanna hoped her friend had called the police. *God, please help me.* She wanted to scream, but she felt numb with disbelief and suddenly recalled her aunt's strange ways and warnings of some mysterious force that would enter her life. Words from the letter laced her mind and Bryanna feared that she had been hasty in dismissing her aunt as mentally off-balance.

She slowly drifted into a pleasant sleep and became barely aware of Trudy pounding at the front door--a sound that melded with the pounding of her heart in her chest.

Fifteen

Bailiwick was in his element. Adoneesis had left him in charge along with Krickall and Mayard. Well, maybe not in charge, but he'd said if there were any questions to ask Bailiwick, because he would know where Adoneesis was at all times. That kind of meant he was in charge, didn't it? Of course, Krickall had other ideas; the two of them had come to an understanding on the first day when Bailiwick tried to direct some of the warrior faeries about their business. With face of thunder, Krickall very calmly told Bailiwick to mind own business. Sensing a will of steel beneath the calm exterior, Bailiwick had been hasty to find another area in which to flex his newfound responsibility.

Dunraven was functioning smoothly. Preparations moved along easily enough that Bailiwick was left with empty time. Everyone pulled together, as if knowing that bickering would only hinder them and lend strength to the enemy. The most excitement Bailiwick had was watching Krickall woo the lady Analiese. Gruff and battle worn, Krickall was humbled by the experience of not being able to simply take what he desired. Newly developed manners and a more giving personality resulted from his courtship. Although he was so obviously in love, that did not deter from the regimented training he instilled upon the warrior faeries. Many grumbled about the harsh exercises and constant drills in preparation for war.

Time had passed quickly as scouts made their way to the borders to caution other faeries of the impending battle and the safety offered by King Adoneesis. Many of those warned packed their belongings and sought refuge at Dunraven during these unsettled times. As they arrived, they were put to tasks such as gardening, preserving and building food stores and erecting temporary places of living for the influx of faeries.

Bailiwick flitted about, but found little chance to exert any authority. Sighing, he floated aimlessly until he came to rest on a tree branch in the lower meadow where he could consider the activity from afar. He was bored and looked for something of interest to catch his attention. It came in the form of Krickall and Analiese. They strolled at a leisurely pace toward his hidden perch. Since their time together was almost over, it was obvious that Krickall grew anxious at the little time remaining to win her heart. Personally, Bailiwick wished that Mayard would win the battle of love, because Krickall scared him with his intense manner and rough speech.

As they moved to stand under the Hawthorn tree he was perched in, Bailiwick crouched behind the clustered white blooms to remain out of sight. Echoes of laughter and teasing interrupted Bailiwick's perusal of Krickall and Analiese. A couple of young buachailleen faeries raced across the field from the west down toward the meadow. Probably coming from the river, they seemed to be playing a game of chase the stag. As they came closer, Bailiwick decided they weren't playing. The two of them were hot on the heels of a drake faerie that cried and pumped his little legs as fast as possible to stay ahead of the older two.

Although pleasant and helpful, drake faeries emitted a rather unpleasant odor, and upon deciphering the insults hurled by the buachailleens, Bailiwick realized that was why the young drake raced across the fields of Dunraven with two buachailleens on his heels.

Krickall and Analiese saw what was happening, and as the younger faeries came within arm's reach, Krickall intervened. With a wave of his hand, he brought the trio to a sliding halt. One out of breath, wide-eyed drake and two red-capped buachailleens with the gleam of mischief in their bright eyes stood before the great warrior.

In a gesture of protection, Krickall placed a large hand upon the young drake's shoulder, gave a reassuring squeeze, and pinned the offenders with his gaze. "Tell me." His voice thundered with certain authority. "Why do you chase my young friend here?"

The buachailleens looked at each other. "You say he's your *friend*?"

"Most assuredly. As a matter of fact, I've promised to teach him how to wield a sword. We begin our lessons this afternoon." Krickall scratched his chin and frowned. "Maybe--it'll be up to my friend here--but maybe you can join us."

A smile lit the features of the harassed drake and mixed with the growing awareness of the power held within his hands. Gasps from the two buachailleens added to the sudden shift of leverage.

"It is always wise to make friends rather than enemies," Krickall cautioned.

A gentle hue of red tinged the drake's face. He looked to the hopeful faces of his former tormentors and saw only pleading in their eyes for the chance to train with the great Krickall. An honor bestowed happened so rarely. In a gesture of decision, the drake stood straight, shoulders back and decreed, "If they want, they can train with us."

Cheers of delight and relief accompanied the drake's words. In their own gesture of decision, the two of them grasped the drake between them and danced about in youthful exuberance. Leaping and bounding away from the tree, the trio stopped long enough to acknowledge Krickall's decree.

"Be in the training area in an hour, we begin then."

Analiese and Krickall chuckled at the antics of the faeries. There were so few young ones around these days it was important to build a bond between them. The young faeries may be the last in a line that reached back in history further than most remembered.

"They are sweet. What is the drake's name? He is not one I've seen too often."

Krickall shrugged at Analiese's question. "I have no idea of his name. Today is the first time I have ever spoken with him."

Understanding Krickall's act of kindness, Analiese smiled.

Very uncomfortable in his awkward position, Bailiwick shifted carefully and peered from behind the blossom. The sweet aroma tickled his nose, and he wriggled about in an attempt to stifle a sneeze. Blast, the two of them had stopped right under the branch where he was hidden and they seemed to be... oh, no, they were kissing. Passionate sounds and light moans drifted to Bailiwick's perch and he now had to stifle a giggle as well as his sneeze.

Analiese's voice broke the passionate embrace. Palms against Krickall's chest she used her strength to push him from her. "Krickall, please."

"Please what?" He pulled her tight against him and kissed her again.

She pushed, more forcefully this time. "Please stop. Your kisses excite me, but this must go no further. I have told you I save myself for the one to whom I give my binding oath."

"My kisses excite you, do they? Well, come closer and let us kiss some more."

Pushing against Krickall, Analiese barely managed to ward him off. "Stop." Suddenly released from his embrace, Analiese almost fell back onto her rear. Instead, she staggered a step and stood with chest heaving. She brushed her rumpled skirts in an attempt to calm her mind.

"Analiese. What game do you play?"

If Bailiwick wasn't holding on to the branch to prevent slipping, he would have been rubbing his hands together in glee. This conversation was definitely more stimulating than flitting around looking for something to do. Brushing a blossom from his nose and leaning forward for a better view, he saw the thunderous look on the face of Analiese. He wouldn't want to be Krickall at that moment.

"Game. I play no game." All signs of compliant passion had left her voice. "I merely ask that you respect my wishes."

"Your wishes are unknown to me." Krickall's expression matched Analiese for fierceness. "You prance yourself around like a mare up for a stud and then pull back when you are taken up on your offer. On one hand, you swear you care for me, yet tomorrow I will no longer be able to even speak with you. That privilege will be Mayard's."

Analiese's face had grown red. "How dare you bring me to task when you are as much at fault as I. If you had only but shown me a moment of respect and love, I would have fallen to your feet. Instead, you treat me like the mare you speak of with no thought to my desires or feelings. You simply expect me to bow down to you and nod my head like a good little faerie to all that you say. Well, surprise, Krickall, I have a mind and a will of my own."

Analiese snapped her skirts as she twirled around and marched away. Her blond hair billowed behind her and her hips swayed with grace and splendor. Tension, thick as winter syrup, mingled with the lonely call of a mourning dove and drifted over meadow grass blowing gently in the breeze.

Bailiwick now felt embarrassment for the warrior instead of fear at his presence. Whispered words were spoken to mix with the mourning cry of the dove. "Analiese, you must know how much I love you." The great warrior's shoulders drooped in resignation. He had failed to win her love and tomorrow she would go to another. One with a tongue of velvet and words of the ancient bards. What chance did he, an uncouth warrior, stand to win the love of one such as Analiese? All this and more reflected in his eyes before he straightened his shoulders, sighed, and made his way back to the outer field where sword practice was in full swing.

"Well, well, the mighty Krickall has a heart." Bailiwick flitted from his perch, which had become increasingly hard on his butt, and floated to the ground. He re-evaluated his personal choice in the battle for a faerie heart. Mayard was pleasing to look upon and his gift with weaving words came second to none, but now that Bailiwick gave the matter thought, he remembered the occasional distinct look of a ferret touching upon Mayard's features. His words may be smooth, but they formed the opinion of whomever Mayard spoke with. Bailiwick could not really remember Mayard having an opinion of his own to stand up for. Not like Krickall, if he believed in a notion fiercely enough he'd take a stand. If he cared for someone, he would protect that person with his life.

Bailiwick slapped his palm to his forehead. "How have you been so blind, you ninny pixie? But wait." Bailiwick worked himself into a frenzy of pondering and he darted about among the wildflowers of the meadow. "I could be wrong. I need to be fair. Tomorrow is Mayard's chance. I'll watch to see his actions. If he only cares for the chase and does not love

Analiese like Krickall, I will need to make sure he does not win. Yes, that is what I will do." He giggled. "Do not worry, fair Analiese, I will make sure your choice is the right one."

~ * ~

Gar stood under the shadow of an ancient elm tree, a place to remain hidden while he feasted his gaze upon the lands of Dunraven for the first time. Coming from the north, he'd left his horse with the other goblins and come ahead as he wanted no interruption from measly underlings while he perused the land he considered his by birthright. With practiced stealth, he'd managed to sneak up and overpower any sentries posted.

Dunraven was all he could have imagined. Granted, Night Gloom throbbed with power, but the land and forest sat heavy with unleashed possibilities and Gar always felt threatened. He felt the eyes of the trees follow him on each hunt and he felt the earth tremor under his feet as if trying to upset his balance. Older than almost any other place in the faerie realm, Night Gloom reeked with forces of old that promised one day to unfold in a frenzy of magic and retribution. Gar shivered at his thoughts. He'd never confided to anyone how he felt about the land of his birth. They'd think he was unfit to rule.

Now, the lands of Dunraven spread before him with pureness. Instead of an aching throb, the lands and forests pulsed with invigorating life and energy. Gar breathed deeply of the scented meadow grass and wildflowers. His eyes filled with the bright contrasts of color that seemed unnatural after Night Gloom's monotone grayness. Yes, Dunraven belonged to him and he would enjoy the bounties offered. It never crossed his mind that his decadent ways would result in the destruction of the beauty he so admired. He would never take responsibility for the anger permeating from the land of Night Gloom. As far as he was concerned, the darkness in the north was a result of the ancient ways. It was time for him to claim his birthright and rid Dunraven of the charlatan who ruled in his place--his half-brother.

He crept ever closer to the activity going on in the settlement. With patience born of need, he took his time until he was close enough to notice a dab of color in the south meadow. A blond-haired faerie making her way back to the cluster of settlement trees. Hmmm, capturing Dunraven would have many advantages. He watched her until the sight of a warrior striding across the meadow drew his attention. The red-haired giant came from the same place as the female and he looked angry. Gar considered the span of chest, sureness of stride, scarred face, and definition of vast muscles straining against cloth. There walked the one Gar would need to deal with in order to defeat the others. A germ of an idea already formed in his mind. From the thundering look upon the face of the one with red-hair, Gar guessed the warrior's weakness. He turned his thoughtful gaze to the blond faerie who directed some garden workers, and was rewarded by the longing look that touched upon her face at the sight of the warrior. Her gaze locked with the warrior's for a split second of joining--a look that confirmed Gar's suppositions. Yes, Dunraven would easily be his.

With a snort of satisfaction, he turned and slunk back the way he'd come. The entire goblin population of Night Gloom waited for him in a small hollow just beyond the edge of Dunraven. Heart pumping at the impending battle, he made his way back as quickly as possible. When he approached the hoard, his presence instigated a surge of movement in the otherwise hushed goblins, but none dared make a move or hasten to a task without direction from Gar. No one dared inflame the temperamental goblin and risk a beating. Gar's hateful gaze fell to his prisoners. Gwepper and Ghilphar, bound, gagged, and locked in a cart with Lapis curled at their feet in a drugged, unconsciousness heap. Gar would be relieved to take over Dunraven, because it had been his dream for so long. He'd also be relieved when the mage was once again locked deep in the bowels of a dungeon. As for Gwepper and Ghilphar, they would amuse him--each in their own way of course.

His sneer of delight melted into a mask of domination as he raised his hand to call the goblins to battle. The time had come--his time, the time to claim Dunraven as his own. Behind him was spread a haphazard battalion of misfits, rebels, and goblins of low morals who would fight to their death for the riches and immortality promised by Gar.

Gar's nose rankled with the sweat, fear, and blood thirst that oozed from his followers, and he thrilled at the power he wielded with his promises. The warriors of Dunraven had not lifted their weapons in battle for many years. He had no doubt that his band of rabble could lay them into their graves with nary a bother. Look how easily he'd dispatched their sentries.

Keeping a tight rein on the horses, the goblins approached from the north. Up the incline of land that gave way to the valley of Dunraven below. He had but a moment to spare at the crest of the hill.

Look at them. He sneered at the faeries moving about the main cluster of trees, obviously the hub of Dunraven's population. *What a feeble attempt they make at war. Like children, they scatter and scurry, while I wait to mash them into the dust.*

Frustration from years of denial of what belonged to him gave strength to his mighty roar of rage. Thrusting his sword into the air in an age-old gesture of battle, he reveled in the sound of his fellow goblins breaking into a melee of snorting, shrieking, and howling, as they rushed down the hill in a wave.

~ * ~

Dunraven rang with the goblin's battle cry--a cry that pierced the very hearts of those who heard and understood its meaning. Krickall reacted to the cry without thought, as instincts became the drive that sent him scrambling to bring a semblance of order. Krickall's answering warrior's cry carried to all reaches of the land, though only those faeries close enough to fight would be any help in this battle.

His cry put into motion a series of pre-planned procedures. With only a minute or two before the goblins were upon them, it was imperative to act fast. The younger faeries scrambled to the main tree, while the female faeries grabbed any food within reach as they also raced for the main tree. Fortifications had been undertaken to strengthen the area of Dunraven immediately surrounding the main tree, with the thought that protecting a smaller area would keep from stretching their battalion thin.

Krickall and the others, weapons constantly on hand in readiness for battle, ran toward the onslaught of goblins, formed their lines, and stood to face the invading army. Krickall spared only a brief thought for Analiese and hoped that she'd made it to safety.

Thundering hooves, feet pounding upon the earth, and the raucous battle cry of the goblins melded together to create an atmosphere of chaos. Hearts pounded and lips moved in silent prayer, as the faeries stood to defend themselves and their lands. It seemed a foolhardy proposition with a gaggle of featherweight pixies, untried warrior faeries, peaceful pillywiggins, and various other faeries standing against the invading goblins that slobbered with inbred rage and fierceness, yet Krickall would bet on the hearts and souls of the faeries who now stood to defend their way of life.

The moment of furious confrontation raised a cloud of dust that blasted skyward only to settle back onto the opposing forces as they clashed together. Many were sent across death's threshold instantly. Fiercely swinging swords, clubs, axes, knives and even hammers, were wielded by some of expert ability, as well as those of middling skill. Equal in numbers, the goblins had the advantage by virtue of their fierce nature and the fact that about half of them fought from horseback.

Krickall expectations were high and his strategy had been honed over years of training. The force of his raw power alone was enough to evoke belief in the others fighting by his side. The faerie fought for their home and way of life and Krickall had done his best to prepare them beforehand for what to expect. That alone helped the faeries manage to push the goblins back ever so slightly. Their hope was to drive them west toward prepared traps and hidden pits. If they could push the goblins to the dangerous area, a portion of the goblin forces would be eliminated and would give a more even balance. Slowly, harshly, the faeries pushed the goblins west. The battlefield became slippery with life's blood as faeries and goblins alike fell in the final wretchedness of battle. Krickall, never one for praying, sent words to the ancient gods to protect them and give them the final advantage. His prayers were ignored.

He watched as gentle-hearted drakes, impish pixies, and staunch brownies fell under the blade of the goblins. Used to the walls that guarded the emotions of his warrior heart, Krickall nearly broke as overwhelming emotion battered him and left him weak at the sight of unrelenting blood and useless death.

Wrapped thusly in battle, Gar's absence had not been noted by Krickall until a sudden change in the atmosphere alerted him. Slowly, the faeries lowered their weapons one at a time. Frustrated that they would give up, Krickall hollered at them, but the battle-worn faeries stood mutely with their weapons in hand and looked about as if uncertain what to do. Eerie silence fell in the wake of the furious battle.

With a snarl, Krickall turned to see what phenomenon had the ability to draw the attention of an entire battlefield. The sight that greeted him sent his already battered heart into a spin of agony. His primal screech of fury and frustration rang over the land. Filled with vitality of a long line of protectors of the faerie realm, the yell vibrated deep inside every soul standing upon the field of confrontation. From within Krickall, previously unexplored and unknown tendrils of ancient abilities threaded their way to the surface. His piercing gaze came to rest on the main tree of Dunraven.

Arrogant and triumphant, the leader of the goblins had found the one thing that would cause Krickall to lay down arms and call for surrender. Gar held Analiese's slender throat within his hoary fingers--the tip of his sword pressed against her life vein. Tendrils of finely spun blond hair drifted in contrast over the scaly fingers of the goblin. Her eyes, not long ago alight with laughter at Krickall's words of jest, now pinned Krickall with their fear.

Without thought, without hesitation, Krickall lay down his steadfast sword and, with a slice of his hand through the air, commanded the rest of the faeries to throw their weapons to the ground in a final act of surrender. They did. Gar's eyes gleamed with the cold wave of triumph, as he ran his hand over Analiese's fine shoulders and down her arms to span her waist.

Krickall growled in protest and tensed to leap to her defense. He knew he'd be dead before he could reach her but his instincts demanded action. Before he was able to make any move to save his love, pain exploded from his head as he was clubbed by something hard. Spots circled within the blackness of his mind, while his senses rang with the bitter taste of defeat and fear for Analiese.

~ * ~

Gar watched the great warrior fall to his knees, and not a moment too soon. For a brief span of a moment, power had oozed from the warrior's eyes that caused Gar to doubt if the battle for Dunraven had really been won. Gar had been pinned in place by the piercing gaze, and the ground beneath his feet trembled as if a creature awakened from a long sleep.

When the warrior hit the ground, Gar breathed in relief, and then, angered by his own fear, he slapped the faerie woman. With a cry of pain, she fell to her knees, and Gar took the opportunity to kick her. Only when dust marred her hair, grass stains covered her clothes, and blood dripped from her lip, did he feel in control.

Once the warrior had been tied and thrown at his feet, Gar allowed himself to survey the domain of Dunraven. As the outcome of battle had become clear, many of the faeries had melded into the surrounding forest, the remaining ones stood transfixed among the bloody aftermath of the battle. Faerie and goblin had lost their lives that day. Gar cared little. His thoughts were of ruling the land of faerie and beyond, into the world of man, as Navarre had promised. As Dunraven now rested within his power, his next desire was to see the look on Adoneesis' face as the dethroned king realized that his precious home had been overrun.

Sixteen

Adoneesis faced the rising of the sun in the east. Restless and discontent, he waited for the females to waken. The woman, Bryanna, hadn't stirred since Bronwen had placed a sleeping spell on her. Adoneesis didn't understand his abruptness in dealing with the flame-haired female, but Bronwen proclaimed Adoneesis would regret his hasty actions that had forced her into placing the spell.

A sound drew his attention, but it was only the hissing of a dying fire that had burned all night to deter predators. Adoneesis shivered as he remembered his recent battle with the muckraker. A moan interrupted his thoughts and he looked over at the sleeping woman, her hair flaming even in the subdued light of the early morn. The pale raspberry colored blanket rose gently with each breath she took--her chest rising and nostrils flaring ever so softly. Adoneesis yearned for an unknown fulfillment.

Even in the dream state achieved when he'd first spied the woman at the place where humans buried their dead, he'd felt the tug at his senses. Then, when he'd seen her standing amongst the books of the ugly human dwelling, the tug had blown into a raging boil of blood. That was his excuse for acting without thought to the sensibilities of the woman. In the confined walls of the small place of books where they'd found her, her eyes had burned into him, made him feel inadequate, made him act irrationally to quell the uncontrollable base urges that had confused and weakened him. After all, he was of the bloodlines of kings, so he shouldn't be overcome by the mere presence of a female. She was the one at fault for enticing him with her beguiling smile.

Realizing the course of his thoughts, Adoneesis kicked the dirt with the toe of his soft leather boot and cursed himself for such arrogance. Visions of Raegar flitted into his mind. Vivid memories of his father beating what he considered a worthless servant, or slaking his lust on the unwilling recipient of some unfortunate female who happened to cross his path. Of course, Raegar had never taken responsibility for his action, always claiming that he'd been pushed too far by incompetence, or deliberately teased until overcome with sexual frustration.

His illustrious father always had a reason.

Adoneesis would not follow the rule of his father.

Therefore, he owed the woman an apology. The weakness had been his, not hers.

A light touch upon his arm jolted him from his self-effacing thoughts. Bronwen's warm voice poured over him, cleansing him, and offering support.

"I sense your struggle, and I also feel that you are harsher with yourself than need be."

"I am as hard on myself as necessary. Lives depend on me. Fangs, the very realm of faerie depends on me. I have not the option of mistakes."

"Oh, I see the arrogance of Raegar creeping into your words."

Adoneesis flushed. Arrogance. Yes, he'd only just accused himself of the same sin, yet he had seen no arrogance in the words spoken to Bronwen. Was that how it started? The slide downward to a level where the very meaning behind your own words blurred. The bloody face of a dying faerie beaten for stealing the king's stag crept into his mind. No. He would never do such. Of that, he was sure.

"You do not understand, prophetess."

He threw the words at her, quickly to realize he'd addressed her formally, as well as arrogantly. She had been right. Raegar's character ran strong within his veins, and it sickened him. He raised his hands in supplication. "Please, forgive me. As ever, you are right. My father has left his mark on me, and I struggle daily with his traits."

"Bah. Your father runs strong within you, yes, but not in the way you imagine. I must beg your forgiveness, as I spoke in haste. I should have realized it was not arrogance that colored your words, but fear." She waved her hand at him. "You must understand, Adoneesis, echoes of bloodlines run in your veins steeped with justice and honor. You could no sooner perpetrate an intentional wrong against someone than you could summon the souls of the ancient ones of the flooded lands. You are only trying to deal with the responsibility that rests heavily on your shoulders. Do not be too harsh on yourself."

Bronwen's words confused him. Honor and justice were not attributes his father had possessed. "You obviously did not know my father well. He was cruel and harsh, with no respect for any save himself."

His words may as well of been ones spoken of disaster and death, such was the effect they had on Bronwen. Her face drained of color and her eyes filled with pain. Before he could ask her what was wrong, a moan drifted to them from across the fire. Their eyes connected and Bronwen gestured with a wave of her hand.

"Go. You need to undo the damage you have done with your earlier harshness. Bryanna must learn to trust you or all will fail. This I know. This I say."

"I had no choice. We could not chance her raising an alarm."

"Adoneesis." Bronwen brushed her fingers gently across his face. "There are always choices. The hard part in life is making the right one."

Her touch soothed, at the same time evoking conflicts of unknown emotions within. For a sliver of a moment, Adoneesis felt as if he were somewhere else and another woman, much like Bronwen, brushed his face with her fingers. Pain and desperation etched deep within the face of the woman, but before Adoneesis was able to grasp the memory, it vanished. He frowned.

"Not now, Adoneesis. The time for questions is later."

"There is much more to you than I know, is there not?"

"Yes, but at the moment, you have a captive woman to placate." Bronwen inclined her head toward Bryanna.

Adoneesis took one look and cursed. Hair askew and confusion from Bronwen's sleeping spell still evident in her eyes, the woman named Bryanna had wakened enough to sit up and was presently surveying her surroundings. She had the hand-woven sleeping blanket wrapped around her and clutched under her chin as if seeking some semblance of protection.

She struggled to fully waken and Adoneesis prepared himself for the battle ahead. The woman's eyes held strength, and when they connected with his, it was as if the earth raged with fire. Heat raced through Adoneesis. Like a doe caught in the light of a hunter's torch, the woman froze, her eyes round with fear, yet etched with the wariness of one who would fight to survive. That aspect of her character pleased Adoneesis, as she would need the will to survive to carry her through whatever lay ahead. The realm of faerie rested on her shoulders and it was his place to make her understand the importance of that.

He frowned. How could he make her understand something that he didn't understand? Tomorrow wavered in a mist of mystery. Doom crept over the land in a cloying cloud of darkness that gave nothing tangible for Adoneesis to grasp. If Bronwen had knowledge of events to come and how to save the dying realm, she gave as little as the darkness. Fangs, he had no idea what to do and frustration ate at his insides until his blood boiled at the injustice. His land and people depended on him and he depended on the fragile human woman who trembled before him.

In one stride of anger, he found himself by her side. She quivered with fear, yet gave not even an inch as he advanced on her. He dropped to one knee and grasped her arm, while she stared him down, and Adoneesis became aware of the sliver of heat that rose from his groin. She must have seen something in his eyes, because she spoke to him as regal and cool as the first breeze of fall.

"If you try to rape me, I'll kill you."

Adoneesis let go as if scalded. Shame filled him, and then anger. Anger at himself. Why did he measure each action of his life by his father's life? He was nothing like Raegar; he would be nothing like Raegar if he died trying.

"I would not bother myself with the rape of a human. You hold no appeal for me." But she did. Oh, how she made him yearn to gather her in his arms and find a meadow of wildflowers in which to lay her. He ached to cleave to her amidst the splendor of nature's beauty. Abruptly, he stood and paced the already trodden grass of the clearing where they'd made camp. Rubbing his hand over his stubbled chin, he glanced at her every few seconds and tried to decide how to handle the volatile situation. Should he tell her everything and let her judge for herself, or should he let her believe she still resided in her own world? Piece by piece, rather than all at once, the truth may be easier for her to handle.

A hoof thumping on dirt belayed Adoneesis' need for a decision, as he and the woman turned to the insistent stamping sound. On the horizon, the morning sun had finally risen above the ragged line of the land, brought warmth and spurred the daily ritual of nature. Sparkling dew, the fresh crispness of a new day, shadows retreating into the forests, all became lost in the ethereal beauty of the creature prancing in the distance.

From the forest's foliage stepped the unicorn--graceful in her beauty, immortal to her soul. Rays from the sun reflected off her pearlescent hide and created an aura of otherworldly light about her body. In a gesture of impatience, she threw her head about, snorted and stamped. Nostrils quivered. Sinew and muscle trembled. Long, silken strands of mane floated in the air and drifted back to her neck.

Bryanna gasped and rose. The tip of her tongue darted out from between her lips and brushed across her lips as she took a step toward the unicorn. Adoneesis made a move to stop her, but a look from Bronwen quelled him.

"No, let her go. As Merlin said, the unicorn is a gift from the Lady. They must make their own path."

So he waited and watched. He watched as the flame-haired beauty stepped around the embers of the almost dead fire, almost tripped over a rock jutting from the ground, and walked barefoot onto the dew-dampened blanket of grass that surrounded their camp. He watched her stare at the mythical creature she must have read about in human books of legends and her face light up with wonder and disbelief. What he couldn't do was stand and watch as the unicorn reared high, hooves striking mightily on the ground as she returned to all fours, and then race directly at the fragile human woman.

~ * ~

Bryanna had awakened with a pounding headache and only a glimmering memory of what had transpired at the bookstore. A wary survey of her surroundings didn't give her much hope that help would be arriving soon. Wrapped in a woolen blanket of faded raspberry, she was laying in the middle of a clearing that was thickly bordered by forest. Moaning, she attempted to sit, only to find herself face to face with the man who looked like Aragorn. Her kidnapper. The man who set her heart to pounding in her chest. The woman, Bronwen, had said his name just before Bryanna had lost consciousness. Adoneesis. What a strangely exotic name.

A tug of attraction pulled at Bryanna, and she silently cursed her wayward emotions. It was wrong to feel a physical attraction to someone who would drug and drag you to the middle of some godforsaken wilderness. Not only that, but he sat across the fire from her and his gaze pinned her in place and held barely subdued flaming desire.

"If you try to rape me, I'll kill you." She said the words, even though she doubted their meaning. If he touched her, she'd melt, and such whimpering folly disgusted her. If he came near her, she should be ready to fight him off with everything that was in her. The man had kidnapped her for God's sake.

"I would not bother myself with the rape a human. You hold no appeal for me."

Oh, how those words stung. Bryanna felt shame for the rampant sexual visions racing in her mind, and took a deep shuddering breath to control her errant emotions. Warily, she watched him pace and throw a disgruntled look her direction every few seconds. Just as she couldn't stand the silence, a sound distracted her.

At first, a brief flash of light overwhelmed her, but she recovered, only to be astounded by the beauty of the creature that appeared on the edge of the forest. Never in her life had she seen such a beautiful horse. Built delicately like an Arabian, the white horse had a larger stature and broader chest than the desert breed of horse, more like one of the rare Andalusian breed. With a tail that brushed its delicate tips along the ground and a mane that swung in long strands of silk, the animal tossed her head and stamped her hoof impatiently. It was then that Bryanna noticed the one major difference between that horse and any she'd ever seen.

Upon the tossing head of the gleaming horse rested the golden spiral of a horn.

A unicorn?

Entranced, yet confused, Bryanna rose and stepped toward the mythical creature. Logic mingled with childhood dreams and imaginings as she raised her hand in a gesture of greeting. Her head thrummed with a voice that she couldn't decipher. So she moved closer to the rearing creature. Fear held no place in her heart. Somehow, she knew the animal would never harm her.

As intense as her desire for the man who kidnapped her rang the singing in her heart for the white unicorn. For a moment, she was no longer a bookstore owner, a young, single woman leading a monotonous life. Suddenly, she was a queen; a regent devoted to the preservation of magic and the protection of all that was good. Voices rang inside her that she tried to decipher, and ancient rhymes whispered their words.

The moment passed, the voices faded, and she was only barely aware that a shift of energy had happened within. Feeling herself again, she faced the unicorn galloping straight at her. A brief flicker of fear touched her heart, but a soothing murmur within her mind bade her to stand fast.

Closer the unicorn raced, hooves pounded upon the ground and nostrils flared with each breath. Suddenly, everything went haywire. Bryanna was grabbed from behind and pulled close into the steely arms of Adoneesis and the unicorn screeched a cry that pierced the ears of everyone within hearing distance. Bryanna felt the warmth of Adoneesis' body close behind her, as well as the coiled strength emanating from his body. The approaching unicorn sent any other thoughts from her mind.

"*Stop.*"

One single word imbued with magical intent stopped the galloping unicorn. Grudgingly, the creature stopped with horn tip placed dangerously close to Adoneesis' throat.

"Adoneesis, very slowly let go of Bryanna," Bronwen bid quietly. "The unicorn thinks you are threatening her."

"Funny, that's what I thought the unicorn was doing."

"I know, but she is protecting the woman, as is her duty."

Adoneesis released Bryanna, and stepped back.

With floating grace, the creature reared high and stamped to the ground inches from Bryanna. Bryanna's kidnappers became lost in a mist, as the bluest eyes of ice she'd ever seen burned into her. Still unbelieving, she searched for the golden horn that nestled beneath the flowing forelock of the horse. Hesitantly, she reached out to brush aside the cream-colored hair, her action revealing a sight that filled her with wonder.

The horn was real, which meant she was touching a unicorn. The unicorn lowered her head and allowed Bryanna to explore the horn further. As soft as the unicorn's hide, hard was her horn. About ten to twelve inches long, the horn was thick at the base where it melded with forehead and then traced a spiral all the way to the tip. Bryanna looked closely and could have sworn she saw strange carvings on the horn, but before she could explore further, the unicorn shook her mane and covered the horn with thick strands of creamy mane.

A strong urge pulled at Bryanna, until she found herself laying a hand on either side of the unicorn's neck. Strength flowed through her veins and she rested her forehead against a muscled neck. Comfort, understanding, and knowledge seeped into her. But that wasn't all. Visions assaulted her. At first, they were visions of a young unicorn playing in meadows and galloping in full abandon among a herd of unicorns. Joy and contentment filled the days of the young creature. Just as quickly, the visions darkened with blood and terror until pain overwhelmed Bryanna. She lived the unicorn's pain and watched the slaughter of others like her for nothing more than a trophy.

She lived the horror, experienced the fear of a young unicorn until she whimpered and slid to her knees. The velvety touch of a muzzle touched her cheek and the pain was gone, but the visions and knowledge remained. A name whispered in her mind. Not spoken a loud, but a part of her. Inherent in her soul. The name of the unicorn.

As if to protect her, the unicorn took a step between her and the others, allowed her the chance to stand up and face the two who had kidnapped her and brought her to this strange place. Confused, she faced the man and the old woman. For the first time, she noticed the minor characteristics that marked them as different from her. Adoneesis had pointed ears and eyes that slanted ever so slightly upward at the outside corner. His physique was that of a man, yet everything was a fraction out of kilter. His arms too long, his shoulders too broad, his hands too large.

Bronwen possessed pointy ears as well, but she wasn't nearly as attractive as the man. Short and shriveled, she also had misshapen, arthritic looking hands. Upon closer inspection,

Bryanna noticed that her hands looked like claws. She gasped and looked up at the woman's face. For a flicker of a moment, as if in a reflection in a mirror, the woman appeared to be tall, golden, and beautiful. Bryanna blinked and was once again looking into the intelligent eyes of an ugly hag. There were no other words to describe her, and Bryanna felt a stab of pity, and then remembered that these two kidnapped her and brought her to this strange place.

Fighting the effects of her visions, Bryanna took a deep breath and wondered if she'd somehow fallen in to the rabbit hole of Wonderland. All of Bryanna's life, her aunt had told her that there was more to life than meets the eye. Late at night, she'd whispered tales of lands that existed even beyond the imagination, and gave warnings of not believing such. Bryanna now knew that her aunt had been preparing her for this moment. The deathbed letter enforced that belief. Bryanna always knew she'd been different; she'd just never been willing to accept that. In fact, she'd spent her whole life fighting such a notion--for all the good it had done. Here she was in a land that defied description, with people who didn't fit the mold. Acceptance that things were not what she knew grew within, just as total acceptance of her bond with the unicorn became fact.

This realization of being taken from her familiar world and brought to this strange but beautiful land sent shivers of fear stabbing through Bryanna, but she warned herself not to show weakness. She must remain strong until she found out her purpose here and what these two planned for her. Locking her gaze on her kidnappers, she demanded, "Who are you? Where am I? What do you want with me?"

The unicorn nudged Bryanna's arm and snuffled. Bryanna didn't know how, but she understood that it was a warning to hold her temper and listen. Jeez, could this day get any stranger?

"Speak, Adoneesis. It is your place," the old woman urged.

He frowned and contemplated Bryanna with a cutting gaze. "I do not think she should be told yet. She is merely a human and could not handle the truth."

Human. Each confirmation of her suspicions only managed to make Bryanna's heart pound more fiercely.

"She is stronger than you think and the blood of the ancients runs through her veins. Do not forget that. Never forget that."

Adoneesis considered Bryanna and she pulled herself to her full height as if that would prove she was worthy of the truth. Something about Bronwen's words evoked a moment of panic. *Ancient blood running through her veins?* Bryanna had no idea what that meant, but she was sure it would open doors that could never be closed. In a flash of distant memory, the words 'ancient blood' prodded her mind until she remembered where she'd heard the term. In her aunt's letter. *Within you runs the blood of ancient ones, and you hold a power that will shape worlds and change lives.*

Bryanna shivered. It was comforting to know that maybe her aunt hadn't been crazy, and Bryanna felt the ache of a life wasted in constant arguments and battles of will. Her relationship with her aunt could have been so different. The fact that it had been distant and fraught with disagreements was Bryanna's fault. She owed it to her aunt to at least try and accept this strange place, with its verdant green grasses, cerulean blue skies, and vivid colors of nature. This place that boasted of colors so crisp they seemed unreal, and throbbed with an eerie, yet exhilarating, strangeness drifting across the land.

Bryanna felt an unfamiliar feeling of connection to the land--a feeling that stimulated a sense of inner power. Combine that with the unicorn and her slightly off-kilter kidnappers, Bryanna knew. Just as assuredly as she'd always been a non-believer, she was now a believer.

Feeling the aching loss of her aunt all over, Bryanna whispered, "Aunt Shirley, I'm so sorry. I'll make it right somehow, I promise." Tears of sorrow and shame fell to the ground and the unicorn shifted uncomfortably--her hooves stamping lightly on the hard packed ground.

Angry with herself and frustrated with Adoneesis' male arrogance, she demanded, "Would you please stop arguing and tell me what is going on here? I have a right to know."

Walnut colored eyes fixed on her, weighed and considered her, as if she were some specimen to dissect. How dare he? First, he kidnaped her, right out of her own store and then he brought her to this strange place and treated her as if he wished he'd never seen her in the first place. She wasn't about to turn into a quivering mass of female fear in the face of danger.

A gentle nudge from a warm nose distracted her from the anger growing inside. The unicorn raised her head and eyes of liquid blue gleamed into her soul. Silent words spoken and understood. Bryanna smiled. The unicorn was on her side, and Bryanna understood that was no small feat. Holding the advantage over the imperious arrogance of the dark-haired, bronzed kidnapper, Bryanna offered the courtesy of a smile. Albeit a smug smile.

"Shadow Dancer thinks you should tell me everything. She says I'm quite capable of understanding, and that you should stop being such a narrow-minded cretin. Her words, not mine," Bryanna haughtily declared.

Her words had the effect of the dropping of an atomic bomb. The long, silent pause as her words hit target and then an explosion of curses from Adoneesis, along with a burst of laughter from Bronwen. Bryanna calmly draped her arm over

Shadow Dancer's neck and waited for the confusion to die down.

Adoneesis was about to say something else, but the old woman quieted him with a wave of her hand. Her gaze touched lovingly on the unicorn. "Shadow Dancer. Yes, sadly that name suits her. A creature born in the light, yet forced to live her life in the shadows."

Remembered pain shot through Bryanna, and a sob escaped her lips. "Yes," she whispered. "She watched the slaughter from the shadows, where her mother hid her. That's how she survived."

"You know of the slaughter?" Bronwen seemed surprised.

"Yes, Shadow Dancer showed me."

"How can this be? None of this makes sense. How can this human know of such things? Even I have not heard the true story of the slaughter of the unicorns." Adoneesis waved at Bryanna in disdain.

"Calm yourself, Adoneesis. Remember who we are dealing with and what Merlin said about the woman and the unicorn."

Merlin? Bryanna frowned, but Bronwen cut her impending question short.

"We have yet to break our fast and I am hungry. Let us decide what is to be done later." Bronwen made her way to her saddlebags, where she pulled out a sack of cloth.

With an affectionate pat on Shadow Dancer's forelock, Bryanna went and sat on the ground by Bronwen. Of course, she gave in to the need to stick her tongue out at Adoneesis as she walked past him. His snort of derision followed her, but she didn't care. The unicorn was on her side.

Sitting on her still unfolded blanket, Bryanna tried for a semblance of normalcy. "You have an unusual name." At Bronwen's questioning look, Bryanna elaborated. "I heard Adoneesis call you by name, just before I passed out. Though, I suppose your name may not be so unusual here--wherever here is."

Bronwen scooped some nuts and raisins on top of some oatmeal she had boiled and handed to bowl to Bryanna, who accepted it gratefully.

"So you realize that we are not in your world."

"It's hard not to realize." She breathed deeply of the air. "Everything here is like home, yet so unlike home. The air is sweeter, colors more vivid, and sounds are familiar, but somehow different. Combine that with how the two of you look, the unicorn, and the fact that Adoneesis referred to me as human, well, I'd have to be dense not to know something's up."

"You can accept all this without doubt?"

"Let's just say that my aunt was kind of unusual, so I've come to expect the unusual." A shaft of pain shot through Bryanna's heart. She so wished her aunt was here, because as brave a front as she presented to her kidnappers, she was scared. Adoneesis glaring at her from across the camp did nothing to ease her nerves. Why was he so ticked with her anyway? She was the one who'd been kidnapped and brought to this place.

"Yes, your aunt understood your destiny and she did her best to prepare you."

"How do you know anything about my aunt?"

Rather than answer, Bronwen motioned Adoneesis to join them, which he did reluctantly. Stealthy, silent, he moved across the grass to sit by Bronwen who gave him an affectionate smile.

"It is for Adoneesis to explain more to you. Your destinies are entwined; your bloodlines call for each other to help the realm of faerie"

"Realm of faerie... I don't... you aren't telling me that you guys are faeries." Bryanna choked on a raisin and found herself heartily slapped on the back. Giving Adoneesis the evil eye, she spat the offensive raisin onto the ground and tried to recover any semblance of composure that remained.

Before she could ask any questions, a rolling thunder sounded in the distance, and Shadow Dancer stamped her hooves restlessly. Adoneesis immediately stood, grabbed his sword from the ground, and drew the scabbard into place through his belt--his hand resting on the hilt. A light veil of mist drifted only inches above the ground and touched softly at their feet. Bronwen tensed, closed her eyes for a second, and then smiled. Slowly, she rose and wiped her hands on her cotton shirt.

"Do not worry, Adoneesis, no enemy approaches. Look, Shadow Dancer prances in anticipation, not fear."

It was true. Shadow Dancer was like a young filly, prancing and shaking the silken strands of her mane as if primping herself. A joyful whinny of greeting echoed through the thickening mist. Bryanna should have been afraid, but she trusted the unicorn, and for some reason, she trusted Bronwen.

On the other hand, Adoneesis stood ready for battle. Nostrils flared, hawk-like eyes piercing the mist, and muscles quivering with bare restraint, he presented a vision of masculinity that threaded Bryanna with desire. In a flash of awareness, he turned his dark eyes to her and the ensuing jolt of craving shook them both. Need crept into his eyes only to be replaced with distrust and anger. What Bryanna didn't know was if the anger was for her, or himself.

~ * ~

Adoneesis locked his gaze with that of the woman, and the heat that filled his limbs almost melted him. It took all that was in him to stand fast and true. He could not let the beguiling blue eyes of a human woman sway him, especially when his land and people lay in danger. He felt useless battling against a threat from an unknown source, and it angered him that this woman held the key to the salvation of the realm of faerie. He was the king, for fang's sake, it was for him to protect the realm of faerie, not this mere slip of a human.

An image of her standing against the stampeding unicorn slithered into his subconscious, and memories of flame hair wafting across her face assaulted him, as she demanded answers. He begrudgingly admitted her bravery, but nothing would convince him that the salvation of faeries rested with her, even if she could talk to the unicorn.

"Then you would be greatly mistaken." The words came to him on an ethereal tendril of mist. He looked for the speaker, but saw only a shimmering glow of iridescent light and then experienced a mellow taste of harmony with his surroundings. Before laying his eyes on the cloaked figure, he knew who their visitor was.

"Merlin."

His whispered statement drew Bronwen's attention, although Bryanna would not have heard. Bronwen smiled and said, "Ah, I see you have touched your own chord of natural abilities."

He snapped at her, "I have no natural abilities. I merely remember the same events occurring when he appeared to us at the sacred moon tree." Her words angered him. He was aware of her watching him at times, expecting more from him than he knew how to give. What did she want from him? Why did he feel the need to ask questions to which he didn't want answers? Yes, he felt the power grow within him at times, and except for the smallest acts of magic, he pushed the power away. He was always afraid that the anger would become the largest part of him and he wouldn't be strong enough to hold back.

Further thoughts were pushed aside at the appearance of the Merlin. The reunion between he and Shadow Dancer was heartfelt and Adoneesis sent a fond look toward Brachus.

"Who is that?" Bryanna questioned. She looked jealous at the attention her newfound friend was giving to Merlin, so Adoneesis thought to tease her.

"Him. Oh, he is Shadow Dancer's owner. He must be here to take her back home with him."

Bryanna's eyes widened, and then filled with disdain. "You idiot, you can't own a unicorn, any more than you can claim ownership of that beautiful creature you ride. No, Shadow Dancer gives love to him because he allows her to be free."

Bronwen's chuckle lifted over their heads and filtered into the now disappearing mist. "She learns quickly, does she not? It only took you your lifetime to realize that Brachus doesn't belong to you. Even then, Merlin had to point the truth out to you."

Adoneesis flushed. He wasn't used to being laughed at or feeling so unsettled with his emotions. He overcompensated by becoming gruff and short-tempered.

"Well, if I had blood of the ancient Gods running through my veins, I'd have her abilities as well."

"You would be surprised at what runs deep within you." Bronwen pinned him in place with a mere flick of her eyebrows. Adoneesis entire body bubbled with unruly energy and heightened sensitivity, until it was more than he could handle. It was as if his body, a mere shell of flesh and bone, was not enough to hold in everything that he was. Desperate, he searched Bronwen's face for an answer, but she broke contact with a mere wave of her finger.

"Bronwen," Merlin warned. "Time runs short. The truth shall out."

A shimmer of tears glittered in her eyes, and she bowed her head to Merlin. "You are right, but I need more time."

"Do not take too long, Bronwen," Merlin warned. "I..." His voice tapered off into a whisper, his gaze touched upon Bronwen's withered face, questioning, seeking, comprehending. In a single gesture of reverence and understanding, Merlin bent one knee to the ground and took her hand to his forehead. "I recognize the essence within you. I had no idea this had been done, my Lady."

"Please, Merlin, rise. You of all should not kneel before me. And I'm sure she would not expect such. I am merely a vessel, while you are so much more."

Merlin rose, clasping Bronwen's hands within his own. "Only the Tuatha could do such, and only with the help of the Lady. The situation is worse than I thought, if she was willing to go to such lengths."

Such cryptic talk worried Adoneesis, but he felt humbled by the presence of Merlin, and even though he had a dawning awareness of the impossible feat to which they referred, he did not feel it his place to speak.

"There will be time for answers to all your questions, Adoneesis," Merlin reassured. "First, introduce me to your friend."

Bryanna lifted her chin and exclaimed in a regal tone, "I've been drugged and taken from my own world, so I would hardly call anyone here friend--except for Shadow Dancer, of course." She rubbed the muzzle of the unicorn, who had returned to her side.

"Yes, it is as it should be. You two belong together, but I think I will miss her company." He held out his hand to Bryanna. "I am Merlin, and you are Bryanna."

"Merlin... I don't think... you can't mean..."

"Yes." His single word confirmed Bryanna's unasked question.

Bryanna's eyes grew wide and her eyes looked to Bronwen for assurance. A prick of disappointment stabbed Adoneesis, because he wanted to be the one she turned to for help. Fangs. He couldn't even offer comfort to a mere human female. Why had the Fates bothered cursing the world with his birth? His own mother had died on him and left him in the hands of a father who never felt him worthy of love. He'd never been proficient in anything while growing up. The one time he tried to show Raegar his ability to start a fire with no firestone, he'd been beaten. Now, he was useless against the danger that threatened the realm of faerie, and had to rely on this female to save his land and people.

Frustration ate at him and boiled inside until he felt the need to explode. He clenched his fists and pointed his narrowed gaze at Bryanna, as if she were the cause of all his problems. Before he was able to expel his anger, Merlin raised a finger.

"Adoneesis. Be calm. I am here to warn you of a certain danger." A deep sigh racked the magician's body and he gestured toward the dying fire. "A cup of calming tea would be most welcome." He settled his robes about him and perched on a blanket by the fire.

Bronwen measured herbs into a battered pot and set it upon the fire to boil and steep. Knowing nothing would be said until Merlin was ready, Adoneesis curbed his anxiety, unstrapped his sword from his belt, and sat upon the ground by Merlin. Bryanna stayed by the unicorn, caressed the silken mane and whispered gently in her ear.

Adoneesis watched them--another stab of jealousy pricking his senses. How had he not seen what was so clearly in front of his eyes? Brachus, his loyal steed. Always ready and willing to bear Adoneesis upon his back, loyal enough to fight with his very life to protect Adoneesis, obviously so much more than a mere horse. Adoneesis should have revered the creature that came to him so mysteriously in his youth, yet he'd taken him for granted. Now, the woman who held responsibility for the realm bonded with the unicorn so easily. Immediately appreciating the treasure offered; the loyalty exchanged unspoken. Bah! He didn't realize his word had been snorted aloud until Merlin spoke.

"King, you are young and have much to learn. Your path is not an easy one, and all that you have lived in your life is to make you strong for what lies ahead. Although you do not feel yourself to be worthy or strong enough, you are." Merlin ran a blue-veined hand over his white beard and scratched his chin, as if in contemplation. "I had not thought to make myself known again so soon, but something has happened. I have not deciphered the signs yet, but it is something of such magnitude to force the Lady's selfless act and stir the Tuatha into showing their presence after so long a time. I also sense a familiar power that has eluded my grasp, I thought him to be dead, but..." He threw a glance at Bronwen, his liquid amber eyes probing for her reaction.

"Yes, Bronwen. It is he," Merlin acknowledged her unasked question. "It seems Gar has the combined forces of a magician, as well as a human with special powers."

His words meant nothing to Adoneesis, but Bronwen gasped, her face turning white.

"Lir told me he still lived, but I had no idea... he would not help Gar, I am sure of it."

"Not willingly, it took a serious threat to make Lapis follow his bidding." Merlin's gaze fixed on Adoneesis.

Bronwen blanched and looked at Adoneesis. "If Gar has Lapis' help, then he knows our plans. He knows about Bryanna and that we are not at Dunraven."

Merlin shrugged. "I am afraid so."

"I don't know who this Lapis is, or why some implied threat against me should win his help. Yes." Adoneesis replied at Bronwen and Merlin's startled looks. "I understand more than just your spoken words. I want answers, and I want them now."

Seventeen

Out of breath and shaking with fright, Bailiwick flitted under an overhanging branch in time to avoid detection by the ugly goblin pacing the dining room and issuing orders. Thank the Lady that he knew every nook and cranny of the main tree. Faith, he probably knew the creases and crevices of every tree in Dunraven better than anyone. Now was not the time to gloat. Dunraven had fallen to that ugly brute lording his presence over the prisoners, and Bailiwick was the only one not in the clutches of the enemy.

Outside, the commotion of the goblins rousting the faeries rang loud and clear. Gar had issued the command to gather up all faeries within the lands of Dunraven and hold them hostage. Muffled by the thickness of the tree, Bailiwick was still not immune to the terror of the screams and the rancid smell of something burning.

A nervous giggle escaped, and he slapped his hand over his mouth afraid that someone may have heard him. He glanced around the room quickly, but no one was paying any attention to his hiding place above the door. Oh, what to do? What would the king do? But he wasn't king. How could he be expected know what to do? Wasn't that what he'd wished for, though? To be the savior of the faeries. To finally do something that would make everyone who'd teased him stand up and take notice of him.

"Ohhhhhhh." The small moan escaped his lips and he slapped his hand over the mouth again. Fangs, he wouldn't save anyone if he didn't shut up.

He needed to find out what the goblin leader was up to and then make plans. Yeah, that sounded like the right thing to do. Presently, Gar sat at the head of the table--feet propped unceremoniously on the wooden tabletop. Standing before him were Krickall, Analiese, Mayard, a couple of fierce looking, slobbering goblins, and an ugly looking human. Thrown into a corner by the fireplace, huddled· some prisoners. A messy looking male goblin, an attractive, female goblin, as well as another figure bound hand and foot and encased in chains with crystals for locks. The third figure, with his haggard features peeking out from behind aged beard, taunted the corners of Bailiwick's memory.

Bailiwick shook his head, but blamed fear for robbing him of his ability to remember the familiar faerie. Who wouldn't be scared? Bailiwick slapped himself in the forehead as realization hit him. Of course, Gar must be here to claim the throne that he probably considered his by right. He was the older of the two sons, which meant he should have inherited. But how could Gar know of his birthright? Raegar had kept his secret so well that Bailiwick had heard nary a whisper of another son. He knew only because of his bond with the crystal, but was sure it was a secret to everyone else.

Slipping off his perch, Bailiwick wriggled his butt backward an inch or two, wedged himself in tightly, and considered the situation. Dog's breath, wasn't this a predicament for King Adoneesis to return to. Oh. No. King Adoneesis and the prophetess would be returning here with the human. He must warn them. Frantically, he searched for a way out, but Gar's goblins where everywhere. He'd have to wait until the room cleared. Worried, Bailiwick turned his attention to Gar, all the while praying the goblin would hurry up and leave the dining room.

"I assume you are in charge here while your king is away."

Gar pointed a gnarly finger at Krickall, whose impassive features showed not a twitch of acknowledgement at the question. Gar narrowed his eyes and looked about to direct another question, but Mayard's strident voice filled the tension filled void.

"King Adoneesis has left us *both* in charge."

Mayard's gaze shifted sideways to Analiese, and Bailiwick could have sworn the scholar's chest puffed out two sizes larger. Unfortunately, since his gaze was elsewhere, Mayard was not prepared for the whip that lashed across his back and felled him to the ground to writhe in pain. Krickall moved like lightning. He grabbed the goblin that'd struck out and with his bicep around the greasy head of the creature, snapped his neck with a mere twist of arm. In a gesture of disdain, he tossed the dead body at Gar's feet.

Gar nodded to another goblin who gripped the whip in hand and a snapping lash rang out and cracked across Krickall's shoulders. With barely a moan, the large faerie stumbled, but didn't fall. Instead, muscles bulging and jaw clenched, he righted himself, to stand with shoulders squared and gaze directed at some point above Gar's head.

Bailiwick felt the whip as assuredly as if it had cut across his shoulders. He whimpered and debated showing himself as a distraction. But, no, what good would that do? He needed to warn the king, and to do that he had to hear Gar's plans and make his escape. Tingling with fear and the urge to flee, he made himself to stay put.

"Ah, a proud one." Gar snorted and slapped a gnarly hand to his thigh. "Won't do you any good to put on airs with me. The answer is that *I* am in charge. Dunraven is now mine, so forget about your weakling of a king and kneel down to welcome your new king."

A collective gasp sounded among the prisoners, while Gar's men nudged each other, slobbering in anticipation of giving punishment to anyone who disobeyed.

King. Humph, King Adoneesis would have something to say about that. Bailiwick puffed his chest indignantly and thought again about flying out to confront Gar. Before he could act, the room exploded in action.

"Eeeeiyah!" Krickall lunged at Gar, grasped the goblin's throat between his hands and squeezed. The two of them tumbled backward onto the floor and rolled about, kicking up a cloud of dust. It took five goblins to shake him loose. By that time, Gar's face had taken on a sickly gray hue and spittle oozed from the corner of his mouth.

Analiese and Mayard backed away from the ruckus--his arm protectively circling her shoulders. Upon closer inspection, Bailiwick could see that Mayard's knuckles were white as he attempted to prevent Analiese from racing to Krickall's side.

Hmmm, not hard to see that beauty cares for the beast, but does she care as much for the scholar? "It doesn't matter now, stupid pixie," Bailiwick muttered. "There are more important things to attend."

The confusion settled to reveal Gar kneeling on one knee and trying to regain his breath, but he'd been able to draw his sword and the lethal looking tip rested against Krickall's throat.

Silence dominated the room, broken only by the sound of a far off scream and a triumphant bellow of release. Bailiwick needed no imagination to know what was happening on the outside and he sent positive thoughts to the poor female hoping that purging herbs would get rid of any unwanted offspring. He shivered at the thought of goblins running free over Dunraven.

Gar's gasping breath had settled to an intermittent wheeze and his fierce gaze was pinned on Krickall. Previously silent, the fierce human took that moment to make himself known. Arrogantly, he felled Gar's hand as he was about to thrust his sword through Krickall.

"Stop. He might be useful to us. If Adoneesis has left him in charge, he must care somewhat for him. A more public death may serve us better in the future."

Gar obviously wanted to slice Krickall to shreds for daring to lay a hand on him, but a pointed glare from the human exerted some kind of control over Gar, who relented. *Interesting.* It seemed the goblin leader played puppet to a human. A fact worth telling the king. Bailiwick applauded himself for remaining as a scout and acquiring useful information.

"Take this creature and throw him in the dungeons with the rest of the prisoners." Gar waved his free hand toward the threesome huddled in the corner--his other hand still holding a steady blade to Krickall's throat. "The rats and spiders have been too long without company." He laughed, slowly moved his sword toward Analiese and dragged the tip from breast to abdomen--the light of greed and lust entering his eyes.

Leaning close, he sniffed her neck. "Mmm, you smell like sweet honey." He traced his slobbering lips over hers, and moved his hand to her breast, but never got that far. Instead, Analiese grabbed his lower lip with her teeth and bit hard. Gar's bellow and the crack of his hand across Analiese's face must have been heard over the entire land of Dunraven.

On the ground, Krickall writhed like a snake, but was too tightly bound to do much more. His muffled curses filtered through the dirty cloth that had been shoved into his mouth.

Gar laughed. "You like her. I saw you slobbering over her, too busy to protect the lands left in your care. No warrior of mine would live after such an act."

Even from his high perch, Bailiwick saw the stricken look of guilt cross Krickall's features and his struggles cease. A sly look of consideration lit Mayard's dark eyes. Oh, trouble brewed there, no doubt about it.

"Go. Get them all out of my sight. I'm hungry." He rubbed his hand over his stomach and then down to his groin. "Later, I'll fill my other hunger." His eyes fell to the prisoners in the corner and narrowed in speculation. "I want the female goblin tonight, along with this faerie bitch. I have a very large appetite." His lewd snigger triggered another round of laughter from his followers.

"Now lock the prisoners in the dungeon, and the females in whichever room was used by dear Adoneesis, then bring me food." He frowned as another scream and some kind of banging like swords on a drum filtered in from outside. "And shut them up. I can't think with all the noise. I need to plan a surprise for the return of the bastard."

"Ahem. Lord, if I may speak?"

The human spoke politely enough, but contempt shadowed his eyes. Bailiwick could plainly see the loathing, and was surprised Gar couldn't. Bailiwick took a closer look at the human who so subtly maneuvered the goblin leader. Was that the slightest bit of point at the tip of his ears? Too hard to tell, because the man kept his dark hair long.

"If you must." Gar sighed and impatiently tapped his fingers on the table.

"I suggest that you keep that one here for a minute." He pointed at Mayard, whose face lost all color.

"What for?" Gar demanded impatiently.

The human leaned forward and what followed was a whispered conference with much waving of hands.

"Fine," Gar growled, giving in to the human. "Take them all, but leave him here." He gestured at Mayard.

Bailiwick perked up. What could Gar want with Mayard? His question was answered quickly enough as the room cleared, leaving only Gar, the human, and Mayard.

"You like the female? The one who belongs to the red-haired giant."

"She does not belong to him," Mayard retorted quickly and then cowered as if expecting to be hit. When no blow was forthcoming, he dropped his arm and tugged the hem of his tunic down.

"Humph, you like her." He shoved his face into Mayard's and sneered. "Do you want to know what I'm going to do to her tonight?"

"I... no... I"

"I'll rut with her 'til she can't move. Standing, sitting, tied up, from behind. If you can think it, I'll do it. Her body is for my use. Tomorrow morning, she'll wish to be dead, but I won't let that happen. No, my loyal goblins would never forgive me." He nudged and winked at Mayard. "You know what I mean. And they won't be as nice to her as me."

Mayard's slender body shook with fear, and Bailiwick saw a darkening stain spread down his trouser legs. He'd peed himself. Jeesh.

The human laughed. "Yes, he will do as he's told. He doesn't have the nerve to do otherwise."

Gar snorted in agreement. "Hmmm, I could be talked out of using her in such a fashion."

Hope glittered in Mayard's eyes, but Bailiwick knew it was a trap. Gar had no conscience and wouldn't give without expecting much in return.

"I will give her to you and keep my goblins from her, if you help me. I need to know everything about Dunraven and Adoneesis." He spat as he said the king's name. "With your knowledge I can lay a trap for Adoneesis when he returns. If you don't help, I'll use that female as brutally as anyone I ever have, I'll make you watch, and then kill you slowly."

Mayard swallowed, his gaze darting about the room and looking for an answer, but there was no choice, not if he wanted to save Analiese. "I will do as you ask."

Bailiwick barely heard the whispered words, but when he did, his heart dropped to his feet. He didn't blame Mayard. He'd probably do the same thing, and at least Analiese was safe--for now, but Gar would not stick to his word for long. He'd get what he wanted from Mayard, and then take Analiese anyway.

Twitching with the need to get to Adoneesis, Bailiwick bit his lip and stayed in place until Gar and his goblins finally cleared the room. It took the course of the day, but finally, he was able to unfold himself from his crevice and creep his way out of the tree. He'd debated trying to get the crystal, but decided it to leave it in its hiding place. That way, if someone caught him, it would still be safe.

The sun was a golden haze brushing the treetops and darkness would not be long in coming, which suited Bailiwick fine, as his escape would be easier in the dark since he knew the land so much better than the goblins. Even if seen, he'd have the advantage. Peering out from the wide blades of meadow grass where he hid, he felt a familiar tug in his mind. The crystal? But how could the crystal call to him from its hiding place? That had never happened before. He'd always needed to hold the crystal in his hand to feel the connection. There it was again, a hum in his head. A beckoning. But Bailiwick felt led, not toward Adoneesis chambers, but toward the dungeon. The soft hum turned to a buzz, and then became a roar, until Bailiwick's stomach roiled and his head pounded. He needed to answer the call, or he'd die, he was sure.

Stumbling, trying to give thought to the presence of the enemy, he quickly found the entrance to the long unused dungeon. The dungeon had been built generations ago, in a time of upheaval only whispered about, but never spoken aloud. A time when the Sisterland of Avalon fell into unrelenting mists and disappeared, never to be seen again. Bailiwick had always wondered what circumstances would constitute the creation of such a place. Yet, he was in the midst of such a time now. He shook his head and peered down the long stairway. The roaring in his head seemed to have subsided enough for him to think clearly.

Long unused, the dungeon's purpose and presence had almost been forgotten by the faeries of Dunraven, until Raegar had opened its musty doors and refurbished the ancient bars of imprisonment. Bailiwick had never been into the dungeon, thank the Lady. He'd never brought the wrath of Raegar onto himself. Built deep under the roots of a tree, backed by the granite rock of a nearby hill, and enforced with bars of solid oak, the dungeon was impenetrable. Good thing too, because it made Bailiwick's task simpler, as there were no guards to sneak past. He was easily able to creep down the winding stair to the depths of a place he would not soon forget.

Whispers crept into his mind, but not the same as the ones that had led him here. These ones were a sad lament to days gone past. Bailiwick didn't want to hear the stories, yet they threaded through his mind like the crystal river waters through the valleys of Dunraven. It was the fault of that damned crystal. Ever since the day he'd touched its cool surface, he'd become a conduit for the emotions of those around him, both past and present. Down here, the pain was fresh, even though generations had passed, and the voices strong, though they lived no more. He shivered.

Overwhelmed, and about to leave this place, Bailiwick heard Krickall's unmistakable voice. His quiet words fell heavy on the muffled darkness of the dungeon, and Bailiwick was easily able to find the red-haired faerie.

Locked in the farthest cell, Krickall was deep in conversation with the figure that had prodded the corners of Bailiwick's memories earlier in the dining area. Bailiwick approached the locked bars and stood dumbfounded when he saw a white bearded figure suspended in some kind of contraption that held him off the ground. He thought he'd been quiet, but must have made a noise, because the figure turned his gaze to Bailiwick, who felt himself pinned by the bluest of blue.

"I see we have company. I hoped you would hear my call," White beard spoke.

Bailiwick frowned. That voice, so familiar. Suddenly, the light of realization struck him and his heart flipped in his chest. "Lapis. Oh, Lapis, we thought you were dead. Where have you been? What are you doing here? What is that *thing* you are strapped into?"

"You know each other?" Krickall's directed his question at Lapis.

"Yes, we were once friends, were we not, little one."

Bailiwick swooped up to the roof and down between the bars that gave wide berth for a pixie such as he. "Yes. Yes, we were friends. Oh, it is so good to see you." Bailiwick laughed in relief and came to rest on Krickall's knee.

Krickall grumbled, but couldn't do anything with his hands and feet bound. Only then did Bailiwick notice the third prisoner, a rather dirty goblin quivering on the floor beside Krickall. Bailiwick nudged Krickall, who groaned in pain.

"Watch it, little one, or I will give in kind when I am free."

"Sorry. Who is that? He looks like a goblin to me."

Lapis replied, "He is Gwepper, obviously a prisoner of Gar's as are we."

"Hmmm. Why would Gar imprison one of his own?"

"We know not. The creature will not confide in us."

"How do you know his name, if he won't talk to you?"

Bailiwick frowned at the goblin, who sat in the corner wringing his hands and muttering under his breath. The words rats, cats, and something about bats filtered through the stale dungeon air to make Bailiwick wonder about the strange creature's sanity.

"Gar spoke his name earlier, when he captured him and the female goblin together. It seems they were on the run from Gar."

A hacking cough accompanied Lapis' explanation and Bailiwick became instantly alert to the chortling sound deep in Lapis' chest. With a flutter of tiny wings, he flitted off Krickall's knee, flew high, and descended to a hovering stop above Lapis. He peered into the familiar blue eyes and pursed his lips. "Hmm, you look terrible."

Lapis harumphed. "That's what comes of being deprived of fresh air and freedom for untold years."

Bailiwick paled at the implication. "You mean, you've been Gar's prisoner all these years?" He touched a narrow finger to the ropes holding Lapis suspended and swallowed the lump in his throat. "Has he kept you like this all that time?"

"Yes, my petite pixie friend, he has."

Even Gwepper seemed disgusted at that thought. His snort resounded in the enclosed area, and his mutterings increased twofold. Bailiwick wondered about the goblin's story. There was a chance he may have useful information. Working up the nerve to approach the nervous goblin, Bailiwick nevertheless alighted on the dirt floor out of Gwepper's reach. It didn't seem to matter, as the goblin ignored his presence but focused instead on whispered words of revenge against Gar.

Krickall and Lapis eyed the situation warily, but neither was in any position to help, so Bailiwick proceeded cautiously in case Gwepper decided to lash out at him.

"Goblin, you don't sound very fond of Gar."

"Gritty, shitty, stupid Gar."

Gwepper raised his eyes long enough for Bailiwick to see the light of intelligence and glint of determination, and then he lowered them to the ground and continued his rant. Attempting another tact, Bailiwick said, "Who was the female goblin prisoner you were captured with?"

You would have thought the walls were caving in, the way Gwepper jumped to his feet and waved his arms. No more questions needed asking. Amidst spittle and fierce curses, the last few weeks of Gwepper's life poured out for all to hear. Finally spent, he deflated into a heap on the floor, his chest heaved, and his eyes dispensed tears of anguish. Not knowing what to do, Bailiwick turned a shocked face to Krickall and Lapis and shrugged his shoulders.

"It seems that the female you care about is in the same situation as the one I care about." Krickall spoke gently. "I would suggest we get Bailiwick to free us and go save them."

Gwepper raised his face and the light of hope was a wonder to behold. Bailiwick made haste untying the knotted rope that bound Gwepper to a metal ring attached to the wall. Finally, the goblin was free. Gone was the desperate, drooling goblin, as Gwepper puffed his chest, jumped to his feet, and stood looking ready to do battle. "Jeez and cheese, you'll help me? Yes, yes, oh, yes, we can save them." He ran to the oaken bars that held them prisoner and pushed with all his might. "No, no. Tits and bits, we're stuck." His shoulders drooped and he slumped to the ground.

Bailiwick's heart went out to the pathetic creature and he flew over to offer comfort. This time he was not afraid to light upon the goblin's shoulder and console him. "Do not worry; we have the greatest magician ever, right here in this prison with us. He will get you out of here."

"Oh, Bailiwick, do not hold your hopes too high. Remember, I have been imprisoned for many years and have not the abilities I used to. Besides, I am not the greatest magician ever. That would be my cousin, Merlin."

"Ohhh, Merlin is your cousin." Bailiwick's eyes rounded in wonder. "You are of even greater blood than I knew." He patted Gwepper on the shoulder. "We'll be fine now. Don't worry yourself."

"We won't be fine unless you free us," Krickall grunted.

It took a lengthy struggle by both Gwepper and Bailiwick to free Krickall from his bonds, which in turn freed Lapis. Finally, the ropes binding the magician were loose and Lapis set his feet upon the dirt. A brief glow of light filled the dark room, and the transformation that overtook Lapis was certainly a sight beyond even Bailiwick's imagination. Lank, gray beard suddenly appeared whiter and cleaner, while clothing suddenly didn't appear so dirty and ragged. For that brief instant of glowing light, Lapis appeared to engulf the entire cell, but in a blink of an eye, once again became the only slightly intimidating figure Bailiwick knew from days gone past.

With a sigh and a brief pat of his clothing, Lapis turned to his fellow prisoners and shrugged his shoulders. "Now what?"

Bailiwick remembered Lapis as a strong character, unafraid of conflict and willing to stake his life for what he believed. His seeming lack of motivation worried Bailiwick, but not as much as the weariness that muddled once twinkling blue eyes. He couldn't stand to see his onetime hero so passive. In a flurry of gossamer wings and with all the best intentions, he flew to Lapis, settled on his shoulder and hoped to rouse him out of his state of apathy.

The result was chaos.

With a roar, Lapis grabbed for Bailiwick and managed to catch him by the leg. The light of anger reflected in eyes that no longer held apathy, but fired with heat and distrust. Slowly, purposely, Lapis drew Bailiwick deeper into his grasp, all the while studying his face with a narrowed gaze.

"Tell me, little one, are you here at our enemy's behest."

"What. Such a suggestion is insulting." His shaky voice ruined the indignant effect he'd been trying for.

"Tell me the truth, or I shall turn you into a toad and then step on you."

Lapis' voice fell to a whisper, yet the surrounding tree vibrated and Bailiwick wondered if it was from fear or merely the power generated from the magician's voice. While Gwepper shivered in the corner, Krickall stepped forward and laid a hand on Lapis' arm in a gesture of restraint that went unnoticed by Lapis.

Bailiwick shivered and his brain flew in circles as he tried to understand what he'd done to upset the wizard. Lapis drew him to eye level and peered deep into his eyes. Dizzy with fear, Bailiwick took a deep breath, but could no more look away than he could have performed the magic that came so naturally to Lapis, not without the crystal anyway.

"Aha. I knew I sensed the power of the crystal upon you."

"You read my mind."

"Yes, now tell me about the crystal, and if I don't like what I hear..."

Bailiwick gulped. "I know about the crystal, but no one else does, I swear." These words seemed to soothe Lapis and his grip loosened. Relieved, Bailiwick thought it best to tell the entire story and not risk Lapis' anger again. "I found the crystal quite by chance, well, maybe not by chance..."

"Get on with it," Lapis growled.

"The main tree was deserted that day--the harvest festival it was. I returned for the king's overcoat, he'd forgotten it and a chill had set in." Seeing the look in Lapis' eyes, Bailiwick hastened to finish his story. "I found the clothing and was leaving the king's room, when my head started to buzz. Every time I tried to leave, the buzzing increased, almost as if calling me back into the room. The need to search the darkest corners of the tree overcame me until I became frantic. I had no idea what I was doing. After only a few minutes, I found a loose trimming of bark in the far corner, under the clothing box."

Remembering the awe he felt upon his first sight of the crystal, Bailiwick lowered his voice. "I pushed aside the bark and peered into the recesses. I saw the crystal. I was stunned with its beauty, but when I touched its surface, I was transported to a place unfamiliar to me. People screamed, fires and floods raged over the land..." Bailiwick's voice broke and his shoulders shook.

"There, there, little one. I believe you." Lapis patted his arm and comforted him. "The crystal called to you for a reason, but now I must reclaim my family's heritage."

"Lapis, this is interesting, but the longer we stay here the more chance of Gar finding out we're free," Krickall reasoned.

"Yes, we must go. But not without the crystal."

"Not without Ghilphar, farts and darts."

"I know, and I must free Analiese as well."

"You are right, young warrior, we must go." With a mere wave of hand, the bars disappeared and the stairs lit with a dim glow. Seeing the questioning looks on the eyes of those around him, he remarked, "It seems I have not lost all my abilities. Let us proceed."

Quietly, with maybe some magic of invisibility from Lapis, the foursome made their way to the main tree. Busy arranging sleeping places and food for twice as many as Dunraven usually held, Gar and his followers had left the main tree virtually unguarded, except for the two burly goblins at the door to King Adoneesis room. Grumbling about being left to guard a female, the two presented little enough of a challenge against the determination of a rogue goblin, the burliness of a red-haired faerie, and the burgeoning magic of a magician locked up for too long. The two drooling, dense, goblins stood no chance.

Krickall and Lapis dragged the two unconscious guards into the room and shut the door. The window shutter closed out any of the day's available light and it took a moment to adjust to the dimness. They heard a rustling and groaning at the far side of the room where Adoneesis' bed sat. Bailiwick raced to the bed, but was outrun by the goblin, which muttered curses and worked fiercely at loosening the bonds of the female goblin.

"But where's Analiese? I thought she would be here, too." Krickall's voice held a thread of fear when he realized that only Ghilphar lay imprisoned on the bed. Bailiwick was about to answer his question, but Lapis interrupted abruptly.

"We must get the crystal, or all is lost. Where is the crystal, little one?"

Bailiwick couldn't resist the direction of the intense blue eyes, or the gentle pull of the crystal that beckoned from the corner. He wanted to answer Krickall, because he knew how the warrior cared for Analiese, but first, he had to get the crystal for Lapis.

Everything happened at once.

One of the guards staggered to his feet at the same moment that the door flew open and crashed against the wall to reveal five goblins, weapons drawn. Gwepper grabbed the now free Ghilphar, while Lapis and Krickall turned to face the intruders. Unevenly matched in numbers, but not in heart and desperation, Krickall and Lapis fell into the pack of mindless creatures. Bailiwick was able to dump a pitcher of water on one of the goblins and turn him toward wall just as Gwepper charged the now wet guard. Throwing his body into the taller goblin, Gwepper sent him flying headfirst into the hard wood wall.

It took only one swipe of Krickall's fist and two guards fell to the ground in a stupor, while Lapis used some magic to put the remaining goblins to sleep. At least, Bailiwick assumed they'd been put to sleep. Before he was able to check, the sound of shouting echoed from outside and caused fear to slice into Bailiwick's heart.

"We have to go. Come on." With a fearful flutter of wings, he flew to the door and peered down the hallway. "It's clear, let's go."

"The crystal."

"Analiese."

The pounding of feet on the lower steps drowned out Lapis and Krickall's pleas. "There is not time. If we are captured, we'll be no good to anyone. Come on," Bailiwick pleaded desperately.

"Yes, the little one is right. We can come back another time."

Krickall's face mirrored Bailiwick's desperation, and for the first time ever, Bailiwick saw the sheen of tears in the giant's eyes.

Ghilphar and Gwepper raced to the door, where Gwepper placed a hand on Krickall's arm. "Bastardly, dastardly Gar will get his. I'll make sure. You and me, we come back another day."

Krickall was intelligent, even though Mayard enjoyed maligning that certain trait on occasion, and he knew he couldn't stand against the entire goblin mass and come out unscathed, which would leave Analiese in worse trouble. As long as he lived, he could come back to save her, but if he died, she would be left to the clutches of the goblin and his masses. With a nod of his head, Krickall followed the others down the back staircase. Above them, they heard the squeal of discovery as the goblins entered the king's rooms only to find their own comrades in a beaten state.

Bailiwick knew a shortcut and led the others as swiftly and quietly as possible around the back area of the main tree. A rustle of grass, a snuffed sneeze, and heavy breathing signaled their retreat, but there was no one close enough to hear. The further from the invasion, the easier Bailiwick's heart beat. They passed from the wildflower garden behind the main tree, and set their feet upon a dirt path the wound through the thickest part of Dunraven's forest. As far as Bailiwick was concerned, they were free and clear.

Until Krickall looked back.

His strangled gurgle stopped their retreat. Flying high, Bailiwick saw the cause of Krickall's bellow. Outside Mayard's tree, the flash of golden hair glinted in the falling sun. Analiese. And gripping her arm was Mayard, locked in conversation with Gar.

"I will kill him. He conspires with the enemy. Go on without me, I have business to take care of."

"NO! It is not what you think." Bailiwick landed on Krickall's shoulder and, in an attempt to stop him from going back, flicked his ear with a finger. Ineffectual, perhaps, but

Bailiwick was frantic. Just a shrug of Krickall's massive shoulder sent Bailiwick flying head over heels.

"Stop him, Lapis. He'll only get us all killed."

"Krickall, he is right. Do not be foolish."

His words fell on a retreating back, and it took a wave of his hand to spear Krickall into a dead stop. Krickall glared at Lapis and his gaze shot daggers.

"Let me go, wizard."

"No, I will not let you waste your life and endanger ours."

"I will die as a warrior, not running from the enemy like a bunch of rabbits."

"You will die, but it will be a wasted death. We retreat so that we may return in a stronger position, not because we are rabbits running from their own shadows."

"I may die, but I will kill the traitor who betrayed his own kind."

"I think the little one may have a word on that subject." Lapis raised his eyebrow at Bailiwick.

"Yes. Oh, yes, you are wise, Lapis. Thank the Lady you are here to save Krickall from himself. You know, I remember when... oh, sorry. No time for stories. Krickall, Mayard is not a traitor."

Krickall snarled. "He stands free among our enemies with Analiese by his side. He has obviously bargained with the enemy."

"Yes, but not the way you think. I was in the eating room-- hiding. I heard everything. When you were taken and Mayard kept behind, Gar gave him a choice, not a very nice choice. Mayard could join with Gar and help him with information, or Gar would use Analiese in disgusting, unmentionable manner of ways and then throw her to his goblins. If Mayard helped him, Gar would let him live and give Analiese to him as a reward. You see, there was no choice."

Krickall struggled with Bailiwick's explanation and the anguish of his thoughts mirrored on his face. Bailiwick's heart beat with pain for him. "Krickall, she's safe for now, thanks to Mayard. We have to go."

"Have to go. Jeepers, creepers. Sorry, but have to go." Gwepper jumped from one foot to another only to have Ghilphar calm him with a gentle touch on his arm. For the first time, she spoke and Bailiwick was humbled by the caress of her voice in the air.

"Gwepper's right. We have to go, Krickall. But we'll come back, I promise."

Sensing Krickall's surrender to pressure, Lapis waved his hand to free him, but stood ready in case Krickall decided to bolt for Analiese. He didn't. Instead, he cleared his throat and studied the forest that awaited them. With a shuddering sigh, he squared his shoulders. "I suggest we raid some of the outlying gardens before we head into the forest. With each of us carrying as much as possible, we should have enough food to last awhile."

He thoughtfully fingered the sword he'd grabbed from one of the fallen goblins. "This is our only weapon. I hope we don't run into any goblins on patrol, or hungry wildlife."

Bailiwick giggled and pointed his finger at Lapis. "You are forgetting our other weapon."

"Yes, my magic has been known to come in handy every now and again." His voice turned serious. "The nights are getting colder, so we'll need some kind of protection. Are there any families living at a distance from the main tree that could offer some supplies?"

"Yes, a few of the faeries like the solitude, but that means cutting around the forest for a ways before we enter." Krickall wrinkled his brow. "If we're careful, we should be all right. There are a couple of dwellings only a half-day's travel west.

We can pilfer some blankets and supplies, then head into the forest. But what then? We are boundaried to the north by Night Gloom and the west offers only mountains. If we cross them, the far west offers the Gateway to the world of man."

"Oh, I forgot." Bailiwick slapped his palm against his forehead. "A human man came into the dining area after you left."

"Navarre." Lapis spit the single word from his lips. "His family is an evil my family has been struggling against for generations."

"But he is only human; surely you are more powerful than he," Krickall questioned.

"He parades as a human for his own warped reasons, but his blood also pumps with faerie blood. Come, let us find a safe place to spend the night so we can start early in the morning."

~*~

Lapis set the pace and left everyone to follow his lead. Bailiwick, Gwepper and Ghilphar were quick to follow, but Krickall had hesitated long enough for one more glance back at the chaos they'd left behind. Determination slowly replaced the look of stark anguish that colored his face a moment ago, and Bailiwick would not have wished to be in Gar's place if Krickall ever got him in hand.

The group moved quickly and always kept to the outskirts of the forest where they could hide if need be. After a lengthy time with no conversation, but much labored breathing, dusk became dark and Lapis directed them into the forest and a small clearing that offered seclusion and protection against prying eyes.

"We sleep here. Gwepper and Ghilphar, gather up pine branches for sleeping and firewood for warmth. Little one, bring as many leaves as it takes us to sleep comfortably. Krickall, we need to discuss our plans."

Pouting at being left out of the planning, Bailiwick gathered leaves at a ferocious pace and bundled them onto the pine branches provided by Gwepper and Ghilphar. He helped them set a fire, and then breathlessly alighted on Krickall's shoulder only to find out they'd finished talking.

"Don't worry, little one. We keep no secrets. The way ahead may be hard, so we need to trust and help each other." Lapis motioned Gwepper and Ghilphar to sit with them. "Krickall and I have decided that the only course of action is to meet with Adoneesis as he returns from the Westland. We need to warn him of Gar's insurgence into Dunraven. We can plan together from there."

King Adoneesis. Yes, that made sense. Bailiwick missed the king and when he settled down for sleep that night, he sent a prayer to the Lady that they didn't pass the king undetected. He dreaded the thought of Adoneesis arriving at Dunraven to find his home overrun and himself taken prisoner, or worse yet, killed.

Eighteen

"I want answers, and I want them now." Adoneesis dark walnut eyes glinted with determination and bore into the magician.

Bryanna comforted herself by running her fingers through Shadow Dancer's mane, while watching the play of emotions on the faces around her. She barely had time to accept her circumstances and the existence of unicorns, and then she was confronted with the mythical legend, Merlin. Wielder of magic. Champion of King Arthur. Protector of the mythical sword Excalibur. He was just an old man sitting on a blanket and sipping a cup of tea.

"You know mostly everything, but what you do not know is not mine to tell." Thoughtfully, he passed his cup to Bronwen to refill, which she did with shaking hands.

Bryanna wondered what secret the old woman guarded so closely that fear shadowed her eyes whenever the subject was broached. Bronwen had been nothing but kind to her, and Bryanna felt sorry for her. Heck, who didn't have a secret or two in the closet? Bronwen reminded her of her Aunt Shirley, and she felt closer to Bronwen than she may have otherwise. As if sensing her thoughts, Bronwen turned to Bryanna and smiled reassuringly, a gesture of kindness almost making her look attractive.

"I should perhaps make it clear to you that you have more of a right to the throne of the faerie realm than anyone, no matter the circumstances of your birth."

"The circumstances of my birth?" Adoneesis looked stunned, but a wave of Merlin's hand squelched any questions.

"I will tell a tale, but it will be one to enlighten our visitor. She has been patient long enough, would you not say?" Without waiting for an answer, Merlin spoke. "The tale begins in the sunken island of Atlantis, where a human female captured the attention of the Thunder God."

"Yes, I know this already," Adoneesis interrupted impatiently. "Niobe's gift of prophecy foretold of a period of disaster and she gave powers to her child. The child she conceived with Zeus. The power would carry through the generations and be called upon when times became unbearable."

Bryanna's heart thudded dully in her chest, and words from her aunt's dying letter echoed loudly. *Within you runs blood of the ancient ones, and you hold a power that will shape worlds and change lives.* Ever since Bronwen and Adoneesis showed up at her store, Bryanna's life had become a surreal sequence of events. A strangeness constantly driven into her mind. A mind already having a hard time realizing that she'd been, oh, so wrong about her aunt. Talk about narrow-minded. But how could she have known she was descended from some ancient bloodline and possessed special powers?

Even as she tried to excuse her lack of awareness, brief memories of her childhood flashed through her mind and she realized the knowledge had been there all along. But she'd blocked so much from her mind. Schoolyard pranks resulting in whispered conferences between her aunt and teacher, with a lot of accusing finger pointing and glances shot with fear turned her direction. They'd move to another town, enroll in school, and everything would be fine until another unexplained incident of flying cats, or bursting pens and then the whole thing started all over.

Her sense of other people's thoughts, an ability everyone possessed--didn't they? That's what she thought at the time, until a boy beat her up for telling her teacher he'd started the fire in the boy's washroom. The young offender then spread rumors about her being a witch. He'd been alone in the washroom, so he reasoned that she had to be a witch to know what he'd done.

Realizing that reading minds was not common and elicited fear in most people--fear that resulted in bullying--Bryanna refused to acknowledge her own powers from that day forth. She rebelled against her aunt whenever she tried to teach her tarot cards, asked her to focus on moving an object, or tried to get her to experience the fulfillment of her powers. As time passed, Bryanna refused to admit any such powers ever existed and she slowly sent her past indiscretions into the recesses of her mind. Only once in awhile, such as when she'd levitated Trudy over the fence that one winter, was there ever a resurgence of power, and of doubt.

A gentle nudge from Shadow Dancer brought Bryanna back to awareness of the present, and before she could stop herself she said, "I'm one of the descendants, aren't I."

"Yes." Merlin fixed his gaze on her as if waiting for more questions.

"So why wasn't I raised here?" A wave of her hand encompassed the surrounding countryside.

"For protection. You see, any offspring of Niobe and Zeus would be in ultimate danger from those wanting control of your power. Until such time as your power, or that of your ancestors, was needed, you were safer there."

"Danger from who?" Bryanna's heart beat wildly in her chest, as she wondered at the extent of her aunt's sacrifice. From the day her parents had been killed, her aunt had been responsible for her life, and knowing that there was danger involved in the task, she'd taken on the responsibility nonetheless--and died for her trouble. Bryanna was suddenly sure that her aunt's sudden heart attack was no accident, which also brought into the question the circumstances of her parent's deaths.

"I know those of your world tell of Avalon and how the magical place came to disappear in the mists of time," Merlin prompted.

"Yes, of course most people don't *really* believe in Avalon. It's folklore, kind of like faeries and ghosts." Realizing the absurdity of such a statement while standing in the presence of the mighty Merlin, and on the very real ground of the faerie realm, Bryanna blushed.

"Avalon did exist. Maybe it still does somewhere in the forgotten mists of memory." Merlin smiled, but the smile touched only his lips. His eyes foretold a remembered pain so intense that Bryanna's heart reacted with a sharp jab of sympathy. The sound of a hoof stamping and the stirring of wooden spoon against the cup intruded on the moment of contemplation.

Adoneesis spoke. "If I understand correctly, Avalon's disappearance was due to the differences of the Christian religion and the natural ways of Avalon."

"That is a rather narrow view of circumstances at that time. Regardless, the result was the disappearance of Avalon. The beings that inhabited the magical place created the faerie realm, but there was no one to rule. At first, it was decided that no ruler was necessary. A natural harmony and respect would be enough. Unfortunately, the faerie realm lies too closely to the human world to function free of greed and disharmony, and a splitting of factions occurred. There were those who thought contact with the mortal world would enhance our growth and we could work with mankind for the betterment of both worlds. Others fought hard to retain the distance from outside influences; therefore, enabling narrow advancement of a burgeoning culture. This utopia allowed for dictatorship of those who were stronger and greedier."

"My father being one of those who set himself up as dictator."

"Your father?" Merlin smiled. "Raegar followed his own father's example, except he had the ill grace to split the realm with his penchant for sexual exploits."

"Merlin." Bronwen's voice rang out sharply causing the great magician to shrug his shoulders.

"As I said, the tale is not mine to tell."

"But what about the Lady and yourself? You could have used your powers to ensure the freedom and strength of the realm."

"No. Avalon was destroyed. Nimue and I were torn apart by Morganna's lies and almost destroyed each other in the process. During the formative years of the new world created after Avalon, the Lady and I occupied a place unheard of by most. A place so cold..." Merlin pulled his robe about his shoulders and a small shiver rustled the woolen material. He whispered, "No sense in dwelling on the past. We both moved on with our lives, finding love with others who eventually died off. The pure blood of the ancients enables us to live longer. Eventually, our misunderstanding came to a head in a fierce battle on the very Tor upon which now stands the doorway to the world of man."

Clearing his throat, he straightened his shoulders and shrugged. "Regardless, we are now one, but the cost was dear as our powers were depleted greatly in the battle to win the power of the sword from Morganna. My powers only enable me to see danger ahead, but are not strong enough to decipher the warning. All I know is that the pathway ahead will test you greatly, and all that can be done is being done."

Merlin and Bronwen exchanged looks and Bronwen's shake of her head elicited a look of disapproval from Merlin. There was that elusive secret again. Bryanna tried to probe Merlin's mind, for the first time in many years using her unacknowledged ability, but she came up with only a vague sense of frustration and hint of anger.

Merlin frowned and shook his head. "Fine. Your secret will remain so until it destroys you."

"Then so be it." Bronwen stared Merlin down, and then had the grace to blush. "Forgive me."

Adoneesis snorted and threw his hands skyward. "When will you both stop speaking in riddles and give me the knowledge I need to save the realm of faerie?"

"You have all you need," Merlin replied. "You have the magic of the unicorn, the woman who holds the power of the Thunder God within her, and Bronwen--who now carries the essence of the Lady Niobe, and you will discover other forces working in your favor along the way."

Adoneesis' startled gaze pierced into Bronwen and silently questioned Merlin's remark. She merely smiled and poured more tea into her battered cup. "It seems the Tuatha and the Lady felt I was a worthy vessel."

Bryanna was confused. The words were simple enough, but instinct warned her that the simple remark masked a wealth of meaning. She watched in amazement as Adoneesis, King of the

Faeries, knelt on the dew-damp earth and bowed his head to Bronwen, who merely blushed and waved her hand.

"Rise. I am still who I have always been. Except now I carry a greater responsibility to make sure you do not fail in your duties as king." In an urgent outpouring of fear, Bronwen clutched Adoneesis by the shirt and pulled him close. "You must not fail. Life back to the very beginning relies on you saving the realm and the forces that reside here. There is nowhere else to flee. The faerie realm must endure."

Rising understanding of responsibility mingled with wavering fear flickered across Adoneesis' features as he stood. A battle between doubt and duty raged silently until he managed to school his features and speak in a calm manner.

"You spoke of other forces. Will you not tell me of these forces?"

"Find strength in your friends and they will offer you what you need."

"Fangs. You place such great burden upon my shoulders and then deny me the information I need to fulfill my purpose." With a glance shot with anger, Adoneesis looked to Merlin first and then Bronwen. When neither said a word, he shook his head muttered under his breath and left the campfire to stand on the nearest hilltop. A lonely figure silhouetted by the now risen sun.

Warily testing her abilities, Bryanna opened herself to his anger and felt the underlying frustration of a king unable to defend his people. Focusing on that frustration, Bryanna breathed deeply in an attempt to delve further, never once giving thought to the fact that she may be invading his privacy. She was easily able to see that the abruptness of his personality housed the uncertainty within his character and Bryanna felt sorry for him. Success made her bolder, and she tried to reach further into his mind, only to find her mind slammed with the force of resistance.

"Ouch." She put both hands to her head to still the dizziness.

"Careful, little one. As of yet, he is unaware of the extent of his power, therefore has no control over them."

Merlin rested a hand on her shoulder and the pain in her head quickly receded until she was able to sit up straight. "How can he be unaware of his powers? Does it have something to do with the secret you two are keeping from him?"

Bronwen blushed and Merlin chuckled. "Your perceptions are sharp and growing stronger by the minute, but you must not to intrude on another's minds without their knowledge. It is a courtesy." Merlin's gaze fell on Adoneesis who paced the edge of the clearing. "Our king has had a cruel upbringing and his journey to self-awareness is slow. The learning of certain information will shake his world. He will need the strength and trust of those around him to win the battle that looms."

"What battle? What's my role in all this? Why not tell him what he needs to know, so he can be prepared?"

"All in good time, I promise."

Bryanna folded her arms across her chest and threw a narrowed gaze at Merlin and Bronwen. "I don't like the evasiveness of your answers and I'm coming to understand Adoneesis' frustration with both of you."

Bronwen laughed. "Good, he needs you on his side."

"I'm not on anyone's side. You guys kidnapped me, remember. The only side I'm on is my own."

"We'll see."

Bryanna considered Bronwen's words. There was a dawning understanding that her destiny was inexplicably tied with this world and these beings--a destiny that caused her blood to boil with an uncontrollable need and gave rise to an aching sense of justice and harmony. As she came to accept her strange destiny, the sudden understanding of the conversation over the past few minutes hit her full force. With a gasp, she turned to Bronwen.

"You carry the essence of Niobe. My ancestor. Is that why you seem so familiar to me? How can that be?"

Water bubbled over the cook pot and into the dying embers of fire and effectively blocked out Bryanna's whisper. This was too much. She couldn't handle another strange occurrence. Heck, she had no idea why the events of the day hadn't already driven her into a blinding mass of drooling flesh. Against her constant rebellion, her aunt's teachings must have become ingrained enough that Bryanna could handle the magical and unexplained with very little question or doubt. But enough was enough, she thought, while she clutched her head in her hands to quell the beginnings of a migraine.

The first tendril of ease was so tender and elusive, Bryanna swore she'd imagined the relief, but as gentle fingers of comfort wound their way through her head and drove the throbbing pain away, she realized someone was administering a form of healing. Lowering her hands, Bryanna opened her eyes to see Bronwen's palms directed at her--her lips moving in a silent chant. The wind picked up ever so slightly, lifting a lock of Merlin's white hair and then releasing it to drift back into place on his shoulder.

Acute awareness of her surroundings and the invisible connection to Bronwen gave Bryanna cause for consideration. She shared the past and the future of this mythical land with her kidnappers, as assuredly as she sat there breathing the scent of pure, unpolluted air. She'd found a lyrical ally with Shadow Dancer, and felt a bond with Bronwen in spite of her part in the kidnapping. Even Merlin, with his warm amber eyes shimmering from beneath unruly hair, elicited feelings of comfort. The lone figure in the distance drew her gaze and enforced the knowledge that the difficult part of her task would be to win the trust of Adoneesis. The king burdened with the responsibility of saving his endangered realm--the king burning with the need to prove himself worthy in the eyes of those who looked to him. Oh, yes, Bryanna's burgeoning senses hummed with the knowledge that the hardest road traveled would be the one that led through the thorny feelings of the faerie who had kidnapped her from her world.

Nineteen

"You and I aren't like everyone else. One day you'll see. You'll come to understand your purpose in life."

Navarre moaned and shifted in his sleep. His father's words echoed through him as they had for so many years. In a dream haze, he watched his father caress the leather-bound book that Navarre's young mind was convinced held the mysteries of the universe.

He hadn't been far wrong.

His mother died giving birth to him and through the early years of Navarre's life, that book had held a place of mystery, not only in Navarre's mind, but also in their home. Occasionally, when his father was especially nostalgic, the book would appear and his father, Jebediah, would bemoan his hapless abilities. Abilities that Jebediah claimed had deserted him when he needed them most.

A mean drunk, Jebediah would curse and slug back another drink until he'd deteriorated into a state of self-pity. "Damn, I almost had everything." He slurped another mouthful. Droplets of liquid amber dribbled down his chin. "I hate him, I hate all of them."

Sometimes, his gaze would search out Navarre, who usually sat in the corner and pieced together the threads of his father's ramblings. Speculation would light drab gray eyes and he'd whisper, as if in prayer, "One day you'll understand your purpose in life. One day, you'll avenge your dear old dad and see that Lir burns in hell."

Once, when his father was quite mellow in spite of the alcohol, Navarre raised the nerve to ask a couple of questions. "Who is Lir?"

Jebediah's head snapped around and the heat of glaring eyes pinned Navarre into the corner. He almost wished he hadn't asked the question, but his father's shoulders gradually relaxed and he sucked another mouthful of rye. "Hmmm, don't know who tole you 'bout him, but guess you should know the truth." He burped and sank into a deeper depression. "Hell, lots you should know."

Jebediah's words slurred and his eyes unfocused, but talking about Lir seemed to sober him. The name alone was enough to instill enough pride to sit straighter and clear his throat. When he spoke, he made an effort to enunciate clearly. Navarre quickly came to realize it wasn't pride that spurred Jebediah into pulling himself together, but a sense of fuming hatred.

"Lir was--probably still is--leader of the Tuatha de Danann. He's the son of a bitch who sent me packing from my own home."

Jebediah touched the book reverently. "He never could see the advantage of using this book. When I tried to convince others... well, that didn't work out well. Because of Lir's interference, I had to leave the faerie realm and travel to this world." He spat his anger and left a glob of phlegm on the tan carpet. "But not without the book. Ha. Showed that sucker. I can't go back, but you will. Oh, yes..." He glared at Navarre. "You'll go back and avenge the injustices heaped on me by the Tuatha and their blasted morals.

"But you gotta watch for the saviour child. Bah! I killed one, and his wife, to keep them from interfering. The daughter got away. You deal with her." He rubbed a limp hand across his forehead and mumbled, "Always someone to interfere. Here or in the other place. Faeries. Stupid... stupid"

His voice drifted into a whisper and Navarre sat there, numb.

He's crazy. My father is crazy. Thoughts raced through Navarre's mind, yet a small part of him wondered what truths the drunken revelations revealed. He'd always felt different-- apart from everyone around him. But the *faerie realm*--that bordered on insane.

A snorting snore ripped from his father's throat and Navarre looked at the book nestled so innocently in his lap. There lay the answers to his questions. Stepping gently on squeaky floorboards, Navarre tiptoed to his sleeping father. With shaking hands, he reached out to touch the embossed, warm cover of the black book. His fingers tingled. Excitement raced a path through his body, and he wound his fingers around the spine of the book and, slowly, carefully, pulled it from his father's flaccid hands.

The prize was almost his when a resounding smack echoed in his head and he dropped the book. In horror, he watched it fall, and knew the noise of the heavy book hitting bare wood, would awaken his father. Desperately, he grabbed. Instead of the rough leather he expected to grasp, he ended up with a fistful of cotton.

"What the..." Dazed, Navarre sat up, quickly realized that he'd been dreaming--again, but something had awakened him. "Goddamn, old man, will you never leave me alone?"

He threw the bedcovers from his naked body and stood. The coolness of the floor made him quickly aware that he occupied one of the main sleeping chambers of the main tree of

Dunraven. In his arrogance, Gar had claimed Adoneesis' chamber as his own. Navarre hadn't argued. The time to declare his intentions would come eventually, but that time was not now. Navarre needed the crystal first. The Crystal of Light. References to its power threaded their way through the book and Navarre had full intentions of claiming the power for himself. That was his purpose. Anger furrowed his brow as his father's words whispered to him.

You'll come to understand your purpose in life.

"My purpose in life, old man, is my own to decide, and I won't waste my life avenging yours." Navarre sneered to the empty room, as if taunting his father to suddenly appear and beat him as if he had done so often before. The one thing he could thank his father for were the whispered deathbed words that sent Navarre to the realm of faerie searching for the power of the crystal.

The sound Navarre remembered the most about that time of death was the hum of hospital machines. His father's insistent beckoning, making Navarre lean closer to hear Jebediah's whisper, a raspy sound nearly drowned out by life-sustaining machines. Navarre's nose had tingled with the hospital smell of death and disinfectant, while his gut heaved at the gaunt features of a dying man.

"The power... in your blood. My blood. You can travel... through the doorway. The book... the book tells you how. Find the crystal. Use its power to avenge me." His father's fingers tightened at Navarre's throat and clenched his shirt in his bony fists. "Dunraven. The crystal rests at Dunraven."

His father died the instant those words crossed his lips, but Navarre didn't care. He had a book to read. Navarre wasn't sure when he started to believe, but tales of magic, feats of bravery, worlds and places beyond belief somehow wound their way into him, and he found himself believing. Echoes of a distant world tingled within him--heating and rising until there was no denying the instinctive knowledge of his ancestry. The words sang to him of beauty, harmony, and disaster. The sinking of a continent that gave rise to a land of enchantment--Atlantis to Avalon.

Raised voices from the hallway jolted Navarre from his reverie. The shuffling sounds of a struggle and then--*smack*; the same sound that jolted him from sleep. He strode to the door ready to rage at whoever dared disturb him, but he hesitated, his hand hovering midair. Knowledge was power. Reading the Book of Time drove that lesson home well enough, with its age-old strategies and manipulations

So, he listened.

"Curse it, Analiese, there was no other choice. Unless you wanted to end up as the whore of the goblin leader." The male voice fell and rose, subtly turning the statement into a question.

Obviously, Analiese heard the implied question, and another smack resounded in the hallway. The sound of a struggle and then Mayard's voice. "You'll not slap me again. I did what was best for you, putting my own life in danger at the same time, I might add."

"You betrayed us. You betrayed the King."

"I saved your life. Do you have any idea what Gar had planned for you? Well, do you?"

"I can imagine."

"No, you can't." Mayard proceeded to tell her of the conversation that had taken place in the dining hall yesterday, leaving out not one of the lurid, sexual details.

Listening to the violent words of lust and imagining the soft, struggling body of Analiese beneath him, Navarre found himself getting hard, but fought the physical reaction and silently cursed the sign of weakness. He had no time for such things. He had a realm to conquer, a goblin leader to outwit, and a king to destroy. But maybe, just maybe, when all was done, he could reward himself and indulge in the physical acts he'd only imagined until now.

A whisper of a gasp from Analiese and a self-satisfied *humph* from Mayard routed Navarre from his fantasies.

"See, I told you it wasn't pleasant. I did what I had to." Mayard lowered his voice enough that Navarre had to put his ear to the thick door to hear. "Gar has no way of knowing whether I speak the truth or not. I can easily feed him false information until we find a way to escape. That's my plan."

"Oh," Analiese sniffled. "I'm sorry, Mayard. But when Gar said he was giving me to you, and that you were helping him, I thought..."

"I know. You thought what I wanted him to think, but now you know the truth. You do know how much I care for you, don't you?"

"Yes."

Mayard cleared his throat. "Do you think that when all this is over..." His voice trailed off expectantly.

"Mayard, we may not live to see that day."

"It's him, isn't it?"

"Pardon me?"

"Krickall. You care for him. Gar said the two of you were together when the attack happened." Mayard spat the words of accusation, anger, and jealousy rising in his voice.

"Mayard. We were only talking." The quiver in her voice negated the words of protest. "I do care for him, but I care for you also."

"Then I have a chance to win your love."

"Mayard..."

"Don't worry; I'll make sure we live through this. Then you'll have to give me a chance."

Navarre grimaced at the words of love and relaxed as Mayard and Analiese's voices faded the direction of the stairs. He wondered how they came to be wandering around with no sign of a guard, but he was glad because he now possessed knowledge that Gar didn't. Mayard's information was false, but should he share the knowledge with Gar? Gar had his uses, but the limitations of the goblin's intelligence dictated that Navarre be careful in his handling of the self-proclaimed king of the faeries.

Adoneesis, on the other hand, offered an undeniable challenge. Sure, the faerie reeked with the blood of the ancients, but had been brought up blissfully unaware of the extent of his abilities. Navarre planned to strike before the king came into his own, and Gar would make a useful distraction. While Adoneesis focused on regaining his throne and heritage, Navarre would be manipulating behind the scenes, and would not be showing *his* true heritage until the time was right. No one knew his background; therefore, no one could guess at his motives. He could weaken both sides, play them against each other, and then strike like a cobra when the time was right. He knew all the angles and was playing for the ultimate goal of total power over all faeries, while Gar and Adoneesis played games with each other for the throne. Ha, what a joke. Gar hadn't the intelligence, and Adoneesis, though intelligent, had not the forethought to use the throne to his advantage. He'd allowed the faeries of the realm to do as they please, when he could have been bending them to his will and shaping a new world of subservience and decadence. Navarre had the advantages of surprise and knowledge.

Knowledge was power, and he loved power.

~ * ~

Gar paced his chamber. Nerves stretched taut, and his mind fiercely roiling. He'd done it. He was in the bedchamber of the king. Now what? He belonged here as much as Adoneesis, more so, since he was firstborn, but how did he keep his hold on the realm? Adoneesis would soon return from the world of man and bring with him the child that supposedly possessed unknown powers. Probably not a child any longer. Gar didn't even know that. He knew nothing, and didn't know what to do about it.

"Curses and rat dung." He slammed his fist into the clothes cabinet, splintered the wood and caused his hand to throb at the same time. "Fangs."

Nothing was going right. His fantasies for last night dashed into dust because of the manipulations of the wizard and escape of the prisoners. Gar had been so furious upon finding out the prisoners had escaped that more than one goblin paid dearly with their flesh flayed under the whip for that mistake. Ghilphar's sweet face hovered on the edges of his mind, just as always. She'd escaped him twice, but when he caught her this time, he'd make sure she never escaped him again.

His trust in Navarre was minimal, and his belief that the human's abilities matched Lapis' ingrained powers, was non-existent. A glance out the window showed a courtyard full of drunken, filthy goblins and his blood beat with anger at their blatant indolent behavior, even if he had been the one who told them to let loose. What if Adoneesis showed up now? How could the rabble splayed on the ground before him defend the newly won Dunraven? They couldn't.

With anger and unslaked lust clouding his mind, Gar let out a bellow and stomped to the door with full intentions of laying into anyone who crossed his path. Yanking open the sleeping chamber door, he found himself face to face with the human, whose calm features further taunted Gar into temper.

He snarled and spat.

"Where are your powers now, human? And what good are you to me?"

Navarre smiled which near drove Gar into a state of frenzy. Before he could explode, the human reminded him, "I still have the book, which is your best means to retain the power you recently gained and now hold so precariously."

Against all needs, Gar was barely able to hold his emotions in check. "The book. Ha! You snivel about this curse and that spell, but what do I see except an old book in your hands." Agitated, Gar paced the room while Navarre stood just inside the doorway. Thumping his fists to his chest, Gar demanded, "It is time for me to read the book. I am king, it is my right."

Belligerently he faced Navarre, whose eyes bore into him with such intensity to create a seed of doubt that maybe he'd pushed too far. But he wanted the book. He meant to have the book and use its power to rule. History of all faeries hinted at unparalleled magic. Lapis was a throwback to ancient blood and abilities, and Gar had seen his power more than once. This human declared to have the abilities of past-times, but had done little to prove himself. Now, the realm of faerie and the rewards of unlimited imagination lay so close that Gar tasted the glory. All would bow down at his feet, declare him supreme leader, and none could dare challenge him--if he could only tap into the secrets of the book. He quivered with anticipation and speculation.

"Calm yourself, Gar. As I have said, the book contains the language of old. You would never understand its teachings. You need me. Besides, we must now focus on our next step in strengthening your hold on the throne."

Thoughts of killing Navarre and grabbing the book for himself flew from Gar's mind as enticements of a secure throne blinded him. He could always dispose of the human later. For now, he was needed. He sneered. "Tell me more."

Seemingly satisfied, Navarre smiled, inclined his head in a gesture of respect, and glided past Gar to stand by the window overlooking the lands of Dunraven. Silence fell on the room long enough for Gar to shift and his temper to rise. Just as he was about to snap at the human, Navarre spoke.

"Tell me, Gar, what do you see when you look over the land?"

"Stupid question. What do you think I see?"

Navarre was looking for a specific answer, but Gar had no idea what was expected of him, so he blustered instead. If the human kept up with his arrogant attitude, Gar would kill him regardless of the book. Someone, somewhere, would be able to read it for him.

"Come." Navarre beckoned. "It's important. Tell me what you see."

Grumbling impatiently, Gar shuffled to the narrow window and looked over Navarre's shoulder. Before them, the lands of Dunraven stretched into a distant horizon. Gently rising hillocks, open fields spotted with glorious displays of wildflowers, the movement of long grasses in the early day breeze, and scampering four-legged creatures at work setting in their stores for another day. Above it all, providing homes, shade and protection, were the trees. Dunraven was laden with trees whose trunks spanned wider than a hundred goblins standing together.

Gar frowned. The human was making him feel stupid again. Not a good thing. His temper and insecurities rose to the surface. Grunting, he turned from the window as if it was not important. "No time to fool around. I've got to wake up some slackers."

"Wait." The command cut the still air in the sleeping chamber, but when Navarre continued speaking; his voice took on a soothing, conciliatory tone. "Forgive my arrogance. I am in possession of facts that are unknown to you; therefore it is wrong of me to expect you to know what answer I seek."

"Then tell me, human."

Navarre smiled and Gar could have sworn he saw a flash of hatred flash across his features. Within that split second, Gar knew the truth of Navarre. He didn't need intelligence to see the human's motive. Instead, age-old survival instincts gave him the true picture of Navarre's nature. The human worked his own plan and only used the situation to his own advantage. Slowly, considering, Gar relaxed his fists, took a step back and knew that the days of the human were short. Now free, his hands rested on the hilt of his sword and threatened without words.

"You need me, Gar. I have knowledge you cannot do without. Not if you want to retain your hold on the throne." He lowered his voice to a whisper. The soft sound slithered into Gar's subconscious and molded his mind into jelly with its promise. "I will share with you the secret. Now, if you desire."

"Tell me."

Navarre smiled. "Of course, Gar. You know Book of Time is a written history and record of lineage of the faerie world."

"Yes, yes. Go on."

"Fine. It is also a book of magic, spells, and gives locations of sources of energy within the realm. We know that Adoneesis' blood is rank with magic, but he doesn't know that. He has it within him to wrest the throne from you with no more than a mere glance if he wants."

With a swift action born of years of swordplay and practice, Gar drew his sword from its protective sheath and held it mid-air. Polished only that morning, the sharpness of blade glistened in the rays of sun slanting through the window.

"Let him try," Gar threatened.

"Oh, he will try and he will succeed, unless you listen to me."

"I'm listening." Gar stood battle-ready, sword raised between he and the human.

"The answer lies in the question, *what do you see when you look out the window?* Trees, Gar. Dunraven, the entire faerie realm, is laden with trees. Think to the teachings of your youth and you will know the answer."

"Yes. Adoneesis carries the blood of the prophetess, so he is connected to the earth."

"I knew you'd figure it out. From the beginnings of time, the alternate worlds of energy have held a special connection to the elements of nature and the bounty of everything living. Even though the faerie realm is closer to the world of man than Atlantis or Avalon ever were, there still remains strong ties in those who carry the blood of The Ones Who Came Before. It's all in the book. If you destroy the trees, you also destroy the homes of the creatures that live there. You cut off the thread of energy that keeps Adoneesis strong. If you destroy the trees, you destroy him, and he won't even know why he suddenly becomes weak. He has no idea of his blood history."

Triumph caused Gar's blood to race through his veins. He was about to avenge years of Raegar's neglect and living the role of second best. He'd wipe them from his mind by a single act of destruction that would bring Adoneesis crawling to him and begging for forgiveness. Destroy the trees and his grip on the faerie realm would remain strong and true. He frowned.

"That weakens Adoneesis, but what of Lapis?" He snorted and pinned Navarre with a narrowed gaze. "You are not powerful enough to stop him from defending the realm should he decide."

A look crossed the human's face--a look that gave Gar reason to consider killing him where he stood. After all, he now knew Adoneesis' weakness, what more did he need the human for. His hand inched toward his sword and he considered his options.

Smooth as steel, and just as cold, Navarre's voice felled Gar's hand. "That would be the last mistake of your life, goblin."

Eyes clashed. Dark mud gray against slashing silver, they measured and considered. Gar dropped his gaze first and hated the stab of fear that licked his spine. His nostrils flared and he covered his weakness with a threat. "You can live for now." He thrust his finger underneath Navarre's nose. "But remember that I can have you killed whenever I want."

Navarre bowed his head. "Of course."

The hint of derision slicing the edges of Navarre's words was not lost on Gar, whose fingers itched to slice the human into small pieces. He comforted himself by imagining what he would do to the human when his services were no longer of use. Gar would enjoy cutting Navarre, and would revel in smearing the dead human's blood all over his own body in a gesture of dominance and triumph. But years of hatred and resentment against Adoneesis stilled his hand. He may yet need the human and his ability to read the book.

Nose twitching and fingers itching for killing, Gar strode from the bedchamber. "Come, human, let's go kill some trees."

Twenty

A searing pain shooting through his head woke Adoneesis instantly. Vividly aware of his surroundings, yet feeling disconnected, he threw off the woolen blanket, clenched his head between shaking hands, and rolled to his knees. The stygian darkness hid his pain from the others, and he struggled to keep from crying out as the invasive pain wended through his body. Distant rumbling in the sky threatened a deluge; yet, Adoneesis sensed something else woven within the approaching storm.

For some reason, the pervasive sense of evil riding the wings of the storm sparked memories of the darkened dungeons of Dunraven. Over the years of Raegar's responsibilities to the realm, Adoneesis had watched his father age, physically and emotionally. The weight of responsibility stretched over centuries could pervade the soul, and he prayed that the progression of character that formed Raegar into a cruel, heartless character would not be his fate.

Another shaft of pain thrust a dagger into Adoneesis head and brought him fully to the present. With supreme effort, he stumbled to his feet and away from Bronwen and Bryanna, both lying innocently in slumber. Merlin was gone. As the sun had set beyond the horizon earlier, the legendary magician had quietly melded into the dusk and left only the warning he'd come with. A warning of unseen, unknown danger.

Pain expanded into a throb of all over body pain, and beads of sweat congealed on his forehead as Adoneesis forced himself to breathe through the pain. Memories of his early years mingled with the pain and forced him to retain his silent composure of suffering. He'd been about five summers old when he tripped over a fallen tree branch. The pain or blood hadn't bothered him and fear of Raegar kept him from acting like a baby, but when he looked to his arm and saw splintered bone protruding from ragged, bloody skin--he screamed, and he couldn't stop until Raegar grabbed his undamaged arm, pulled him to his feet and demanded that he stop sniveling. After all, one day he'd be king, and kings don't cry.

"No," Adoneesis mumbled as the pain in his head subsided somewhat. "Kings don't cry, but we sure as hell feel pain."

With the mild relief of pain came an insistent need--the need to return to Dunraven. He didn't know why, but it must have something to do with Merlin's warning. Most likely with the pain he was experiencing as well.

Suddenly the distant rumble in the heavens stopped and gave way to a darkness of sky never before seen by Adoneesis and a haunting stillness that exaggerated all sound. The stamp of a hoof, the scrape of branch upon branch--the very land shivered with energy that seeped into her soil--and Adoneesis was painfully aware of the disruptiveness calling him home, to Dunraven. Quiet at first, a breeze drifted in from the surrounding mountains, carried on its gentle gusts and shattered shards of fear and pain. Increasing in tempo, the breeze scattered dried leaves and carried puffs of dust, sending them swirling around Adoneesis.

The need to return home increased with the wind. It was that fierce urgency building within that convinced Adoneesis something was wrong, and drove him into panic.

~ * ~

Someone shook her hard. If that hadn't wakened her, the insistent yelling in her ear would have. Physically, Bryanna had a hard time waking, but her senses snapped into alert awareness. Something wasn't right. When had her bed started feeling like hard-packed, uneven ground? And she was sure she hadn't left her bedroom window open last night, so how could the sweep of a breeze brush across her face?

Someone yelled again, causing yesterday's events to crash into her mind and leave her breathless. Adrenaline's potent elixir raced through her blood as Bryanna threw the blanket off and scrambled to her feet.

Fervent chaos greeted her.

With precise, quick movements, Bronwen was in the midst of packing the cookware and utensils. Already saddled and bridled, Aurora and Brachus snorted, stamped impatiently and rolled their eyes nervously, as if sensing a danger not apparent to anyone else. Adoneesis kicked dirt on the still burning embers from last night's fire.

Not sure what was going on, or what to do, Bryanna looked to Bronwen for guidance. For a brief moment, the sun's glint reflected a face of glowing beauty, quickly replaced by familiar wrinkles and sagging of age. Bryanna shook her head and thought she must still be dreaming, but and recalled a similar moment when she'd first met Bronwen. Before she was able to ponder the conflict, Adoneesis grabbed her and pushed her toward Brachus.

"We have no time to watch the sun rise, woman. Have you not heard a word I have spoken?" Adoneesis punctuated his impatient growl with another push.

Still unable to see reason for such urgency, Bryanna's temper rose and she shook free from the unwanted grasp. Lifting her chin and rubbing her reddening arm, she glared at Adoneesis. Darkest eyes of walnut brown stared back and unfamiliar shivers tickled Bryanna's spine and caused her to sway, suddenly unsteady on her feet. Adoneesis radiated a haughty demeanor. His nostrils flared in impatience.

Bryanna lost all manner of civility. She stamped her foot. "Goddamn it. Who the hell do you think you are? You kidnap me from my own store, heck, my own *world*, and you bring me to this place." She waved her hands carelessly about, encompassing the surrounding countryside. "You expose me to a world full of legends and pie-in-the-sky myths, which you expect me to believe without question. Then you shake me from a sound sleep, scream in my ear and shove me about like some piece of meat. A person can only take so much you know."

Adoneesis stared her down, not moving, not flinching. Finally, the corner of his mouth twitched slightly. "I didn't scream in your ear."

Bryanna didn't know whether to laugh or cry, so she stood staring at the King of the Faerie and letting emotion wage war within her.

Bronwen spoke, taking the decision from Bryanna. "Adoneesis is right. We need to hurry." Her black eyes reflected worry and a hint of fear as they darted from mountains to trees and searched for something. "Merlin was right to warn us. Something is wrong. I am surprised you felt the energy before me, Adoneesis. Your powers are stronger than you realize."

"Humph!" Adoneesis turned to tighten the cinch on Brachus' saddle. "I have no special powers. I'm merely heeding Merlin's warning."

"Oh, then why did we not leave last eve for Dunraven?" Bronwen questioned.

Adoneesis flushed and Bryanna wondered if his arrogant assertiveness merely covered his insecurities and uncertainties. An interesting thought to pursue later. He turned to her.

"Come, I'll help you up." He extended his cupped hands to help her up into the saddle.

"No."

"Blast, woman, we do not have time for your single-mindedness. Dunraven is in danger."

"I mean, I don't need to ride with you. I'll ride Shadow Dancer."

A whinnying trumpet heralded the unicorn's arrival. Regally, magically, she broke through the forest's leaves and the early morning sun dancing shadows and light upon her.

"You cannot ride the unicorn, she has no saddle."

"It doesn't matter." Bryanna stroked Shadow Dancer's velvety muzzle. "I've been riding since I was five. The first pony I ever learned how to ride was bareback. I'll be fine."

Adoneesis snorted. "And how do you propose to direct her with no bridle?"

A valid question, but Bryanna somehow knew she'd need no bridle. Already the thoughts of the unicorn settled themselves in her mind, as if they were her own thoughts. The emotions of fear and urgency prompted her to grab a handful of mane, step on a nearby rock, and jump up to Shadow Dancer's back. "You're right about one thing; there is danger ahead. We need to hurry."

"How do you know what lies ahead?" Adoneesis placed a foot in the stirrup, swung himself onto Brachus, and threw her a challenging look.

"I know because Shadow Dancer tells me so. She is vibrating with tension and fear."

Bronwen's chuckle broke the mood. "Not even here a full twenty-four hours and already she listens to animals better than you, Adoneesis. You would do well to take a lesson from her."

Bronwen swung onto Aurora's back with a grace that belied her aged appearance, and Bryanna once again harbored suspicions that the old woman was not all she appeared--she was much more. Obviously not in the mood for comparisons that left him on the bottom end, Adoneesis spurred Brachus into a gallop and left the others to follow.

Bryanna could have sworn that when he glanced over his shoulder and saw her still seated, a flash of disappointment crossed his features. *Ha, arrogant jerk. I'll show him.* Before the idea of going faster had become more than a glimmer of a thought, Shadow Dancer increased her stride. The pumping energy and streamlined legs brought them easily alongside Adoneesis and Brachus. Bryanna spared them not even a glance. She remained intent on keeping pace and didn't bother to analyze why she felt such a great need to prove herself.

~*~

The sun rose and crossed the sky slowly, yet Adoneesis and his group did not stop. Bryanna was barely aware of the passing scenery. Gracefully rolling hills, open fields, a distant horizon presenting visions of snow-peaked mountains. They galloped through countryside not long ago ripe with spring's ritual of rebirth that had given way to summer's fruits and blooms.

Bryanna's muscles ached in places she'd never felt; yet, still they pushed on. Cripes, the animals would need to rest soon; they couldn't keep up this deadly pace. Another mile, then another, and still no slowing of pace. Shadow Dancer's mane whipped Bryanna's face and shafts of fiery pain shot up her legs until she worried about falling off at the breakneck speed they traveled. Suddenly, Shadow Dancer slackened her pace to a stamping halt.

Bronwen and Aurora followed suit, leaving only Adoneesis and Brachus racing ahead. Once Adoneesis realized they ran alone, he pulled Brachus around and trotted back.

"What's wrong? There is no time to rest."

Bronwen replied. "Shadow Dancer must be tired. She decided it was time for a break."

Adoneesis frowned. "But Brachus has barely broken a sweat, and here I thought a unicorn would be at least as able to travel distances as a dragon steed."

Bryanna threw a thankful look to Bronwen for explaining, and with a grateful pat on Shadow Dancer's neck--for the unicorn still breathed at a normal rate, but understood Bryanna's need for a break. She threw her leg over the unicorn's cream-colored back and onto the ground. That's where she lost it. More than rubbery, her legs had lost all ability to stand on their own, so Bryanna slid to the ground in such an ungainly manner that there was no covering the action from Adoneesis.

Embarrassed and in pain, Bryanna sat on the ground and swore. A shadow fell across the grassy ground in front of her. Bryanna heaved a sigh and looked up expecting to see Adoneesis smirking at her. Except he wasn't smirking. He looked concerned. He knelt by her side and brushed her hair from her cheek. The aching need for more of his touch was as unexpected as this entire adventure. His dark eyes rested on her causing her heart to beat fiercely.

"I have a feeling that in your world, that word you just muttered is something like fangs would be here."

Bryanna smiled. "Worse."

"I see. Would I be correct in assuming that you're regretting your decision to ride bareback?"

Bryanna bristled, imagining a hint of sarcasm in his tone. "You could have warned me that we'd travel this far without a break." Slowly, she stood and stretched her legs.

"You insisted on riding the unicorn. I didn't have the heart to dissuade you." His eyes sparked with humor and dark swirls of walnut mingled with accents of gold. "I suppose I could have warned you that dragon steeds, faerie horses, and unicorns can outrun the horses of your world without thought."

"Yes, you could have."

The humor disappeared, replaced by the haunting fear Bryanna had seen in his eyes first thing that morning. Adoneesis shrugged his shoulders. "I am sorry, but we must ride. You are in no shape to stay on Shadow Dancer, so you will ride with me."

Bronwen already sat atop Aurora's back but had her gaze fixed on the horizon. "Adoneesis is right. We need to go now." She spurred Aurora into a gallop and left them to follow.

Bryanna eyed Adoneesis and knew there was no way she could climb back up on Shadow Dancer and be expected to stay. Reluctantly, and with an exaggerated sigh, she stepped into Brachus' stirrup--the single motion sending her muscles into a silent, screaming protest. With a single, easy sweep, Adoneesis swung Bryanna onto Brachus' wide back. The dragon steed snuffled gently, his fire-shooting nostrils flaring with the breath, but he stood statue-still as if sensing Bryanna's weakened state. Without use of stirrups, Adoneesis leapt up behind Bryanna, and, none too gently, pulled her against him. A flick of his wrist sent Brachus into a leaping melody of muscle and sinewy speed.

If Bryanna had thought they were traveling quickly before, now she would have to say they flew. Flashing hooves barely touched the ground. She would have sworn there was no sound of hoof striking earth. The silence hung over them in a way that made her able to understand the saying, *deafening silence.*

Moving with the lengthy rhythm of Brachus' stride, it took Bryanna a few minutes to realize that she'd settled far too comfortably against Adoneesis. Warmth engulfed her as both his arms weaved under hers--one pinning her to his chest, the other directing Brachus by means of braided leather reins. Each motion of stride rocked her against Adoneesis thighs and groin, and each motion took on a sensual, hypnotic quality.

Her face flamed. Thank God, she faced away from Adoneesis so he wouldn't wonder what she was blushing about. A quiet chuckle tickled her ear.

"I suppose now wouldn't be a good time to tell you that faeries are well-known for being highly attuned to the environment around them."

Bryanna gritted her teeth and forced herself to concentrate on anything besides the movement of body against body. "That's interesting, but I have no idea what you're talking about."

Adoneesis tightened his grip and brought her close enough that every fiber of her felt tangled with him. She may have moaned, but she wasn't sure. Of course, she could always blame it on her stiff muscles.

Adoneesis laughed. "No worries. I am King of the Faerie. I would never mate with a human."

Before Bryanna was able to retort, Adoneesis spurred Brachus into even faster speed. In no time, they caught up with Bronwen and Aurora but gave Bryanna time to consider the insulting statement. King of the Faerie. Huh. Big deal. Was that supposed to make him better than her? Why did he think she'd be interested in any kind of sexual relationship with him, anyway? Bryanna fumed, hoping that anger would give her the ability to ignore the unsettling closeness of her kidnapper.

It didn't work, damn him. She prayed that they'd reach their destination soon, so she could get down from this horse and away from the arrogance of her captor.

"Do not worry, we're almost there."

"Stop reading my mind. You may have control of my physical body, but don't you dare invade my mind."

His body flinched against hers as if he'd been slapped, but his answer is what surprised her the most.

"You are right. Your thoughts are your own."

"Hmmm, a faerie with a conscience," Bryanna muttered.

The two of them fell into an uneasy silence. The closer they came to journey's end, the more Adoneesis tensed against her. His nerves hummed so tightly, that Bryanna's own nerves wound through her stomach, expanded into her chest, and made it hard to swallow. Adoneesis' eyes focused on the horizon-- never wavering, trusting Brachus to maneuver the rough terrain.

Racing beside them, Bronwen tensed visibly as they approached another small hillock. Her small, veined hands gripped Aurora' reins, and she whispered, "Something is missing."

"Yes," Adoneesis replied, as Brachus' lengthy stride brought them to the base of the hillock. "Lives have been taken, but more than that--I feel the absence of greatness." Brachus brought them to the crest of the hillock.

"The absence of greatness," Bronwen repeated the ominous words--her uneven voice lending a chilling reality to the unknown. She pulled Aurora to a stamping halt on the hill's crest. Faerie steed brushed against dragon steed as if seeking comfort.

The ride up the hill had been short; fooling a stranger into believing they the way down would be just as easy. Only as they crested the hill was Bryanna able to see they'd been climbing steadily and easily for some time, until they now stood atop a small mountain. The way down the other side presented a precarious trail of twisting, rocky terrain.

But the panorama spread before them was beauty itself to behold. The trail melted into a lush valley nestled safely among surrounding mountains, and carried on to a forest of trees like Bryanna could never have dreamed possible. Gnarled trunks spanning the distance of a large house extended their limbs as if reaching for the heavens.

Squinting her eyes against blazing sun, she saw that someone must have been logging, as one of the trees lay on the ground in pieces.

"Wow, what some of the lumber companies back home wouldn't give for just one of those massive trees."

"We do not lumber our trees here."

Adoneesis spoke harshly, but Bryanna was vividly aware of the shaky timbre and threat of tears within his tone. Something was very wrong. Her gaze touched on the fallen tree and small details became clearer. The tree hadn't been cut, it had been butchered. Splintered wood exposed newly carved scars of fresh wood, uneven chunks haphazardly littered the ground, and massive limbs lay strewn in a macabre fashion. What once held beauty and grace now lay stripped of all dignity.

Bryanna choked with the oppression of the scene below them, even though she had no idea what they faced. Time seemed to halt, as a single tear wound a pathway down Bronwen's face and Adoneesis withdrew into a hard shell of pulsing anger.

"Duir," he rasped. "They have destroyed Duir. I did not think such a thing was possible."

Mesmerized and appalled by the scene of destruction, Bronwen replied, "They could not unless..." She choked back a sob. "Unless Toran no longer lives."

A shuddering sob heaved through Adoneesis, almost unseating Bryanna from the saddle. "Let us ride." Fervently, as if hoping against hope, Adoneesis spurred Brachus into a flying gallop that left Bryanna gasping.

Aurora's hooves pounded behind them, and Bryanna knew the old woman followed closely, even on the treacherous descent down the mountainside. Each time Brachus slipped on a rock, the dragon steed recovered, each time the descent looked unmanageable, the steed's steady stride carried them through.

Partway down the mountain, Bryanna became aware of a pulsing pressure building in her head and flaming her senses. It was as if a thousand flies buzzed around, teasing and taunting her with their constant tirade. She may have moaned, she wasn't sure, but Adoneesis slowed Brachus long enough to ask if she was all right.

"Yes... no, my head hurts. It feels like a symphony of rotten musicians blasting away in my mind."

Adoneesis frowned and lay a settling hand on Brachus who pranced and snorted impatiently. "Have you a history of subtle communication with other beings?"

"What?" Bryanna hurt too much to understand him.

"He is asking if you are psychic. That is the word in the human world, Adoneesis." Bronwen held her pace and directed Aurora to stand still. "It does not matter much if she was. The fact is that here in the realm she is obviously able to pick up on the emotions and energies of those that surround her."

Bronwen reached out to pat Bryanna's clenched fist. "It will recede shortly. You are being blasted and have not learned the control that we have. Just breath deeply and relax."

Another shaft of pain threatened to unseat Bryanna and she mumbled to Bronwen's retreating figure. "Ow, that's easy for you to say."

Adoneesis spurred Brachus and caused Bryanna to clasp the arm that held her close and to pray that they soon made it to the bottom. They did. Then she prayed the pain would recede. It didn't.

The ground leveled to a grassy cover and enabled Brachus and Aurora to let loose until they came to the butchered tree. Up close, the destruction battered the senses more sharply than from the mountaintop. A disentangled quality hung in the air and stifled Bryanna. She could only guess that Bronwen and Adoneesis felt the pain more deeply in their souls than she did. This place was their home, while she remained an outsider.

Their faces held the pain and a disbelieving glance between them intensified the hanging emotion. Afraid to speak, Bryanna bit her tongue to belay the questions firing her brain.

"I see no sign of Toran." Adoneesis scanned the debris. "Do you think he survived?"

"No. If he lived, this would not have happened. You know the way of the dryads; their life is forfeit before the life of their tree. He was old, but his powers ran strong enough to destroy whoever threatened Duir."

Confused and unbelieving of what she was hearing, Bryanna was about to ask for clarification, but a swift rustling in the forest brought Bronwen and Adoneesis to full alert. Brachus and Aurora perked their ears. Bronwen moved her hand to her waist, where Bryanna knew was sheathed an archaic, yet lethal looking knife, and Adoneesis moved his hand to the hilt of his sword.

Alert, expectant, grieving--they waited.

Twenty-one

Adoneesis hand touched upon the smooth hilt of his sword. Because of the woman seated in front of him, he would have to execute a left-handed draw, but a lifetime of practice had honed his skills to account for any eventuality. He could kill as easily with his left hand as with his right.

The rustle in the bush turned to muttered curses and Adoneesis' gut wrenched in fearful anticipation. He had never seen the true face of battle, yet his mind, body, and spirit rang with the age-old throb of survival, and Raegar's lessons ensured that Adoneesis could endure any form of physical mistreatment. Hours upon hours of standing on one leg, then the other, all the while holding his sword in one hand, while his body rebelled with vicious shaking and a constant ache for water. Raegar would pass by the training field now and again--a smirk on his face and threats of punishment for failure. Punishment more torturous than the exercise itself and the main reason Adoneesis had closed the dungeons to the light of day once he became king. He needed no reminders of time spent below the earth with no food, no water, and daily beatings.

Before his mind could wander too far into the past, someone broke through the forest bush and into the decimated clearing. Instantly recognizing a goblin, his sword was in hand and

Brachus was spurred full gallop toward the goblin standing among the debris that had once been Duir.

Sanity held no place in that moment, and Adoneesis crossed over the boundary into a mindless state of vengeful fury. Bellowing a pain-filled roar, he lost awareness of everything and saw only the hateful face of the one responsible for destroying an icon. History itself lay slaughtered on the ground that had given life to the mighty tree.

But something was wrong. The edges of his vision revealed a hazy familiarity. Voices screamed. Were they in his head? He couldn't be sure. The focus of his rage had not moved. The goblin's ugly face registered fear mixed with silent pleading. A warning screamed in his brain and Adoneesis was sure he was going crazy, until he realized the familiar vision was Krickall. And his life-long friend was waving his arms madly and rushing to stand in front of the goblin.

Fangs, if he did not pull up, his sword would kill for sure, but it wouldn't be the goblin, it would be Krickall. As the thought was born, Brachus ground his hooves into the dirt and brought them to a grinding halt with the sword tip mere inches from Krickall's white face.

"By the Lady, Krickall, what are you doing? I almost killed you." Adoneesis pushed Bryanna aside and jumped from Brachus--his shaky legs barely able to support him. He thrust Krickall aside and punched a finger toward the goblin. "Why do you risk your life for this slag? Does he hold any responsibility for this destruction?"

Only then did Adoneesis realize that others stood nervously behind Krickall. Another goblin, obviously female based on length and color of hair, as well as the rise of her breasts as she inhaled sharply when his gaze fell to her. Arm protectively wrapped around her shoulders stood a male whose very presence invoked sensations of wistful nostalgia. Tall and gaunt with white hair to match tatty beard, the stranger wore simple clothes and no shoes. Adoneesis' stomach heaved, and a brief flash of regret stabbed him in the chest. Regret for what, he had no idea.

Before he was able to question the stranger, he was assaulted. Something slammed into the side of his neck and tried to choke the life out of him. His first reaction was of defense, but the high-pitched screech in his ear stilled his sword hand.

"Oh, King, we have found you. I thought you were dead. Oh, you have no idea what we have been through. Have you found the child? Are you coming to save Dunraven?"

Adoneesis allowed Bailiwick his moment of reunion. "Ouch, Bailiwick, settle down. Who would have thought such a tiny creature holds such strength in his skinny little arms."

"My arms are not skinny," Bailiwick retorted indignantly and pulled back to hover, his hands on hips, just beside Adoneesis. "Humph! That's the thanks I get for saving everyone." The pixie whirled about mid-air and landed back on Adoneesis shoulder. "Oh, it is soooo good to have you back again."

His antics raised subdued chuckles among the mismatched group, but faded into an awkward silence as Adoneesis raised his hand. "It would seem I have missed much in being absent from my lands. I need answers." He stabbed a finger at the offensive goblins. "Why are these disgusting creatures in my sight? Who is this stranger who so resembles Merlin?"

Adoneesis hadn't missed the stranger's resemblance to the ancient magician. Although his eyes were ice blue rather than amber, they sparked with the same intelligence and wisdom, while his aura oozed power and strength. Maybe not as disciplined as Merlin, but then Adoneesis would wager the stranger had not attained the great age of Merlin.

"What did you mean, Bailiwick, about having saved everyone's life? Krickall, why have you left Dunraven unguarded? And what in the name of all the ancients happened to Duir?"

His voice cracked with emotion. The force of many eyes burned into him even as he strained to retain the strength expected of him. He panicked. This was more than he could handle. Krickall's presence could only mean that Dunraven had fallen to the enemy. Yet, two of the enemy stood here as if welcome by the others. The great tree that had once been Duir, now lay good for nothing but firewood. By the stars, such a waste. All this was his responsibility. He was King of the Faerie Realm, and as such, all lives were his to protect, whether they be faerie, beast, or nature.

The softness of a voice whispering in his ear was the only thread to sanity he held. "Calm yourself. The time of your destiny is upon you, and you will find the strength within yourself to handle all that transpires."

Adoneesis looked into ice-blue eyes of the white-bearded stranger and noted the weariness of his gaunt features. Who he was, Adoneesis had no idea, but the urge to trust him sang strongly through his blood. A thread of understanding connected them, and Adoneesis took a deep shuddering breath as he turned to face the onlookers.

It was then that he noticed the tears pouring down Bronwen's face. He would have thought she cried for Duir and the demise of Toran, but her gaze fixed steadily on the stranger. For but a brief flash of time, her features changed and beauty shone from her. Then, with a gasp, she hid her face in her hands and turned away--her shoulders shaking with sobs.

Chaos broke loose in the clearing.

From deep in the forest, a gray shadow exploded into the group of bystanders, and from high on the mountain they had just descended, the pounding of hooves struck desperately upon stone. A gray wolf and a cream colored unicorn.

Adoneesis was shoved aside, almost falling to his knees, as a large wolf leapt toward the stranger. Automatically, Adoneesis reached for his sword, only to withdraw when the wolf knocked the stranger to the ground and used a large, sloppy tongue to wet his face.

Tattooed arms wrapped around the wolf and the stranger hugged the huge, furry wolf close. "Gray Wolf, my friend, how I have missed your company. Now get off my chest so I can breathe."

At that moment, the unicorn skid to a stamping halt and screamed a defiant battle cry. She reared high and brought her hooves to the ground by the butchered tree. Her nostrils flared in protest. Adoneesis was sure he saw the light of tears in her eyes. Did unicorns cry? Nothing would surprise him on that day.

He watched helplessly as Bryanna advanced on the rearing unicorn, but he'd learned his lesson and left her to soothe the wild beast. If anyone could, it would be her. He let his gaze wander to the motley crowd and shook his head. Two goblins-- his sworn enemies, a stranger who resembled Merlin and held some hold over Bronwen's wolf, his friend and trusted companion, Krickall, the prophetess, the human woman, a unicorn, a wolf, and last but not least, Bailiwick. What manner of fate brought them here to stand amidst the destruction of Duir? What state did Dunraven lay in that Krickall had abandoned the lands? And what, oh what, was he to do about it all? He felt far too inadequate to deal with whatever circumstances tested him on that day.

With a sigh, he shook his head, took a deep, shuddering sigh, and raised his voice to override the din. "Enough. It is time for answers. Bailiwick, build a fire, but use Duir's wood only at threat of your own life. Bronwen..." he lowered his voice to a respectful level. "Please prepare a meal. I think we could all use food. Krickall, I want to know what has happened and who these goblins are that you bring them with you as friends."

His gaze fell to the longhaired stranger. "I would have your name also."

"Lapis. I am called Lapis."

A familiar name. Adoneesis had heard it whispered by others when he was young, only to have them hush and scurry off as they became aware of his presence. A name that haunted his dreams and became the creator of his youthful imaginings of a great and mighty warrior who threw magic from his hands. Instead, before him stood a gaunt man of indiscriminate age or bearing.

"But *who* are you? Where do you hail from? What is your purpose here?"

"All will become clear. Now, King, if you would excuse an old man, I am very weary and would like to rest. Krickall is more than capable of filling in the details."

Lapis bowed respectfully and found a secluded spot where he lay on the ground, pulled his clothes closely about him, and curled up as if to nap. Rather than be insulted by his refusal to explain himself, Adoneesis admired how Lapis retained the right amount of respect for his king, yet still did just what he wanted in the end. Subtle diplomacy.

His gaze quickly assessed that Bailiwick and Bronwen were performing their requested tasks. Bryanna had managed to calm the unicorn and now helped Bronwen prepare a meal, while the unicorn snuffled her nose about the debris as if searching for something. Gray Wolf trotted over to Lapis and, head up and perusing the area in a guard position lay down beside him. The goblins, unsure and afraid, huddled together. The male goblin muttered under his breath only to flush when the female shushed him.

Adoneesis threw his arm over his friend's shoulder. "Come, Krickall. Tell me of your ordeal, and give me a very good reason not to slice the heads off these offensive creatures."

A glimmer of satisfaction rushed through him at the look of terror that lit the faces of the goblins. If he found out they were in any way responsible for the death of Toran and the destruction of Duir, he would not take their heads. That was too fast of a death. No, he would make sure they suffered greatly before they died.

~ * ~

Bryanna threw more carrots in to the hastily prepared broth of vegetables. Her gaze wandered to Adoneesis and his giant red-haired friend and touched briefly on the strange looking goblins, and over to the sleeping figure and watchful wolf.

"I thought Gray Wolf belonged to you," she addressed Bronwen who silently sliced up some field potatoes Bailiwick had found on his search for wood.

Pain crossed through Bronwen's eyes. "Gray Wolf belongs to no one, no more than Shadow Dancer does." Black eyes sought out the wolf and his companion. Fires of emotion flamed briefly, and then her gaze returned to the potatoes, as if looking were a crime. Tears glazed Bronwen's eyes and she whispered, "I had no idea he came from Lapis. We have not seen each other in many years. When Gray Wolf appeared at the time Lapis disappeared, I suppose I should have realized... but so much was happening."

"You love him, don't you?"

"Gray Wolf, of course I do."

Bryanna laughed. "You know who I mean." Thoughtfully, she set the wooden spoon onto a nearby rock and fixed her gaze on Bronwen. "Can we talk?"

"I thought that is what we were doing."

"No, I mean, can we be honest with each other? *Really* talk. Just you and me."

Bronwen frowned. Her eyes softened in resignation. "Yes, Bryanna, we can talk."

"Good." Now that she'd opened the door, she had no idea what she wanted to say. All her life, she'd shied away from what she considered her aunt's strange ways. Now, Bryanna's wildest imaginings paled in comparison to the situation in which she found herself. "Oh, Aunt Shirley, if you could only see me now."

"Aunt Shirley?" Bronwen prompted.

"My father's sister. She raised me after my parents died in a car crash. The police said alcohol was a contributing factor, but neither of them ever touched the stuff."

"How old were you when they died?"

"Six. I was with a babysitter when the police came knocking on the door and changed my life. The next few days passed quickly, in a haze of tears. Right up until the day my aunt came to pick me up at the foster home I'd been sent to, I insisted that my parents would be coming to pick me up. I sat by the window day after day and waited. When the yellow cab pulled up out front and my aunt stepped out of the cab, I knew the truth. My parents were gone."

"I am so sorry, Bryanna." Bronwen sighed and made a move as if to speak. Instead, she cut up another potato and threw it into the pot.

"It's all right. At least I thought it was."

"What do you mean?"

"The letter. My aunt died recently..."

"I know. I am sorry for that as well. Your life has taken many turns that have battered your emotions, but the pain is now part of who you are and will be there to lend you strength when needed."

Ignoring most of Bronwen's words, Bryanna's attention focused on the first two. "You know. How can you possibly know that my aunt is dead?"

"Come, Bryanna, think back to the cemetery and use your new-found understanding of what is possible."

Bryanna remembered her aunt's funeral, the despair, and the condolences from people who never knew her aunt, and the cold, bitter weather. But what she remembered most about that day was afterward--when she was alone in the cemetery, the wind biting through her light jacket and silk dress and flinging her hair about her face in reckless abandon.

Understanding dawned. "That was you? I remember the mist and then I heard singing, but there was no one around. I didn't feel alone, yet I couldn't see anyone. I felt a familiar sensation." She gasped. "That was you. My God, you came to me when I was younger as well, didn't you."

"Yes. I was able to cross the lines between our worlds twice. The first time with no effort, it took me unaware and unprepared. The second time, I intentionally set out to make a mind connection with you. I am surprised you remember my first visit."

"Aunt Shirley was so upset when I fainted and then woke up to tell her I'd heard voices and seen a face. She kept repeating, *It's begun. It's begun.* We moved immediately after that, as if we hadn't moved enough already. I chalked it up to her usual crazy ways that I now realize weren't so crazy after all."

"She was trying to keep you safe."

"I know."

Bronwen shot her a look of calculation, as if measuring how much to tell her. "You also know that your parent's accident was no accident."

Yes, she knew, but that didn't stop her heart from clenching in a knot of pain, or her eyes from welling with tears. She managed to whisper, "I know. Aunt Shirley left me a letter."

"Oh." Bronwen raised an eyebrow. "What did the letter say?"

Bryanna recited the contents of the letter to the best of her memory while Bronwen ceased all pretense of peeling potatoes. Her black eyes focused intently on Bryanna's face and weighed her words.

"Your aunt was extremely well informed. How did she know come to know so much about your destiny? A destiny that should never have come into being."

"I don't know. She was into a lot of stuff, you know, tarot cards, psychic readings and such."

"I do not know much about any of those things."

"The way she used to explain it was to say that she was in touch with the energies around her. According to her, very thought and emotion, past and present, are in the atmosphere for anyone to access if only they open themselves up to the possibilities. Something like the tarot cards, for instance, were a tool to stimulate her senses and help her read the energy all around her."

"I see. Your aunt was a very wise woman."

"Yes," Bryanna agreed. "Much wiser than I ever gave her credit for while she was alive. It's strange, you know, that I can accept all this so easily, as if a part of me always knew the truth. Maybe that's why I rebelled with such fervor against everything she tried to teach me. If I denied it and suppressed that part of me, some inner part of me thought I would live a normal life."

"Who knows what the heart holds. The fact is that you are here now and fate has been set into motion, whatever the outcome."

Bryanna noticed Bronwen's gaze flick over to Lapis and then back to the flickering fire. "I would say that you have a very good idea what your heart holds," she teased.

Bryanna was surprised to see the hint of a blush spread across Bronwen's wrinkled features, only to be replaced by a haunted look of longing. She immediately felt sorry for teasing the old woman, and wondered at what kind of fate would make friends out of two such different beings under such extreme circumstances. She laid her hand on Bronwen's shoulder.

"Sorry. I shouldn't have teased you."

"No. You speak the truth. We're really talking. Just you and me. Remember?"

Bryanna laughed. "Okay, your feelings for Lapis are obvious, but I'm confused by the way you look at Adoneesis." She carefully set some plates on the ground to serve the stew. "Care to tell me what's going on there."

As much as Bronwen's face had colored at the mention of Lapis' name, it went stark white at the mention of Adoneesis. Her shaking hand stopped midway to adding some potatoes into the pot and her eyes filled with tears. Recovering quickly, she dropped the potatoes into the boiling water, her lips pressed firmly together.

Immediately contrite, but extremely curious, Bryanna hastened to apologize. "Bronwen, I'm sorry, I didn't... I just..."

"It is a very emotional subject to discuss, is it not?"

Lapis' voice cut into the tense moment. He had awakened and managed to come upon their conversation without their hearing him. He looked not quite as gaunt after his brief nap, and his blue eyes sparkled with restrained emotion as they rested on Bronwen.

Bronwen looked to Lapis and the air cracked with unspoken words, almost as if the two of them communicated on another level of understanding. Bryanna made a move to leave, but Bronwen gestured for her to stay.

"No. Lapis and I will go from the sight of others to talk." Her gaze flickered to a squatting Adoneesis who was listening intently to whatever tale Krickall told.

~ * ~

"You tell me that Dunraven, the home of my birth, entrusted to me for safe-keeping by all the generations who have come before me, is now in the hands of a goblin and you expect me to remain calm." Adoneesis snorted and rose to his feet with one snapping motion of anger. He ran a hand through his hair and rubbed it vigorously across his aching neck. Fangs. Roiling with frustration, he turned on Krickall. "How could you let this happen? I trusted you with everything."

A stricken look crossed Krickall's face and gave way to one of resignation. He bowed his head and Adoneesis felt instant regret for directing his anger where it did not belong. He knew Krickall would have let the goblin spill his blood on the lands of Dunraven rather than give up.

"Tell me, friend, what made you lay down your sword in surrender?"

Krickall, the fiercest of faeries, spoke with the tremble of tears in his voice. "Analiese. The goblin held a knife to her throat and would have sliced if I had not surrendered." With shoulders shaking, Krickall knelt on the ground before Adoneesis. "I know you can never forgive me, but I beg you to make sure Analiese is taken care of, even if it means she mates with Mayard. I trust your sword's cut will be smooth and swift."

He leaned over. Adoneesis stared at the back of Krickall's neck in confusion, until sickly realization dawned. Feeling nauseous, he grasped Krickall by the shoulder and pulled him to an upward kneeling position.

"Stars in heaven, how can you even think I would do such a thing? We are not primitive beings here. Fangs, Krickall, I need you by my side to win back Dunraven and save the realm."

"But, it is the way of honor in battle. I failed you; therefore, my life is yours to take."

Adoneesis snorted. "Well, if that is the way of honor in battle, then I choose to be dishonorable. You will live. I have spoken." Seeing the stricken look on Krickall's face, Adoneesis softened his voice. "Krickall, I do not know of love and its grasp on the emotions, but I know I would have done the same as you if any faerie that trusted me had been in such a situation as Analiese." He thrust his hand out and held it steady for Krickall to take hold.

"Come, we have much planning to do. Besides I am anxious to find out more of this magician whom I have never heard of until today. Mayhap his powers will help us regain Dunraven."

Wary, but relieved at still being alive, Krickall grasped the hand extended before him and rose to his feet. It was a powerful moment as their eyes connected, forming a bond much more than friendship--an unspoken alliance of blood for blood, life for life.

Adoneesis smiled. "Yes, what a waste it would be for me to take the life of one who would give his own life for me."

A flicker of movement from the campfire drew Adoneesis' attention. Bronwen and the mage made their way from the fire towards a nearby copse of trees, and he wondered what situation would entail them looking for privacy. A high-pitched screeching from the forest where Bailiwick had been collecting wood brutally interrupted his questioning thought. Adoneesis and Krickall covered their ears at the same time as they set themselves into a high-speed race to the source of the wrenching sound.

On their heels followed Bryanna, as well as Bronwen and the mage. Adoneesis set the pace and covered the terrain quickly. The screeching subdued into a more recognizable sound, and Bailiwick's babbling cry of distress formed words.

"Toran. I have found Toran. Oh, come quickly. Hurry. He needs help." Another screech of fear and dismay followed.

Adoneesis broke into the small clearing first. His gaze connected with Bailiwick's fluttering form and pale face and then fell to an indescribable mound on the ground. Only when the mound moved, did he realize it was Toran, and the tree faerie still lived--barely.

Racing to the dryad's side, Adoneesis threw himself on the ground, intended to help, but he had no idea how. Toran was of no substance. His life-light usually reflected bright, vivid colors, but Adoneesis was hardly able to detect a flicker and cried out in frustration at his lack of understanding of the ancient faerie.

The others arrived, including the goblins, but it was Lapis who knelt by Toran. Laying blue-veined hands over the fading aura of light, Lapis closed his eyes and breathed deeply. Slowly, but obviously, a shaft of light formed between Lapis and Toran. Glowing and intensifying, the light gave strength to Toran who raised his head and smiled a feeble smile.

"Ahhh, I had given up hope. I held on as long as I could."

"Do not tire yourself." Adoneesis warned. "We are here now. We will heal you."

"No, it is too late. I am held here only by the shared energy of the mage."

His light form shivered and wavered, but Lapis gave more of his own to sustain Toran's connection. The effort cost Lapis greatly, and his hands trembled.

"I must hurry. The thread weakens." Toran looked to Bryanna. "I see you have the child--a woman now. Good, good.

Hear me. The verse to stimulate her memory and powers was in Duir. It has been destroyed, and I have no strength left to relate the words."

"But what of Raven?" Bailiwick cut in excitedly. "He was there at the plan's inception, remember, he must know the verse."

Toran moaned and shifted position. "He died when the Lady's energy passed on to the prophetess. Another ellyllon knew. Kypher was his name, but I have not heard of him in many years. Toran's voice weakened and Adoneesis leaned closer to hear his words. "The secret may be locked in the prophetess along with the Lady's energy." He took a shuddering breath, fighting to stay alive. "One more thing. Find... crystal... light."

"The Crystal of Light," Bailiwick whispered and then clamped his hand over his mouth in dismay. His remark earned a calculating look from Bronwen before she turned a worried look to Lapis before resting on the fading dryad.

Adoneesis wondered how the little pixie knew of the Crystal of Light that Toran spoke of, when he had never heard of such a thing. He also wanted to know what past Bronwen shared with the mage. Her eyes bespoke of strong emotions either forged over a long period of time, or seared instantly through tragic circumstances. Maybe both. No matter, questions would be asked and answered later.

"Toran," Adoneesis had one question that needed asking now, "who committed this horrendous act of destruction and death?"

A brief flame of light invoked by anger faded to a barely discernable flicker. "H-humaaan. Gar." More a gasp than spoken word, yet simple enough for all to understand.

Releasing the connection from Toran's aura, Lapis sank back on his heels and rested his head in his hands. Toran's essence that once burned so brightly now rose above the assembled group and dissipated into nothing more than the pale light of dusk.

With the absence of Toran's light, came the vibration of urgency and a rising fervor for revenge. Adoneesis stood, carefully, thoughtfully, wiping dirt from his knees. No one moved while he looked at each individual in the mismatched group. As his gaze came to them one by one, they felt the assessment and judgment passed. They were at war, and Adoneesis was king. If he so desired, he could order the death of any one of them with no explanation.

He narrowed his gaze at the goblins and noticed how the female stood tall and returned his stare, while the male dropped his gaze to the ground and shivered in fear. But, what was that? A nudge and a whispered word from the female, and the male lifted his face and squared his shoulders. Hmmm, interesting.

"I understand that Gar is no friend of yours, and you helped in the escape of the others." Adoneesis directed his remark to the male goblin, which immediately lowered his head and mumbled something.

"Speak up, goblin."

"Gar is a wormy, squirmy, germy, goblin."

Adoneesis couldn't help it. He chuckled. Krickall had told him of how Ghilphar and Gwepper were prisoners, and how they had fought just as hard to escape Gar's grasp. He would give them the benefit of the doubt, but he would watch them very carefully.

He extended a hand. "Welcome to our group."

Gwepper eyed the offered hand, awkwardly took it in his, and then proceeded to practically shake Adoneesis arm from its socket by vigorously pumping.

"Enough, Gwepper," Ghilphar cautioned. "Leave him energy to wield his sword."

Adoneesis turned his gaze to the mage, fully intending to remain in control this time and find out just who Lapis was and why he'd been a prisoner of Gar. Just as he opened his mouth the question the mage, Bronwen spoke.

"Come, I know no one is hungry, but we need to eat to keep up our strength."

With mumblings of accord, the saddened group made their way to the fire and food and left Adoneesis with questions unanswered and the distinct feeling that Bronwen had deliberately interrupted his attempt to question the mage.

Shaking his head, he strode to the fire and settled on his heels. Bronwen handed him a plate piled high with stew, but before she could withdraw her hand, he grasped her wrist and quietly declared. "You have your way now, prophetess, only because of my regard for you, but my questions of your relationship to the mage will be asked and answered. Dunraven and the future of the realm are more important than any secret you may hide."

Bronwen withdrew her hand from his grasp and smiled wistfully. "King, your questions will be answered, but I take offense to the inference that either Lapis or I would withhold information that would result in any harm to the realm of faerie."

Their eyes connected and the resulting surge of energy threatened to overwhelm Adoneesis, yet he held the gaze. Bronwen was the one to drop her gaze, but not before Adoneesis detected a hint of satisfaction flash in her black eyes. He was confused. He had stared her down, yet she seemed glad, almost proud. Females, there was so much to learn about them.

"Fine, I will trust in your loyalty to the realm, but do not wait too long. I will know of your relationship to the mage."

"Of course. Now eat, you will need your strength."

The meal passed quickly. No one felt the need to speak, each one lost in his or her own thoughts. Adoneesis silently cursed the disappearing sun, as he knew the darkness would limit any ability to travel to Dunraven. Himself, he would have traveled through the darkest of nights, but he was responsible for the safety of the group and could not risk them in the dangers of the night.

Startling the group from their quiet time of restful respite, he declared, "Tonight we rest. Tomorrow, we ride for Dunraven."

Twenty-two

Gar looked at Mayard's perfect features and soft hands. Revulsion flared within him and he snarled, satisfaction ringing through him at the look of fear that wrenched the faerie's milk-white face.

"Time now for you to earn your reward." Gar's gaze ran the length of the dining area to rest greedily on the light-haired faerie female. "If I think you lie to me, I will take quick action." He punctuated his words by drawing his sword midway from its sheath, the sound of steel scraping against the wooden scabbard.

Mayard swallowed. Hard. "I understand," his rasping whisper barely rose above the snickering of the assembled goblins.

Gar raised his hand to quell the rising din and secretly enjoyed how he could manipulate with fear. His goblins laughed at Mayard, but every one of them dreaded the possibility of being centered out or brought to task. Such a thing never boded well, and Gar maintained that fear with beatings and other forms of torture for any slight against him, imagined or otherwise. His gaze flickered from left to right, always searching, always reassuring himself that he held total control.

Usually he did.

Until the wretched human had entered his life.

Navarre stood to Gar's right and looked out over the goblins. A sneer caught the edge of Gar's lip before he was able to control himself. Would not do any good to let the human see what he really thought of him. Wretched beast. If not for Navarre's promise of complete power, Gar would have had him killed long ago. In fact, now that he sat upon the throne of Dunraven and Adoneesis was wandering the human world looking for a child who probably did not exist, Gar was of the mind to have the human thrown into the dungeons. He should probably have him killed, but what fun in that?

He had given no order yet, only because the human held a certain amount of magic and understood the words written in the book. Maybe Gar could use him. Although he doubted the ragged old book held much that would be of any help. Clod's feet, he himself--Gar, King of the Goblins--had taken over the throne with no help from the human or the book. Yes, Navarre's time ran short, but first, he needed to put his attention to the quivering faerie kneeling before him.

"Stand up, you poor excuse for pig's breath."

Mayard stood, fear clinging to him worse than the stench of pig's breath Gar accused him of being. "I have done everything you have asked of me. I have shown you the store of weapons, and directed you to the various paths in and out of Dunraven." His voice cracked. "Please. I have proven myself to you. What more do you want?"

"You did not show me the tree of knowledge. I needed the human to tell me of the tree."

Mayard's eyes darted around the room, as if seeking escape. "I... I thought it to be just a tree as any other."

His word earned him a smack across the face. "You lie." Gar narrowed his gaze and said. "You can regain my trust if you show me the treasure of Dunraven."

Mayard's face lit with confusion. "No such thing exists."

Gar slammed the blunt side of his sword against Mayard's head; the blow sent him sprawling onto the hard-packed dirt floor.

Analiese gasped and made a move to help, but Gar's goblins restrained her. Gar motioned for her release and she rushed to Mayard's side. More snickers, accompanied by murmurs and lip smacking sounded among the goblins, most of whom eyed Analiese with intense sexual fervor. Gar snarled and chopped his hand through the air for silence. She belonged to him, no matter what promise he had made to Mayard. Greedily, he eyed her slender form and wished she had more girth, but her silken hair and other female attributes would make up for the lack.

Navarre whispered in his ear and rudely interrupted the direction of his thoughts. "Do not let yourself be led astray yet. The throne of Dunraven still rests shakily under you. Attend to those matters first, and then you may indulge your warped fantasies."

Incensed at the correction given so freely in front of his goblins, Gar snatched Navarre's throat between his gnarly fingers and slowly tightened his grip. "Do not ever speak to me in that way. You live only by my good wishes."

Piercing silver eyes clashed with mud-gray. Gar fought for dominance, but felt the thread of his power weakening against the human. He narrowed his eyes and sent all his hatred tunneling through his gaze until the thread strengthened. As satisfaction grew, so did his tenuous hold over Navarre until the human broke the silent struggle. His gaze fell from Gar's-- silver eyes flashing briefly. Only then did Gar loosen his hold on Navarre's throat.

"Yes. Do not ever forget that I am the one in charge." Gar turned his attention to Mayard who was attempting to stand with help from Analiese. "The book tells tales of a great treasure. The human here tells me the treasure lies here. Do you call him a liar?"

A dawning sense of futility Mayard's face. "No, I do not call him a liar, but I know of no treasure." Desperately his eyes searched out Analiese, as if hoping she could supply him with an answer, but she just shook her head and tears shined in her blue eyes.

Gar snarled and struck out at Mayard with his fist. "I want the treasure." In a fit of frustrated anger, the goblin wheeled to face Navarre. "Do you lie, human?"

Not a breath sounded in the room. Even Analiese's sobs stilled, as Gar's question hung in the silence. This time when Navarre met Gar's gaze. It was not with defiance, rather with certainty and assurance.

"The treasure exists. My father spoke of it on his deathbed and I would stake my life upon the truth of those words."

"You do stake your life on those words, so you better hope your father told you the truth."

Navarre bowed his head in acquiescence. "Yes, Gar."

"It is King Gar. Now leave me. I am tired of your human face." He waved Navarre from his side as if he were an irritating bug, which is exactly what Gar considered him to be.

With a twitch of his lips, Navarre left the room. Gar watched his retreating back with satisfaction. He had handled the human well. Now, he needed to handle the scholar and plan his defense of the throne.

His eyes fell to Mayard who stood on shaky legs. "You." He pointed his sword. "Have you told me all you know of the pathways into Dunraven?"

Mayard nodded, and then winced in pain. "Yes, I have told you all I know."

"You better hope so. Take him to the dungeons," he barked the order to the guards standing by Mayard.

"But you told me if I co-operated, you would spare my life."

"You are alive, are you not? But if you have lied to me, I will know just where to find you so I can flay your flesh from your bones with my sword."

Mayard blanched.

"Is there anything else you need add to your information?" Gar prompted.

"No. I have told all. What of Analiese?"

Gar's lip raised in a ghost of a smile. "She will be taken care of."

The guards grabbed Mayard and dragged him protesting from the room. "You promised. You said you wouldn't hurt her. You said she would be mine."

His voice echoed from the hallway and the goblins slathered and sniggered in anticipation. All eyes moved to Analiese, who backed into the corner. Gar let the goblins advance on her and stifled her with their very presence and obvious intent. Shivers rushed through his body as her face mirrored the fear of what was to come and his hand rested on his burgeoning groin. Gnarled hands grabbed for her clothes and she screamed. The sound of fear made Gar grind his hips into his own hand. Fangs, he loved fear. Nothing gave him sexual satisfaction as much. But he was not about to let such a beauty be wasted. She belonged to him, and if he let the hoard become too riled, even he would have a hard time controlling them.

"Enough." His voice slashed into the melee and brought the rabble to a reluctant halt. Relief registered on Analiese's face, until she looked into Gar's eyes. Then she shivered. Yes, she would be so much fun to control. "Grud, take her to my room.

And if you touch her you'll feel the tip of my blade sliding into your wretched body."

As Grud wrestled Analiese out of the room, Gar sat back and snorted. "Adoneesis will be here soon. We know about the secret pathways, so we hide there until he returns, and then we attack him. Only when he's dead can we celebrate our total control over the realm. All of you will be with me as I become the undisputed King of the Faerie Realm."

His goblins cheered and the din of excitement rose until Gar covered his ears with his hands to block out the sound. He sneered in satisfaction. Mindless idiots, they were as easy to control as the human was.

~ * ~

Navarre left the dining area quickly before he lost control of his emotions and blasted that damn goblin from the throne he held so tenuously. Taking the stairs two at a time, he swore that when the time finally came he would make Gar suffer. So close. That son of a bitch had come so close to dying and Navarre had barely been able to hold his powers in check when Gar had challenged him. To think, the dirty creature actually believed that he was the stronger of the two. Ha! Gar's arrogance would lead easily to his downfall.

The only thing that stopped Navarre from killing Gar with a thought was the knowledge that Gar's goblins would have killed him in a matter of seconds. Navarre's powers were not strong enough to direct against all the goblins at one time. He needed the crystal.

At this point, he also needed Gar to destroy Adoneesis. He didn't need the lineage of Adoneesis in the Book of Time to tell him that the former king was more of a reckoning of power than he could handle. It made sense to have Gar attempt to kill Adoneesis. If by some chance he succeeded, great. If he didn't, at least the act would leave Adoneesis weakened and distracted and make it easier for Navarre to kill him.

He slammed open his chamber door and entered the tiny room that Gar had bestowed upon him. Another blatant insult. Pacing the room to alleviate his anger, Navarre cursed his father for dying before revealing the exact location of the crystal. Gar's treasure. Thank God, he had not been more specific when he'd told Gar about the treasure hidden at Dunraven. While the stupid goblin searched for some mythical treasure that didn't exist, Navarre could search for the crystal.

Once found, the crystal would enhance his powers to such a state that no one could stop him from doing anything he wanted. With Adoneesis and Gar dead, Navarre would rule the realm of faerie. But that was just the beginning. Once he understood and could control the power of the crystal, he would go beyond the faerie realm. He would return to the world that had given him life and had done nothing but spit in his face. He'd return to the world of man.

Comforting himself with thoughts of revenge, greed, and ultimate power, Navarre settled into the only other piece of furniture in his room besides the narrow bed--a skinny wooden chair. Silently cursing the unforgiving hardness of the wood under his butt, Navarre vowed to make Gar pay. His gaze drifted to the flickering candle and his dark mind developed one torture after another for each insult heaped upon him by the arrogant goblin since they'd met.

Oh, yes, the future held such consummate rewards and possibilities.

~ * ~

Gar paused outside his chamber took a deep breath and settled his shaking hands. The blond-haired faerie waited for him on the other side. She'd been locked in there for a few hours now, long enough to worry and fret. Gar enjoyed his earlier manipulation of her fear when he had set the goblins on her in a pack, and he hoped she would show her appreciation at calling them off and leaving her unharmed. Yes, there were many ways she could show her appreciation.

A trickle of drool marking his chin, Gar shoved open the door, puffed out his chest, and made his entrance. At first, he saw nothing, but a movement of cloth at the window quickly drew his attention. The female sat half way through the window--the hem of her lavender skirt tucked up around her legs to reveal a length of smooth, creamy flesh. Only one leg though, because the other one hung out the window.

Gar growled. Upon hearing the feral sound, Analiese snapped her head around and locked her startled gaze with Gar's. His groin throbbed as fear roiled off the female in waves of tension. Gar curled his lip in a half smile and stepped toward her. She whimpered and frantically tried to shove herself through the too small window. Gar stepped closer and grasped her hair in his fist. With a mighty yank, he pulled her against his fully aroused body and snarled in her ear.

"Is this how you repay me for saving you earlier?"

Her heart beat a fierce staccato against him and she quivered. The delight of it raced through Gar. She was probably so scared she would not even be able to talk, just rut. Maybe scream a little. Yes, a scream or two would arouse him even more. He pinched her tit to illicit one of those screams and was not disappointed. He threw her to the bed and kicked off his boots.

Analiese sat up and spat on the ground at his feet. "You saved me only to use me yourself. Do not expect any thanks for that, you animal."

Surprised that the she had any courage left, Gar grabbed Analiese's shirt in a fist and jerked. The sound of ripping material rewarded him. His eyes fell instantly to the exposed flesh and he grunted his approval at the sight of her tits. She tried to cover herself, but he grasped her hands in one of his and pulled them above her head. Writhing on the bed, trying the break free, she only enticed Gar more. His cock rose hard and he knelt upon the bed, one leg on either side of the female. She was his and she was going to find out all that that entailed. Freeing his cock from his restrictive pants, he muttered, "Tonight, you will find out what it takes to be the property of Gar, King of the Faerie Realm."

Intent on his warped pleasure, Gar barely registered the muffled words spoken by the female.

"Krickall, I need you."

Before Gar could attain the pleasure he was so intent on, a knock sounded at the door. "Leave me alone," he hollered.

The knock sounded again, but this time more timid. "Gar, the human says he needs to see you. Now."

With a roar of frustration, Gar pushed off the bed, adjusted his pants and strode to the door. "Now, you say. You dare to give me orders."

The hapless goblin delivering the message cringed. "N-no. The human, Navarre, he says it's urgent."

Gar struggled with his lust and anger at Navarre for daring to send a lackey to give orders. But, maybe Navarre had seen something in a vision. He glanced at the quivering faerie on the bed and smiled. Anticipation was a powerful aphrodisiac and the female was going nowhere. He'd go see what Navarre wanted.

Twenty-three

Adoneesis woke abruptly. He shook his head to clear it and tried to decipher what had awakened him. The sound of rustling and muttering in the dimness of early dawn alerted him and he reached for his ever-present sword.

"No need for that, King, 'tis only I," Krickall whispered as he pulled his boots on and rolled his blanket into a roll.

Sensing something amiss, Adoneesis thrust off his blanket and jumped to his feet. "Krickall, we have no plans to leave so early this morn." A wave of his hand encompassed the still sleeping forms huddled under blankets of wool and cotton. "We have yet to eat the morning meal."

"I meant to leave without disturbing anyone." Krickall grabbed a saddle and moved toward Aurora. "I must leave. Now."

Fearing the worst because he trusted Krickall, but not sensing any danger nearby, Adoneesis waited for an explanation. Krickall did not disappoint him.

"Analiese is in danger. In my sleep, I heard her calling to me." His rough voice cracked with strained emotion. "She needs my help, so I ride for Dunraven."

Adoneesis placed a restraining hand on Krickall's arm and winced inwardly at the knotted tension of muscles. By the

Lady, his friend was of a powerful build. "You cannot go alone. We will all ride with you."

Krickall shrugged off his hand. "I will go faster alone."

"Then you will die alone as well," Adoneesis snapped back at him. "We need to work together, or we will all die, Analiese included. You know my words to be true. Stop being so stubborn. Besides, there is not a steed here that will let you mount them."

Krickall hesitated, and then tossed the saddle to the ground. "Then I will run." A tear formed in the corner of his eye and Krickall did nothing to wipe it away as it wound a crooked path down his cheek. When he spoke, his words sounded like a mere trickle in a mighty river. "She is alone."

Heart breaking for Krickall, but needing to instill logic in the midst of emotion, Adoneesis asked, "Is she alive?"

"Yes."

"Good. She is stronger than you or Mayard ever gave her credit for. She will survive until we get there. Together." He narrowed his gaze, stared Krickall down and hoped against hope that he would not need to make it an order.

Torn emotions ravaged Krickall's face and he hesitated as if weighing his feeling of love against loyalty to his king.

"King Adoneesis is correct. We must all ride together if we want to win against what faces us." Lapis hovered like a wraith in the shadows.

"We know what faces us. A rebel goblin has taken over Dunraven and proclaimed himself king," Adoneesis stated.

Lapis chuckled, but it was not a nice sound. Within the depths of the simple sound rang a hint of fear. Adoneesis shivered. If the mythical Lapis held fear, the faeries must face an enemy greater than the goblin, Gar. "If you know something we do not, you must tell us."

"I know only what rides on the currents of the wind. Open yourself up and listen. You will know everything I do."

Adoneesis shook his head. "I do not have time for such babble. Lives rest on my actions, and my actions are based on knowledge I hold. Tell me what you know."

"Pity you do not understand your own powers, King. When you do, you will be better able to face what awaits you, not only at Dunraven, but within yourself."

Adoneesis struggled with the urge to trust Lapis, as nothing he had ever heard about the magician directed him to think ill of him, yet the responsibility of the realm rested on his shoulders and the urge to demand answers rang strong as well. Saddle leather creaked, Krickall awaited Adoneesis' command, and the blazing edge of the sun rose above the distant horizon as Lapis and Adoneesis locked gazes. Dull blue eyes ridden with pain flashed at Adoneesis--waiting, measuring, seeking something that Adoneesis was not prepared to give. Something of himself that he did not understand enough to give. Trust.

Bronwen's soft voice ended his internal struggle. "Adoneesis, feel with your heart and act accordingly."

Trust had never come easily for Adoneesis. He had trusted his own father, yet Raegar abused that trust until Adoneesis closed a part of himself to anyone. Now, the prophetess was asking him to open that part to a virtual stranger. No matter the myths of the mage, Adoneesis was not ready to give the fate of the realm into the hands of a stranger. Yet... a memory, or understanding, flashed in his mind. His heart fluttered with an aching sweetness of what could have been. Bah! None of it made any sense. His eyes probed Lapis' gaunt features. Not exactly sure how or why, Adoneesis came to a sudden belief that the mage would never cause harm to the realm or any faerie who resided within.

"Fine. I will trust that you hold no harmful knowledge from me."

"It is not just me you need to trust. It is yourself as well." A haunted smile touched Lapis' lips at the same time as a waft of mist drifted up from the dew-covered ground. Shrouding the mage in swirling tendrils, the mist suddenly disappeared leaving an empty space where Lapis had stood.

"What..." Adoneesis and Krickall exclaimed.

"He has gone to regenerate his energy. The last years have been so very hard on him that I'm surprised he survived." Bronwen's wistful gaze rested on the very spot where Lapis stood but a moment ago. Then, with a snap of the blanket she still held, she retorted. "Come, let us wake the others. There is much to do."

Adoneesis would know the past between Lapis and Bronwen, but now was not the time. "Yes. Bronwen, wake the others and get them to help prepare a quick meal. No time for a fire, we must ride. Krickall, you saddle the horses. We will need to double up."

Calculating in his mind, Adoneesis wished he could command Bryanna to ride with him, but the unicorn would not let anyone else sit upon her back without the human woman. Damn, he would not put Krickall with her. His friend was far too virile and a shaft of jealousy shot through him at the thought of them locked in close rhythm on the back of a galloping horse. No, there was only one way to go.

"Gwepper will ride with Bryanna, Krickall, you ride with Bronwen, and Ghilphar will come on Brachus with me. Bailiwick can rest on whoever's shoulder he wants; he weighs naught but a smidgen anyway. That way, the steeds will be evenly matched for weight and we can make better time."

"Yes, King." Krickall seemed satisfied that Adoneesis took his premonition seriously enough and he hastened to saddle Brachus and Aurora.

Hastily awakened and rushed through a meal of yesterday's cold oatmeal, everyone sensed the urgency and did surprisingly little grumbling. The only one who grumbled at all was Gwepper upon finding out he was expected to ride upon the unicorn.

"Rats, bats, and hats. I'll not ride on that beast."

Already mounted and trying to control the prancing unicorn, Bryanna held out her hand. "Come on, Gwepper, she won't hurt you."

Bailiwick, sitting on Bryanna's shoulder because he seemed to have developed an admiration for her, also encouraged Gwepper, who only shook his head and hunched his shoulders. "No, no, she is an evil creature. Gar said so."

Bailiwick flew into the air doing a double flip, while Bryanna gasped and looked for Adoneesis' reaction to Gwepper's declaration. His face darkened with thunderous rage. "You have done naught to make me distrust you until now, goblin. The unicorn embodies all that is good and light in this world. Gar is the evil one. If you cannot accept this, tell me now." His hand rested gently on his sword.

His dark eyes gleaming with fear at the threat, Gwepper cringed and looked helplessly to Ghilphar, already seated behind Adoneesis. His twisted features clearly showed an internal battle being waged. Finally, muttering and slobbering, Gwepper accepted Bryanna's hand, and in one agile leap, landed on the unicorn's back. A sigh of relief passed through the onlookers and Adoneesis felt Ghilphar's tense muscles relax against his back.

"All right then, we ride for Dunraven. As we get close, watch for my signal to stop. I know a way into the main tree and a room we can hide in while appraising the situation. Am I understood?" His gaze fixed on Krickall who nodded glumly in acknowledgement.

"Fine. Then let's ride. Let us hope Lapis does not tarry long. His help will be sorely needed." With a pointed gaze at Bronwen, who nodded as if reassuring Lapis would reappear in due time, Adoneesis spurred Brachus into a rearing charge and elicited a fearful squeal from Ghilphar. Shadow Dancer held a steady pace beside them, with Aurora galloping directly behind. A dragon steed, a unicorn, and a faerie steed thundered across the valley. Adoneesis would have appreciated the impressiveness the sight would have made, if the situation were not so dire.

~*~

Adoneesis and his group rode hard and stopped just outside Dunraven's limits to hide the horses. That was when Lapis magically appeared, his presence radiating a more steady force. Without hesitation, he approached Bailiwick and squatted down to the little pixie sitting cross-legged on a rock. Gently, he spoke. "It is time. I need to know now."

"Lapis, what..."

"Shhh." Lapis raised a hand to quell Adoneesis question. "Bailiwick knows of what I speak."

Bailiwick's shoulders slumped. "I guess it was stupid of me to think a dumb pixie would save the faeries."

"No, pixie, it was not a stupid hope. But time runs short and if we work together we have a chance of saving the realm."

"Together. Hmmm, I can live with that."

In a breathless barrage of words, Bailiwick told Adoneesis and Krickall about how he'd found the crystal and how Lapis sensed this just by touching him in the dungeons. Adoneesis was shocked that such power resided in his own sleeping chamber and he'd never known. Even more surprised that Bailiwick had kept such a secret from him.

"Fine," Adoneesis said. "We now have two feats to accomplish. Rescue Analiese and retrieve Lapis' crystal. Bailiwick, you know the pathways better than anyone, so you lead the way."

Making sure that Bronwen, Bryanna, and the goblins were well hidden, Adoneesis and the others left for Dunraven to rescue Analiese. "Even that laggard, Mayard, if necessary," Krickall muttered. Adoneesis smiled at Krickall's remark.

It had been easy to sneak past the patrolling goblins. With a combination of Krickall's scouting skills and a touch of magic from Lapis, the three of them made it without incident to Adoneesis' secret room atop the tree.

"Wait here until I return," Lapis gave a stern warning and then disappeared.

"Blasted magician." Adoneesis grumbled, but said nothing more aloud. The time would give him a chance to decide how to find Analiese without detection. It would be no easy feat to find her and get her out.

Twenty-four

Gar sniffed the air and grunted. "I can't smell him. Are you sure he's coming?"

Navarre gritted his teeth and calmed himself before replying. "I said he would come today, and he will."

Gar paced the yard outside the main tree of Dunraven, while he'd divided Grud and most of the other goblins to the different routes into Dunraven. Not a one had been left unguarded. "Humph, how you can know fuddles my brain, but I will give you time to prove your words."

Fuddles his brain, indeed. He'd need a brain in order for it to be fuddled. The uncharitable thought flashed through Navarre's mind along with a flash of doubt. Maybe he'd misread the leaden gloom permeating the air, or the expectant hum of anticipatory vibes that prodded him. No. Navarre would not doubt the senses that he'd honed through years of strident meditation and daily practice.

Unfortunately, Gar was not patient, and if Adoneesis did not show today, Navarre's life would stand on precarious ground. If worse came to worse and Gar turned on him, Navarre could escape using minor magic, but the crystal remained here at Dunraven, and without that, he'd never have the power to rule Gar's goblins and the realm of faerie. He needed to stay in

Gar's good graces until he held the power of the crystal in his own hands. He cursed his weak half-breed blood and the limitations his human blood put on his powers. Oh, how he'd love to flay the skin from Gar's living body and watch the goblin writhe in agony, all the while screaming for mercy.

With a sigh of resignation he replied, "Gar, my instincts have never steered me wrong. Last night, the Hunter's Moon hung high in the night sky. The feeling rang true within me. The king returns today. I feel his presence, not to mention the presence of the magician who escaped from your dungeons." Navarre enjoyed mentioning the escape. It steamed Gar no end and this time was no exception.

Gar thrust his face close enough that saliva spittle landed on Navarre's face. "I am not as stupid as you think, human. I know when you bait me. I do not like you and you do not like me. The time soon comes when we will see who is the smarter one, and I will not lose to a human half-breed." He spit on the ground at Navarre's feet. "Now leave my sight. You distract me."

"Fine. I am glad we understand each other, goblin. But mark my words, you have no idea the powers you are dealing with and I have no intention of letting a living example of scum such as you stand in my way." So much for staying in Gar's good graces.

Gar drew his sword and thrust it toward Navarre. Silvery steel flashed in the afternoon sun. "I have what I want, so I don't need you. Your words are empty, and the book you hold is nothing more than words of long ago that hold no power over me. I don't need it any more than I do you. Go, or I will kill you now."

"Gladly." Navarre strode from Gar and felt as if the goblin were about to stab him in the back, but a quick glance backward showed the Gar staring off into the distance awaiting the arrival of Adoneesis. He was happy not to kowtow to Gar anymore, but he needed the crystal, and what better time to search than now. With the onset of the coming battle, he'd have free rein over the main tree, and that was where he felt the power of the crystal the strongest. Yes, the crystal laid hidden in one of the thirty some odd rooms of the main tree of Dunraven.

He hadn't been lying when he said he felt the presence of Lapis. When the two of them had bonded by Gar's wish to search for the child, the mage's magic had imprinted itself on Navarre, and he felt it now. Insidious and stifling, the magician invaded Navarre's mind.

Navarre crossed to the staircase and tried to decide whether to start his search upstairs or downstairs. A flicker of movement from the corner of his eye drew his attention to the front door. It was empty, but he knew then, as clearly as he knew his own name, that Lapis was after the crystal and was using magic to track him. Well, he wasn't going to get it, not after Navarre spent years planning this takeover of the faerie realm. Besides, Navarre considered the crystal his payment for years of abuse from his father. A worthless father's legacy. A book and a crystal--a legacy with which to rule the world.

A gentle finger of breath whispered across his earlobe and he slapped at the invisible force. "Damn you, Lapis, I know you are here. But the crystal is mine." The gentle whisper increased to a roaring crescendo and Navarre had trouble keeping his balance on the stairs. Fighting the invasive energy with his own mind, Navarre grasped the wall of knotted wood and reached deep within him. Gathering himself, he shot out a neutralizing thought to dispel the roar back to a mere whisper.

His lip curled into a grin. "You see, Lapis, I am the stronger one. You have years of decaying power to regenerate and not the time to do it in. I will possess the crystal--not you."

Defiantly throwing taunting words to the empty air, Navarre waited for an answering shot of pain. Nothing happened. The stupid mage probably wore out his powers trying to scare him into running. His chest near exploding with the triumph, Navarre took the stairs two at a time until he reached the top. A choice of rooms lining both sides of the hallway faced him. Where to begin? Taking a deep breath, he cleared his mind and focused on a mental image of the crystal he'd formed over the years.

Although the book never described the crystal in detail, Navarre somehow knew the stone was roughly hewn, not polished, or smooth with the ages. His mind's eye had seen the fist-sized rock shimmer in the light and reflect shafts of prism-like colors from its very core. Vibrating with power and stunning in its basic simplicity, the Crystal of Light was pure, white light energy and Navarre ached to hold the crystal. He'd spent the years since his father's death planning for the moment he could run his hands over the surface of the stone and make its power his own.

As if thinking about the crystal gave him a connection, he suddenly felt an insistent pull toward Gar's sleeping chamber. Pushing aside the uneasiness of feeling an unseen gaze on him, he entered the chamber. An immediate stab of pulsing energy thrust itself at him and he had to take a deep breath to clear the buzzing from his head. Strange, he'd been in Gar's chamber before and felt no such reaction. Could the crystal be reacting to the anticipatory hum in the air?

Shouting and scuffling sounds from the courtyard distracted Navarre and prompted him into action. Snarling and grunting indicated it was merely a couple of those slow-minded goblins that fought amongst themselves, but it was also an indication of the state of unrest that settled on Dunraven. He needed to find the crystal before the situation fell into total chaos.

Fervently, he searched. Throwing aside anything that got in his way, he made a thorough search of the chamber. With grasping hands, he tore apart woven wooden furniture, ripped to shreds cotton bed coverings, threw across the room the hand-made pottery, and finally stilled when a sudden flash of knowledge assaulted him. He knew where the crystal lay. Scrambling to the far corner of the room, he knelt and peered into the shadows. At first, he saw nothing, but as his eyes adjusted, he came to see an indent in the natural contours of the tree. Thrusting his hands deep into the darkness, he fumbled around. His fingers scraped against rough bark and his nails caught on splinters. His skin crawled with the thought of what bugs may be hiding in the hole.

Sudden heat burned his fingers as they touched on a surface so unlike the tree. He knew it had to be the crystal. His entire arm throbbed with heat, as he grasped the crystal and hastened to pull it from its hiding place. With a shout of glee, he pulled it forth. Sunlight gathered. The crystal drew the rays into its very depths and transformed light into a glorious, luminescent glow. Navarre opened himself to the power of the crystal, but a voice interrupted him before he could feel the fulfillment.

"I appreciate your efforts in finding my crystal. Now, if you would be so kind as to hand it over."

The glow of the crystal turned to blazing heat, and with a scream of pain, Navarre dropped it to the floor. "Damn you, Lapis. The crystal is mine."

Lapis stepped into the bedchamber and gracefully reached down for the crystal. The moment his hands touched the stone, the blazing heat subsided. Its light returned to a subdued glow. A glow that encompassed the damned mage as if greeting a long lost brother.

Navarre snarled. "Give it to me now, and I might let you live."

Lapis smiled. "Your words are as empty as your mind is evil. As weakened as I am, my powers far exceed yours at their best."

He sounded so sure of himself that Navarre wavered. If the mage were right, he would need both the crystal and the book to become powerful enough to fight Lapis. His mind raced with alternatives. He could not tolerate being so close to the culmination of his dreams and have it torn from him by the arrogant magician. There had to be a way to get the crystal. He narrowed his eyes and fixed his gaze on Lapis.

"Pity your friends didn't stay to help you. After you helped them escape the dungeon, it would have been the least they could do."

Lapis tucked the crystal into a deep pocket of his robe and fastened the pocket closed with the twist of a strap. "You will not fool me into giving you any information, Navarre."

"Ah, but I have all the information I need. I know your secret."

Lapis hesitated only slightly. A brief flash of uncertainty crossed his face then disappeared. "I have no secrets."

"I know that Adoneesis is your son. Yours and Bronwen's. I also know that Adoneesis has no idea of his heritage."

Navarre had hoped that revealing this knowledge would scare Lapis into some kind of negotiation. He was wrong. A flare of heat shot up his legs and banged into his head with such force that Navarre thought he would explode with pain. The sensation ended almost instantly, but Navarre was left weak and with a newfound appreciation for the powers of the mage.

"You will never threaten those I care about again, or I will not release you from pain so easily."

Before Navarre could respond or react, the sound of footsteps echoed in the stairway. With a pointed look of warning, Lapis quickly waved a hand and disappeared, taking the crystal with him as if he'd never been there. Navarre could have screamed, but didn't want Gar to know he was there. Kicking a broken piece of furniture, he ran from the room and down the back stairs before Gar found him. He needed to re-evaluate his plan. It was going to be hard to get the crystal from Lapis, unless he found something to bargain with.

Gar must have reached his bedroom, because a bellow of anger echoed through the tree. Goddamn, he'd have to make a run for it. No way could he explain the mess to Gar without explaining why Lapis had been there. The goblin would surely kill him if he knew Navarre had kept the existence of the crystal from him.

Gar's bellow drew goblins to the main tree and Navarre cursed his misfortune. There was no way to make it to his room and grab anything without someone catching him. He wanted the book, but he also wanted to stay alive.

Pausing at the doorway, he peered around the back end of the tree to ensure the way was clear, and then he sprinted for cover of the forest. He tested the air with his mind and found that the magician's energy was still behind in the great tree, but he sensed something else that pleased him greatly. The answer to his dilemma. A way to bargain for the crystal, and it lay not too far to the east.

Satisfied with what he considered flawless plan, Navarre set out at a full run. Lapis would be sorry for interfering. Oh, yes, he would be very sorry.

Twenty-five

Only moments had passed before Lapis suddenly reappeared from nowhere--a skill that Adoneesis found decidedly disconcerting. Forming first as a wavering mist, a form not quite there, the magician soon became as solid as Adoneesis, Krickall, or Bailiwick.

"Can you not give us a warning or something?" Adoneesis queried.

"Sorry," Lapis said, but the twinkle in his eyes belied his amusement.

"Did you get the crystal? Did you? I am sure you did, after all, you are a great magician."

"Pixie, you wear my patience thin," Krickall snapped.

Lapis raised his hand for silence. "Yes, I found the crystal, thanks to you, little one."

Glee lit Bailiwick's pointed features and Adoneesis allowed him a moment to bask in his glory, and then crossed to a gnarled knot in the tree and twisted. Silent as the veil of early dawn, a small door slid open to reveal a tunnel leading down into the dark. Now, with the crystal safely tucked in Lapis' robe, it was time to find Analiese. Adoneesis stepped into the dark maw of the tunnel. His mind raced over the possibilities of where she could be, and and he worried about Krickall, if they failed to find her. The darkness of the tunnel hid much as he led the others forward, but a flutter of wings against his cheek alerted him to Bailiwick's presence on his shoulder and a thought occurred to him.

"Bailiwick," he whispered. "I need you to fly back to Lapis and warn him to be ready in case we do not find Analiese."

"Ready?"

"Yes. To deal with Krickall."

"Oh, yes."

Another flutter of wings and Bailiwick was gone. A grunt, and a warning to Bailiwick to bloody well watch where he was flying, raised a bittersweet smile from Adoneesis. Krickall was in a sour mood.

Adoneesis bumped into a wall. The action turned his smile into a frown and signaled the end of the passageway. Darn this darkness anyway. He rubbed his scraped nose while waiting for the others to catch up, and then carefully pulled a large knot of tree inwards enough to let a crack of light into dark. Wood was a natural sound insulator and Adoneesis was surprised at the chaos of movement and sound that greeted them even through the small crack.

"Fangs," he whispered.

"Not a word I want to hear." Krickall pressed against his back and tried to peer out the crack.

A sinking feeling wound its way into Adoneesis stomach, but maybe things would work out. He hoped so, for Krickall's sake. "Before we jump to conclusions, let's get out of here and get a better view of the surroundings."

A tangled mess of purple and red hydrangeas and climbing ivy hid the knothole into the tree. This allowed the foursome to climb from the tree and hide easily in the natural barrier where they had a reasonable view of the main area of activity.

Fewer goblins scattered the yard than Adoneesis would have thought with all the noise they were making, but then, goblins were not known for being light-footed. Cowed and beaten, a few faeries dotted the area and each one attended to some task or burden. A slender, kind-hearted brownie slugged rocks; pixies with bent or broken wings were forced to walk on tender bleeding feet, while offensive goblins hurled crude taunts and pinched the female's breasts.

These faeries were entrusted to Adoneesis, and just look at their state. His blood raced into a fierce boil and it took Lapis' firm grip on his arm to keep him from jumping from the bushes and fighting to his last breath to free the faeries.

Just then, a haughty shout sounded from a window directly above their hiding place. Adoneesis feared detection, but it was only Gar yelling abuse at the goblins racing about the yard and flailing at any faerie unfortunate enough to find themselves in their way.

"You measly rats. The human has fled and I think he stole something. Find him and make sure he takes nothing of importance. Hurry or I'll flay your stinking hides into a bloody pulp."

His words set the goblins into high gear, and if the situation had been any less serious, Adoneesis would have laughed at them banging into each other and tripping on their big feet as the scrambled to do Gar's bidding.

"Get out of my sight," Gar screamed and a spray of spit showered onto the hydrangeas and elicited an exclamation of "*yuck*" from Bailiwick.

"Shhh," Adoneesis cautioned just as a flash of gold sweeping against a slash of red drew his attention to the middle of the yard, just this side of a cluster of tree lodgings. What he saw turned his heart cold. Analiese wrestled with a goblin intent on pulling her towards the main tree. Krickall's growl a split second later signaled that he noticed the commotion as well. Adoneesis was quick to lay a restraining hand on his arm.

"Not yet, my friend. Gar has sent the goblins out to find the human. We'll bide a few minutes until they are gone."

"Grud," Gar hollered. "When I sent you to fetch the female, I thought you capable of handling her." His words prompted the goblin's efforts to increase and he managed to throw Analiese to the ground.

It took the combined efforts of Adoneesis, Lapis, and even Bailiwick's slight weight to hold Krickall in place. The silent struggle caused little more than a rustle in the surrounding underbrush, nothing more than a gentle wind may have caused, yet a fierce battle of will and intent it was.

"Let. Me. Go," Krickall demanded, his muscles straining in an attempt at freedom.

Adoneesis hissed, "Damn, Krickall, use your head. Analiese is fine, but if we go racing out there now, we stand no chance of defeating the goblins. We will wait until the goblins have cleared."

Krickall's blazing eyes bore into Adoneesis, who could see Krickall was in no state to be reasonable. Fangs, he didn't blame him either. If he cared for anyone the way Krickall obviously did for Analiese, he'd move heaven and earth to save her and let nothing, and no one, stand in his way. However, he needed Krickall, and the faeries needed him. Not relishing the thought of having to carry Krickall, who had at least seventy pounds on him; Adoneesis clenched his fist and readied himself to render him unconscious, for his own good of course. He'd deal with recriminations later once they were safely away from Dunraven.

Before he was able to land a felling blow on his friend, the sound of a slap and another struggle between Analiese and the goblin distracted Adoneesis. Instinctively, he grabbed Krickall's arm and raised his fist. The situation was now critical, and he could tell by the look of fury that wrenched Krickall's face.

Like flicking a bug, Krickall shoved Adoneesis away from him and rose from his crouched position, when his face suddenly turned a hurtful shade of reddish purple, and he collapsed onto his butt.

"What... Krickall, are you alright?" Thoughts of punishing Krickall for shoving him down disappeared, replaced instantly by concern and the fear of losing his friend, especially now, when he needed him the most. His mind flashed with youthful memories and some of the pranks they used to harass the other faeries. Life without Krickall would be an empty one, no doubt.

Lapis laid a restraining hand on his arm. "No worry, just a restraining spell. It shall pass momentarily."

"Curses on you, Lapis," Krickall managed to rasp out, his face returning to a more natural color.

"You are lucky that's your only punishment after treating your king in such a manner, as well as endangering all our lives," Lapis snapped. "If this is indicative of the level of discipline in the realm these days, I worry for our very survival."

Krickall's face flushed red, although this time it was a natural color of embarrassment.

"Look," Lapis directed.

Bloodied and bedraggled, Mayard had appeared from somewhere. He argued with the goblin and put his arm about Analiese's shoulders in a gesture of protection.

"Mayard," Krickall whispered, his voice breaking with emotion.

"He looks fierce. I do not remember ever seeing him look so fierce. He looks as if someone's beaten him. Badly. Maybe he will save her. He did before. Remember, I told you how he saved her in the dining area."

"Bailiwick, be quiet," Adoneesis ordered.

The argument lasted only a few seconds with both Mayard and the goblin trying to lay claim to Analiese. The goblin gestured toward the main tree and tried to make it clear of his intensions to take Analiese to Gar. Mayard's face mottled with anger as he hollered at Gar.

"You cannot have her. I will kill you first."

Gar spat, the stream of gob and saliva landing in the bushes beside the hidden foursome. "Bah! She is mine. I'll take her as I want," he bellowed.

"No, you can not," Mayard screamed.

"No? *No?* Who are you to tell me anything, you faerie scum? I am Gar, King of the faeries." He thumped his chest. "You are nothing. You betrayed your king, you lied to me, and I do not know how you escaped the dungeons, but now you die."

Before anyone knew what was happening, a knife flashed through the air and its silvery tip slid into Mayard's shoulder. Chaos reigned. Blood flowed. Mayard crumpled to the ground and a near silent thump became the only sound until Analiese screamed. Krickall rose in spite of Lapis' earlier act of discipline.

Some movement or sound must have alerted Gar, because he shouted to Grud. "Intruders. We have intruders in the bushes."

Only a few goblins remained close by, but Gar's warning brought all of them running toward the main tree and directly to the place where Adoneesis, Krickall, Lapis, and Bailiwick crouched in hiding.

"Fangs, it looks as if we'll be fighting after all," Adoneesis moaned as he drew his sword and stepped from the bushes to face the onslaught of swaggering goblins.

"My life with yours," Krickall declared fiercely as he stepped from shade to sunlight.

"Me, too. Me, too." Bailiwick flew high in the air and came to a fluttering hover beside Krickall and Adoneesis.

Lapis quietly parted the bushes and stepped forward to stand with the others but spoke no words. His presence exuded a force beyond words.

Used to battling defenseless faeries living on the outskirts of the realm, the goblins were hesitant about fighting against someone adept at defending themselves. They snarled at each other, each one waiting for someone else to make the first move.

Silent faeries stood against dancing goblins.

"Kill them, you cretins," Gar shouted. "I'm on my way."

His voice incited the goblins to charge. Adoneesis and Krickall met them with flashing swords, while Lapis relied on weakened magic. Bailiwick couldn't do much more than direct warnings about impending attack. His shrill voice mingled with the clash of steel and grunts of exertion.

"Look out behind, Krickall. Yes, no... another one approaches from your left. Oh, good one, Lapis, his face is turning red. King, oh, look out behind."

It went for as short a time as a span of breath, or as long as the passing of a life. Adoneesis sank the sharp tip of his sword blade into another writhing goblin and twisted. He hated to kill, but knew his enemy would give no second thought to draining the life from him. Besides, there were other lives to protect. A brief flash of silken auburn hair, and radiant blue eyes burned his mind and caused him to falter and lower his sword tip long enough to make himself vulnerable to an attacking goblin.

A spiked club descended, seemingly in slow motion, and Adoneesis quickly raised his sword to protect himself, but knew he moved slower than the incoming attack. He buckled his knees and fell into a roll. The spikes deflected off his shoulder and the club smashed into the ground beside him. Fierce pain ripped through him and the warmth of flowing blood arced a trail down his arm. Before the goblin could muster for the finishing blow, his gray eyes sparked in pain and he fell. A tiny spear protruded from his temple.

Relieved, Adoneesis looked for his savior and saw Bailiwick twirling in circles directly above the fallen goblin. Lady preserve him, Adoneesis never would have accredited the tiny pixie with such a heroic action. But, as he'd come to find out today, he knew little about the ever-present pixie.

With no time for hesitation, Adoneesis saluted Bailiwick, jumped to his feet and, switching his sword to his left hand, silently thanked Raegar for the hours of tedious sword practice.

The odds had started a dozen against four and slowly dropped to eight against four. It was at that moment that a mighty growl of anger punctuated the battle. Gar broke from the main tree at a full run. He held his sword at arm's length and parallel to the ground and with the lethal tip pointed straight ahead--directly at Adoneesis.

"I will kill you. You bastard son of immoral parents."

Weakened from the brief battle as well as his wound, Adoneesis was barely able to deflect Gar's sword, but he did. Snarling, Gar spun about to face Adoneesis and crouched low ready to spring for another attack. Such hatred shone from his eyes that Adoneesis shivered. Around them, the end of the battle rang strong and deadly, but neither one moved. Even as the last goblin fell to Krickall's slashing blade, Adoneesis' focus remained on the crouched goblin leader. With his peripheral vision he was aware when Krickall came and stood by his side and noticed that Lapis stood a short distance away, his arm around Analiese's shoulder. Adoneesis held his sword steady and took a shuddering breath of relief that his friends still lived.

Narrowing his eyes, he slowly tipped his sword toward Gar. "Give up, Gar, you have no hope. There is no one here left alive to help you."

"I need no help to kill you." Gar thrust his sword toward Adoneesis who easily side stepped and deflected the thrust with a flick of his own sword.

Adoneesis raised his hand to stop Krickall who had taken a step forward. "Tell me, goblin, why do you feel such a great need to kill me? If you give up now, I will let you live."

"I will die before I give Dunraven back to you." He thumped his chest with his free hand and declared, "I should rule the faerie, not you."

Hate sparked in Gar's eyes so intensely, that Adoneesis could have sworn he felt the breath of heat burn him.

"We need to leave. I hear the goblins returning," Krickall warned.

"Fangs, they must have heard the fighting," Adoneesis replied.

Gar looked between Adoneesis and Lapis, and some expression or stray look must have given them away, because he stood taller and brandished his sword defiantly. "You look scared. My goblins must be returning. Dunraven will remain mine, and I will take over the rest of the realm. You cannot stop me, you bastard son of whore."

Bastard son of a whore. The words wound their way into Adoneesis' mind as he tried to understand their meaning. He had been born to Raegar and a female faerie that died at his birth. He was no bastard. His mother had been no whore.

"Dunraven is mine by right of blood and I will not let a slimy usurper such as you take what is mine." Adoneesis charged Gar and knew that time ran short because he could now hear the approach of the goblins. Distant still, but the sound of stamping feet vibrated the ground as they moved quickly to return.

"The right of blood is mine, not yours," Gar snarled as Adoneesis' sword skimmed his shoulder. He countered with a swift thrust to Adoneesis throat and almost succeeded in slicing open the vulnerable area, but Adoneesis stepped back and spun around to bring his own sword directly in line with Gar's heart.

"You lie." Adoneesis thrust forward his sword. Gar moved, but not fast enough, as the sharp blade sliced a path that paralleled his lower rib. Its sharp tip lay open cloth and then flesh.

Spittle flew from his mouth as Gar screamed in pain. "I tell the truth. You do not even know who gave you life. How can you be so stupid?" Blood surged from his side, but still the goblin managed to sneer a final sentence before falling to his knees. "No blood of Raegar's runs through you. You are the bastard offspring of the bitch, Bronwen, and the weakling magician, Lapis."

Shock bore a trail of fire through Adoneesis. He was tired and had trouble wrapping his brain around the words. Voices echoed, words spoken that hadn't made sense to him. Still didn't make sense to him. *Your heart races with true magic blood.* Words spoken by Merlin, who would know of such things. But what did it mean? And how did it relate to Gar's babbling declarations?

"I only know that you are about to die, goblin." Adoneesis flushed with anger and his blood surged with the need for vengeance. He curled his lip and made a move to raise his sword for a final reckoning between him and Gar, but before he could, Krickall grabbed his arm tightly.

"We must leave now or die."

Adoneesis struggled to shake off the adrenaline of battle and the confusion of information thrown out by Gar. Sounds of snuffling and approaching footfalls on the ground sounded to be just beyond the nearest tree. His heart jumped with renewed fear. The rest of the goblins were almost there and there was no way his weary group could battle them all. Krickall was right. They needed to leave. Now.

"Go through the pathway. That way." He motioned for Lapis, Analiese, Krickall and Bailiwick to take the same path that had led the prisoners from the dungeon when they'd made their escape.

"Not without you, King," Krickall decreed.

Adoneesis hesitated. He wanted to find out more from Gar, but he also knew Krickall wouldn't leave without him and he couldn't put anyone else's life in jeopardy. Gar's sly look of triumph jabbed him as if a sword had struck him. Fangs, he hated to leave Dunraven to such a cretin.

Lapis and Krickall prodded him into a run, but as he reached the entrance to the path, he whipped about to face Gar. "I'll be back for justice, Gar. This I swear on the blood of my ancestors and the lives of those you have taken so callously."

"First you need to know the blood of your ancestors." Gar's raunchy laughter followed Adoneesis into the dimness of the thick forest.

They needed to hurry. Gar would send the goblins after them, and though unfamiliar with the path, they wouldn't be too far behind. Fear raced through his heart, and branches slapped his face as he leapt over a fallen tree stretched across the pathway, all the while hoping the others wouldn't fall too far behind. The urge to return to Bronwen and find out the truth drove him as nothing else could have.

Twenty-six

Bronwen tried to shake off the pervasive sense of fuzziness. Her eyelids were stuck shut and she lay prone on a cold, hard surface. "Fates have mercy." Before she could remember what had brought her to such a state, something wet and rough scraped across her face and brought her to instant awareness.

"Gray Wolf." She opened her eyes to face the piercing eyes of the wolf, and everything rushed back. "Bryanna." Bronwen pushed to her feet. Her head still woozy, she surveyed the surrounding camp.

Gwepper knelt by Ghilphar, who had also been blasted by the surge of power from the human when he'd burst into camp. But she'd recover; the human's power was strong, but not enough to kill with a thought. Few were capable of such a thing. If Bronwen hadn't been caught unaware, she would have been able to stop him before he invaded the camp and... Bryanna? *Oh, fates preserve us.*

"Bryanna," Bronwen yelled as she ran to Gwepper and the now conscious Ghilphar. "Where is Bryanna? Have you seen her?"

It was futile. The same person who had snuck past Bronwen's mental defenses and rendered her unconscious had taken Bryanna. What kind of power did the human hold that he could accomplish such a feat?

"Sorry, Bronwen, the last thing I remember, I saw Gwepper returning with the flask of water from the creek." Ghilphar moaned and clutched her head while Gwepper awkwardly patted Ghilpar's back and shot Bronwen a look of concern.

"No worries, goblin, Ghilphar will be fine in couple of minutes." She narrowed her gaze and fixed it on Gwepper. "You're obviously unaffected by the human's thrust of energy. I suppose you weren't as close to Bryanna and the energy blast as we were. So, why did you let him take Bryanna? Cowardly behavior is unacceptable. Too many lives depend on trusting each other."

Gwepper mumbled a reply.

"Speak up, goblin." Bronwen wondered if the goblin had purposely let the human leave unchallenged, and there was no act of cowardliness involved. Without thought, she raised her hand to fell the goblin should her suspicions prove correct. "Why did you not try to stop the human?"

"I did," Gwepper choked the reply and moved a hand to his side.

"Turn around and let me see what you are hiding," Bronwen commanded.

Gwepper stumbled to his feet and stood crookedly in front of Bronwen. His pleading eyes fixed on Ghilphar, and he dropped his hand.

Bronwen gasped. "Sweet fates, Gwepper, why did you not say something?"

Dark red blood seeped from a long wound in Gwepper's side. Upon closer inspection, Bronwen could see the only thing preventing the blood from flowing freely, was a paste of herbs applied like a poultice.

"Gwepper, you need to sit," Ghilphar pleaded as she took his arm and pulled him to the ground beside her.

"Yes, sit still while I prepare a poultice." Bronwen ran to the forest edge and searched frantically until she spied the tall, spiky flower of the prunella plants. Yanking a handful from the ground, she gave a brief apology to the flower faeries for not showing due respect, but hastened to add that this was an emergency. Running to her saddlebag, she withdrew some items, and returned to Gwepper's side. Quickly plucking the leaves from the stem, she threw them into a small pot and proceeded to grind them with her pestle. "This will make a paste to stem the bleeding and promote healing, though I must say it was quick thinking on your part to apply some lavender. It will help prevent infection.

"Farts and carts, I am not just a stupid goblin," he mumbled and flinched in pain as Bronwen cleansed the wound and applied some healing ointment.

"No one thinks you are a stupid goblin. Me, least of all," Ghilphar soothed with a gentle pat on Gwepper's arm.

Bronwen worked swiftly. She had no idea if the human would return, although she doubted he would. He had Bryanna. There was nothing else here for him. She prayed silently that the crystal was not also in his possession.

Gwepper grunted in pain, and Bronwen realized she was rubbing the poultice a little too vigorously on the wound. "Sorry. And I'm sorry for doubting your loyalty. It took great courage for you to stand against the human. He obviously has strong powers at his disposal... somehow." She frowned and whispered, "I hope the others return soon."

No sooner had the words crossed her lips then a shout from across the clearing alerted her to their return. Adoneesis surveyed the clearing, his face stricken with fear. Bronwen's heart near stopped beating, but she realized that the others probably--hopefully--followed closely behind. The look of fear on his face was understandable considering the bloodied rags, strewn pots and saddlebags, and signs of a scuffle in the dirt.

"Drats," Bronwen gave a final pat on Gwepper's arm. "There, you'll be fine." She rose to greet Adoneesis, all the while dreading telling him the news.

"What has happened? Where is Bryanna?"

No use in delaying anything. Besides, there was no time to waste. "She is gone. The human came and took her."

Adoneesis grabbed her by the arms and yelled, "And you let him?"

No one had manhandled Bronwen since Raegar. An intense, brief moment of anger rose so starkly within, that she had to grit her teeth to prevent herself from waving a hand and sending Adoneesis battering into the nearest tree. It took her a second to calm herself and it frightened her how close she had come to losing her control amidst the shifting memories.

Quietly, calmly, she spoke. "The only reason you are not flat on the ground now, is because I understand you are upset, but I would highly suggest you unhand me this instant."

Reason slowly returned. Bronwen could tell by the change of color in Adoneesis eyes as they mellowed from a blazing purplish-brown to his more normal walnut brown. His grip loosened on her arms until he finally let her go altogether.

"Forgive me." He looked about the encampment and asked, "What happened?"

Before anyone could answer, Krickall, Lapis, Analiese, and Bailiwick ran into the clearing. Bronwen allowed herself a moment of sheer joy to see Lapis alive, but waves of disruptive energy rolling off Adoneesis quickly overcame any emotion. Something was very wrong, and it had nothing to do with Bryanna's abduction.

"Adoneesis, what happened with Gar?"

349

Adoneesis did not seem to hear her question. His gaze darted from the disheveled campsite to Krickall and the others. Bronwen sensed his desperation and could only imagine how that he felt responsible for Bryanna's abduction. His untapped abilities were of such strength that Bronwen feared for his sanity if she didn't calm him down. With one thought of intent he was capable of retreating into a world of his own making--the phantom world that existed in the dark recesses of the mind--and since he had this ability, he was in danger of unintentionally doing just that.

"Adoneesis," she snapped at him. It was then that she noticed his blood encrusted sleeve. Damn, no wonder he was fading in and out. Muted colors swirled in his eyes, but Bronwen could detect no awareness of his surroundings. He'd closed himself off from reality as easily as that. She slapped him. An action that elicited protest from Krickall, but Lapis restrained Krickall easily enough. Bronwen slapped Adoneesis again--the palm of her hand stinging from the harsh contact--but a look of awareness lit deep in his eyes rewarded her. Shaking his head, he looked at her.

"What?"

Bronwen breathed in relief and admonished, "You must stay strong. Do you understand me?" After she spoke, she applied some of the poultice she'd mixed for Gwepper.

Another brief spurt of panic lit his eyes, followed by pain from his wound. Then he nodded. "Yes. Yes, I understand." He looked helplessly about then his eyes settled back on Bronwen and she felt the icy stab of anger, but didn't understand the reason.

By that time, the others had come to stand beside them, their faces alight with worry, but Bronwen was hasty to reassure them. Krickall had somehow managed to grab a couple of goblin horses when they escaped Dunraven and although not as strong as the faerie steeds, they would come in handy for extra mounts.

While Krickall's hand rested on the hilt of his sword and Analiese hovered behind him, Bailiwick flitted over the rest on Gwepper's shoulder. The goblin shrugged and grunted, but looked resigned to allowing the pixie his resting place.

"Where is Bryanna?" Krickall asked.

"She is gone. Taken by the human. Shadow Dancer followed them," Bronwen replied, hoping to give Adoneesis a chance to regain his equilibrium. He needed to take control of the situation and resolve his unbidden anger.

"Navarre has her. Oh, the fates are playing with us this day." Lapis reached inside his robe. "We have the crystal, but we've lost the woman."

The crystal revealed in the palm of Lapis' hand radiated such beauty and light that Bronwen took a step back. It sang to the part of her that was the essence of the Lady, and Bronwen did not know if she could withstand the images that raced through her mind--the sensations of times long past that thrust into her soul. Overcome, she was not able to subdue the crystal's power over her until Lapis closed his hand and blocked the crystal from her sight.

Bailiwick giggled. "It is powerful, is it not?"

"Yes, little one, it certainly is." Bronwen watched Lapis put the crystal back into the folds of his robe, and then looked to Adoneesis.

"Unfortunately, we need the woman as much as we need the crystal," Lapis remarked.

Adoneesis strode to Brachus and readied to mount. "Yes, we do. We must leave now to save her."

"No," Lapis spoke.

"No? You dare to contradict me?"

Bronwen gasped. Oh, fates above. *Adoneesis knew something.* It was not the situation that disoriented him. It was sudden knowledge of a long buried secret that gave rise to the anger he was trying to control. Shivers rushed through her body.

"I don't mean to contradict you." Lapis' soothing voice calmed the situation. "But there are other considerations. Gar must have sent his goblins after us by now, and unless we elude them, we will be of no use to Bryanna. We do not even know what direction they headed."

"But..." Bailiwick protested, the single word falling into a stunned silence of confusion.

"There is one other consideration," Bronwen offered. "Can he use Bryanna's powers without the crystal?"

"No. He may have been able to if he possessed the Book of Time, but I sensed the book at Dunraven. For some reason, Navarre fled without it."

Bronwen sighed with relief. "Then Bryanna is safe with him until he can access her powers, which he can't do at this point."

"Yes. Good news for us," Lapis said.

"But not for Bryanna." Bailiwick flipped and landed on Adoneesis shoulder. "We can't just leave her with him." His pleading eyes bore into Adoneesis who shifted uncomfortably.

"We cannot just abandon her. We brought her into our world and made her our responsibility. We owe her our protection."

Adoneesis set his foot into Brachus' stirrup as if to mount, but Bronwen's hand on his arm stopped him. His seething gaze would have felled most, but Bronwen stood firm. She ached when she saw the struggle within her son. His emotions bore strong upon the wind, and his feelings for the woman had somehow weaved themselves into intense passion and caring. *Fates that be, please let him make the right decision.* Too many lives rested on his words. But even with the lives resting upon his shoulders, Bronwen sensed that he wavered toward chasing after the woman. She could not let him.

"King Adoneesis. We flee, not only for our lives, but the very existence of the realm. The cold season is almost upon us. We are on the run from goblins, low on supplies, some of us are wounded, and we have no shelter. How can we be of help to the Bryanna, if we cannot keep ourselves alive? Besides, we have no idea where this Navarre person has fled with her. Do you remember the bargain we made when I agreed to help you?"

His face blanched. "Yes."

"You gave your word to me and now I call upon your honor to heed my words."

Adoneesis fumbled with Brachus' saddle as if he attempted to cover his shaking hands. All eyes fell to him. Afraid he would rebel, Bronwen prompted him, "You gave your word to obey me when this time came. Without question."

Adoneesis' eyes hinted at the emotion warring within him, but Bronwen held fast. Now was not the time for weakness or sentimentality.

"We will pack quickly and head out before we are overrun by goblins and forced to fight another battle that none of us is capable of winning." Adoneesis shot a bitter, distrustful look at Gwepper and Ghilphar. "If you two would like to remain, your friends will be here shortly."

Gwepper snarled and it was only Ghilphar's hand on his arm restraining him from leaping for Adoneesis.

"Gwepper was injured while trying to keep Navarre from taking Bryanna," Bronwen remarked pointedly, causing Adoneesis to level a measuring glance at Gwepper. "Now, as you suggested, let us pack and ride."

"But where do we ride to? Where will we go?" Bailiwick wailed.

Silence reigned.

Bailiwick's question stopped everyone mid-motion, until a distant sound vibrated the ground and signaled the approach of the goblins. The threat moved everyone into preparations for a hasty departure.

Still, Bailiwick's question went unanswered.

Gwepper broke the silence with a mumbled remark.

"What did you say, goblin?" Adoneesis demanded.

"Rats and cats. I said; why not go to Night Gloom?"

"Night Gloom?" Adoneesis frowned as he swung into Brachus' saddle.

"Yes. It is empty. It is shelter. And there is lots of food."

Adoneesis looked to the others who stood expectantly, and extended his hand to Gwepper. "Come, since the unicorn is gone, you ride with me. Ghilphar, you ride with Bronwen, Analiese with Krickall, and Lapis you take the black horse. He looks the weakest, so you travel alone on him."

Everyone mounted and fear grew evident with the approaching sounds. Horses snorted and stamped, awash with the emotions of their riders.

"Which way, King Adoneesis?" Krickall asked.

"North. We make our way to Night Gloom."

Those words thrust horse and riders into a full gallop away from the goblins, toward a destination most of them would have avoided if given the choice. Bronwen shivered and sent a silent prayer to the heavens for all their sakes.

Twenty-seven

The dream started out calmly enough. His father's voice reaching into his mind--urging, prompting. *"You and I aren't like everyone else. One day you'll see. You'll come to understand your purpose in life."*

Navarre moaned. Tried to placate his phantom father. "I know. I know. That's why I'm here."

"Not good enough. You lost the Book of Time. You're a failure. I always knew you'd fail. Everything I worked so hard to gain for you is gone because you were too stupid to hold on to what I gave you."

Kicking off his heavy blanket, Navarre thrashed about on the cold, hard ground, knowing he was dreaming, yet unable to wake up. Cold breezes blew down the mountains they'd crossed earlier that day and whipped across his body. He shivered. Goose bumps left uneven trails on his skin. His father's insidious voice invaded the deepest part of Navarre's mind.

"You failed. You have nothing. You'll return home and die just like I did. With nothing... nothing..."

"NO!" With a jolt, Navarre thrust his body upward and sat, panting in the dark. Had he spoken aloud? There was no sound from the woman, Bryanna, and the skittering sounds of nightlife carried on as usual. He must have screamed inside his own mind. The mind his father invaded more frequently as time passed.

Damn him to hell and perdition.

The fingers of dawn barely smudged the horizon as Navarre stumbled to his feet to check on his prisoner. Last night, he'd tied rawhide around her wrists and one ankle and bound her to the nearest tree to ensure she wouldn't escape. The rise and fall of her chest beneath the blanket was barely visible, but attested to the fact she was still there. He sighed with relief. She was his bargaining tool for the return of the crystal.

Damn Lapis to the Netherland of Tarnished Souls.

With the gurgle of hunger rippling deep in his stomach and frustration licking at his intestines, he stoked the fire and cursed fates that had brought him to this miserable place in such a weak position of power. Gar was likely to kill him on sight, he'd lost the crystal to Lapis, left the book behind at Dunraven, and he was in unfamiliar territory, devoid of supplies or a plan.

He took out his anger on the nearest object. The sleeping woman. One swift kick planted firmly at her blanket-covered form elicited a satisfying yelp of pain. "Wake up, bitch. I'm hungry."

Startlingly blue eyes peered at him from beneath the blanket. Eyes whose depths sparked with fear and a hint of defiance. No matter, he'd beat the defiance out of her if she proved difficult. "Move or I swear I'll leave you behind and tied to that tree. You won't last long before a muckraker or wildebeest chomps on you for breakfast."

Bryanna awkwardly pushed the blanket off and held her bound hands toward Navarre. "I have to pee."

"So. Go."

She flushed and her gaze faltered. "I need privacy and I can't do it with my hands tied."

"Fine. I'll untie your hands, but the ankle tether remains in place. You can go as far as that will allow you. Other than that..." He shrugged his shoulders. "I'm hungry and you're making breakfast, so make it quick."

"Dammit," she mumbled, as she snapped the rawhide behind her and headed toward the trees. "Kidnapping me wasn't enough. He has to make me wait on him as well."

She reached the end of her restraint and, with a glare of triumph directed at him, squatted behind a small bush. Stupid woman. If she knew how little he cared about any brief flash of her skin he might possibly see, she'd be insulted. The sounds of scuffling and crunching reached him from behind the bush and he smiled. She must be scavenging around for leaves to use as toilet paper. Good. He hoped she was miserable. What made her so special anyway? He'd like to know. Sure, she descended from ancient blood--powerful bloodlines. So did he. She was somehow the answer to the problems faced by the faeries. So what. He'd find out how to use her powers to his own advantage.

He threw another log on the fire and snorted. Adoneesis traveled all the way to the world of man to kidnap the answer to his problems and then loses her. What an idiot. Navarre wouldn't make the same mistake. The woman would remain his prisoner until he managed to retrieve the crystal from Lapis. He didn't need the book, because he'd memorized the only important section. How to use the crystal to control the powers of nature.

Bryanna's return jolted him from his musing. He motioned to the supplies. "Oatmeal. And make it quick, I'm hungry."

She put the pot of water onto the fire, grabbed the sack of food supplies, and pulled out what she needed. "They'll come after me, you know."

"No, they won't."

Bryanna's motions slowed and she pinned her gaze on him. "If everything they told me is true, and I believe it is, they need me. They'll come."

"No, they won't."

"How can you be so sure?" Fear and doubt crept into Bryanna's voice.

"Because, they'll go to Night Gloom."

He was only guessing, but logic dictated that they would need to regroup, restock, and plan. The only place for them to manage that safely and comfortably would be the goblin stronghold.

"Here."

Bryanna plopped a wooden bowl of porridge in front of him. Hunger licked at his stomach and he greedily spooned a mouthful of the oatmeal into his mouth. Satisfaction turned to distaste, and then anger. He spat the oatmeal to the ground.

"Damn you, it's not even cooked and it tastes like crap. How much salt did you put in the water?"

"Oh, sorry, it looked done, and a handful of salt in the water seemed about right. You did say to add salt to the water."

"A touch of salt, you useless bitch." He threw the bowl to the ground and started packing. "Forget it. Pack. We're leaving."

"Where are we going?"

Navarre smiled. "To Night Gloom, of course."

~ * ~

She protested as Navarre grabbed her arm and shoved her toward the horse. She dreaded the thought of riding thigh to thigh with Navarre for the day. Anger and frustration rolled off him in waves of stifling energy, and with her awakening sense of powers, Bryanna reacted to such emotions much more strongly than before.

Navarre climbed into the saddle in front of her, and spurred the horse into a gallop. Since the horses of the faerie realm possessed the ability to run full speed for hours at a time, Bryanna knew hours would pass before they would stop.

~*~

Navarre and Bryanna rode hard and fast. The sun passed across the sky. Scenery flashed by in a brilliant blaze of color. Bryanna had time to think about the last few days and came to realize that she belonged here, in the faerie realm. Never had she felt so alive, so a part of everything that surrounded her. She'd even come to care for her kidnappers, and was certain the feeling was mutual. From Bronwen at least, because Adoneesis didn't trust her. He was jealous of her, and he was attracted to her. Trying to get him to like her would be a little difficult.

At that moment, a soft nuzzling of a familiar feeling tugged at the edge of her mind. Shadow Dancer. Her heart soared. The unicorn hadn't deserted her, and she was close enough to send mind feelers. The horse they rode sensed something as well, because his stride broke and he slowed down. Navarre cursed and spurred the animal back into a gallop.

Idiot. But it was to her benefit he couldn't be bothered paying attention to his horse.

Her powers were supposedly latent within her until invoked by some verse or something, but Bryanna's insides roiled like misty tendrils simmering below the surface looking for release. She was sure she could tap into those powers and when the time was right use them against Navarre.

~*~

By the end of the third day, Navarre and Bryanna reached Night Gloom. She knew they'd arrived because the vivid hue of the landscape faded to gray, and the tingle of connection to nature dulled to throb of unease. The latent power in the dominion of the goblins awaited release, much as her own power. And it wouldn't take much to incite ancient powers.

With sureness born of familiar territory, Navarre wound a path through the dwelling trees and a section of newly built log structures that Bryanna was sure went against all faerie belief. They passed all the trees and came to a place that was nothing more than a small hill covered by branches and twigs. Navarre pulled the horse to a stop. "We're here."

"Here? There's nothing here." Bryanna slid off the horse and looked around for some form of shelter.

He reached over and cleared the branches away from the hill to reveal a shadowed entrance. "We'll be staying in here." He removed the supplies from the horse, thrust most of them at Bryanna, and slapped the animal on its rear to send him galloping away. "Let's go." He opened the door and shoved her unceremoniously into the dark and down a set of narrow stairs.

An occasional hole drilled into the earth above and supported by hollowed logs lit their way. The resulting light was feeble and, unfortunately, did nothing for the smell of rot and urine that engulfed Bryanna and caused her to gag. Navarre shoved her. "You'll get used to the smell."

"Get *used* to it? Why should I get used to it when there are trees above that are empty?"

Navarre didn't bother to answer. He was busy checking out some of the cells. His face turned white at whatever he saw in one of the rooms. "Let's try another room." He opened the door across the hallway and gave a nod of satisfaction. "In here."

Bryanna stepped in to the small room and it was then she realized that this place below the earth was a dungeon. Restraints lined the walls and a stain of what she assumed to be blood darkened the ground. One small hole reinforced with dried mud and twigs lent light to the room, but the corners remained dim with the shadows of dark.

"You can't be serious."

"Why not? You see..." He took the knapsacks from her and threw them on the ground. "...when your friends get here, I don't want them to know we're already here."

Hope flared. Then died. Adoneesis and the others would never find her here. Navarre was right about that.

"I'm hungry. Let's eat, and then get some sleep. I have a crystal to steal and a realm to destroy."

Even in the dark, fanatical light gleamed in his eyes. Bryanna had no doubt he meant exactly what he said. Whether he could accomplish such a feat was another story, but Bryanna would do whatever she could to keep him from destroying the place she'd come to care about in such a brief time.

They ate quickly. Dried fruit and a mixture of nuts. With no patience or consideration, Navarre shoved her into the back corner shadows, chained her to one of the hanging metal rings, and then stretched out on his blanket. Tense and nervous, Bryanna lay in the darkness and listened to Navarre's steady breathing that soon gave way to snoring. Sounds of Night Gloom's nocturnal life provided a chorus that melded with snoring and Bryanna shivered.

She was alone with a madman.

Twenty-eight

Gar sniffled and kicked at the offending rock that had tripped him. His head hurt and his rib was bleeding where Adoneesis' blade had sliced a fine line. But he'd beaten the bastard. Ha. He was the true ruler of the realm. The cruel taunts of the bitch whose belly he'd sprung from no longer mattered. Her, with a sullen face, swigging another glass of malt brew as she staggered to sit by the fireplace in their tree. A tree left empty by another faerie family because they'd outgrown the small elm. The remembrance of her slurring, sniveling voice, still made him cringe.

That bastard, Raegar, forced himself on me and deserted me when he found that his seed had caught. That's how much he hated the thought of a bastard son. You. It's your fault he left me in this hovel trying to survive on handouts and garbage scraps.

Stupid bitch. His life had been a holy hell because of her, and it was during those long, dark nights and frequent beatings that hate had been born. Hate, simmered with bouts of anger. Hate, given life and breath by the viperous words of a scorned goblin bitch. Hate directed at a deserting Raegar and his favored son--Adoneesis. Bah! He'd beaten the shining king and proven himself stronger and faster. Now he ruled.

Gar stomped into main tree of Dunraven and turned his nose up at the offending odors of rotten food and malodorous goblin aroma. Scraps of food lay stuck on the earth-packed floor, spit there by ill-mannered goblins. Ransacked clothing, obviously not suited to the looting goblins, lay strewn about. Straw from the stable and mud from the kennel added the final touch to the filth. The shining victory that had been Dunraven resembled the goblin hold of Night Gloom more each day. Gar limped up the stairs and yelled for Grud to follow him. Mumbling all the way down the hallway to the room that used to belong to Adoneesis but was now his, Gar slammed open the chamber door and strode in.

"Grud. Grab those useless goblins lazing about the yard and make them clean the tree. If there is one scrap of food or one piece of clothing, dirt, or furniture that does not belong, someone will pay. Understand?"

Grud's eyes rounded at the unusual command, but Gar didn't bother explaining himself. He didn't ponder his need to keep Dunraven the shining jewel he'd conquered. He only knew he didn't want it to slide into the pit of filth and gloom that had become Night Gloom.

Bowing, Grud made a move to leave the room. "Of course. Right away."

"Not now, you stupid nit. Tend to my wounds first," Gar bellowed.

Flushing, Grud hastened forward and carefully lifted the tattered shirt and washed the wound. "Tis a clean cut. Should heal easily."

"Easily. Huh. Maybe you would like to have such a wound and see how easily it will heal." His hand hovered over his nearby sword, but Grud's heartfelt--fearful-- apology soothed him enough to let the comment pass. After all, if he harmed Grud, who would tend to him so proficiently? None of the idiots milling about downstairs would have the brainpower of a gnat.

Grud kept his head lowered and his mouth shut as he finished dressing the wound. Gar moaned, shifted in his seat and mumbled for Grud to hurry. He hated the sight of blood. In an attempt at distraction, he grit his teeth and looked around the room. He'd kept it clean. A true feat for a goblin. First thing he'd done was throw Adoneesis bed out the window and had it burned, and then he'd replaced it with one of fresh straw and a cotton blanket newly filled with down. A blazing fire burned in the fireplace and brought warmth to a chill that Gar couldn't shake. He hoped that Dunraven would offer comfort, whereas Night Gloom had only offered nightmares. Conquering Dunraven couldn't have come at a better time. Night Gloom seeped with a sense of pervasive intent aimed at harming him and had only grown over the last years. Fingers of dread had kept him shackled indoors most of the time and he'd run out of excuses so the other goblins wouldn't lose faith in him as the leader.

"Finished." Grud's voice jolted Gar back to awareness.

"About time. Now go." He waved the fawning minion away from him. "Wait. Better idea. Make the faeries clean the mess. Why should goblins waste time when we have slave faeries now? Go. Make sure the tree gets cleaned."

Grud didn't move. He averted his face and mumbled something. In no mood for games, Gar slammed his fist onto the nearby tabletop. "What?"

"I said--most of the faeries have fled." As he said the words, he cringed and backed up a couple of steps.

"What? How did this happen? Who is responsible? I will flay his hide with my sword, soak him in sweet honey, and then leave him for the fire ants to feast on."

"Lord, when Mayard broke from the dungeon, he knocked out the guard posted at the tree where we imprisoned the faeries. They ran, but we managed to recapture a few."

"Imbeciles. Why were they not locked in the dungeons?"

Grud swallowed. "You... you said there would not be enough room for them all. You suggested the tree."

"You dare to blame me?" Gar raised his fist to strike a blow.

As if knowing he'd made a mistake, Grud tried hastily to correct himself. "I put the thought in your mind. It is my fault. I take responsibility."

"Now you dare to say that you have the power to sway my thinking. You need a lesson in humility." In a movement so swift, it was a blur, Gar drew his sword and sliced a bloody streak down Grud's right cheek. Thrusting his face close to Grud's, he spat at him, "Know your place, goblin, or die."

With a shaking hand pressed tightly against his bloody cheek, Grud offered an awkward bow and backed his way toward the door. But before he had a chance to leave, Gar bellowed, "Wait." Fear kindled anew in Grud's face, as he stood stone still. "Take that blasted thing with you." Gar waved toward a book resting on his bed. "I never read. Why would you bring such a thing into my room?"

"It was Navarre's book and since he's gone, I thought..."

"Of course. The book." Gar narrowed his gaze and reached out to touch the leather bound surface. Worn flecks of gold smattered the surface, and the late day sun shimmered in the golden design. Though worn, the book held regal power. Gar held some faith in magic and sorcery, but doubted the power of the book. Although, it wouldn't hurt to find out. Especially now that he sat upon an empty throne. He was furious that he'd finally fulfilled his dream to take Dunraven and the rule of the realm from Adoneesis, and there was no one to rule except his own goblins. Bah. The battle was not over yet.

"Grud, I never listened when the human spoke. Tell me, what did he say about this book?"

Grud swallowed and his gaze darted about the room as if searching for an answer. "I... something about magic and bloodlines."

Frustrated, Gar snapped, "I know that. But what else? Where did he get the book?"

"Oh, I remember. He said his father stole it from the Tuatha De Danann."

"Yes. That's right." Gar paced the room--his injury presently forgotten. A hint of a plan wormed its way into his mind. "The book holds much power. That's what Navarre said. Did he lie?" Gar fixed his eyes on a nervous Grud and willed him to answer.

Panicked, the goblin sputtered and spit in an attempt to speak. "I think we should find out."

A corner of Gar's lip rose in a distorted smile of accord. "Yes. We should find out." His finger, tipped with long, yellowed nail, stroked the book cover, and then flipped it open. Gibberish. Page after page of scratchings and marks that resembled nothing Gar had ever seen.

"Who would know the language of the Tuatha?"

"The traitor, Mayard," Grud offered.

"Bah. That does me no good. I killed him."

"I saw him trying to crawl away. I think he's still alive."

"Well, go find out. If he still lives, bring him here. And stop dripping blood on my floor, or I will mark your other cheek."

Grud scrambled from the room and Gar heard his footsteps clunking down the stairs. He waited to the sounds of shouting and a scuffle in the yard below. Thud. Thud. A struggling Grud appeared at the doorway and dragged a dead-looking Mayard behind him. The only evidence he still lived was to be seen in the twitching of his mouth and fluttering of eyelids. Grud heaved him to the floor and straightened with a sigh of relief.

"He lives. But barely."

Gar grabbed the hilt of the knife that still stuck out from Mayard's shoulder. He twisted. Mayard screamed and his eyes fluttered open.

Gar glared at Mayard. "Tell me what I want and I will let you live."

"I don't..."

"Tell me about the book."

Mayard's glazed eyes flashed in confusion and then he noticed the book Gar gestured toward. Understanding mingled with fear. "The Book of Time."

"Yes, so you do know of it. Can you read it?"

Mayard shook his head slowly.

"Do not lie to me. Your life rests on your answer."

"I cannot." Mayard gasped and dropped his head to the floor in exhaustion.

"Who can?" He grabbed Mayard by the shoulders and shook until the faerie screamed in pain. "Tell me who can."

Blood ran freely from Mayard's wound and his voice gurgled with vomit. "Take a flying leap." He hawked a bloodstained wad of spit onto the floor at Gar's feet and turned defiant, somewhat glazed, eyes at the goblin.

Gar exploded with rage and, grabbing Mayard's arm, dragged him to his feet, out the door, and threw him against the wall in the narrow corridor. "Grud. Get outside, see if you can find a faerie that hasn't escaped, and bring him to me."

Grud clattered down the stairs. With a grunt, Gar heaved Mayard down after him. The thud of bone against wood and Mayard's sharp cry of pain soothed Gar's anger somewhat and he grinned in satisfaction as he clumped down the stairs and purposely kicked Mayard while stepping over his sprawled form.

"Sit up, you mangy creature." He propped Mayard against the wall, but the unconscious idiot slid back to the floor. Gar looked around, but the room offered nothing except a couple of broken chairs, a table, food scraps on the floor, and a wooden jug. He picked up the jug and sniffed. Yuk. Rancid mead. He poured it over Mayard and was rewarded with sputtering and open eyes.

Grud returned. Held firmly in his grasp was a young male buachailleen struggling and cursing--his red cap sitting askew on his head. He threw the young faerie to the ground at Gar's feet. "I found this scrapper hiding under a pile of wood. Practically peed himself when I grabbed him."

Gar grinned. Quick as a flash, he reached out, grasped the young lad by his collar, and shoved him to the floor by Mayard. One swift kick of his booted foot elicited a sharp scream of pain from the buachailleen and a flicker of understanding to light in Mayard's eyes.

"Yes." Gar rested his sword tip on the young one's cheek just under his eye. "You may not care for yourself anymore, but I will thrust this sword through his eye and into his brain unless you tell me what I want to know."

Sobbing, the young lad knelt as still as possible, but his thin shoulders shook with the force of the shivers racking his body. A whimper escaped his white lips and he turned his pleading, terror-filled gaze to Mayard.

"Bastard," Mayard spat through split lips and broken teeth.

"Good. You understand," he spoke slowly and at the same time traced a slice down the cheek of the young faerie.

"Stop. Let him go."

Gar's hand closed around the throat of the quivering faerie and lifted until the young lad's feet kicked the air in desperation and his eyes bulged. A chortling gurgle signaled the frantic struggle to breath. "I will let him go when you tell me."

"Tuatha," Mayard screamed. "One of the Tuatha de Danann, or..."

"Or what?" Gar growled, shaking the faerie.

"Possibly one of the Lady's emissaries. I'm not sure."

"An ellyllon?"

"Yes."

"Ahhh." Gar let go of the buachailleen, who fell only long enough to scramble to his feet and stumble from the tree. Gar barely acknowledged his exit. "A Tuatha de Danann or an ellyllon." He turned a considering look to Mayard and barked at Grud. "Kill him. He is of no use to us anymore."

He barely acknowledged Mayard's death rattle as Grud's sword sank deep into his chest. He stepped to the doorway and fixed his eyes on the horizon. The Tuatha or an ellyllon. He had no idea where to find the Tuatha de Danann, but he knew where to find an ellyllon.

"Grud. We return to Night Gloom." He shivered. But the rewards of being able to read the book outweighed his dread at returning to the place that repelled him.

Twenty-nine

Adoneesis pushed the group hard. Bronwen, Ghilphar, Gwepper, Krickall, Analiese, Lapis and Bailiwick, each one obviously tired, yet gave him no complaint at the breakneck speed. Seething with resentment and questions, he set a spine tingling pace with Brachus and left the others to follow as best they could. Gar's taunts echoed persistently, *you are the bastard offspring of the bitch, Bronwen, and the weakling magician, Lapis.* He pushed harder but as Night Gloom approached, he found his anger replaced by a tug of familiarity. Tugging Brachus to a stop, he searched the countryside, looking for something to explain the strange sensation.

The long break allowed the others to catch up and Krickall drew up alongside him. "What is the urgency? We are tired. The horses need alonger break. Can we rest for the night?"

"No. You may rest the horses and then follow me. I'm continuing on." Adoneesis spoke, his voice far and distant, disembodied from the moment. "Delicate weavings of mist wend through me. I feel things such as I have never felt and I must find out what draws me forward. If I don't, I fear insanity will replace the mists and control my mind."

Krickall frowned. "I don't understand, but then I am not a king." With a sigh of relief, he motioned for the others to dismount. He grinned. "We're taking a break."

Adoneesis gathered the reins and directed Krickall. "There's not much further to go, so don't rest too long. I'll see you there." On some level, Adoneesis realized he was being unfair to the weary group, but once they arrived at Night Gloom, they would have the chance to rest longer.

Spurring Brachus forward, he ignored the commotion behind him as he heard Krickall explaining that Adoneesis would not be stopping with them.

It wasn't long before Brachus' stride carried them up a steep ridge and they crested to the panorama of immense forest below. They'd arrived. Adoneesis drew in a sharp breath at the fierceness of thought that assaulted him. Pressure constricted his chest, his heart pounded, and he found it difficult to draw a breath. Trees grew in abundance and were possessed of such immense size they shamed even the trees of Dunraven. Gnarled trunks presented a macabre image of misshapen beauty. Dark, thick, and cut deep into the trees, the bark provided deep textures and shadows that played with the light making it seem as if the trees moved. Night Gloom. An apt name; yet Adoneesis sensed depths beneath the obvious cloud of dark abuse shrouding the forest.

His heart sang. His forehead beaded with sweat. Tendrils reached from the forest and bid him approach. He did. With no thought to those who followed, he spurred a reluctant Brachus down the slope and to the timberline. Pulses, not unlike words sung, entered his mind, and tightened the tendrils that urged him. His first step into the forest increased the intensity of the songs. Familiar verses raced through him and prodded memories of the time he'd found Wyllow Wood. He reined

371

Brachus a direct route toward the center of the forest and forged through thick brush and grasping branches. A bed of fallen leaves muffled any sound Brachus might have made with his hooves and the ensuing silence amplified Adoneesis internal upheaval.

Finally, he and Brachus broke into a clearing and the sight surpassed even Adoneesis first sight of Night Gloom's forest. There stood a tree to overpower all trees and possessed of roots that encompassed the clearing and beyond. They rose and undulated from the ground like waves on the sea. This tree was not dark--rather it glowed and emitted thin streams of light into the forest. The light strands attached to the roots of other trees and pulsed with alternating colors.

"Fangs," he whispered and Brachus shifted nervously.

As if aware of his presence and greeting him, the tree swayed gently and lifted its branches. Even with its immense size and gnarled structure, the tree possessed grace beyond words.

Hoofbeats sounded in the distance and Adoneesis broke from his reverie. He needed to let the others know where he was, but before he could leave, a wisp of a touch upon his shoulder stopped him. Spoken in the language of the wind, yet given substance by the tree, he heard these words.

> *Adoneesis, son of great lines*
> *Your presence is at the worst of times*
> *For too long we've been victims of greed*
> *And hoped for an answer to fulfill our need*
> *So here you stand, surging with blood of old*
> *The answer--our last hope if truth be told*
> *Oh, friend of my daughter, Wyllow Wood*
> *I give to you my name--Wyllow Root*

And I bind you to the trees of Night Gloom
To break this bind will bring you doom
Honor bound--our tree protector
Our lives are with you, entwined forever

The tree finished her song and extended a shaft of pulsing light that connected with the center of Adoneesis' forehead. Energized, yet soothed, he felt at one with the mingling trees and, for the briefest flash of time, their song became his. Root bound to the earth, wind bound to the heavens, his essence mingled with times past and times yet to be. When the connection was broken, he felt bereft, but Wyllow Root comforted him.

The bonding of ages invisible may be
But as one we are, you and me
My life for yours, yours for mine
As it shall be on through time

Shouts from within the forest distracted him and with one last glance at Wyllow Root, he made way to find the others. Before he came upon them, a flying pest of a pixie assaulted him.

"King. We looked *everywhere* for you. We've looked for hours. Where have you been? Are you all right?" Bailiwick flipped in the air and came to rest on his shoulders.

"Hours? But..." He realized that the sun had descended toward the far away mountains, and confusion shook him. "Where are the others?"

"Gwepper took them to main tree. Although, I understand it's not a standing tree. Gar had the nerve to chop down trees of the forest to make some kind of a place to live. Can you believe that? What a dufus."

"Take me to them."

~*~

The main structure stood surrounded by a few smaller ones of similar construct, all forming a circle around the main one. Roughly hewn trunks stacked upon each other, chinked with mud and grass, Gar's stronghold would assuredly provide shelter and maintain heat within, but when Adoneesis stepped down from Brachus and placed his palm upon the logs, he felt no life. No vibrating pulse that he depended on so much in his own main tree of Dunraven. He shook his head. To remain in such a place would render one weak. Everyone knew that the life breath of trees provided life breath to the faeries. What rank stupidity would prompt anyone to build such a place?

"Farts and darts, we can enter over here." Gwepper motioned his four-fingered hand toward a door hinged with strands of rawhide to the above beam.

"No. We are not staying in this lifeless place. Show me the trees where you used to live."

Gwepper frowned and pointed. "Around that turn in the path." Reluctantly, he shuffled along the path, mumbling, "Rats and cats. Silly, nilly, willy King."

Ghilphar set stride beside Gwepper and whispered in his ear. He blushed, stood straighter and nodded. "Here. Trees are here. Lots of trees left empty. Smart idea, King. Smart, tart idea." His smile brightened and he looked to Ghilphar as if seeking approval. She smiled at him and gave him a gentle pat on the arm.

Gwepper was right. Trees hollowed out and etched for living purposes stood desolate on the far corner of the inhabited area of the goblin's lands. Not too far, just as Gwepper had said. The deserted trees stood close to the line of forest that ran thickly around the living area. Encroaching tree branches had extended their reach to encompass the now empty trees, as if offering comfort.

In the quickly fading sun Gwepper, Ghilphar, and Bronwen opened a couple of the trees and grabbed corn stalks to sweep with. A waft of dust and dirt blew out the door, into the air, and settled on the earth whence it had come. Analiese sat on a rock and watched, her expression blank, while Krickall tried to entice her to have a look inside the trees. Analiese blinked her eyes, but Adoneesis feared she was lost in the meanderings of her own mind. Thoughtfully, he watched Krickall try again to rouse Analiese from her hypnotic state. To no avail. Krickall's look of desperation filled Adoneesis with pity for both of them. Analiese had assuredly endured some terrible time at Dunraven and he only hoped that with Krickall's care and attention she would recover.

Fierce intent colored Lapis' voice when he came to stand beside Adoneesis. "Gar has much to atone for."

"Yes, he does." Adoneesis' mind raced with the faces of panic-stricken faeries that had mistakenly trusted him, Toran and Duir's deaths, Bryanna's kidnapping, and his newfound responsibility to the trees of Night Gloom. Burning stronger than all those emotions was the need to find out about his birth.

"You have a right to the answers," Lapis echoed Adoneesis thoughts. "But keep in mind that history and events unfold in a way dictated by the fates. Do not judge too harshly, as the mists of emotion sometimes hide the pure intent of actions."

"You seek to confuse me, when all I want is the truth."

"Adoneesis, the rising of each sun lends strength to your abilities. Soon you will not need the answers you seek. You will act with assured belief in yourself, regardless of the past."

His words were true. With each passing day, Adoneesis became less who he had been and more who he was going to be. His bonding with Wyllow Root caused his blood to tingle with sensations, and he was painfully aware of the abuse that hung like a cloak in the forest of Night Gloom. But that awareness was encouraging, because he never would have sensed such things before. So maybe the truth of his ancestry was not paramount to survival.

"Come." Lapis put a hand upon his shoulder. "Let us pitch in. Darkness is now upon us and hunger prompts the swift work of the others. Gwepper will know where the food stores are."

With their combined efforts, and Gwepper's knowledge of the place, it took no time to start some fires, clean a couple of trees, arrange sleeping chambers, fill water basins and prepare food. Of the two trees cleaned, one of them had a larger area and a place on the ground floor for an eating area. Assembled there, they finished off some sweet yams and peas. Because their base comforts had been taken care of, the group's mood lightened and tension eased.

Adoneesis sat back and took stock of the gathering. Gwepper and Ghilphar. Two goblins on the faeries' side of the fight. Adoneesis felt nothing evil in either of them, and no longer thought they were spies for Gar. Bailiwick. Cheerful, giving and caring. He'd be the light that kept shining in the darkest of hours. Adoneesis smiled as the speck of whirling green streaked out of the tree to *patrol the perimeter*. The little faerie yearned to feel important or accomplish some great feat.

Krickall--loyal friend, ruthless warrior. Raegar would have skinned Adoneesis alive for giving Dunraven to Gar to save the life of one faerie--a female no less. But Adoneesis vowed that they would regain Dunraven and free the faeries. Krickall could be trusted. He would give his life saving those imprisoned by Gar.

Analiese was the one who sparked unease. Her eyes held fathomless depths of emptiness and he felt a creeping warning from an unknown source. He was learning to trust his instincts, so she would bear watching.

Lapis. Their eyes connected and the room and its occupants receded into a far distant thrum of conversation. Lightness weighed Adoneesis body, and the room darkened. He watched in fascination as a wavering thread of light wound its way from Lapis' forehead to his own. The ensuing connection jolted Adoneesis with ice-cold fire through his veins. As the intoxicating force of emotions subsided into a thrum, awareness rose. A confirmation of Gar's taunts.

Adoneesis gasped and his gaze flew to Bronwen. Her black gaze bore into Adoneesis and her aged face whitened to a deathly hue. Her voice was only a whisper loud enough to carry to Lapis and Adoneesis.

"What just happened?"

"It was a bonding of sorts." Adoneesis frowned at Lapis. "Maybe Lapis can explain."

"I didn't instigate the thread of bonding. It came from you." Lapis scrutinized Adoneesis with ice-blue eyes.

"I have no idea how to do such a thing."

"Sweet Heavens." Bronwen's hand flew to her chest. "A thread of bonding." Her wild gaze flew to Lapis and her hands grasped his arm. "Did he see the truth?" Her eyes fluttered wildly and she collapsed into a ratty heap on the earth packed floor.

Everyone rushed to her side and Ghilphar immediately gave directions. "Krickall, carry her to her room. Gwepper, warm some water and bring cloths and my bag to her room." She looked at Lapis and flushed. "I am sorry, maybe you should..."

"We both can. Your abilities will lend me strength during a healing."

Fire shadows danced on the walls while Lapis and Ghilphar did their best to make Bronwen comfortable and restore some strength to her. Lapis knelt at the edge of the bed. His eyes closed in concentration, while he slowly ran his hands down the length of Bronwen's body. An occasional glimmer of light jolted between his hands and her body. Then, he was done.

With a sigh, he stood. His usually ice-blue eyes had dulled to cobalt and his voice rasped with emotion as he whispered, "I fear she dies. Life seeps from her and there is naught I can do."

Bronwen lay on the straw bed, tucked under a pile of blankets in an attempt to quell the shivers that wracked her frail body. Ghilphar dipped a sponge into warm water and wiped her brow in an attempt to warm her.

Adoneesis watched helplessly. It wasn't right. Not now. Not when he had so many questions to ask. When he'd come to be sure enough of himself that he could appreciate her wisdom rather than be angry at her for not being there for him as he grew up. "But she has the essence of the Lady within her, and that alone should lend her strength."

"It has. It enabled her to make the trip to the world of man and bring the woman here. That was your request of her and she has done her duty."

"It is not her duty I worry about. I do not want her to die."

"She is cursed. She will die."

"Cursed? But how? Who would do such a thing?"

Lapis' hand hovered over Bronwen's brow and, with a gentle sob, Ghilphar slipped quietly from the room. The glimmering of the fire's shadows on the wall was the only movement, while a distant owl and the cracking of some creature fumbling in the forest echoed in the distance.

Adoneesis thought his question would go unanswered, until Lapis placed the cloth back in the bowl and turned to face Adoneesis.

"Raegar cursed her."

"Raegar? Why?"

"Because he was jealous. He never loved her, but he possessed her, and when Bronwen and I fell in love..." Lapis rose slowly, painfully, to his feet and stretched his back. "Raegar banished Bronwen from Dunraven. He fully expected that she'd die by the hands of a beast or nature when he sent her the mountains with a group of faeries as escort. In case she survived, he ensured her eventual death by cursing her to grow old at an escalated pace. Not wanting to leave her at the mercy of the cold hand of the mountains, the faeries breached Raegar's order and left her at the base of the glacier line. She survived. But Raegar allowed for every eventuality by decreeing that if she ever returned to Dunraven, she would set into motion the second part of the curse, the part that rots her from the inside out. She now ages rapidly and her organs are shriveling."

Adoneesis was shocked at such a curse. The hate that must have instigated such a thing. "Sweet Lady, it was by my urging that she returned." Gasping for a deep breath of air, he sat on the edge of the bed. "She dies because of me."

"No. She dies because of Raegar. The choice to return to Dunraven was hers and nothing you could have said or done would have forced her return if she had chosen otherwise."

Adoneesis watched the shallow rise and fall of Bronwen's chest. A low rattle in her throat mingled with the crackling of the fire and the pounding of his heart. Lapis' assurances aside, Adoneesis felt responsible for Bronwen's state.

"We can't just let her die. It is just a curse, which means we can reverse it. I can't believe that you sit there and do nothing except watch her die. You are a great magician. Use your powers to counter the spell."

Lapis didn't move, yet the room vibrated with the force of magic-hued anger. "I allowed you to question my integrity when first we met, but I will not allow even you to question my devotion to Bronwen."

Adoneesis bowed his head. "I meant no disrespect. The ties of your love weave strongly between you. I just didn't understand that love until you explained the curse."

"Yes. Bronwen's aged appearance would cause confusion." Lapis brushed a stand of gray hair from Bronwen's cheek and let his fingertip trail down her withered cheek. "Would you believe that she was once as beautiful as the dawning of the day? Glorious color brightened her cheeks and her hair would cascade like strands of silken honey down her back. The first time I saw her, she stopped my breath in my throat."

"But what happened? When Raegar cursed her, why didn't you try to stop him? Follow her? Something."

Lapis didn't respond; he merely stared at Bronwen's shrunken features, as if his gaze alone could return her to health. With a sigh, Adoneesis wandered to the window and stared across the shadow of night.

"You are my father, aren't you?"

Silence lent fear to Adoneesis. Fear of rejection of a truth he knew to be so.

"Yes. I am."

Simple words, yet they shattered a lifetime of struggling to understand himself. The truth of his heritage alleviated the worry that Raegar's vicious streak ran in his veins. And he was relieved. Not angry or resentful, as he would have thought.

"Lapis..." So many questions, but did any of the answer really matter? Focus needed to be maintained on their present situation. They could share past experiences later. He sighed. "Tell me about the trees of Night Gloom."

Lapis looked relieved that the question was not one that would entail revelations of a more personal nature. "I will tell you. You know the tale of the sinking of Atlantis and how some people, Niobe included, were lucky enough to escape the island before it tore apart and sank into the ocean."

"Yes."

"Niobe, carried with her water from the fountain of the Ancients and upon arriving here, she threw the water into the Chalice Well that exists upon the Tor. The Well gave birth to the land of Avalon and was ever the source of power for the land of mist. When Avalon became lost, it gave way to the land of the faerie realm. Needing a source of power for the realm, just as the Tor was for Avalon, a cup of water from the Chalice Well was brought to Night Gloom and used to water a tree. Nurtured, fed, watered, and bathed in magic, the tree grows somewhere in Night Gloom and is the source of power for the realm."

"Stars in heaven. Gar never knew the power he held at his fingertips," Adoneesis exclaimed.

"It wouldn't have mattered. Wyllow Root gives of her power as she wishes. No one can force her. But by abusing her and the trees of the forest, Gar has made an indefatigable enemy."

"Wyllow Root is the tree of power?" Adoneesis asked.

"Yes. As I said, she shares her power with some." Lapis frowned and then understanding seemed to dawn in him. "That is how you were able to form a thread of bonding."

"I suppose. All I know is that I felt the power of the forest long before we arrived. Before you and the others arrived, I entered the forest and found Wyllow Root. She connected to me, called me tree protector, and said we were entwined forever. To break the bond would bring me doom."

"A tree bonding with the life-giver. Adoneesis, it is an honor rarely given."

Adoneesis shrugged. "I *feel* that it is a great honor and I understand the responsibility, but I'm still not sure of the implications."

Lapis nodded. "You share a connection with the earth and the trees. You are bound to the elements of nature that allows you access to powers beyond realization. But I warn you, practice wisdom along with these abilities. To do otherwise would entail great repercussions."

Thirty

The night passed quietly. Lapis and Adoneesis stayed by Bronwen's bed, each one of them drifting in and out of sleep. It was the hacking sound of Bronwen coughing that woke Adoneesis, but before he could check and see if she was all right, he was unexpectedly jolted by a crashing thud to his head.

"Bailiwick, how many times have I told you to control yourself?" Adoneesis cradled his ringing head in his hands. "Tiny you may be, but your sliding landings into my head pack a wallop."

"King. Oh, King, I am so sorry. You must come with me." Bailiwick flipped in the air. "We need the prophetess or Ghilphar or even Lapis. But we have to go now, or he shall die. I am sure of it."

"What are you blabbering about, Bailiwick?"

"The dungeon. I heard sounds and went to check it out. I'm not sure how I got the nerve; it's really quite scary--and stinky--down there. We should do something about cleaning the place."

"Bailiwick," Adoneesis warned.

"Sorry. But I found someone." Bailiwick lowered his voice to a conspiratorial whisper. "He's still alive."

"Well, don't waste time. Take me to him."

A murmur of voices crossed the clearing from one of the nearby trees and he recognized the two goblin voices.

"Ghilphar, Gwepper, I need your help. To me, now."

His urgent tone waylaid any questions and they quickly fell into step beside Adoneesis. The dungeon lay on the furthest boundary of the circle of trees. Bailiwick flitted into a nearby opening and left the others to follow through the door. At first, it wouldn't open, so Adoneesis threw his shoulder into the heavy door and shoved. The scrape of wood against wood cut the night and as the door swung open, stale air wafted from the underground cavern. Adoneesis gagged as odors of urine, feces, mold, and putrefying wood assaulted him.

"Hurry, hurry, this way." Bailiwick flipped and flitted down the rickety stairs.

"Gwepper, is there a torch to light or any way to light it better down here?" Adoneesis asked.

"Sorry." Gwepper shrugged. "Never been here. Rats and cats, thank the fates."

Suddenly a dim circle of light appeared in the midst of black. Hovering in the air, the circle threw light enough to outline the walls and shadow the stairs so they could proceed cautiously.

"Hurry," Ghilphar instructed. "I can't maintain the circle for long."

Moving quickly, the trio followed Bailiwick. The shallow, gasping breath of someone struggling to breath greeted his or her descent into the rancid pit.

"Lady above, someone still lives," Ghilphar said.

The first door at the bottom of the stairs stood open. The room itself offered nothing except a small bowl that probably once held water, but now stood empty. No window to the outside, no pot for body functions. Nothing except the bowl.

Adoneesis peered around the room. He heard breathing, but couldn't see anything.

"There." Bailiwick pointed. "He lies over there."

The skeletal figure melded with the tree wall and the shadows--no more than a mere shift of contour that a hasty glance could easily overlook. Ghilphar moved quickly. Kneeling by his side, she placed her fingertips on a dirt-streaked throat.

"His pulse is weak. He needs fresh air. I can't know what else he needs until we clean him up and I can examine him in better light. King Adoneesis, you should have no trouble carrying him, if Gwepper could run ahead and heat some water. We'll use my room, as it has already been prepared. Please, Gwepper, make haste." She shooed the goblin out the door and stood aside for Adoneesis.

~ * ~

Gently lifting the sickly faerie in his arms, Adoneesis hastened to leave the oppressive atmosphere behind and breathed deeply of the night. A muffled moan and shivering gasp resulted as the prisoner breathed in fresh air for the first time in the Lady knew how long. Working together, it took but a few moments to get the haggard, dirty faerie disrobed, bathed, and laid onto a comfortable bed of straw and sheets, soft as down.

Ghilphar poked and prodded, careful not to irritate existing wounds. "I feel no broken bones, but there is a lot of internal swelling. He's been beaten and abused badly. He is most assuredly in a lot of pain, as well as starving and dehydrated. He needs rest, water, and some broth. I will prepare a cream to smear on his body." She stood and stretched. Her blue eyes settled on Gwepper and she smiled. "Gwepper, you know the area best. I think I have cat's claw and ginger, but I need calendula. There should be some late blooming flowers around. Can you have a look for me?"

"I think I saw some in the forest just beyond the felled and constructed tree houses," Adoneesis said.

"Flowers and showers, I know where. I'll go." Gwepper bolted for the door, but stopped and turned. A light flush crept up his face. "Ummm, what do they look like?"

Ghilphar smiled. "You may know them better as marigold. They have golden-orange or yellow flowers and grow tightly in bunches."

"Yes. Yes, I know." His uneven gait took him from the room and clattering down the stairs.

Ghilphar sighed and looked at the resting figure. "Gar possesses cruelty beyond measure. I wonder who the poor wretch is?"

Adoneesis looked at the newly freed prisoner. Now that the filth had been cleaned, his features stood out clearly. Gaunt as he was, he was obviously of faerie blood--regal features and fine-boned stature. He frowned. "I would say he is one of the ellyllons, but that is impossible. I have heard no tale of one missing."

"Maybe not, but he has been imprisoned for a very long time."

Then, without warning, the prisoner jolted to a sitting position and grasped Adoneesis arm. His gaunt face radiated desperation. His thin body was barely able to support itself. His mouth opened and snapped shut, attempting speech, but the only sound he produced was a mournful whimper. He grunted. He tried again. Tears squeezed from pitiful eyes, and a low raspy sound wound its way from his throat. "Hheere khiss chiidd."

Ghilphar tried to push him back onto the bed. "You need rest. You can talk to us later."

Frustrated, he shook his head. "Nnnooo." He took a deep breath, a motion that drained him. His shoulders slumped. This time, though he still spoke low, his words were more easily understood. "Where is the child?"

Adoneesis jerked. "The child. What do you know of her? Who are you?"

"Must say the words." Ragged blond hair hung about his face, his blue eyes faded through ages of pain and torture. "Kypher. I am... Kypher."

The name rang memories in Adoneesis and he struggled to remember. He did. "Kypher. I remember. Raven mentioned that you'd disappeared. Everyone thinks you're dead." He knelt to the ground to face the ellyllon. "You know the words to release her powers. You have to tell me."

Kypher shook his head. "I have to. And it must be soon." A cough wracked his body, his slight shoulders shaking with the effort. "I've held on as long as possible. Bring her to me before it's too late."

Panic rose in Adoneesis. "She's not here. She was kidnapped."

"Noooo." Kypher slumped back onto the pillow. "Futile. All these wasted years of pain. I will not live beyond the day--this I know. Oh, Wyllow Root, forgive me."

"Wyllow Root. What has the tree to do with this?"

Too far gone in pain, Kypher seemed not to hear the question. Adoneesis pleaded. "Kypher, please, you must focus. What has the tree to do with all this?"

"It must be a tree-bonded faerie who speaks the words. When I die, Merlin will be the only one able to release the powers of the woman."

Adoneesis breathed deeply, elation bursting his chest full. Only out of respect for the dying ellyllon did he remain calm. "I am tree-bonded. Tell me the words and I can fulfill your duty."

"You?" Kypher squinted at Adoneesis. "Yes, I can see the radiance about you." Relief lent color to his dying features. "You must hold both her hands in yours, your eyes should never waver from hers, and you must be close enough to mingle your life's breath with hers. Then you will speak these words.

> *"Thunder from the heavens so vast*
> *Powers from the ancients of past*
> *Formed in Water,*
> *Forged in Fire,*
> *Earth bound, Heaven bound*
> *Destinies wound*
> *Charge within the powers without"*

Exhausted, Kypher whispered the last words and fell into a faint. Ghilphar placed her fingers on his throat and ran an open palm over his body. Sadness touched her eyes as she spoke. "He gave all the life left in him to recite the verse. Let us hope it was not in vain."

"I'll make sure it wasn't." Adoneesis turned from the ellyllon claimed by death and strode from the room. "I'll make sure no death of late has been in vain."

Thirty-one

Navarre took his hand from Bryanna's mouth and pushed her back into the corner. "They're gone, and it sounds like they found someone still alive in this rat's hole." He paced the room; his fingers brushed against his stubbly, unshaven chin. "Now is the time. One of them mentioned that Bronwen's on her deathbed, and now they have a sick prisoner to care for. It's the ideal time to take my revenge."

Bryanna had no idea what he was talking about, but his comment about Bronwen worried her. On the other hand, it was great to know she wasn't here alone anymore. With the others at Night Gloom, there was a chance for rescue. She pulled carefully at the chains that bound her to the wall. She'd been able to loosen the metal loop and peg inserted into the hard-packed earth. If she could keep Navarre talking, he might not notice the occasional clink of metal upon metal.

"What exactly do you think you can do? I mean, look around. We're hiding out in a dungeon, it's you against some pretty powerful faeries, you left your book behind, and you don't even have that crystal you keep talking about."

Navarre ignored her taunts. He was too busy emptying his sack and preparing what looked to be a mini altar. Reverently, he laid out some items. A small knife, a couple of candles, some herbs or incense, and some various colored crystals.

He spoke, "A weak mind is so easy to manipulate."

He lit the candles.

"And even easier to crush."

He knelt by the altar.

"But first, I'll use the weakness to my advantage."

Bryanna's stomach muscles knotted. She needed to stop him. She didn't know why, or how, just that she couldn't let him do what he was doing. She increased her efforts to pull the loop free, but to no avail.

Minutes passed. Sweat beaded on Bryanna's forehead as Navarre drifted further into a state of crazed mutterings. She would be scared for her life except for the fact that Navarre seemed to have forgotten her presence. But that gave her a chance to work the loop more intently. She found a sharp stone and dug at the dirt surrounding the peg. She was having success when Navarre startled her by letting out a bellow. She jumped and hid the stone behind her back, but he still sat on the ground and rocked to some unseen rhythm. Though open, his eyes glazed with a fevered sheen of madness and his chanting rose and fell with each breath he took. Jeez, she needed to get away from here. Next thing she knew, he'd be offering her up as a blood sacrifice or something.

Before she was able to continue her digging, the door creaked open. A female figure stood outlined against the dim light from the outer hall. Before Bryanna was able to shout out a warning, Navarre rose. It was only when the female stepped into the wavering circle of candle light that Bryanna was able to see her features.

She had to be Krickall's faerie, Analiese. The one he'd given up Dunraven for. His description of her barely did her justice. She was beautiful. But something wasn't right with her.

Bryanna squinted, trying to see what didn't fit. Then she realized. Analiese's face was slack, and her eyes stared without blinking. She extended a closed fist to Navarre. Still chanting, he reached out and opened his palm below her fist. In that split second when Analiese opened her fist, the room flashed with a burst of blinding light.

"Ouch." Bryanna cursed and covered her eyes. In the moment it took to recover, she came to understand Navarre's words. He'd somehow taken over Analiese's mind and used her for something. But what?

Navarre shoved Analiese into the corner by Bryanna. "You've served your purpose. Neither one of you are any good to me now. Now that I've got the crystal, I don't need anyone."

The crystal. Bryanna remembered Toran mentioning a crystal just before he died.

Navarre opened his hand to show his prize. Nestled in his palm, slightly larger than a goose egg, lay a crystal. Bryanna gasped and reached out to touch it, but Navarre snatched it back.

"You are not worthy enough. Besides, time is running out. As soon as they notice this one missing, they'll search for her. I need to utilize the power of the crystal now."

Whatever he had in mind, it couldn't be good. He was mad and driven by a blinding need for revenge and power. Bryanna quickly started pulling at her chain. "Help me. We need to get out of here and warn the others." She may as well not even exist for all the notice Analiese took of her. Analiese sat on the dirt floor. Her shallow breathing and unblinking stare sent chills up Bryanna's spine.

"Damn." Bryanna yanked harder.

Navarre didn't notice. He was too busy rolling one hand over the crystal and sprinkling herbs over it with the other hand. Unsheathing his knife he moved toward Bryanna, who tried to shrink into the surrounding darkness. The fire flame reflected off the blade as he made a slashing motion, and Bryanna felt a shaft of pain run up her arm. Navarre bathed one hand in her seeping blood while holding the crystal with his other.

"By right of the Tuatha blood that flows in me, I call upon the powers of the crystal." He smeared Bryanna's blood over the crystal. "Vengeance upon those who shunned my father. Destruction to the land that gives them life."

The crystal began to vibrate with a low hum and throw light enough to dispel the shadows in the corners. Bryanna's arm hurt and her heart raced. If he gained the power of the crystal, God only knew what kind of havoc he could cause. Her fervent efforts to free herself were futile. A sharp breath of frustration shot from between her teeth and she threw the chain against the wall.

"Analiese, please. We've got to get out of here. Don't you want to see Krickall again? I know how much he cares for you."

Did Analiese's eyes flicker? Bryanna couldn't be sure and there was no time to waste. Navarre's ritual was causing the room temperature to heat to an unbearable degree as shimmers of light radiated from the crystal. Dread clutched Bryanna. There had to be a way out. Wait a minute. What an idiot she was. Why not use the power of the crystal? She had as much right--if not more--to its powers, than Navarre.

Deep breath. In. Out. Clear the mind. Relax. The crystal's shimmering light touched her face and her blood cooled, became weightless. It felt as if someone had poured water over her. The cool became bitter cold and then exploded in a surge of heat. Empowering her. Filling her with strength beyond her own ability. With one jolting tug on the chain, she was free. My God, it had been so easy.

"Come on, Analiese. We've got to go now." She grabbed the faeries' hand and forcefully pulled her from the dungeon cell. She glanced back and thanked God that they'd made it out. Navarre and the crystal sat in a bubble of protection, but flying dirt and gravel battered the rest of the room. As if imbued with life, dirt and gravel whirled around the room, smashed into walls, and crashed against the ceiling in a morbid attempt to find a way out.

"Jeez." With a breath of relief, Bryanna slammed the door shut and pushed Analiese toward the stairs. Her heart pounded. She hoped the others were still close by and that they were okay. She also prayed that they knew how to stop Navarre before he brought the crystal under full control and destroyed the realm. If such a thing was even possible.

Bounding up the stairs, she threw her shoulder into the heavy door. It opened slowly, revealing the welcome rays and warmth of the sun. "It's okay, Analiese. We're free."

They stepped out of the oppressive dungeon. Bryanna would have knelt and kissed the earth, but one thing stopped her.

Gar and his goblins blocked their path to freedom.

Thirty-two

The closer they came to Night Gloom, the more miserable Gar became. He kicked his frothing horse to keep the lazy animal galloping. If the stupid beast fell in exhaustion, there were other horses. Anger and resentment spurred Gar. His victory at Dunraven left him with nothing but empty trees and fields that needed tending, but no faeries. Elusive and desperate, they had all escaped. He blamed his goblins. Lazy, drunken, slackers couldn't even keep a bunch of faeries in line.

But that wasn't what vexed him the most. He thought that possession of Dunraven would put an end to the empty, nagging sense of failure. He ruled his goblins with an assured demeanor of uncompromising force. No one knew that he felt unworthy, and taking Dunraven from the bastard whelp-- claiming what belonged to him--should have quelled the unworthiness. Instead, he was left with a bitter sense of failure. Dunraven sat empty. Taunting him with his hollow victory.

"Bah!" He yanked his horse to a halt, and the animal stood on trembling legs. It was at that moment he noticed the fresh tracks and turned earth. "Clod's feet." The irony was not lost on him. Adoneesis and the others had lost Dunraven only to flee to Night Gloom. Laughter roiled out of his chest and exploded into a cacophony of snorting. He turned to his goblins, who must assuredly have thought he'd lost his mind.

"It seems you wastrels have a chance to redeem yourselves. Our enemies have fled to Night Gloom. My orders are simple. Kill everyone you see. If it moves, kill it. Faerie, animal, human. I want them all dead, except the prisoner, Kypher. I need him."

Gar touched the leather bound book he'd shoved in his saddlebag. If Dunraven hadn't given him fulfillment, mayhap the book would provide him with the answers. He would not die as a bastard nobody who'd done nothing more than lead a bunch of ragged, idiotic goblins.

His rage boiled and mingled with the foreboding sense that had plagued him constantly at Night Gloom. But something was different. He sniffed the air. The forest's brooding atmosphere was rancid with a chilling quiet. Intense panic flooded him, as well as the urge to issue an order to return to Dunraven, but he stopped himself. Idiot. There was nothing there that a sharp axe and muscle couldn't cure.

One swift motion of his hand, and his sword was free from its scabbard. "We circle around and attack from the west." He set the pace. Each beat of horse's hooves upon the ground melded with the beating of his heart. Thoughts of killing Adoneesis occupied his mind until they drew within the boundaries of Night Gloom, when the fact that something was wrong became startlingly apparent.

The wind whipped into a whirling spiral of dirt, grass, and leaves. Tree branches bowed with the wind until some limbs snapped under pressure and, snatched by the storm, twirled an awkward dance before they plummeted to the ground with a resounding crash. Gar frowned and his unease sharpened his breath. Was this Night Gloom's way of welcoming him home? Still he fought the urge to turn round. He wanted Kypher to read the book and he wanted Adoneesis dead. Nothing less would satisfy him, so he pushed his goblins forward in spite of their grumbling.

They slowed their approach. He wanted to quiet the sound of hooves and use surprise to their advantage. An icy breeze sliced through Gar. Forced from the nearby mountains by the billowing wind no doubt. But it passed on. No one spoke as they rounded the first trees of the settled area. Gar signaled to stop at the entrance to the dungeon. There was a good chance they could retrieve Kypher and be gone with no one the wiser. That was if the prisoner hadn't been found yet, and assuming that Gar was not in the state of mind to decimate his enemies. No. There would be no skulking away.

Gar thrust his sword skyward and was about to bellow his battle cry, when the dungeon's outer door swung open and out stepped two females. Ironic satisfaction lit Gar's heart. Could he force surrender as easily as he had at Dunraven? Why not? Standing within his reach was the woman who'd instigated that surrender, as well as a woman who must be the human woman so valued by Adoneesis.

Recognition lit Analiese's eyes and she opened her mouth to scream, but Gar's shout drowned out any sound she might have made.

"Grab them."

The ever-increasing howl of the wind battering and thrashing the forest successfully drowned out his command.

Thirty-three

I am not completely without heart; after all, we will share a child. The curse will be lifted if you can find someone to love you regardless of your appearance... love you in spite of... in spite of...

How? Memories of the reflection of her haggard face staring back from a quiet pond, and visions of her gnarled, wrinkled hands flashed through her mind. Who would love her? Bronwen tossed, reliving the nightmare that consisted of Raegar's abuse and eventual curse. With his taunting words echoing from the past, Bronwen forced herself awake. Sweat beaded her forehead and she was only barely aware of her surroundings and the fact that she was not alone. Her body ached. Her insides felt as if organs had shriveled into pebbles of stone, but the worst was when she looked upon Lapis' face. Love so fleeting. Doomed to destruction before having a chance to bloom. Worry etched crevices on his features and Bronwen reached a wavering hand to brush a wisp of hair from his cheek.

His blue eyes fixed on her intently. "You're awake."

"Yes," she croaked, her voice as weak as she. "Lapis, I won't live out the day."

"No. No, don't talk like that." Desperation lit his eyes and he clutched at her arm and rubbed up and down as if he could stimulate life into her veins.

"So much to say, so many regrets. One regret I don't hold is that we loved on that day so long ago." Sweet memories wound through her mind. She sighed and closed her eyes.

"Bronwen, we may have loved physically on that day, but in my mind I've loved you every day since."

"Until you faced a hag these few days past." She laughed quietly--softly.

"No." Lapis cradled her face in both his hands and held her eyes with his. "No. I love you still, no matter your appearance. I see into your heart. I feel into your soul. You and I are one. Now, always, and forever." Leaning forward, he pressed his lips to her forehead.

Though weak and barely conscious, his words warmed her limbs. She smiled. At least, she thought she did, but wasn't sure if her lips moved. Lapis sat back in his chair, but the pressure of his lips stayed. The center of her forehead tingled. The tingle grew to a pulse of heat that wended a path through her body. Her heart skipped a beat, then another, and she knew the end had come. But instead of stopping, her heart continued to beat. Fierce, indomitable, the life-giving organ pulsed blood through her body until she felt more alive than she had for a long time.

She opened her mouth to speak, but the distressed look on Lapis' face quelled her. He jumped to his feet--the abrupt motion sending his chair clattering to the ground.

"Something is wrong." He closed his eyes briefly. "The crystal. I don't understand what's happening, but I feel the turbulence of an unnatural storm approaching." He frowned. "I have to go. But..." He looked at Bronwen, torn between duties and spending the last minutes of life with the one he loved.

She waved him away. "Go. I'll be fine."

He gently ran his fingertips over her cheek as if saying a final good-bye. Tears of regret and sorrow glimmered in his eyes, and then he turned and ran from the room. Bronwen watched him go with a mix of wonder and worry. Was it her imagination, or was she feeling stronger? Had his words of love and eternal bond of commitment set a reverse course to Raegar's curse?

Carefully, testing her strength, she pushed herself into a sitting position. She clenched her hands and they closed without their usual needle pricks of pain. Still weak, she swung her legs over the edge of the bed and placed her feet on the floor. Afraid, yet exhilarated, she attempted to stand and found that, though wobbly, she was able to put full weight on her feet. Again, without the aching pain she had grown accustomed to over the years.

Fates above! A sob choked its way up her throat and she was about to muster the nerve to look into the oval hand mirror by the bed, but was hindered by shouts and clamoring from beneath her window. She shivered with the sudden fierceness of the wind and chill in the air, and her heart about leapt from her chest when Shadow Dancer's familiar scream pierced through all other sounds.

Thirty-four

Kypher's death had spurred Adoneesis outside looking for an outlet to his frustration. He spent the next hour swinging an axe, splitting some nearby deadfalls for firewood. With Dunraven in Gar's hands, Bryanna kidnapped, Bronwen dying, and Kypher dead, Adoneesis had to fight feelings of failure and desperation. *Thwack!* Wood splintered and chips flew in all directions. He swung the axe high and brought flashing steel to wood. Sweat from his forehead burned his eyes and the salty taste puckered his lips.

His way was clear. Now that he knew the verse to kindle the powers instilled within Bryanna, he had to find her. Night Gloom provided safe refuge for the others, so as soon as... He swung the axe with ferocious intent. As soon as Bronwen passed on, he'd leave to rescue Bryanna. For whatever reason, and for whatever transpired, he knew that she was needed to counter the forces set into motion.

A chilly wind wrapped around him and cooled the sweat streaks on his body. He shivered. When had the weather turned so cold? Wiping the back of his arm across his forehead, he rested the axe on the chopping block and looked into the distance. Ominous clouds approached, their dense black color lending a surreal hint to the landscape. Soon, the clouds would cover the sun, and if the whipping wind was any indication, they were in for a major storm.

Adoneesis frowned. Something wasn't right. His recent connection to the elements hummed a warning. Then everything happened at once.

Lapis burst from the tree. The stricken look on his face shot the fear of loss into Adoneesis, but it was not Bronwen's death the magician ran to declare. Instead, he grabbed Adoneesis and spun him to face the storm clouds.

"You see those clouds? They are unnatural ones created by the misuse of the crystal. Someone is using the power to destroy the realm."

"The crystal? But the crystal is in *your* possession."

"Not any more. While I was with Bronwen, someone stole it from my room."

"I don't see how that can be. Someone would have to sneak past all of us, steal the crystal, and hide somewhere in the shadows of Night Gloom."

At that moment, Krickall's shout carried above the rising storm and mingled with the scream of a horse. No, not a horse. Across the clearing, by the dungeon door, Adoneesis watched in shock as Shadow Dancer reared on hind legs and crashed down on a cowering goblin. One goblin in a troop of goblins. Leading the goblins and swinging his sword uselessly at the prancing unicorn, was Gar.

Time receded into a murky fog of dreamlike events. His eyes must be deceiving him, because there stood Bryanna, her flame hair tossed about by the blustery wind. She was trying desperately to pull Analiese from Gar who snarled and shoved Bryanna to the ground. Between them and the goblins, Shadow Dancer was on a killing rampage of flashing hooves and razor-edged teeth. Blood flew and goblins scattered in terror. Above it all, Gar bellowed orders. Obviously having trouble holding a squirming Analiese, Gar stamped his foot and screamed for Grud to help him.

But Gar was beyond help. Krickall's warrior cry of fury meshed in harmony with the raging storm as he charged forward to save Analiese. Adoneesis gripped the axe handle and raced to the melee. Out of the corner of his eye, he saw Gwepper and Ghilphar follow, both armed with clubs. Axe held in hand and swinging with ferocious intent, Adoneesis let out his own cry of battle. The blade that a moment ago had split wood now split bone and flesh.

Amidst raging storm and flying debris, Adoneesis and the others quelled the goblins and most of them ran for the cover of forest once they realized it would not be a battle easily won. Their desertion left Adoneesis, Lapis, Gwepper, and Ghilphar breathing with fatigue, but unhurt. Gar's scream of anger followed his goblins, but Krickall wouldn't allow Gar the luxury of escape. Thrusting and parrying, his sword backed Gar away from Analiese and into a corner by the dungeon door. It was as if fury had been born and given life to breath for those brief moments of battle.

Obviously aware that death faced him Gar fell to his knees and raised his arms in supplication. "Please, don't kill me."

"Did you give the faeries you killed a chance at life?" Krickall snapped the tip of his sword to Gar's throat and angled it forward. "What about Toran? Did he beg for his life?" His shaking hand tightened its grip on the sword handle. A trickle of blood etched a dark pathway down Gar's throat. "And what of Analiese? Did you give her a chance to deny your abuse of her?"

Adoneesis saw Gar's death reflected in Krickall's eyes and he made a move, thinking to save Gar and find out about the crystal, but Lapis stopped him.

"He doesn't have the crystal. Let Krickall cleanse his anger and avenge Analiese. They both need to see Gar die."

And die he did. Krickall's cry tore from within and put to shame the storm's ravaging echoes. His sword crunched into Gar's throat, and the goblin's death sounds mingled with Analiese's sobs. Quickly withdrawing his sword, as if contact with Gar tainted the blade, Krickall put his arm around Analiese and gently drew her to him. The easy act of caring contrasted greatly with the brutal act of killing.

The storm increased in intensity.

Bryanna stood by Shadow Dancer. As if ensuring that the animal wasn't injured, she frantically ran her hands over the unicorn. Satisfied, she turned her gaze to Adoneesis.

Fangs, she looked amazing, even with dirt smeared on her face and her clothes wrinkled and torn. Concern for her tore at Adoneesis.

"Are you all right? What happened? How did you get here?" A torrent of questions flew from his mouth unbidden.

"I'm fine. But there's serious trouble." She was breathless. Her voice quivered with panic. "Navarre has the crystal and he's using it to create this storm. He means to destroy the realm and kill everyone."

Adoneesis grabbed her by the shoulders and elicited a whinny of protest from Shadow Dancer. "Navarre has it. Where is he?"

Bryanna answered, but the ferocity of the storm tore the words from her mouth and tossed them away. Wind whipped twigs and leaves into a dangerous torrent that pushed Adoneesis a step back. He leaned closer to Bryanna and tried to speak again, but Ghilphar grabbed his arm and yelled in his ear. "The verse. Use it now."

Fangs, he'd almost forgotten. Mouthing the words, *trust me,* to Bryanna, he enfolded both her hands in his and looked into her eyes. Ice blue, like the unicorn's, she stared back at him with uncertain trust. He leaned close enough to mingle breath with hers and spoke the words.

> *Thunder from the heavens so vast*
> *Powers from the ancients of past*
> *Formed in Water,*
> *Forged in Fire,*
> *Earth bound, Heaven bound*
> *Destinies wound*
> *Charge within the powers without*

Each word deepened the color of Bryanna's eyes until they became the indigo blue of a starry night sky. Her breath came in gasps and she wavered as if to fall. Adoneesis kept his grip firm to lend her strength. The life's breath that passed between them tingled with unknown depths and a circle of radiant light pulsed around them and expanded to encompass the group of weary faeries, and finally, the entire clearing.

Beyond the clearing, the storm raged its relentless destruction. As Adoneesis spoke, the last word of the verse to Bryanna, Navarre burst from the dungeon and screeched.

"Who *dares* to defy the crystal?" Cradling the crystal in both hands, he extended his arms above his head and began chanting in an unfamiliar language.

The storm pressed against the circle of light and forced it back toward them again. Adoneesis swore and tried to grab the crystal from Navarre, but the human was protected by some kind of electric charge that zapped Adoneesis. He glanced desperately at Lapis and hoped he'd know what to do. But the answer came from the most unexpected source.

"We must join hands and circle around Navarre."

A collective gasp of disbelief greeted Bronwen's words. Adoneesis knew her only by her voice, because the vibrant female standing beside Lapis in no way resembled the shriveled hag he'd come to know as the prophetess.

Lapis stared unblinking, his face parchment white with shock. Bronwen gave no time for questions. "Hurry. I'll explain later. But if the storm manages to destroy the circle you've woven, it may be impossible to rebuild. Join hands and form the circle."

Her tone brooked no hesitation and everyone hurried to her bidding. Adoneesis thought that Navarre would fight the encompassing group, but he seemed oblivious to the activity going on around him. His body glowed with unearthly light and his voice rang out.

As their hands connected in a single ring, the ensuing shot of adrenaline almost knocked Adoneesis to his knees. By the startled expressions of the others, he assumed they must have experienced the jolt. But they held firm.

Suddenly, Bryanna's voice rose in a melodious pitch of unfamiliar words. The same language used by Navarre. Their voices met. Words crashed together within the circle--shards of sound creating their own duel. Navarre faltered and his eyes cleared for a moment, and then he resumed his chanting.

Adoneesis felt the chain of power passing from one member of the circle to the other--each adding a portion of their own essence. The wave of potent energy passed through Adoneesis and the temptation to use it to blast Navarre was strong. But it wasn't his place. The energy they gathered was meant for Bryanna. He passed it to her. She glowed luminescent. Her voice resonated like the booming of distant thunder. All encompassing, her words bore Navarre into desperation.

The crystal gradually lost its luster. Navarre spewed words at a faster pace, but their sound was empty, hollow. He screamed his defeat. Useless to him now, he threw the crystal to the ground and attempted to flee, but there was no escaping the circle of faeries surrounding him. Before Navarre could escape, Adoneesis smashed his fist into Navarre's jaw. The well-aimed shot was laden with a final, cleansing burst of uncontrolled anger that welled up within. Adoneesis was free. No longer did he fear that unknown part of himself. No longer did he question his past or his future.

The storm melted away into nothing more than an occasional clap of thunder and even that died into the distance. The clouds wafted on the settled breeze. Their ominous shadows dissolved and allowed the rays of the sun to touch the weary group.

"Farts and darts. Is it over?"

Gwepper's remark released the disbelieving tension. Ghilphar let go of his hand and rushed over to Analiese who looked on the verge of collapse. Adoneesis was encouraged, because though weak, Analiese had lost the dazed look that had followed her from Dunraven.

"She needs rest and food," Ghilphar declared. "Krickall, would you help her to her room so I can tend to her?"

Krickall looked to Adoneesis questioningly.

"Go, my friend. She needs you more than I do right now."

With a grateful look of relief, Krickall put his arm around Analiese, kissed her on her forehead, and helped her to the tree. Ghilphar and Gwepper followed.

"The crystal." Lapis bent to retrieve the innocuous stone. Sighing with relief, he folded it into a pocket inside his robe.

Once the crystal was safe, he turned his attention to Bronwen. They spoke not a word, yet the air pulsed with their exchange as understanding was given.

Still stunned, Adoneesis had so many questions, but didn't know where to begin. Helplessly, he looked at Bronwen and saw her in her true form for the first time. Her blond beauty was subtle, regal like a willow tree. She met his eyes and squared her shoulders, as if expecting him to condemn her for past lies.

"I can see why Lapis fell in love with you. But how..."

"It was his very love that broke the curse. Raegar decreed that if someone loved me unconditionally, even at my most ugly, the curse would be lifted."

"Such a simple thing?"

"Not so simple when the person you love shrivels--their face ugly enough to send even the brave into hiding. No, many would not have made the commitment that came so readily to Lapis." She smiled at Lapis and then looked to Adoneesis--searching, pleading for forgiveness. "We need to talk, my son."

My son. Adoneesis heart filled and tears came unbidden, but Lapis' exclamation cut short any further conversation.

"The book is also near. I sense its presence." He scanned the windswept area, but it was Shadow Dancer who solved the whereabouts of the book when she approached with a torn saddlebag clenched in her front teeth. Giving thanks, Adoneesis took the saddlebag from the unicorn and rummaged through the contents until he felt the hard edge. With reverence, he lifted the book and cradled it against his chest. His body shivered with the force of a deep sigh.

"Finally, untold years after making my vow to the Tuatha, I now hold the book and the crystal in my possession. The power held by these two artifacts is such it takes the combined wisdom and knowledge of the most ancient of all faerie races to hold them safely." He stood and smiled at Bronwen. "There is so much to talk about, but first I need to return these to the Tuatha."

"I understand." She flicked a wrist to Navarre, who lay unconscious on the ground. "I think he should be returned to the Tuatha as well. After all, he is of their blood. They will deal with him in their own manner."

Lapis laughed. "Yes, I am sure they will take in to account his father's betrayal as well as his own when they mete out justice. It will indeed be a punishment to fit the act and intent. Unfortunately, I fear I am drained and will need to rely on the archaic form of transport called a horse." He looked at the unicorn who at moment was soaking up Bryanna's solicitous attention. "Shadow Dancer, could you tear yourself away and round me up a couple of horses?"

The unicorn snorted and tossed her head.

Lapis rolled his eyes. "Fine. *Please.* Now, if you'll excuse me, I'd like a private word with Bronwen." He put his arm around her shoulder and they ambled away.

Adoneesis shook his head. He was still shaking, yet the two of them acted as if they had not a care in the world.

"I'm happy that things worked out for them. They obviously love each other very much."

The soft, dulcet tones of a familiar voice sent quivers through Adoneesis and he turned to face Bryanna. They were alone for the first time since she'd been kidnapped. He wanted to say how sorry he was for not protecting her. Fangs, for bringing her here in the first place and exposing her to the danger.

"It's okay, Adoneesis. None of this is your fault."

He frowned. "Have you not learned yet that it's impolite to touch someone's mind without permission?" Was that his voice sounding so cold and proper?

"I didn't have to touch your mind. Your face tells me everything I need to know." She crossed her arms and turned away from him.

He clenched his hands into fists and tried to figure out a way to deal with this female. What was it he wanted from her? She'd saved the realm; so by all rights, he could take her back to her world and let her go. But that was the last thing he wanted to do with her. That realization hit him with the full force of one of Bailiwick's awkward landings, with ten times the force. He didn't want her to leave because he wanted her to stay. It was as simple as that. But he couldn't be that selfish. He had to let her go.

"Bryanna. I'm sorry. That was rude of me."

She shrugged. "It's okay; I'm just a little tired and probably more sensitive than normal."

"Tired. Of course, you're tired, and here I am giving you a hard time instead of letting you rest. You have a long journey ahead of you. I wonder if Lapis could be talked into going the extra distance after he visits the Tuatha."

"My journey? Lapis?" Her voice dripped with crystals of ice. "After all I've done for you and your realm and you're sending me *back*? Not only that, but you can't even be bothered to take me yourself. You pawn me off on someone else. Great. Why the hell did I even save your stupid realm? Don't worry; I won't bother resting. I'll leave right away, so you won't have to look at this *human wench who holds no appeal for you.*" She turned and strode toward the tree--anger setting her pace.

He cringed. His own words had been thrown back at him. He hadn't meant them then, and he certainly didn't think that way now. He had to make her understand. His stride was twice hers in length and speed, so he caught up to her easily. Without thought to his strength, he grabbed her arm and spun her around.

"Are you saying you want to stay?" Fear lent wings to his blood and it raced through him until he felt as if his head would explode.

"Of course I want to stay. I belong here, and if you can't see that then you don't have the intelligence or compassion that I credited you with."

Her blue eyes swelled with tears as she shook his hand off her arm, and Adoneesis realized how tightly he'd been gripping. Red marks marred Bryanna's skin and he knew they'd turn to bruises. He thought he had his temper under control. His shoulders slumped and he sighed.

"It seems I owe you another apology."

"Damn it, Adoneesis, do you always have to be so formal?"

"No. But I'm not sure I understand what you want from me."

"I want you to kiss me. Is that so difficult for you to understand?"

Fangs. His heart jumped to his throat and a sense of calm followed. "Strangely enough, that's exactly what I want to do."

So they kissed. And that single kiss almost blew Adoneesis into another realm. Ultimate fulfillment mingled with a driving need for more as he gathered her body closer and moaned against her lips. Desire licked his groin and he was about to suggest they find somewhere a little more private, when he was butted roughly from behind. Alert to danger, he thrust Bryanna behind him, drew his sword, and turned to face an unknown enemy.

Shadow Dancer pawed the earth and snorted a warning.

"You rotten bugger. Do you realize what you just interrupted?" Adoneesis sheathed his sword and crossed his arms over his chest. "Well, am I going to have to teach you some manners, or can we come to an understanding?"

Bryanna stepped from behind him and her quiet laughter eased any remaining sexual tension. "She's just telling us that there's a time and place for things like that, and now is not the time or the place."

Adoneesis snorted. The unicorn snorted back. "Fine. She's probably right." He looked around the bedraggled clearing. "We need to clean up and make some decisions." He shook a finger at the unicorn. "But I'll be keeping an eye on you, trouble-maker."

Shadow Dancer trotted away and flipped her tail at Adoneesis in what he thought was a very disrespectful manner.

~ * ~

The day ended in a glorious display of colors as the sun settled beyond the horizon. Ghilphar and Gwepper had prepared food and Krickall had built a fire outside. He claimed that he didn't feel like sitting in the confines of the tree. They were damn fortunate to be alive and they should give thanks by enjoying the bounty of nature.

Analiese sat by Krickall's side. She had recovered enough to feel mortified that Navarre had used her to steal the crystal while everyone was busy. Everyone reassured her that it wasn't her fault.

Navarre was tied to a tree. He and Lapis would leave for the land of the Tuatha in the morning, while Bronwen remained here to recover some of her strength. Raegar's curse nearly killed her and although she'd regained much, she was still weak. Adoneesis was glad to have the chance to spend time with her, because he was sure that as soon as Lapis returned, the magician would claim most of Bronwen's time for himself. And rightly so, as they had many lost years to recover.

"Krickall." Adoneesis decided that now was as good a time as any. Bryanna and he had a chance to talk earlier and they'd made some decisions. "My vow to Wyllow Root dictates that I stay here and help restore the forest, so I'll need someone to care for Dunraven. I know the faeries trust you and you'll have the best chance to restore much of what Gar destroyed."

"But, it was because of me that Gar gained control in the first place. No one will listen to me. Besides..."

"Besides, nothing. You and Analiese will go to Dunraven and the faeries will return. Of that I have no doubt." He laughed and pointed toward Gwepper. "I am replacing you with Gwepper. He has offered to be my second and guard me well."

Gwepper blushed, but nodded his head in agreement.

"Thank you, Adoneesis. Analiese and I appreciate your trust."

Analiese nodded and spoke her first words since her ordeal at Gar's hands. "Bryanna, Navarre would have killed me in that dungeon, so I owe you my life. Would you consider coming with us to Dunraven? It is a beautiful place."

"Oh... I..." Bryanna stuttered and looked at Adoneesis.

"Bryanna will be staying here. With me." He emphasized his intent by placing an arm across her shoulders.

Bronwen laughed. "A tree-bonded faerie and a newly initiated descendent of the ancients. It should prove for some interesting times."

Laughter rounded the fire and just as the final thread of unease left the weary group, a strange sound carried to them from the forest.

"Oh, my goodness." Ghilphar jumped to her feet as the sound came closer.

Eeyah. Eeyah. A high-pitched, grating sound filled with indignation.

The sight of Gray Wolf herding Glory the mule was one that no one could ever forget. Recognizing Ghilphar, Glory pumped her short legs with all haste to her side and proceeded to pour out her entire story with an occasional snort the direction of Gray Wolf, who merely sat on his haunches and appeared to grin.

"Well, it seems as if we're all here now." Adoneesis laughed and raised his cup. "To loyal friends, the blessing of family, the wonder of love, and the magical creatures who give us their devotion."

With hearts filled with joy and amidst much laughter and relief, they raised cups all around the flickering fire and renewed hopes for the future.

Meet Catherine Anne Collins

Catherine lives in rural Ontario, finally living her dream of country living--animals and all. Amidst walks in the woods, playing with her animals, gardening... oh, and working, she loves imagining other worlds and creating magic as she weaves her tales of fantasy and romance.